Emily Purdy, also known as Brandy Purdy in the US, is the author of the historical novels *The Confession of Piers Gaveston*, *The Tudor Wife* and *Mary & Elizabeth*. An ardent book lover since early childhood, she first became interested in history at the age of nine or ten years old when she read a book of ghost stories which contained a chapter about Anne Boleyn haunting the Tower of London.

Visit Emily Purdy online:

www.brandypurdy.com
www.brandypurdy.blogspot.com

The
BOLEYN
BRIDE

Emily Purdy

piatkus

PIATKUS

First published in the US in 2014 by Kensington Publishing Corp., New York
First published in Great Britain in 2014 by Piatkus

A CIP catalogue record for this book
is available from the British Library.

ISBN 978-0-349-40595-7

Printed and bound by CPI Group (UK) Ltd, Croydon, CR0 4YY

Papers used by Piatkus are from well-managed forests
and other responsible sources.

MIX
Paper from
responsible sources
FSC® C104740

Piatkus
An imprint of
Little, Brown Book Group
100 Victoria Embankment
London EC4Y 0DY

An Hachette UK Company
www.hachette.co.uk

www.piatkus.co.uk

AUTHOR'S NOTE

This is a work of historical fiction based on the life of Elizabeth Boleyn. Certain events, dates, locations, and characters have been altered, condensed, or invented.

Life is but a cherry fair.

—A popular medieval English proverb
about the transience of life

*Then I looked on all the works that my hands had wrought, and on
the labor that I had labored to do: and, behold, all was vanity and
vexation of spirit, and there was no profit under the sun.*

—Ecclesiastes 2:11

PROLOGUE

May 21, 1537
St. Peter's Church, on the grounds of Hever Castle, in Kent

They're all dead or dead to me now. My husband, Thomas, and Mary, my sole surviving daughter, are as strangers to me—the first by choice, the second by my grievous fault, my unforgivable failings as a mother. While the others molder into dust, bones crumbling into buff powder as delicate as ashes, most of them lost in the sweet innocence of childhood, babes born still or blue, who scarcely or never drew a breath, the two who lived and thrived, only to fly, like Icarus, too near the sun, sleep uneasily in the blood-, sin-, and scandal-stained infamy of treason, incest, and adultery in a crypt beneath London's Bloody Tower.

This churchyard used to be a beautiful, peaceful place to come and sit upon the white stone benches and reflect upon life, love, the wages of sin, ambition, and vanity, and, of course, one's own mortality; in a graveyard, such thoughts spring readily to mind. I would sit for hours and contemplate the graves where my lost children slept, resting in the protective, embracing shadow of a tall white marble cross, mounted on a little hillock, rising like a miracle, a resurrection, out of a dense mass of sweet white woodruff, planted all around with a small orchard of apple, cherry, plum, peach, pear, fig, and quince trees, my husband's prized "Paradise Apples," from which our cook baked his favorite pies and made quince jelly. But not now, not now, things are different now. . . .

Welcome to my private Hell. Pass through the portal, the old sagging, groaning gate, twined with stinging nettle, not quaint, picturesque ivy; walk in amidst the thorns, thistles, and grasping blackberry brambles; chance the poison, if you dare, when a prick or a graze, a carelessly plucked leaf or nibbled berry, even a beautiful yellow flower, could be your own death knell; and gaze your fill upon the ugly, foul, festering fury that is the raging, bitter as gall and green wormwood, black and red soul of Elizabeth Boleyn, Countess of Wiltshire. No calm ladylike embroidery or genteel paints for me, nor the masculine chisel or a knife and block of wood or stone to carve out my grief and anger, oh no; my pain wants life, and I've given it that. I've brought it all to full, furious life in a grotesque garden of prickles and poison, flourishing rampant in a place where only beauty and blessed, blissful peace should exist. But peace has no place here anymore. Not since the ax fell. There is not a drop of sweet tranquility left in my soul.

When I came here first as a bride of sixteen there were not even half so many graves. Now I am two years past fifty, and the churchyard is filled with them, populated with white stone crosses and brass scrolls that bear the names of Thomas, Henry, Geoffrey, Margaret, Amata, Alice, John, Edward, James, Eleanor, William, and Catherine, a dozen dead babies, all lost without grief, but not without regret.

How could I *not* regret all those months wasted carrying a child that came lifeless into the world or left it after only drawing a breath or two? The toll each one took upon my beautiful body: the strain, the bloating and swelling, the kidney fevers, the pushing, tearing pains, the gross thickening of my waist, heavy, sagging breasts, and the tracery of lines left upon my belly as a constant and ugly remembrance of a woman's lot and purpose in life. I am a vain woman, I freely admit, brought up to be a beautiful ornament, so how could I *not* regret the toll all that fruitless bearing took on me?

But not *all* my dead dear ones lie here—Anne and George will never come home again, and if they will ever rest in peace, murdered and with their names so vilely slandered, spoken with scorn in wicked whispers, destined to be reviled by posterity, people being ever wont to believe the worst, I do not know. I can only pray that the truth will shine a golden light one day, to show the world their innocence and set them free from the shackles of this undeserved infamy. Think what you like of me and their father—our indifference, vanity, ambition, and avarice. My children were not depraved and wicked monsters.

Doubtlessly when I die—and I think it shall be soon, as the poet Wyatt, who loved my daughter, so aptly said, "These bloody days have broken my heart," and already I cough up blood—Thomas, *my venerable and esteemed husband* (Read those words with bitter, biting gall like a scorpion's sting or a serpent's deep-piercing fangs!), will send in the gardeners to restore order and beauty, the stately perfect precision of pruned boxwood hedges and intricate knot gardens like embroidery brought to life, all the expensive elegance he thinks befits him as every year takes him further and further away from his London shopkeeper origins.

When I was being fitted for new gowns, and I saw the merchant's shrewd and canny gleam in his eyes accompanied by the telltale twitch of his fingers that told me he *longed* to reach out and test and scrutinize the material, to caress it like horseflesh or a lover's skin, and draw it close to his eyes for a better look at the weave, I used to taunt him, adopting a haughty yet exaggeratedly, and, I hoped, maddeningly casual tone. "You're a draper's son, *Bull-In*"—I pointedly pronounced it just like that and persisted even after he had changed the spelling from *Bullen* to the more elegant and refined Frenchified *Boleyn,* though not without experimenting with several variations first; at one time or another he signed the family name as *Boullan, Boulen, Boleigne, Bullegne, Bolen,* or *Boleyne*—"feel this velvet, and tell me, is it worthy of the Duke of Norfolk's only daughter?"

Every time without fail he turned a pinch-lipped frown on me and, with ice in his voice and eyes, coolly corrected me; it was his grandfather, he said, not his father, who had made his fortune as a cloth merchant—a *silk* merchant, he emphasized the difference, making it clear that the late Geoffrey Bullen had handled naught but the finest. But I could not resist it; I *never* let a chance go by to remind him that he was a new man, who had risen via a determined mixture of sheer perseverance, ambition, intelligence, and marriage to me, not by right of blood and pedigree. He was a self-made man, a parvenu, who had married up, bought himself a highborn bride with a fortune founded on cloth—it was *still* cloth even if it was fine silk!—and barged and bluffed his way into the Tudor court and made himself useful to the King, or indispensable, as Thomas liked to think he was, ignoring the truth that we all knew and were raised with from birth—*everyone* who served crowned heads was disposable and only there at their whim and fancy. *Nothing* is more fickle than royal favor. Thomas Bullen was the perfect court toady, rewarded with crumbs and bones tossed from the royal table and a pat on the head from time to time. That was my husband, and he *loved* every moment of it. If he had ever lost the King's favor, it would have been like the sun going out of his life. He would even condemn and kill his own children to keep it, it meant so much to him; he could not live without it.

Calling him *Bull-In* was also my way of reminding him, rubbing it in, that he made love like a bull, without grace or finesse, but a grim and brutal, grunting and sweating determination to get things done, to fill my womb and go on to other business. *Bull-In,* I always said through my tightly clenched teeth each time he entered me, like a bull thrusting his pintle into a cow solely for the purpose of breeding more cattle for sustenance and profit; for in truth that is all it ever was. The children I gave birth to bore the name of Bullen and were intended to go out into the world and grab their greedy share of gold and glory before they died. The sons were to sire and the daughters give birth to children who would push the barefoot farm boy who had walked to London to make his fortune further and further back into the dim and distant past. There you have it— the intimate, behind the curtains truth of our marriage bed. No love, no pleasure, only the duty and obedience of a good Christian wife.

But the Bullen bull could never fault me. I did my duty. I was the perfect, outwardly good, and obedient Christian wife, just as my father and brother had promised him I would be. The pedigreed patrician ornament and trophy arrayed in jewels and gorgeous gowns of silk and velvet and a gracious smile that Thomas had always wanted beside him when he went abroad in society, and, at home, presiding over his table with charm and grace, ordering his house, and bearing his children, to take the next generation even further away from the Bullen shopkeepers of London.

I was born beautiful, with hair black as ebony, skin white as snow, eyes bewitching and dark, lips as luscious, red, and sweet as the ripest cherries, and a deceptively icy exterior with a secret sizzle hidden inside that it always delighted me to reveal to those I chose to share the secret with. Oh how I *relished* their surprise! And, sometimes, just for fun, I let them think that they were the first to melt the ice, that I was cold with everyone else.

I was raised to be perfect in every way, well schooled in all the social graces and domestic virtues. My manners were flawless; I never blew my nose on my sleeve or wiped my greasy fingers on it, or squatted and relieved myself beneath a table or behind a tapestry. Every time my father heard of a new book written for the instruction of young ladies or new brides he immediately bought a copy for me. Whenever we passed one another in the corridor or sat down to dine *en famille* he would test me until he was satisfied that I had made good use of the gift of knowledge he had given me. I spoke fluent, impeccable French, wrote an elegant hand, and knew how to keep a neat and accurate household ledger. I embroidered, danced, and dressed exquisitely. I had imbibed an abundance of both frivolous and practical knowledge—trivial, mundane, and vital—so I could hold a conversation on almost any subject, and, most importantly for a female, I knew when to keep my mouth shut and to just nod and smile and let the man do all the talking, and to *never* interrupt, contradict, or disagree with him, even when he was obviously in error or showed himself to be an absolute fool. I said my prayers like every good Christian woman should and endeavored to obey the Ten Commandments and live by the Lord's teachings whenever it was convenient. I hawked and rode to hounds with a modest exuberance, yet always knew when to dig in my heels and pull back the reins and let the men charge on ahead of me. I recited poetry and sang in a good, clear, and unwavering voice, pleasant to all ears and not too shrill, and always with properly restrained emotion, and was a competent and skillful performer on the lute and virginals—more precise than passionate, but in my father's, brother's, and future husband's eyes, correctness counted for far more than feeling.

By the time I was sixteen, I knew how to order a manor house from top to bottom, chastise a servant for pilfering plum jelly from the larder or a vial of rose perfume from the stillroom, prepare a poultice of comfrey to ease a painful bruise or help knit a broken bone, plan a spontaneous picnic for a hundred guests beneath the trees in the Great Park, and arrange a banquet, right down to where the Pope should sit if perchance he ever came to supper.

I maintained a perfect facade. The smile upon my face always stayed in place. And Thomas Bullen was well satisfied that in marrying me he had made the greatest bargain ever. But there was never any love between us. In marriages of arrangement there seldom is, such is the way of the world we live in, though most find a tolerable affection, or friendship, within their marriages that also eluded us. I didn't want his friendship or his love, and I daresay he didn't want mine, only a trophy to prove he had won the perfect, pedigreed bride, and to be seen, whenever an opportune occasion arose, with the glittering prize on his arm, gorgeously gowned and bejeweled and smiling graciously at all the right people.

Appearances are *all* that matters to Thomas Bullen and men like him. He really didn't care what I did as long as the children were his and I was discreet and did not make him a laughingstock in his cuckold's horns to be sniggered and pointed at in the corridors of the King's palaces or in the city streets. And I was amenable to that. After all, it was the same thing I would have wanted for myself if our positions had been reversed and I had been the man in this marriage and not a woman condemned from birth to serve and obey, to be gracious, graceful, and agreeable, and to always keep smiling.

I kept my end of the bargain and played my role to perfection; only once did Thomas ever have cause to complain of me . . . when I failed to become the King's mistress. But I had my reasons.

Walk inside the stone church of St. Peter's, bask in the scarlet, blue, purple, green, and gold rainbow of the stained glass windows, and admire, by golden candle glow, the magnificent brass table tomb my husband has had made for himself, showing Sir Thomas Boleyn, the right honorable Earl of Wiltshire, in his prime and glory with his hair thick and dark instead of stringy, sparse, and gray, in the full crimson velvet and ermine robes and regalia of a

Knight of the Garter, his hands devoutly clasped in prayer. Smile and nod over the sanctimonious hypocrite's lavish tomb. Wink, plant your tongue firmly in your cheek, try to stifle your spurted laughter, and don't be fooled—see him for what he *truly* is. Don't let a pleasing face and pious mien coupled with high honors fool you. The Devil was ever fond of disguises. Here someday will lie a man who sacrificed his children's lives and honor, who lied with a straight face and blackened their names with the foulest sins, all to satisfy a king's caprice and carnal lust, and retain his place on the winning side—the *only* one that matters, Thomas would be so quick to tell you, as he spent years drumming this lesson into our children's heads.

I truly do not care what Thomas does after I die, and whether my poison garden withers or thrives; it has already served its purpose. Life and death spring many surprises on us before they are done with us. Who knows? I may outlive him. He is ailing too. We are running a race against the reaper, Thomas and I. And I want to win, just to thwart him, just so I can have the last laugh. I want to dance on his grave in my bare feet, with my skirts tucked up, a bottle of wine in hand, and a lusty lad young enough to be my grandson at my side, and have my wanton way with him right on top of that splendid tomb! I am not supposed to know this—Thomas would account my possessing such knowledge most unseemly—but if I die first, after a year of mourning, of course, since form must be seen to be observed, and hypocrites like Thomas and King Henry are so particular about such things, he will marry the King's niece, Lady Margaret Douglas. It's just another pat on the head from the King to his favorite lap dog, his way of saying, "Well done, good and faithful servant. Here—I toss you a bone—a semi-royal bride!" God send me victory: Let Thomas perish first, just to deny him this last great honor, the chance to have wedlock bind him even closer to his beloved sovereign.

And if not, if I die first . . . well, let the picks and axes, shovels, and hoes come! Bring them on, Thomas, and the King and Margaret Douglas too! I challenge you all! Uproot this vile patch of teeming thorns, noxious weeds, tangled roots, malicious berries, and corpse-stinking flowers, cockleburs, thistles, stinging nettles, and lethal toadstools that I have unleashed like a witch's curse, or a blight upon the land, to strangle and tangle the graves, benches, gates, and fruit trees, and trip and tear the flesh of any who dare venture here. It will in truth change *nothing;* ugliness is garbed in beauty every day. The truth remains even though you try to hide it as you may. *Nothing* is impervious to Time; every wall *will* crumble. In the end, *all* will be revealed. Truth will have its day, bold, bare, and naked. It will stand defiant in the full blazing sun, even if it blinds and burns the beholder. I am not afraid.

That day in May, one year ago today, when word came from London that Anne and George were gone, my two brightest candles snuffed out, I ran outside and with my own hands—hands that had inspired poetry for their alabaster loveliness and grace, and in their day been likened to doves, snow, lilies, and white roses against the pulsing pink of the pricks they gripped—I ripped up every pretty flower I could find by its ugly, matted roots, sending soil, beetles, and worms scattering as I screamed, wept, and howled, watched by servants and gaping peasants who kept a nervous and wary distance, cowered and crossed themselves, and whispered that I was a woman driven mad or possessed by a demon—a demon named Grief. Even my own mother-in-law, who had known me since I was sixteen, was afraid of me.

What a strange and frightful sight I must have presented, this frenzied and crazed, weeping and wailing woman—my behavior at such a startling and sharp variance to my appearance, the epitome of courtly elegance and gracefully aging beauty arrayed in silver-braided black satin embroidered with fanciful swirls of silver acanthus leaves; ropes of pearls and a diamond collar to artfully conceal the sagging skin of my throat; diamonds on my fingers and at my breast; and a pearl-bordered black gable hood (before the veil caught, and it fell away and my silver-streaked black hair tumbled down to catch on and be torn out by the grasping thorns).

There I was, a madwoman, "a howling, deranged banshee," my Irish mother-in-law said of me, attacking the flowers as though they were my mortal enemies. Even the roses—*especially* the rose garden! Where King Henry had come to court my daughter, my husband himself—*God blight and damn him!*—had set the scene: a garden of roses and a green gown! It *had* to go! Every petal, root, and thorn! Even though some, believing that the fragrance of roses is the breath of God, thought this a great sacrilege, I *had* to do it. I could not let it live when Anne was dead; and Henry, her murderer, was celebrating her death, toasting it with wine, and about to wed another; and my husband, that Judas, his creature, that ever faithful lackey, still basked and preened in his favor, having earned his thirty pieces of silver several times over by going on his knees before the King and volunteering to preside over the court, alongside my brother, another Judas, that would sit in judgment upon my children.

While I ripped up the rose garden with my bare and bleeding hands, my husband was even then in his luxurious apartment at Hampton Court with his tailor being fitted for new clothes for the wedding ten days hence—a silver-threaded and silver fox-furred doublet of Our Lady's blue because the color reminded him of the wholesome and pure Mistress Jane Seymour, that bland and boring little nobody who was placid as a garden pool devoid of frogs and fish and pink and white lilies to give it life and interest, who would soon be our gracious Queen. The lifesaving antidote, her doting and eager bridegroom said, to the poison that had been Anne Boleyn. While I wept, Thomas debated what gift would best please this queen-in-waiting. I know he chose not to give her the gift I so thoughtfully sent—a dead snake in a box filled with grass I had ripped up by its dirty, matted roots from Hever's fine lawn he used to boast was like a carpet of spring green velvet. He was ever a tactful man, my Thomas. He sent a note that, since he knew me to be unwell, he had taken it upon himself to select and send a *proper* gift to the soon-to-be Queen Jane in my name.

Every time I looked at that garden, I could see King Henry pursuing Anne like a relentless hunter stalking a deer, a fleet-footed doe with terror in her dark brown eyes, and hear the lovelorn Thomas Wyatt reciting the words that made her famous—*"And graven in diamonds in letters plain there is written her fair neck round about: Noli me tangere, for Caesar's I am, and wild for to hold, though I seem tame."* And Memory—my foe, and yet I find now my friend also—played its kind and cruel tricks and let me see Anne and George, laughing and gay as they used to be, sitting on the benches, bent over their beribboned lutes or dancing amidst the sweet, breeze-swaying roses. I could hear the music. I could hear them singing, composing verse together, and completing each other's sentences, like a circle, complete, with no end and no beginning. My Gemini—twin souls though not twins by birth—that was how they always described themselves. *Oh the torment; I could not bear it!* The roses *had* to die, like my son and daughter. I would have no peace as long as they remained to remind me. Their beauty was too painful to behold. Red and white, the Tudor rose that symbolized the union between the Red Rose of Lancaster and the White Rose of York, blood and snow, passion and purity, fire and ice, hell and heaven, sinner and saint, conquest and surrender, whore and virgin, the red dazzle of rubies and the nacreous lustrous shimmer of pearls, innocence born from a bloody womb, the blood is the life, the cold white marble of death—a tomb effigy; red roses for the blood of martyrs. It was *all* there in those two colors, those red and white roses that seemed to nod knowingly in the May breeze, commiserating with a mother's loss, forgiving me for killing them, seeming to say, " 'Tis better to die young and beautiful than to grow old and wither upon the vine."

Heedless of the thorns' stabbing—I *welcomed* the pain!—I let them tear my flesh with ugly, ragged, stinging, bloody gashes, and mark me with scars that would never fade, a silvery cobweb tracery like a snail's shimmering tracks that still mars the snowy whiteness that men's lips used to delight so to kiss. But none of that matters now.

My youth and what was left of my beauty are long gone. When I look in the mirror now I see a skull, a death's head, a memento mori, to remind me that Death is always looking over my shoulder, peering out from beneath the wealth of silver- and white-streaked black hair, where once a vain beauty dwelled, a frivolous, gay coquette, sitting before her mirror, preening and perfuming herself, preparing to meet her lover.

It's an exquisitely painful irony—I was untrue with many; I even dallied with two of the men who stood accused with my daughter. I had *many* lovers, but my daughter, who died condemned of cuckolding the King with three of his favorite courtiers, her own brother, and one lowborn musician, had none. She came a virgin to the King's bed, and no other ever had carnal knowledge of her.

And the holly! I *screamed* for an ax, and none dared deny me.

One of the gardeners scurried off to fetch one for me. When it was brought, I flew at the holly with the vengeance of a soldier facing a mortal enemy in the heat, sweat, and bloodlust of battle. As I swung and chopped and suffered the stab of the glossy evergreen's dagger-sharp thorns, I sang in a hoarse voice, coarsened by tears, the song Henry gave to Anne one Christmas, telling her "eternal and evergreen shall ever be my love for you."

> *Green groweth the holly, so doth the ivy.*
> *Though winter blasts blow never so high,*
> *Green groweth the holly.*
>
> *As the holly groweth green*
> *And never changes hue,*
> *So I am, and ever hath been,*
> *Unto my lady true.*
>
> *As the holly groweth green,*
> *With ivy all alone*
> *When flowers cannot be seen*
> *And greenwood leaves be gone.*
>
> *Now unto my lady*
> *Promise to her I make:*
> *From all others only*
> *To her I me betake.*
>
> *Green groweth the holly, so doth the ivy.*
> *Though winter blasts blow never so high,*
> *Green groweth the holly.*

I brayed those lying words over and over again until my voice was a raw, rasping croak, and I collapsed, with bloodied, blistered hands and no tears left, and let the servants carry me inside and put me to bed and dress my wounds.

In the churchyard, where my children, left to molder under the Bloody Tower's chapel floor, were denied their final rest, I replaced all the prettiness with poison, putrid as a rotting corpse lying bloated in the sun, ugly as the vilest sins, harboring destruction within its deceptive, dangerous beauty. Unfettered, I let death and pain flourish and thrive; I unleashed the evil and gave it free rein. As I planted and nursed my noxious seedlings, with every breath I cursed my husband and the King he had served so well, kissing the hands that had signed Anne's and George's death warrants.

That night as I lay alone in my bed, my blistered and torn hands swathed in bloody, seeping bandages, my eyes and face swollen red and raw from all the tears I had shed, and my cheeks scratched like trails of bloody tears from the thorns, I could not rest. I disdained all the poultices and potions offered by my maid and mother-in-law in the kind but vain hope of bringing me comfort like a pair of favored slippers. I preferred to suffer the throbbing pain instead. Nor would I allow a physician or my husband to be summoned.

Nay, better that Thomas stay far away from me, else I claw his eyes out. In truth, I did not believe for a moment that he would forsake the King's nuptial festivities to come to me. He was too busy choosing a collar of sumptuous sapphires to "bring out the blue" in the soon-to-be Queen Jane's weak and pallid eyes while I tossed in the bright blue-tinged whiteness of the moon pouring in through my window, like a sea of grief to flood my soul. I was gasping, tossing and turning, drowning in grief, staying stubbornly afloat when all I wanted to do was sink to the bottom and die.

I kept thinking of Anne and George, their broken, headless, mangle-necked bodies, thrown naked to rot for eternity in their ignominious graves. My own husband, their father, whose seed planted in my womb had grown their lives, had sat, rigid-faced, stiff-backed, and tearless, in his bloodred velvet robes on the jury and, when called upon, had stood and spoken loud and clear the one word—*"Guilty!"*—calculated to curry favor with his royal master, to retain his posts, privileges, and honors, like a dog loath to lose his precious hoard of bones. Loyal to the last, Thomas Bullen did his master's bidding. To earn his head a pat and the certainty of future boons, he told the world his children were sinners, a "vile incestuous pair," and sentenced them to a traitor's death upon the scaffold.

Such is the man I married! He takes care to always stay on the winning side, and he wants his bread buttered instead of plain, or even better with a slab of melted cheese and a fat slice of mutton! *Oh how I hate and despise him!*

I knew the poison that filled my heart would slowly seep out and kill me. I could not bear the agony; I knew it would be worse than the lung rot that would inevitably take my life in God's good time. I had to find another way to unloose the venom, to ease the agony. When I finally slept, my dreams were filled with deadly nightshade, lacy florets of hemlock, yellow flowered henbane, screaming man-shaped mandrake roots, speckled spires of fox-glove, and dangerous beautiful spikes of deep purple-blue wolfs-bane. Thus were the first seeds of my poison garden planted.

With the dawn I rose from my bed and went out to rend and rip the churchyard to lay the soil bare for the baneful roots I would soon bring.

Thomas is at court now, where I am no longer welcome. My black eyes burn with fierce, undisguised hate whenever they light upon our sovereign lord, King Henry VIII. Unrelenting and un-flinching, they make His Majesty supremely uncomfortable and re-mind him of a pair of bewitching black eyes that once flashed like vivacious black lightning. So I am excused, to retire from court, to Hever Castle in Kent or Blickling Hall in Norfolk, whichever I will, for the sake of my health, to reap the benefits of the country qui-etude and clean, fresh air, though we all know nothing cures the lung rot. But, go I must, for it is not meet to make the sovereign squirm and prick his conscience to see if it will bleed ruby red guilt. God's will be done in heaven, but not apparently in England.

For the same reason, I am told, my granddaughter, the erstwhile princess now called Lady Elizabeth, is also banished from the royal gaze. Her flaming hair and milk-fair skin are true Tudor, visible proof for any doubter, but the rest of her—her black diamond eyes, the shape of her face and the features upon it, and her long-fingered musician's hands—is *all* Anne. No wonder Henry cannot stand the sight of her! It is a stab in his murderer's heart! No doubt he fears Anne's spirit will return to accuse him through their daughter's dark eyes. I almost wish she would. He deserves every torment and damnation the Devil can devise.

I sometimes wish we two Elizabeths could bear each other company. But I know that can never be. They would never trust me to be left alone with her. I would tell her the truth about her mother—the *real* truth, not Henry's rewritten and revised history of a dark-eyed enchantress who bewitched him and cast a spell, causing him to commit countless atrocities, even murder, in her name, and turned his whole world upside down, then betrayed him with "over a hundred men," cuckolding him with his own intimate and favored body servants. In any case, I would be ill company for any child; I was never any good with little ones, and with my hacking cough and bloody expulsions, mayhap even a danger to her very life. And Elizabeth is the *one* Tudor I do not curse. She is Anne's legacy, not just Henry's. I want her to live and do Anne proud, so that her blood will not have been spilled in vain. I want her to defy the odds, though Henry has stripped her of her title of "princess" and had her declared a bastard, and no one believes she will ever be Queen of England or anything. I want her to grow up to prove Henry wrong and show him that a "useless" girl can rule England and make a better queen than he ever did a king. Though her hair is Tudor red and her skin white-rose pale, it is my dearest wish that someday when she is grown, when she is queen, a *great* queen, people will look at her and remember that she is Anne Boleyn's daughter, that she didn't become the woman she is all because of Henry.

So I stay here at Hever and faithfully tend the poison garden Thomas indulgently calls my "strange and morbid fancy," my "melancholy madness"—he was ever a one to paste on labels, my shopkeeper-sired spouse, just like an apothecary marking his vials and bottles with a neat and efficient hand, everything so precise and orderly, lined up just right on the shelves, neat as a regiment, to make the best impression and a swift sale—with a greater fidelity, it shames me to admit, than I ever gave to any person, including my own children. But I am honest where my husband is false. I own my faults, unhesitatingly. I confess them freely. I make no excuses and take full blame. I confess them, but I don't look for forgiveness. I've gone through life feeling entitled to a great many things, but absolution isn't one of them. Being shriven of my sins would bring me no comfort. But even as I damn Thomas, I take comfort in knowing that though I damaged them in their earliest youth with my indifference and neglect, my vain preoccupation with myself and my own pleasures, and carelessly afforded them glimpses of a moral laxity I should never have allowed their tender eyes to see— they *must* have known about the men who visited me at Hever when their father was away and slept in my bed—at least I did not conspire to murder them. I did not stand up in open court, stare hard at them, and say the word "Guilty!" when I knew them to be innocent of all the charges laid at their feet, and would, if I could, have fought for them unto my very last breath. I would have braved the royal wrath and defended my son and daughter if I had been able even though I knew full well that in that crooked court if the King desired it, evidence and what it proved or disproved be damned, the jury would find that Abel slew Cain instead of the other way around.

At the heart of this poisonous patch stand three humble monuments. For my two dead children that I cannot bring home, and for the one who still lives and yet is also lost to me, the one I fear would snub me if I swallowed my pride and put pen to paper and wrote, "Daughter, please come home." I've tried so many times to do it, but I'm too afraid she would not come, and if she did, it would only be to repay me in kind, to hurt and rebuff me the same way I did her.

Mary was the lucky one, though it took me a long time to realize that; she got away from us. She renounced our world of corrupt power and heartless ambition, and even, in the end, her own beauty. She fled the court and followed her heart. She married a penniless soldier several years her junior who loved her for herself, even fat and faded, with a purse as empty as his own. She, the golden girl who knew from the start how worthless gold is, found the love she deserved and had longed for all along.

In defending her actions, she wrote declaring that she would rather be a beggar and a vagabond and tramp the world with him than live in luxury and rule as the greatest queen in Christendom. If I didn't know my sweet-natured golden girl as well as I do, I would have taken those words for a poisoned arrow aimed straight at Anne. But Mary never thought that way. She was too frank and honest; she always spoke straight from her heart without pausing first to consider the consequences of honest speech—a tendency that always simultaneously delighted, vexed, and worried me. I never wanted to see her hurt or taken advantage of. But that was a fate I could not spare her; there is only so much a mother can do. She had none of the duplicity and cunning, the callousness and ambition, it takes to succeed at court, and that is why she fell too far to ever warrant her father's forgiveness.

And I was angry too, for a time, with what I thought was good reason. At the height of Anne's glory, when Mary could have used her position as the Queen's sister to make a grand marriage, perhaps to even wed a scion of royalty, and secure her children's future, and a comfortable and luxurious life for herself, she threw it all away for a soldier of fortune, a happy-go-lucky mercenary. A younger man we all expected would be mean and beat her and eventually leave her when he found out being married to the sister of the Queen wouldn't fill his purse or advance him a jot. But we were all wrong about Will Stafford, *completely* wrong. He was a good and honest man who genuinely loved Mary for herself, not her family and royal connections. He wanted as little to do with us as we wanted with him. All he saw, and wanted, was Mary.

But I fancied myself a woman of the world, sage, seasoned, and sophisticated, cynical and jaded, diamond hard as well as bright, a woman who knew more than she should about younger men who were not her sons, and my husband was a diplomat and favor-currying courtier nonpareil, and we both thought—it was one of the few times when Thomas and I were in complete accord—that our firstborn daughter was a fool.

I recalled that long-ago day in the nursery at Blickling Hall when Nurse Margery had dropped my beautiful baby, slippery and naked, fresh from her bath, and Mary had banged her pretty chamomile- and lemon-sodden head upon the floor. She teetered on the verge of tears for only a moment, seeming more surprised than hurt, then sat up and smiled, rubbing the bump rising beneath her curly yellow hair, and held up her arms for Nurse Margery, beckoning her to come get a kiss. Oh, my sunshine girl! Mayhap with that fall, I used to think, the part of your brain that governs good sense had become hopelessly addled; yet now I think she was the wisest of us all.

The bright yellow button blossoms of tansy bloom alongside orangey gold marigolds and rosemary for remembrance in a tub of tarnished gilt to honor my own tarnished golden girl. These cheery flowers, so out of place in this vile patch I have created, remind me of her dimples and golden curls, and conjure up memories of the tansy cakes and tasty tansy puddings we shared when we went a-Maying together, the two of us skipping along barefoot, gowned all in green, as the legends said Queen Guinevere had been when she went a-Maying, gathering May flowers, singing, dancing around the beribboned Maypole, and granting kisses to admiring gallants. Even when she was just a little girl, Mary was always free with her kisses and would give them to anyone who asked or whom she deemed deserving. Now I know I should have been more vigilant. I should have been stern and reprimanded her. I should have warned her to have a greater care for her virtue and reputation. But back then, when she was just a little girl, I thought it harmless, sweet and charming, so natural and unfettered; yet I see now I should have cared more about corseting my daughter's uninhibited nature than I did about her waist. I should have taught her to govern herself better, even when I didn't govern myself, only hid behind a thick veil of discretion.

I would like to make my peace with Mary before I die, but I fear I've left it too long. I tell myself I don't have the strength to try, but that is a lie; 'tis courage I lack, not strength—my will would sustain me if I would but try. But I know I won't. I fear failure, humiliation, and rebuff too much to even try it. My husband was always right about one thing—if you doubt you can succeed, why even bother to try? Never invite failure into your life if you can possibly help it. Yet another of the life lessons he drummed into our children's heads.

Next, from out of a little mound, a false grave for one who is condemned to lie elsewhere, rises a speckled spire of bold pink and white foxglove, each flower like a little upside-down wine cup, for George, who never left a wine cup without draining it to the dregs. Some aptly call this poisonous beauty dead man's bells. When the breeze gently blows them, they toll for my lost boy, my "Dark George," always so moody and melancholy, always seeking something he could never hope to find and searching for solace in wine cups, reckless nights of gambling, and a rapid succession of lovers of both genders, no sooner embraced than they were discarded.

Around it, like a frilly border of frothy lace, hemlock flourishes, its stems eternally spotted with red splotches known as Socrates's blood in memory of the ancient sage who was forced to drain that bitter cup. There is also a blue-veined marble cross and affixed to it a scroll of brass on which I had engraved a verse my daughter wrote while she was awaiting "the Sword of Calais," as they called the headsman who had been chosen, on account of his great skill, and as testament of the great love King Henry had once borne my daughter, to take the head of an anointed queen. I didn't think Anne would mind if I gave those words to George.

> *Defiled is my name, full sore*
> *Through cruel spite and false report,*
> *That I may say forevermore*
> *Farewell to joy, adieu comfort,*
> *For wrongfully you judge of me;*
> *Unto my fame a mortal wound,*
> *Say what ye list, it may not be,*
> *You seek for what shall not be found.*

Aye, he loved her, more than any, as his venomous wife would rightly say, but it was for his loyalty that he died, not any sin or carnal lust, for there never was anything of that kind betwixt the self-styled Gemini. George would have fought for Anne to his very last breath; he would have spoken out against the injustice, recklessly and wildly revealing the truth to one and all, as indeed he did at his own trial when he revealed something that was meant to be kept secret. It would not have been safe to let him live. Even in prison, George would say the truth would set him free. Even if they had cut out his tongue, they could never have silenced him; such was his love for Anne that George would have found a way. He was her one true champion. Sir Loyal Heart, as Anne affectionately called him, from a character he once played in a masque in which they danced together. And she was his Lady Perseverance, indomitable and proud.

And for my daughter, the ugly dark brunette duckling I could never bring myself to love until she surprised me by becoming an elegant and fascinating black swan, there is a bush of roses, so deep a red they appear almost black, rising like the night from another false grave, along with a black marble cross and a brass scroll inscribed with the last poem her ardent admirer, Sir Thomas Wyatt, wrote for her.

> *So freely wooed, so dearly bought,*
> *So soon a queen, so soon low brought,*
> *Hath not been seen, could not be thought.*
> *O! What is Fortune?*
>
> *As slippery as ice, as fleeting as snow,*
> *Like unto dice that a man doth throw,*
> *Until it arises he shall not know*
> *What shall be his fortune!*
>
> *They did her conduct to a tower of stone,*
> *Wherein she would wail and lament alone,*
> *And condemned be, for help there was none.*
> *Lo! Such was her fortune.*

How amazingly apt those words are! And what visions they conjure! My daughter, a gambler at heart, being wooed by a man, a king, she could never like or much less love, but choosing, all the same, to take the ultimate gamble and become a queen, to make the world bow down to her, a queen who reigned for a thousand days, then ended her life a prisoner in a tower of stone.

These are the only tributes I can render them when all the world would erase Anne and George, and those loyal and loving friends who died with them, from human memory. Their portraits have been taken down and burned or else hidden away, the names removed so that time will rob them of their identities when a day finally comes when there is no one left alive to remember and put a name with the face. The court, filled with self-seeking survivors, likes to pretend that these men never lived or loved, laughed or cried, danced or dined or died at all; all that matters now is the future, fawning on the King and his new Queen—Jane Seymour, the wholesome and pure yet boring white milk that replaced the spicy-sweet, intoxicating and exciting dark wine that was my daughter Anne.

I festooned my husband's precious fruit trees with mistletoe, laughing when I recalled what one of Anne and George's witty friends—I think it was Francis Weston or perhaps William Brereton—once told me about quinces, saying of the glowing yellow globes of its fruit called *Pommes de Paradis,* or Paradise Apples, as he tossed one up and down in his palm: "They have the perfume of a loved woman and the same hardness of heart."

I draped the mistletoe over those trees with all the joy of a lady decking her house for the Twelve Days of Christmas, willing it to thrive, to hug their branches like the most tenacious cobwebs, like a spider ravenous for a new caught fly. *"Hold them tight and never let go!"* I whispered, caressing the tiny leaves with the featherlight touch I once used to coyly stroke my lovers' cocks. I know how to provoke a man to ecstasy with just a brush of my fingertip. And then I trained creeping ivy and strangling vines over their trunks and limbs to twine and tangle and squeeze the life out of any fruits that dared try to ripen there. "These trees shall be barren," I regally decreed.

Panting, my jagged, broken nails caked with black dirt and lichen, I leaned my flushed and sweaty brow against the bark of an apple tree and remembered Henry Norris.

Many years ago he had been a tallow-haired youth newly come to court. I found him sitting by the fire at Greenwich one winter's day, trying hard not to cry. He had just been scorned by his first love, a haughty, flippant auburn-haired coquette, who mocked and deplored his clumsiness and inexperience in the art of love. I took him to my bed and, over a series of delightful afternoons, taught him well.

I always did fancy younger men; I relished the role of instructress. Or perhaps I just liked being the first, the one they would *always* remember no matter how many others came after. Young girls often harbor amorous fantasies about their tutors, so I reversed the roles and made the dreams real.

But that was long ago. That winter ran its course, and though remembered fondly, was never repeated. He was amongst those who died with my son and daughter, declaring from the scaffold, "I know the Queen to be innocent of the charges laid against her, and I would rather die a thousand deaths than speak false and ruin an innocent person." For those brave and true words I will always honor his memory. When everyone expects a groveling scaffold speech, flattering and glorifying the monarch, to keep his ire from turning on the relatives one leaves behind, it takes great courage to speak the truth, plain and unvarnished, and in simple words that all, even the humblest and unschooled, can understand. I'm sorry, John Skelton and Thomas Wyatt—the two poets who loved black-haired Boleyn women—but Henry Norris's frankness puts all your poetry to shame.

As I wove blackberry brambles over the graves, to honor the old superstition that they would keep any unquiet spirits within—though I do not fear the dead, especially not those innocents who lie here—I recalled the traitorous Master Smeaton, Mark, whom I would rather forget.

He alone lied and confessed his guilt in the vain hope of saving his life. The fact that he was tortured does not absolve him in my eyes. My son, George, always loose-lipped and wont to confide his amorous escapades to any near and willing ear when he was in his cups—a practice that probably explains why so few of his lovers re-mained his friends afterward—recommended that I try his latest plaything. "A pretty bauble: It plays well, and it sings too," he said. The lad was always generous with his toys. What can I say? A lie would serve no purpose at all. And if I cannot tell the truth now, why even bother telling the story at all? I was bored. I did as he suggested and sampled Master Smeaton's wares. My blood has al-ways been hot, sizzling in my veins, beneath the marble pallor of my skin and the haughty, patrician face many have described as cold, remote as the highest mountains, and expressionless as a chaste marble Diana. What more can I say? The truth is the truth; it is what it is.

George was right. Smeaton was amusing—for a time, a *very brief time*. Then he became petulant and whining, wanting *all* my love, when I had no love to give him—that belonged to another; and what we did together was *never* about love—craving more time than I cared to squander upon a boy who was just a moment's diversion to me and nothing more. His shrillness grated upon my nerves. He wanted to be the possessor, not the possessed. He wanted to call the tunes, not play them, and seemed to believe all the sentimental lyrics he had ever sung about love. I wanted to be rid of him. Poor lad, he wasn't jaded and hard, cynical and blasé, like the rest of us; he really wasn't equipped to play the game. He should have gotten out, married some sweet girl, and become a music teacher or returned to work in his father's carpentry shop, before he got in over his head. It was inevitable—I soon got bored with him, just like George did.

As for Anne, the one Smeaton *really* loved, even if she had cared a fig for that lovelorn lute player, she knew the stakes were too high for her to ever dally even if she had been inclined to. She had made her bed—a *royal* bed—and was well content to lie in it alone or with her wedded husband, bullish, insufferable boor though he was with a temper to match his Tudor red hair. His infidelities kindled her ire, but not recklessness and a desire to pay him back in kind.

Whatever people may think and say of Anne, she was no fool. And she was never wanton or given to amorousness like me. Even though she spent her youth at the French court, and there is no more licentious place in the world, Anne held herself proud; she knew her worth, even when others didn't. She had the wit and wisdom to govern herself even when other girls ran wild. Anne knew that, if she played her cards right, virtue would be its own reward. She knew when to hold her cards close and when to lay them down.

Mayhap Smeaton's confession was his revenge upon the Boleyns for scorning him? We each used him in our fashion—some might even go so far as to say that we misused him—and he never could understand why our "love" didn't last. To George and me, he was a plaything, a toy we soon tired of; to Anne he was a lute player, a musician—granted, one of the most talented—hired to play as bidden for the court, nothing more. All I know is that he is the one dalliance amongst my many that I regret. Because of him, I will always wonder, did someone spy me, a slender, black-haired woman in the shadows indulging in some quick and indiscreet intimacy with Mark Smeaton, and mistake me for Anne because the light was dim or because there was already malice in their mind? Did I unwittingly, with my own indiscretions, help condemn my daughter? I will never know.

Yews, "the cemetery tree," hide this hideousness in cool and murky shadows. In the mighty Caesar's time, suicide by drinking the juice of the yew tree was a favored means for tired old soldiers, those too weary to flee or stand and fight, to avoid the sad ignominy of defeat. It was a way to die nobly, by taking your life in your own hands.

Deep purple-blue flowers of wolfsbane, also called monkshood, bloom in profusion. How deceptively beautiful they are! Anyone who did not know better would think them a harmless posy to pluck, tall spires of clustered flowers, to fill a vase or adorn a lady's hair. But, take care—they will stop your heart and steal your breath away in less time than it takes to say a paternoster. I remember when I was a young girl, a neighbor's cook mistook monkshood for horseradish. The sauce she made killed her master and his guests; she found them all slumped dead around the table, facedown in the sauce, brows pillowed on their portions of roasted mutton.

And there is beautiful belladonna, deadly nightshade, growing with a lush, dangerous beauty in the dampened shadows beneath the yew trees, mingling with monkshood and toadstools, like old friends meeting for a gossip on the church steps or witches consorting at a sabbat. Their berries remind me so much of Anne. They start out a cool, icy green, then ripen to a deep, luscious red, before they reach their polished, gleaming black perfection—watching them is just like watching my youngest daughter grow to dangerous and desirable womanhood all over again. They say that witches make a salve from the purple-veined yellow flowers that makes them feel like they are flying through the air to find ecstasy in the Devil's arms. And ladies in Italy use it to make the pupils of their eyes becomingly large, risking their sight to tempt the men whose attentions they desire. Ah, we women risk so much for lust and love! Is it ever *really* worth it? Even without belladonna, I sometimes think we are doomed to blindness anyway.

Then there is pennyroyal, with its pale purple blossoms and

strong mint scent. For good or ill, depending on the circumstances, it can be brewed into a tea to prevent conception, bring on a woman's laggardly courses, or end an inconvenient pregnancy. And hyssop for purges, and spurge for an even more potent one that brings a violent griping, burning heat, and even death if one imbibes too much of its milky juices, which can also, when applied externally, remove warts, even the hardest calluses, and cure fistulas and carbuncles.

And I have planted bitter wormwood; white oleander; stinging nettles; thistles with prickly leaves and tufted purple-pink heads; that bold, smelly little weed herb robert, whose red-tinged flowers are said to play host to little red demons that make mischief in the surrounding countryside during the night; and mandrakes, whose roots buried underground take the shape of a man and are said to utter bloodcurdling screams that will drive any who hear them mad when they are wrested from the earth.

And lords and ladies, evilly handsome, these sleek, sophisticated, floral, phallic spears are the subject of all manner of rude and titillating names—I myself like to call them the Devil's Pintle. They harbor poisonous red berries within and reek of rotting corpses, attracting hoards of hungry flies. The stench grows worse as their waxy petals unfurl. Some men swear they are a heaven-sent aphrodisiac and, ground into potent red wine, they will make even the limpest man ardent, so hard he imagines he has become a marble statue of Adonis with the strength of Hercules and his cock is his mighty club. But there is *always* the Devil to pay afterward, and many a man has perished with his ecstatic smile transformed into a grimace of pain, and his berry red and grossly swollen, rock hard pintle pointing like an accusing finger straight up at heaven as he lies dead upon the floor or tangled in his lover's sheets. Sometimes, if one acts in time, a poultice of sour milk will save his life and stave off his discomfort, and he will live to find a new kind of bliss in limpness; but only *sometimes,* if one acts quickly and there happens to be a pitcher of sour milk fast at hand.

As I sit upon a thorn-embraced bench that snatches like a greedy child at my already tattered black skirt and trailing mourning veils, with clinging burrs taking the place of ornamental buttons and embroidery, serenely regarding my pernicious plants, sprawling in tangled, snarled, and matted masses across the graves and climbing the stone crosses and innocent fruit trees, I cannot help but marvel what a far cry it is from the neat and orderly beds of sage, fennel, mint, rosemary, thyme, basil, chamomile, dill, and rue in the walled garden behind the kitchen. If I have my way, by the time I die, it will be a wild, impenetrable jungle that none dare penetrate unless they desire death or like to gamble with their lives.

I hope Thomas has the very devil of a time, and the Devil to pay, restoring it all to the order he desires. I hope it blunts every ax his men bring and forces him to part with more coins than he counts on. I laugh to think of him tangled in convolvulus, which some call hellweed, bindweed, and the Devil's guts and garters. It strangles the life out of every plant it touches. Beneath the soil, it weaves itself into a nightmare of tangled roots so deeply entrenched it will never completely die; it will *always* come back. The white flowers it breeds are like church bells. They look so sweet and innocent, wholesome, pure, and virgin white; they close demurely as the day ends. Some daring souls use them as a purge to rid their bellies and bowels of unwelcome or uncomfortable contents, and to try to lose weight, but unless the dose is minute and liberally mixed with sugar or honey to sweeten it, or even a spice such as cinnamon strong enough to disguise the flavor, the gambler, fool, or desperate woman who dares take it may die squatting over their chamber pot.

I hope my wicked plants fight Thomas's every attempt to conquer and eradicate them with all the vengeance of a wronged woman and those unjustly defamed and done to death. I am no witch, but this curse I lay upon my husband and his land, even though this patch of land is sacred, consecrated to the church, sans regret, still I make it.

I alone walk fearlessly in this place, letting my black skirts and scarred and roughened fingers trail aimlessly amidst the thorns and brambles, never starting at the now familiar pricks. I suck the blood welling from my fingers and go on as though it were nothing at all; the prick of an embroidery needle or a lover's kiss I have grown bored with. My passion has been quelled; all that remains is the anger and furious pain and lust for vengeance. Nor do I shudder when the snakes and vermin that shelter in the knotted roots and twisted weeds slither and rustle past my feet. I don't fear them

either. There's so much poison in me, I think I have become immune. Nothing here can harm me. And if, perchance, I am mistaken, I do not care. If one day they find me lying dead in a nest of
stinging nettles, bindweed, and blackberry brambles, poison
welling from my pricked fingers or berry juice staining my lips, so
be it. I've had my life, and I am ready to leave it.

❧ 1 ❧

That blustery November day in London, 1501, when the century was still new and it felt *so* good and exciting to be alive, would change my life forever. But, of course, I did not know that at the time. God seldom does one the courtesy of sending an angel down from heaven to wake one on the morn of a monumental day with the solemn pronouncement: *This will be a day that changes forever the course of your life.* Back then, my head was still filled with the usual dreams a young girl harbors—going to court; serving the Queen; being surrounded by dozens of admirers, who would write songs and poems about me and give me gifts; and finding a wealthy, highborn husband who was also handsome and lusty; and being rich, popular, and happy for all the rest of our days.

I was sixteen and wearing a new gown of the richest sapphire velvet, edged with broad bands of black velvet and lovers' knots fashioned of golden braid. Shod and hooded in gold- and pearl-festooned black velvet, I stood fearlessly amidst the jostling crowd lining the street, eagerly waiting to catch a glimpse of the newly arrived princess from Spain.

Catherine of Aragon, the beloved youngest daughter of Ferdinand and Isabella, had come to marry our Prince Arthur, who, God willing, would be our next king. And hopefully, for her sake as well as all his courtiers, far more fun than his severe, taut-lipped, penny-pinching father, that old gray miser, Henry VII. Today she would make her official entry into the city of London, and soon I, my father had promised, would marry a man worthy of my rank and beauty, and come to court to serve her. And—though he could not promise it—she might even single me out and bestow upon me the honor and precious gift of her friendship. Certainly there was no one more deserving than I of such a privileged intimacy. She was after all only seventeen, a scant few months older than myself, so it was possible we might have much in common and become the best of friends. I could hardly wait! Surely my dreams *must* come true! I was born to have the best of everything. I smiled and clasped my hands and hugged them tight against my pounding heart. Soon I would be dancing every night, the radiant, beautiful beacon of hundreds of admiring eyes, my name on smiling, adoring lips that praised me as the most beautiful lady at court, mayhap even in all of England or even the world. And my father would choose the richest and handsomest and finest of those gallant gentlemen to be my husband, and ours would be not only a marriage of duty but passionate, lusty love!

"You have only to wait, my love, and everything you desire will be handed to you as though upon a golden plate," my father always used to say to me; and I saw now that he was right. Everything I had ever wanted or spent my young life dreaming about was suddenly within grasp. I could hardly wait to reach out and take it.

Everyone was so eager to see her and wondering what she would look like. A babble of a hundred questions seemed to fill my ears. Would she be tall or short, slim or fat, dark, ruddy, or fair? And what would she wear? Something exotic, dripping with gold or silver spangles, embroidered with fantastical oriental arabesques, encrusted with a rainbow of gems or the cold glitter of diamonds or paved with the snowy nacreous luster of thousands of pearls? Would it be somber, bright, dowdy, daring, showy, or meek? What would it be? Would she be veiled or show us her face? Would she be coifed modestly, covering her hair, or in some exotic headpiece the like of which had never been seen on English shores? I could hardly wait to see. Surely she would set fashions we would all rush to follow. Would she be exotic as a peacock or plain as a sparrow? And what would it be like to serve her? Would she be a kind mistress? Or hard and harsh, a stern taskmistress, lofty and remote? Or even worse a jealous, spiteful one who took pleasure in meting out petty little cruelties and punishments? Would she be fun-loving and leave her ladies free to do as they pleased, or a strict and pious mistress who sought to mold and shape us, the kind who cared more for our souls than our selves?

I had long since lost—and gladly—Matilda, my bothersome, vexsome maid, whom I often had cause to swat and slap away. I *hated* her red, chapped hands that were always tugging so insistently at my arm, and her whiny voice hissing or screeching that I mustn't do this or mustn't do that. She was like smallpox on my nerves. I could not stand the way she had been pulling at me, at the same time whining and pleading, even stooping to wheedle, that I must come away at once, that it was not proper for the Duke of Norfolk's daughter to mingle with the common populace, dirty, stinking people who were doubtlessly up to no good and would pluck the gold beads from my gown and use them to buy beer.

"Free at last!" I crowed, elated, when I could no longer see or hear her.

I had never been on my own like this in public before. I had spent my life cosseted and closeted, always properly chaperoned, with maids, governesses, tutors, and retinues of servants sheltering me, surrounding me, stifling me until I sometimes felt I could hardly breathe, fencing me in, protecting me from harm, and shielding me—or so they claimed—from the coarseness and ugliness of a world full of improper and unsuitable persons with dubious intentions, so I found any moment when I could slip away and do any little liberating thing that those who had charge of me would frown upon as heady and exhilarating as getting drunk on strong wine for the very first time.

I wasn't afraid. No one would be such a fool as to dare harm the Duke of Norfolk's daughter. Imperious as a queen, I boldly tossed the long gold- and pearl-embroidered black velvet lappets of my gable hood back over my shoulders, and smiled at the goodwill that surrounded me as the people waved and cheered and called out blessings upon the royal family and the newly arrived Spanish princess. I was eager to enjoy myself, to watch the royal parade pass by. At that moment, I had no other care in the world. Everything else, including any punishment I might face, could wait; I would worry about it later.

Heralds and trumpeters in the Tudor livery of white and green came first, their banners embroidered with red and white Tudor roses fluttering with gold fringe. Then, looking as peevish and glum as a mourner who had bumbled into a wedding instead of the funeral he meant to attend, came the King, Henry VII, graying, pinch-faced, and dour in plain and obviously old black velvet trimmed with ratty fur that had clearly seen better days. Apparently he had not deemed this a fit occasion to order new clothes, and one could only hope that he had felt differently about the wedding to come, otherwise the foreign ambassadors would soon be gleefully spreading the word of our monarch's moth-eaten apparel abroad and making a laughingstock of the English people. I shuddered to think what they would say of him in Paris! He offered the occasional curt nod to the crowd but mostly kept his squinty gray eyes trained straight ahead as he rode past on a horse that would have suited a brewer's cart better than the sovereign lord of England.

How can such a beautiful woman bear such an unbecoming old miser? I wondered as I beheld the Queen, the beautiful Elizabeth of York, fair as a white rose, with vivid blue green eyes and red gold hair. She wore a sumptuous gown of rose red velvet, trimmed in gold and black and rubies and pearls to match the trim on her black velvet gable hood. A necklace of gold and enameled red and white roses encircled her throat, and her slender fingers blazed with rubies and diamonds as they delicately gripped the reins of a snowy mare caparisoned in cloth-of-gold and red silk fringe. How we all loved our beautiful Queen! Those who knew her said she had a gentle manner, kind and gracious, and that her husband, the King, could deny her nothing. Looking at her clothes, it *must* be true—she was too beautifully garbed for the King to enforce his miserly, penny-pinching ways when it came to paying her dressmakers.

The royal bridegroom came next—Arthur, Prince of Wales. He was mounted on a handsome white steed caparisoned in cloth-of-silver, ropes of pearls, and grass green velvet. Our prince was a handsome lad of fifteen in white fur and sea green silk broidered with swirls of silver, emerald brilliants, and seed pearls. But all the finery in the world could not disguise the fact that he was alarmingly frail of form; one might even go so far as to say that he looked "sickly"—the sort one imagined a gust of wind would knock right off his horse. Like his mother, he was fine-featured and white-rose fair, but even his red gold hair seemed pale, and his washed-out blue eyes peered out of dark, purplish blue circles. Sleep, I guessed, did not come easily to him.

With a shy, becoming smile and a timidly raised hand, he acknowledged the crowd as he rode past, followed by a cheeky and vibrant ruddy-haired lad, like a fat little rooster preening in gold-embroidered tawny velvet trimmed with the red fur of foxes. The ends of his chin-length red gold hair curled as though they might tickle his plump pink cheeks and be the reason for his smile. A peacock plume jauntily crowned his black velvet cap and seemed a most fitting touch for one so obviously, and with every reason to be, proud and vain. Prince Henry, our fun-loving Duke of York, grinned and waved at the crowd with the greatest gusto as he cantered past on a chestnut gelding caparisoned in green and white velvet emblazoned with red and white roses.

All around me the cheers grew louder and people pressed closer at the sight of him as though they longed to reach out and touch and hug and kiss him. They clearly *adored* him.

Though only ten, Prince Henry had such a way about him; he was so charismatic, like the always-alluring flame that moths could never resist. No witch or wizard could ever cast such a powerful glamour as his smile and eyes did; simply put, he was spellbinding. As his blue-gray eyes swept the crowd, he made each person feel special, as though his smile were a special gift intended solely for that privileged individual and no other. He truly was the people's prince. He collected hearts and kept them.

What a pity such a one was destined for the church! Though I did not doubt for a moment that his sermons would be immensely popular and well attended—with his charm they could *never* be dull—and I would wager every jewel I possessed that ladies too numerous to count would flock to him for spiritual consolation and to give him their confession. Indeed, my fluttering heart told me, if he matured as well as I imagined, I was likely to be amongst that smitten throng.

I should like very much to play the penitent Mary Magdalene to his Jesus Christ, I thought, savoring the wicked wanderings of my mind as I imagined myself kneeling at his feet with my hair unbound and flowing over my naked breasts. *What a wicked one you are, Elizabeth Howard. Your soul is as black as your hair,* I chastised myself, though I wasn't really the least bit sorry. *Maybe he will take me over his knee and spank me,* I thought. *I sincerely hope so!* I giggled and exchanged smiles with the rustic old beldam standing beside me with a sheepish grin, a guilty expression, and a blush spreading brightly over her wizened cheeks that told me that her mind was meandering down a sensual path very similar to my own.

Then the Spanish heralds came in a vivid, dizzying sea of yellow and red, fluttering satin banners dripping with gold and silk fringe, and blaring gold trumpets that gave way to a flock of red cardinals, in voluminous velvet robes and wide-brimmed hats, prayer books and rosaries clutched in their red-gloved hands, and next a solemn mass of pious, black-robed priests with bowed heads, each one carrying a silver crucifix clasped tightly against his chest.

All of a sudden there she was—the one we had all been waiting for, like a single precious white pearl washed up upon the shore in a tangle of garish shells and dark seaweed. We had never seen anyone like her before, and she took all our breaths away.

Petite and plump and golden-haired, she was clad all in the purest, most radiant white. The full skirt of her satin gown was draped over a stiff farthingale that billowed about her like a great bell, swaying with her every step to reveal dainty white leather boots worked with gold embroidery and fringed with gold about the ankles. Her hair fell like a cloak made of abundant golden strands down about her hips, flowing from beneath a broad-brimmed white hat, just like a cardinal's except for its pure, virginal color, tied with gold laces beneath her plump little chin, and adorned with a bit of jewel-studded gold trimming with peaked edges around the crown to suggest the crown that would be hers one day when she became England's Queen.

The crowd went wild, deafening me with their cheers, throwing posies and nosegays of sweet-scented herbs and pretty flowers at the princess, welcoming her, praising and blessing her, and the future fruit of her womb.

Suddenly a little girl broke from the crowd, an adorable, dirty-faced, barefoot cherub whose head was a riot of springy tawny curls. She had never seen anything like the stiff farthingale that puffed out Princess Catherine's skirts and wanted to feel, to find out if this foreign princess was really shaped like a giant bell. Boldly, she reached out and embraced the full, billowing cloud of white skirt, smiling up at the princess with such innocent, radiant joy that it made every heart melt.

There were sighs and smiles and good-natured chuckles all around as her blushing mother hastened to pull her away, though not even she had the heart to utter a word of chastisement, and the Spanish princess smiled and bent down to caress the child's face with a gold-embroidered and fringed white kid glove. She took a pearl rosary from where it hung at her waist and pressed it into that dirty-faced little angel's grubby little hand as a remembrance of this joyful day.

Then she was gone, walking past, so that others might see her, and two dozen dignified, solemn, and serious-faced Spanish ladies took her place, led by the princess's formidable duenna, Dona Elvira. They walked with their chins up, as though in silent comment on the great stink of London, and their hands folded demurely at their stout, matronly waists, clasping dark-beaded rosaries with dangling golden crucifixes replete with the suffering Christ frozen forever in mute agony. All of them were clad in dark, dour opulence. They marched past without acknowledging us, in high-collared, somber-hued Spanish and Genoese velvets trimmed with discreet daubs of muted gold, wearing headdresses that looked like rotten dark brown or black pumpkins that had been cut in half, hollowed out, and studded with pearls and shimmering, winking, and faceted jet, garnet, smoky- and honey-hued topaz, and antique gold beads before being crammed onto their heads to hide each and every hair of their severely pinned tresses. By the look of them, they followed the old fashion of shaving back their hairlines to make their foreheads appear even higher, which had the effect of making them all look bald beneath those ludicrous beaded pumpkins. In the crowd around me, some poor and ignorant people wondered if it was indeed the fashion for Spanish women to shave their pates after the wedding.

As the procession wended past on its way to St. Paul's Cathedral, to celebrate a special mass of thanksgiving for Princess Catherine's safe arrival, the crowd about me began to disperse with much talk of alehouses. It was then that I realized my predicament.

How was I to make my way back to Baynard's Castle for the banquet that was to follow the mass? I hadn't spared a thought for that. A proper conveyance—a coach, barge, litter, or horse—had *always* been provided for me. I had never had to ask or arrange such things myself. I took it for granted that it would always be there when I wanted or had need of it, and it always had been.

Where was Matilda when I needed her? I stamped my foot and wished my maid would miraculously materialize standing right beside me so I could slap her. I would be sure to tell my father that she had abandoned me, deserted me when I needed her most, and left his young and beautiful only daughter entirely unchaperoned, all alone on a public thoroughfare where I had, only by some miracle, escaped being ravished at the hands of some crude and uncouth stranger. I might have been raped by a rat catcher or one of those foul ruffians who collected manure from the city streets! He'd have her lashed for this! I was sure of it. And I would be right there, standing beside him, smiling up at him adoringly with my hand on his velvet sleeve, listening to the annoying music of her screams as her back was being flayed open. My father always took care of me; "naught but the best for my Bess," he always said, even though I detested being called by any diminutive of my Christian name.

Fuming and frustrated by my sudden, and unexpected, helplessness, I spun around, anxiously searching the street, hoping to spy some passing conveyance that I might hail or some familiar face I might prevail upon for some chivalrous assistance. It was then that I noticed *him*. A rather rotund—or *fat* as a cruder, more plain-spoken, and less refined individual might have said—young man, tall, dark-eyed and -haired, and with a light growth of beard adorning his big, round as a pie face, slumped casually against a wall in his humble rusty black doublet and hose, both well-worn and oft-mended. He was like a great big baby—so soft, lovely, pink, white, and fat—yet at the same time unmistakably, undeniably a man, but I still wanted to hold and play with him. He looked *delicious,* and my hot blood gave a mighty sizzle. I suddenly wished with all my heart that I had a bouquet of sweet and spicy pinks so I might invite him to play a rather naughty game peasant girls played in which they secreted the blossoms in their clothes and invited the young men they favored to search and find them, then trade them all for kisses.

A stray lock of unruly dark hair fell like an upside-down question mark over his brow as his intense, warm brown eyes pierced me like Cupid's arrow. It was the most peculiar sensation! His eyes seemed to strip me bare, layer by layer, down past my flesh and bones straight to my naked soul, making me feel even more naked than naked; I hated and loved it at the same time. In one hand, he held what appeared to be a small, light scrap of pale wood, whilst the other clutched a stick of charcoal. He was drawing me.

Though I was rather flattered, I thrust my chin high, gathered up my skirts, and, regal as a queen, made my way across the street to stand before him.

"Let me see that!" I imperiously thrust out my hand.

When he stood up full straight, he towered high above me, but I wasn't afraid.

"How dare you draw me without my permission?" I demanded. "I did not give you leave to sketch me! Do you know who I am?"

With a lift of his brows and a slight little smile that suggested he found this absurd, he turned the drawing around so that I might see, keeping, I noted, a possessive hold upon it rather than relinquishing it to me.

The brows I labored with my silver tweezers to keep plucked into fine, thin, graceful, perfect black arches shot up in surprise.

It was only my face! The way his gaze had made me feel, so hot and penetrating, like I imagined a phallus would be, I had expected to see my whole form, perhaps even unclothed in some lewd pose. But it was only my face as perfect as I saw it in my mirror each day. He had captured every line, every nuance, flawlessly. He had actually done justice to my beauty!

"It is rather good," I coolly admitted without abandoning my haughty stance.

I fumbled for my little velvet purse, but he shook his head and hid the sketch behind his back, silently adamant that he would not part with it.

"Now don't be absurd!" I cried. "What artist does not want to sell his work?"

He shook his head again. "I need it . . . for my work."

He spoke softly, in a shy voice with just a whisper of a French accent.

"For your work?" I repeated, my brows arching high in disbelief. "And what pray tell is that? You are obviously not the average artisan since you shun payment for your humble scribblings."

"I am a doll maker," he said, turning and pointing proudly to the modest wooden shingle that hung above a door set like a jewel into the wall he had been leaning against. *Remi Jouet, Doll & Toy Maker,* it read, carved in elegant Italianate letters painted with weather-faded gilt.

"This is *your* shop?" I asked incredulously. It had never occurred to me that such a young man of clearly modest means might be the proprietor of his own shop, an apprentice boy, yes; indeed I had taken it for granted that that was what he was, but not a craftsman in his own right.

"Would my lady care to see inside?" he asked with a certain shy pride imbuing his voice that at the same time betrayed a fear of rebuff.

He was clearly not a man accustomed to conversing with ladies as beautiful as I, so I took pity on him. I nodded, and without waiting for him to open the door, grandly swept inside with a pleasing swish of sapphire velvet.

The large front room was a fine, orderly place, well lit and clean, and not too cluttered, the tables and shelves all neatly arranged, like a well-ordered jewel box, so each toy could be seen and admired in its own right instead of in a careless, tangled heap that must first be sorted and straightened out like the beaded necklaces I often threw at Matilda, screaming for her to unknot them so I could wear whichever one I pleased; though more often than not, I would end by capriciously flinging them right back into the box, to become tangled again, and slamming the lid. It never really bothered me if such rough handling broke them. My father would always buy me more; I had only to ask him.

There were toys for both humble and highborn children, boys and girls. There were gaudy rag poppets, floppy-limbed with embroidered eyes and smiles, and mops of bright yellow or red yarn hair; stump dolls carved out of a single block of solid wood, hard and unmoving, but good enough for a poor little girl to cherish and love; and more expensive, ornate models with wax, painted plaster, molded clay, or carved alabaster faces, dainty white hands and feet, with bodies of stuffed linen or leather, some even with jointed wooden limbs, with full heads of beautifully curled or braided human hair, and garments of silk, satin, damask, brocade, sarcenet, and velvet so fine that, had they been life-sized, would have been fit for the court. Some even had jewels; the more humble had a string of colorful clay beads, polished pebbles, or a wolf's tooth on a leather cord to ward off illness—"a nice touch for a sickly child," Remi shyly explained—and the more elaborate, and expensive, had glass or even carnelian, jet, or coral beads. Some even had pearls artfully woven through their hair and around their throats or stitched onto their dresses, and gold or silver pendants, crucifixes, or brooches studded with real gemstone brilliants. Perched on the highest shelf safely behind the counter I even saw one with high-piled golden curls, held up by pearl- and diamond-tipped pins, resplendent in a court gown of black velvet replete with a long train sewn all over with tiny twinkling diamonds.

There were lady dolls and baby dolls, the princesses every little girl dreams of being. And, for the boys, soldiers and knights replete with full metal armor and weaponry, some mounted on horses; gentlemen in hunting leathers accompanied by hounds or with hawks on their arms; and that beloved rogue Robin Hood armed with his bow and head to toe in Lincoln green, from the simple stump dolls to elaborate wooden jointed figures. Some of these even came equipped with strings so that the lucky boys who owned them might enact their own jousts or battles. There was something for everyone and every purse; Remi, I would later learn, insisted upon it.

On a table before the front window, there was an array of edible dolls, gingerbread figures adorned with edible gilt, sugared dough that when picked up gave a tantalizing rattle to reveal that there was a prize hidden inside, and bread dolls made in the likeness of various saints, the kind mothers liked to give their children in the hope that by eating them they would be blessed with the same virtues as that particular saint.

There was even a small table artfully draped with silver-embroidered rose-colored silk arrayed with a variety of pincushion dolls and exquisite tiny dolls—I hesitate to call them rag dolls as that usually suggests a homemade plaything made of scraps, simple and cheap, and these were crafted only of the finest materials, and they also had slender wire skeletons secreted inside to stiffen them—that decorated beautiful needle cases, sewing baskets, and trinket boxes.

Standing tentatively beside me, Remi silently picked up a red apple–shaped velvet pincushion atop which stood an exquisite little lady gowned in pearl-studded, gold-blossomed, flesh-colored brocade, her long, sleek black hair braided with gold and crowned with a coronet of exquisite tiny seed pearl flowers. There was a knowing, sensual look in her dark eyes as she held out a tiny ruby red–enameled apple in her outstretched hand while a serpent woven of gilt threads and emerald glass beads twined around her, embracing her limbs through her skirt. I saw the hesitation, the uncertainty and fear of rebuke or refusal in his dark eyes, but the battle he was fighting within himself passed quickly, and he conquered his fear and pressed the pretty bauble into my hands.

"I . . . I would like you to have this," he said haltingly as a blush set his cheeks aflame.

I let my haughtiness fall away from me, like a gown of silk pooling around my feet, and simply said, "Thank you," and held the beautiful trifle tenderly clasped against my breast, and, to give him time to recover himself, I continued browsing his shop.

Besides the dolls, there were rattles, tops, sets of toy soldiers, a wooden Noah's Ark filled with carved and brightly painted pairs of animals, similar sets of barnyard beasts, board games like Fox and Geese, hobby horses, gaily painted shields, wooden swords, and sets of ninepins. Some made plain for poorer children, and others with great detail and embellishment fashioned from more costly materials for his wealthier patrons.

I paused beside the shelf that contained the finest dolls, mounted higher than the rest, beyond the reach of most eager little hands and meager purses.

"Shall you make a doll of me, I wonder?" I said as my fingers idly caressed a skirt of vermilion silk with a pattern of golden poppies worn by a little lady with a mass of golden curls crowned by a wreath of red silk poppies.

"The most beautiful doll I have ever made," Remi promised, his eyes shining with sincerity and ardor. "With her face, hands, and feet carved of the purest white alabaster, and hair like the finest ebony silk. I will dress her in deep blue velvet trimmed with golden lovers' knots just like you are wearing today so you will always remember."

I took a step toward him, just as he stepped toward me. His strong fingers closed around my delicate wrist. My pulses pounded, and my heart leapt inside my breast like an eager, nervous frog. I *relished* the knowledge that he could have snapped it if he had wanted to, but I knew he didn't. This shy, gentle, soft-spoken, and soft-bodied man who made dolls would *never* wantonly destroy any object of great beauty. I would always be safe with him! Then I was in his arms, and he was kissing me with such a *furious* hunger I didn't know whether he was angry at himself for desiring me or at me, a beautiful, proud, highborn, well-bred young lady who should have known better, for submitting to a common artisan's ardor.

But there was no time for questions. As we broke apart, staring at each other, speechless, in blushing and bewildered silence, the door opened and there stood that breathless and gawping idiot Matilda sobbing out an apology for losing me in the crowd.

"It's about time!" I snapped. "I've been waiting for you for what seems like hours! I merely stepped inside this shop as I did not think it meet that I, a duke's daughter, linger in the street like a common trollop looking for trade! My father would never approve, and he will be sure to flay the hide off you if I decide to tell him that you left me to fend for myself alone in the merciless streets of London. I might have been molested by a fishmonger or groped by a grocer! Or abducted and sold into a brothel to spend the rest of my days satisfying the base lusts of low men, or even had my purse snatched!"

As Matilda continued to weep and blubber words I did not even bother trying to decipher, I turned to the doll maker and graciously gave him my hand.

"Make me a doll, Master Jouet," I said. "When it is finished, and you are *certain* that it is worthy of me, send it to me, and—this time I insist—I will pay you, and well." I spoke these words, husky and soft, with a bold gaze and sensually parted lips that I hoped would convey that I meant to give him so much more than cold hard coins.

Without waiting for his answer, I thrust my chin up high and turned, letting the train of my gown slap Matilda's ankles like a velvet whip, and headed for the door.

"But how will I find you again?" Remi called after me. "I don't even know your name!"

On the threshold I paused and looked back at him. "Look for the grandest and most beautiful lady at court; by the time you have finished your doll, that is who I will be!"

And with that lofty boast, I left him, confident that a day would come when I would see him again. Life just couldn't be so cruel as to deny me!

We reached Baynard's Castle just in time to join the lords and ladies hurrying into the Great Hall. I paused for just a moment to catch my breath and straightened my gable hood as Matilda knelt to smooth my skirts and swipe the dust from my hems and velvet slippers even as I kicked at her for no better reason than I wanted to. When I married, I vowed, and this became my everyday world, not just a wonderful place I came to briefly visit when the occasion warranted it, I would send Matilda to work in the laundry and have another, and better, maid to serve me, a Frenchwoman perhaps, someone with enough wit and sophistication to be worthy of serving me, who could help me enhance my beauty even more. Just then a young man, a low common clerk in the midst of his twenties, or some dull, dreary bookkeeper, by the look of him—his cold, muddy gray eyes and mirthless mouth; his boring, blunt-cut, mud brown hair framing a gaunt and grim face; and the plain charcoal doublet, hat, and hose he wore—dared to most familiarly touch my arm, as though he presumed the right to such an intimacy, and asked if he might have the honor of escorting me in to dine.

"You may not!" I cried, snatching my arm away and glaring at him as though he were a scab I wanted to rip off just to make the wound bleed. "*How dare you touch me?* Do you know who I am?"

Without waiting for him to answer, I thrust my chin high and flounced, alone, into the Great Hall.

As for that impertinent clerk, I didn't deign to favor him with another infinitesimal thought. I had put that insignificant toady in his place, and that was an end to that. It *never* occurred to me that I would ever see him again, not even standing in a crowd; he really wasn't worth the attention of the Duke of Norfolk's daughter.

Later that afternoon, after Princess Catherine had been prevailed upon to show us how the ladies at the court of Spain danced, with slow, graceful steps, and castanets clicking in her plump little white hands, I discreetly stole away. As much as I liked being at court, there were moments when I found it all rather tedious, especially when I knew more pleasing pastimes were readily at hand if I went in pursuit of them.

"Life is dull," I always said with a languid sigh I imagined made me appear fashionably world-weary. "And one should grasp every diversion that presents itself." And I was never one to let a precious opportunity pass me by; that was one of the few things I would have in common with the man who was to become my husband.

As the sun sank like a ball of fire, I lay, clad in only my sheer white lawn shift, upon my lover's bed, reveling in his passionate and skillful touch that made me feel as though my soul had been set aflame.

John Skelton, so aptly named, as he had a very gaunt, cadaverous frame—I often teased him that I could count every rib—was the poet laureate of England (I had crowned him so myself) and tutor to Prince Henry. He was a man alternately passionate and pious; one moment he lived and breathed all for love, boldly proclaiming he would lay down his life for just one kiss; the next he was mired deep in melancholy and claiming he wanted nothing more than to renounce the world, retreat to some austere monastery, become a monk, and live out his days as a hermit and a recluse. He had penned many poems he said were inspired by my beauty, as well as many popular jests at the expense of the court worthies that even the common people loved to recite, especially when they saw the subjects passing by in gilded barges on the river or being carried in elegant litters through the filth-strewn streets of London.

Our affair had begun two years ago, when I was a slight, pert-bosomed maid of fourteen, the very night of a masque in his honor, when I, in a gown of gold brocade woven with a pattern of silver acanthus leaves, stepped forward to proudly crown him England's poet laureate. How I preened at having been chosen to play such a role! As I solemnly placed the wreath of gilded laurels upon his brow, he glanced down my bodice and smiled. When he bent and kissed my cheek, to thank me for this honor, he whispered poetic compliments about my bosom and stuck his tongue in my ear, making me lose my composure for a moment and giggle like a common milkmaid.

Later, when the wine was flowing freely at the banquet tables, he doffed his crown of laurels and donned a coronet his own nimble fingers had fashioned from humble garden vegetables, playing the clown and poking fun at his own reputation. He asked me to dance. I readily agreed. I was flattered to have caught the attention of a poet, and dreams of becoming his muse fluttered and whirled like giddy dancers through my girlish mind. When he begged me for one look at my unclad body, to inspire his verse to greater glories, I instantly agreed. Why ever should I not? His verses would make my beauty famous and immortal! Even when my bones had crumbled into dust, I would live on eternally, immortally beautiful in his words. He was giving me the gift of immortal life! Only a fool would refuse that!

He hurriedly whispered directions to his chamber. I made my excuses, whispering some vague and hasty words hinting at the onset of my courses in my stepmother's ear, and left the Great Hall, and a little time later, he followed.

As I stood naked, the first time in all my stark-fleshed glory before any man, he knelt worshipfully at my feet, reciting impetuous verses to me, until I grew bored, and lay down on his bed with my legs splayed wantonly wide to show the secret pink heart of me and beckoned for him to join me and "See what inspiration awaits you here, Sir Poet."

I never would share his passion for poetry. Though it was flattering at first being his muse, the novelty soon paled. I already knew I was beautiful—my mirror and men's admiring eyes and women's jealous ones told me so every day—and those looks told me more than all the poetry in the world ever could. And I think, upon reflection, it was my nature to prefer things more straightforward and simpler. Plain speech and perfect understanding were, to my mind, always better than a whole bouquet of flowery words with the meanings all hidden beneath pretty petals and ribbons.

I was often bored and greatly annoyed when, suddenly inspired by our lovemaking—such as it was with my frustratingly intact maidenhead being avoided like a leper despite my urgent pleas that he relieve my agony and pierce it—he sat up, snatched a quill, and rolled me onto my belly to use my back as a makeshift desk for his impulsive scribbling, ignoring the annoyed little shrieks I uttered whenever the point pricked me through the paper and left black ink spots on my snowy skin. These writing sessions frequently lasted longer than our pleasure, and while John's pen scratched across page after infernal page, often for *hours,* I consoled myself with the plate of raisin-studded saffron buns or gilt-iced marzipan cakes he always left on the bedside table as a treat for me, "his beautiful muse."

But that afternoon, as he covered my body with blazing kisses, I kept seeing the doll maker's face, as though Remi Jouet's likeness were painted in vivid colors on the insides of my eyelids. I could not stop thinking about him!

How curious that I should think of him. I had always before yearned for hard bodies, lean and muscular; those were the kind of men who figured in my dreams, partnering me in the most intimate dance of all, when the finery of the ballroom was doffed, and it was only skin against skin, perfume, heat, and sweat, and yet . . . I wanted him as I had never wanted anyone before, and I knew I would never rest content until I had him.

I moaned and groaned and caught at Master Skelton, trying to pull him onto me, into me, as I begged him to come inside and ease me; I was in such torment. But, as always, he demurred. I wanted to pound him with my fists and scream, *He wouldn't be afraid to do it! He may be a doll maker, but he is more man than you are!* I never intended the words to be the rather obvious jest reflection shows they were—*I can tell by his eyes, his hand around my wrist, and the way he kissed me!* But of course I didn't. John Skelton may have been my first real lover, in the sense that I took all my clothes off and permitted him greater liberties than some hurried fondling and a few stolen kisses, but already I knew better than to discuss one lover with another. Any excitement or adulation I might have felt at being caught between two rival admirers would have soon been transfigured into annoyance. I like excitement, it's true, but I also like things to be peaceful, free of conflict, fear, and argument.

"I cannot pierce you, Bess"—he always called me Bess even though he knew I loathed it—" 'twould be the death of me if I, a common poet, deflowered the Duke of Norfolk's daughter."

The apology and regret in his voice only made me angrier, and it was all I could do not to kick and pummel him from the bed. "But you are not a common poet; you are the poet laureate of England!" I whined, even though I knew a sulky demeanor ill became me.

"But"—sensing my simmering frustration, he lay full upon me and soothingly stroked my hair, as though I were a lapdog frightened by thunder and he was trying to calm me—*"I rather would thy lippés bas, than Saint Peter his gates y-pass."* He recited one of his most famous lines, the one wooers often resorted to, as he bent his head and kissed me long and deep.

I wrapped my arms around his neck and thought of Remi Jouet and wished that he were kissing me instead of John Skelton. If only wishes were enough! What I wouldn't have given at that moment to feel the delicious weight of him upon me, skin against skin, and his lips devouring mine! But at least someone was kissing me, and, for now, that had to be enough. Life often, I find, boils down to making the best of things.

The next morning, as Matilda was finishing lacing me into a black velvet–banded buff velvet gown, while I leisurely sipped the last of my breakfast ale and nibbled daintily upon a honey-drizzled oatcake crowned with succulent, fat raisins, my brother knocked brusquely and came in without waiting for me to call out my permission.

Though only two years older than myself, Thomas, my father's namesake and heir, was one of those men who even when young seem old. Pinch-faced and crotchety, humorless and dour, stingy with his smiles as well as with his coins, my brother loved full money boxes and worldly honors, like dukedoms and deeds to rich manors, more than he ever did flesh and blood. Even his mistresses were a luxury equated with velvet robes and gold-embroidered slippers; he wanted only the best and discarded his women the way he did old or worn-out shoes. In years to come, when his wife complained of the humiliation she suffered because he had left her bed for her own coarse, red-handed laundress, "a blowsy strumpet," my brother stripped her bare, bound her wrists and ankles to the four posters of the bed, and donned full armor and rolled upon her naked body until she spat up blood and was bruised all over. She never dared complain about his infidelities again and was naught but the soul of graciousness to her laundress.

Miserly with his words as well as his money and any kindness that might have been lurking, buried deep, within his soul, Thomas merely said I must come with him and took my arm so quickly I scarcely had time to turn back and hand Matilda my nigh empty tankard and snatch up the black velvet hood I had worn the day before.

Without benefit of a mirror, I was still struggling to set it properly on my head and make myself presentable as I hurriedly followed Thomas along the palace corridors, grumbling all the while at his tight-lipped, straight-backed silence.

"You might have the courtesy to tell me what this is about!" I fumed, wishing he were Matilda so I might kick him without fear of repercussions; but kicking their brothers was something highborn well-bred ladies simply did not do, especially in palace corridors where other nobles or their servants might see and spread gossip about it, so I had no choice but to curtail my violent emotions.

Thomas paused outside the door to Father's lodgings.

"There is someone Father and I want you to meet," he said simply as he opened the door and ushered me inside.

The first thing I saw, standing directly in front of me, was that lowly, presumptuous clerk I had had the misfortune to encounter the day before. I had forgotten all about him until this moment.

Taut-mouthed and grim, with an indecipherable gleam in his gray brown eyes, there he stood before me in a brown velvet doublet with a discreet shimmer of gold braid adorning the seams.

I froze, bristling with contempt. Had the fellow *dared* complain of me to my father? I squared my shoulders, bracing myself for a fight. He would not get away with this! How dare he tattle on the Duke of Norfolk's daughter?

Father was talking, and, to my astonishment, I soon discovered that this person was not a clerk at all but one of the rising stars of the Tudor court, an Esquire of the Body to Prince Henry, with a seat at the royal table, and the privilege of carving the prince's meat, sometimes entrusted with minor missions abroad on account of his intelligence and excellent French. He was a good friend of my brother Thomas. Indeed they might have been twins; beneath the skin they were two of a kind. Ambition was their guiding star. They had made a pact to work together to rise above the mistakes of the past—the low birth of one and the grave and disgraceful mistake my family had made in the past when they backed the loser, Richard III, in the war that ended with Henry Tudor taking England's throne.

This Thomas Bullen, I would learn, despite his clerk's brain, fluent French, and that oily, ingratiating, insinuating, slithering-snake, worshipful manner that appealed so to the vanity of the Tudors, was born of lowly merchant stock.

His grandfather, Geoffrey, a barefoot farm boy determined to make his fortune, left the family farm and walked to London. There he found work as a hatter's apprentice. Later he eschewed millinery for cloth, becoming one of London's most successful silk merchants before he was done. But he didn't stop there. Oh no! The Bullens, with their bull-like tenacity, had ambition instead of blood in their veins; they were on the rise, determined never to fall back down. "I never want to see a haystack again unless I own it," he often said. Geoffrey Bullen, the silk merchant, married one of his best customers, a fat and frumpy but *very rich* widow named Denise, who was over the moon with happiness to have a handsome young man in her bed, and only too glad to instruct him in the social niceties; thanks to her, his days of wiping his knife and blowing his nose on his sleeve were soon past. If I really cared, I would light a candle for her. But the exuberant joy of wedded bliss soon wore out poor Denise's heart; she was not a young woman after all. Denise Bullen was barely cold in her grave before greedy Geoffrey was betrothed to a Bedfordshire heiress, the Lady Ann Hoo. Through this lucrative and fortuitous union, he acquired manors, a knighthood, became an alderman, and later Sheriff of London, and eventually Lord Mayor. When he died he left one thousand pounds to the poor, a showy, vulgar gesture just to display how far he had risen from the barefoot farm boy who had walked to London to make his fortune.

His only son, William, Thomas's father, followed in his father's footsteps, acquiring over time a tart-tongued Irish heiress, Lady Margaret Butler, the daughter of the Earl of Ormonde, for a bride, a few more manors, and a knighthood, and lots more money without having to sully his fingertips with dye from new cloth, even if it was the finest silk, or deal with flighty and indecisive customers, like his father had in his ambitious fortune-seeking youth. Oh yes, with each generation, the Bullens were rising higher and higher. Thomas hoped to trump them all before he left this world.

My father, still in his wine velvet dressing gown, silk-tasseled nightcap, and gold-embroidered slippers, smiled broadly and opened his arms to me, his adored only daughter, and I went into them gladly.

So stunned was I that I didn't even feel his embrace or his lips upon my cheek. As though from the bottom of the sea, I heard my father speak that lowborn toady's name—"Sir Thomas Bullen," coupled with the words *betrothed* and *husband*.

I bit my tongue and tasted blood. I felt faint. A red mist obscured my sight. There was a loud humming, like a swarm of angry bees, which made me imagine there was a beehive on my head where my hood used to be. I could hear nothing else, so I did what I was raised to do—my duty—and nodded and smiled while Father's voice droned on and on, while inside I was raging like a madwoman, screaming and rattling the bars of her cage.

How could my father do this to *me,* his only daughter, a girl so beautiful and well-bred? The insult was beyond belief! I stood there smiling and blinking, dumb as a cow, willing myself not to fall down and embarrass myself by sprawling at the feet of one who was not worthy to wash my own. And, in those few moments, it was done. My future was decided, like a black velvet curtain being drawn over the bright sun. I was doomed. My father had thrown his most precious pearl down before a swine, and I knew then how truly little he valued me. So much for being adored!

My affianced husband executed a gallant bow and kissed my hand.

Long schooled in ladylike obedience, I had dutifully extended it to him without even realizing what I was doing. I was too stunned to even think of slapping that smile of victory right off his cunning weasel face.

"You snake!" I wanted to scream and trample him beneath my feet, but you would have never known it by my face; I kept smiling.

My father was saying something about my betrothed's bright future, how "great things will come to him," a jumble of meaningless words about service abroad and impeccable French, and how high he stood in the royal family's esteem, but my mind couldn't string them together in any way that made sense. And then, I don't even remember how—I have no memory at all of curtsying and leaving that room or walking back down the corridor—I was back in my bedchamber.

Behind my closed door, all hell broke loose. I was as a woman possessed by a hundred demons. I wept and screamed, kicked and stamped, and struck out blindly, at Matilda, the room, and all its luxurious contents, breaking and smashing and tearing everything within my reach.

I ran to the elegant little gilt-embellished oak bookcase Father always insisted travel with me everywhere I went, so the precious knowledge that would make me the perfect wife, mother, and chatelaine of my husband's castle would always be within reach of my fingertips in case a spare hour for study suddenly presented itself, even if I were only coming up to London, to visit the court, for a few days. I yanked out all the tomes of etiquette, cookery, and housewifery, the herbals, books of household hints, child rearing, and midwifery, and began tearing their pages from the costly blue leather bindings with their titles and my family's crest and my initials in gilt lettering upon the covers and spines that Father had chosen just to please me.

When Matilda tried to stop me, I turned on her, snarling like a savage beast, wielding the book I held like a weapon. I smashed her nose in with *The English Housewife* and watched as she fell back with blood spurting from her red and flattened nose. I had broken it, but I didn't care; at that moment I had more important things on my mind.

Soon the floor was littered with elegant but empty blue leather bindings and hundreds of torn pages, their edges glinting knife-edged with gilt, stained with Matilda's blood and my furious tears. I kicked at them viciously, sending pages flying, scattering like the wings of a flock of frightened black, white, and gold birds.

Thousands of words, centuries of wisdom, I in that moment rejected; I *refused* to squander it all on the likes of Thomas Bullen. I had spent my life learning to be perfect—for *this!* I felt so betrayed! I stood for a long moment, gasping and reeling amidst the ruins of my perfect life, and then I collapsed, weeping on my blue velvet bed amidst the wafting feathers of the pillows I had ripped and the gold fringe I had torn from the bedcurtains and coverlet.

It was so unfair! I was born for far better things than to be the wife of Thomas Bullen! I deserved better than better; I deserved the best! How could life be so cruel and unkind to me when I was so beautiful? I was far above rubies and a silk merchant's grandson!

❧ 2 ❧

We lingered in London long enough to attend the royal wedding, but with my own nuptials looming and Thomas Bullen
by my side—gazing at me, the prize he had just won, with greedy,
gloating, calculating eyes, tallying up the advantages, the prestige,
and the connections my highborn pedigree would bring to him—I
could not enjoy a single moment of it.

We sat prominently amongst the privileged, as I, the Duke of
Norfolk's daughter deserved, inside St. Paul's Cathedral and
watched the gold-clad Prince Arthur and Princess Catherine, in
soft, solemn voices, exchange vows, then joined the jubilant nuptial
feast at Baynard's Castle. But the food might as well have been
ashes in my mouth. For once, I didn't feel like dancing. When I
must rise and leave the banquet table to take my part in the
masques arranged in honor of the newly wedded couple, I felt as
though some mechanics, like clockworks, were inside my body,
guiding my velvet shod feet and graceful arms. My heart and head
certainly weren't in it. I didn't even care about all the new dresses
my father had ordered for me, telling me to spend whatever I
pleased. Even the velvet-lined coffers the jeweler opened before me
left me cold. It was as though some automated force guided my finger, compelling it to point and my mouth to utter the requisite

word *that* as I made my selections. I was merely doing what I had to do because I had to do it. I didn't really care about any of it.

Even my lover's kisses failed to rouse me, even when I closed my eyes and dreamed of Remi Jouet's big, soft, warm, delicious dumpling of a body, still I felt like weeping, and frequently I did. I unloosed the tears and let them fall freely. I knew my time as Master Skelton's muse was fast drawing to its inevitable end and that he would take my tears as affectionate proof that I lamented this. So I let myself have the comfort of weeping in his arms and being consoled by his kisses and the clever things his tongue could do. Sometimes it proved a good distraction, and sometimes I wept all the harder because it did not. And I feared that such pleasures would soon be forever behind me. I was certain I would never experience the like with Thomas Bullen; I doubted that clod even knew what to do with a woman.

I felt like I had been sleepwalking through life and Thomas Bullen had awakened me with a sudden hard slap across my face. I recognized all these fantasies for what they were now—dreams destined never to come true. Were the doll maker of my dreams and I to meet again how could I even face him after my boast that I would soon be the greatest and grandest lady of the court? In truth, yoked to Thomas Bullen as his broodmare, I would be ashamed to face him. I would feel humbled in his sight. Even though I was a lady and he a tradesman, being Thomas Bullen's bride would tarnish me and make me feel like a false coin of base metal dipped in gold paint. It was the worst blow my pride had ever been dealt.

I took a perverse delight in slighting my affianced husband. In every way I could, I tried to provoke him, hoping against hope that he would change his mind, that my recalcitrance would make him turn his eyes on some other pedigreed damsel with a sweeter and more obliging and amenable nature.

I suffered a number of headaches that conveniently coincided with times when he wished to see me. I spilled wine, sauces, and gravies at banquets, ruining his clothes or mine so that I must flee and could dally over making myself presentable again. I neglected to answer the letters he sent me. I rejected the gold collar with the snorting, fierce, ground-pawing, ruby-eyed Bullen bull that had belonged to his mother the moment the smiling goldsmith laid it before me. It was too wide and pinched the tender flesh of my throat, I said, after I most unwillingly deigned to try the hideous, cumbersome thing on. It reminded me of a dog's collar, I announced as I dropped it disdainfully onto the stone floor, delighting in the clatter, not caring one whit if it were dented or the gems jarred loose by the fall.

When my betrothed sent me a bolt of sumptuous green velvet and asked that it be made into my marriage gown, green being a fertile and lucky color for brides, I flung it aside, causing Matilda, with her nose still bandaged, to shriek as it fell perilously near the fire and an edge was slightly singed.

Willfully, I chose red instead; scarlet for the harlot I would rather be than Thomas Bullen's bride, a passionate color flaming bright as my hatred of him.

I bade my dressmaker make me a bodice, under-sleeves, and petticoat of silver tissue latticed with golden braid punctuated with diamonds and dripping pendant pearls that would shimmer and sway with every move I made. And for my unbound head, a delicately woven filigreed gold circlet blooming with flowers fashioned of pearls and diamonds. I stood firm and turned my back upon her superstitious protestations that these "emblems of tears and sorrow" were unlucky adornments for brides. She pleaded with me to choose something else, but that was precisely why I had chosen them. I had a point to make, and I wanted to make it so plainly and boldly that even an idiot could comprehend the message I was sending to those who would sit in the church and bear witness to my unhappy nuptials. I *knew* this marriage would bring both sorrow and tears to me. I ordered my bodice cut indecently low and rebelliously pushed my gown down to bare my shoulders and the ripe alabaster mounds of my breasts, remembering all the times John Skelton's kisses had blazed a trail over that pure white flesh and suckled upon those rosy nipples. *Goodbye, Ecstasy!* I cried with a doleful sigh. Thomas Bullen's touch was sure to make my skin crawl like an infestation of vermin, and shrivel and shrink as though his kisses inflicted frostbite or leprosy. Oh how I *hated* him! He was neither lusty nor handsome, entirely lacking in fun and frivolity. His conversation bored me to tears; he was solely occupied with his lofty ambitions. To his mind, diverting pastimes were not an occasion for respite, pleasure, and mirth, merely something to do in order to rub shoulders with, gain the ear of, and be seen with the *right* people.

Our marriage was little noted, not the grand affair I had dreamed of all through my girlhood; instead it was lost amidst the shuffle of court pageants and celebrations, and the many other young and comely couples who chose to be married at the same time in honor of the Prince and Princess of Wales.

For a fortnight there were weddings almost every day, and the royal couple smilingly attended each one, including our own, showering the bride and groom with gold coins poured from a great golden loving cup held over their heads; poor petite Princess Catherine had to stand on her tiptoes every time.

How Thomas frowned at the sight of my red gown and the amount of bosom I was displaying in church upon our nuptial day! But, most surprisingly, the shopkeeper's grandson was too well-bred to mention it, though it was more likely that he had learned his manners like a monkey aping others' antics. I saw the anger in his eyes, but I only smiled. To all eyes I was serene and pleasant, smiling at his side as I spoke the requisite words, pretending I was reciting a lesson my tutor had set me as I cemented my doom by pledging myself "to my wedded husband, to have and to hold from this day, for better, for worse, for richer, for poorer, in sickness and in health, to be bonny and buxom in bed and at board, 'til death us depart, if Holy Church will it ordain, and thereto I plight thee my troth."

Our wedding night was dismal, the disappointment I knew it would be. With the businesslike efficiency of a clerk, a doctor accustomed to examining the human physique, or a dentist pulling his ten-thousandth tooth, Thomas Bullen mounted and entered me. He ignored my pain, uttering not a single soothing or sympathetic word. Nor did he caress me or attempt to comfort, or even pleasure, me with his touch. He never asked how I fared during the entire procedure. *Procedure*—that is the most apt word for what transpired behind the curtains of our marital bed. There was not a shred of tenderness throughout. He grunted once as he spent his seed, then rolled off and went to sleep with his back to me. As he softly snored, it was all I could do not to tiptoe from the bed, seize the poker from the fire, and bash his head in as he slept. I *hated* him *so much!* I lay awake for a long time wondering if a jury would believe I was so upset by this brutal assault upon my modesty that my sanity had temporarily fled. If I cried prettily and said I was sorry, mayhap they would pardon me, but nay, I couldn't take the chance. I was never all that keen on gambling. Besides, a pardon would surely mean the convent, and I could never abide that. My vanity would never suffer me to don a nun's habit and shut myself off from the world. *I suppose,* I sighed, *there are some things worse than being Thomas Bullen's bride!*

When the royal couple departed for Ludlow Castle in Wales, Thomas and I set out for Hever Castle in Kent.

Beneath a slate gray sky, with an icy wind that portended snow tugging at the long, trailing skirt of my blue velvet riding habit and the dyed celestial blue ostrich plumes in my round velvet cap, I sat morosely on my mount, twirling my riding crop between my kid-gloved fingers, and stared longingly after Princess Catherine's gilded litter.

With her went my dream of serving the woman who would, God willing, one day be England's Queen, of being the most beautiful and brightest of her ladies-in-waiting, the adored and acknowledged beauty of the court, the muse of poets, the inspiration of artists, the one whom every man wanted to bed and every woman wanted to be. Instead, I was on my way to Kent, to become mistress of a country manor house, to immerse myself in housewifery, to squander my beauty upon the laundry and the larder, and to, as my husband so elegantly phrased it, "get started breeding" his heirs. Before the groom cupped his hands beneath my heel to boost me up into the saddle, Thomas had given my belly a little pat and told me to exercise great caution riding lest I jostle out his heir should he happen to be already growing inside of me.

My dark eyes flashed furiously at him. Defiantly, I raised my arm high, brandishing my whip, and brought it down with a hard, stinging smack on my ginger mare's flank, and took off at a plunging, reckless gallop. Riding breakneck without caring that might indeed be the end result.

"My lady wants exercise," I heard Thomas say to our astonished retainers, to try to save face and gloss over his wife's disobedience, before he dug in his spurs and hurried to catch up with me.

He grabbed my horse's reins and glared at me.

"That is enough, Elizabeth," he said, a warning concealed inside his quiet words and glacial eyes. "Do not make a scene. Either lag behind or match your pace to mine; if you pass me again, your flank, not your mare's, shall be the next to feel the whip." His words were so soft, his face so calm, he might have been commenting on the weather and whether it might snow again before we reached Hever.

I nodded and smiled as best becomes an obedient Christian wife and let my horse fall into step beside his; I would be damned if I would follow meekly behind one who was so far below me. Oh how I *hated* him! He was dead and boring and had no passion except for acquisition, to rise high, and to always be on the winning side—the *only* side that matters, according to my sage "lord and master" Thomas *Bull-In*.

When we arrived, windblown and weary, lightly dusted with snowflakes, I thought we were stopping for the night, lest we be caught in heavy snow. When my husband told me nay, we were home, I thought that dour clerk's exterior concealed an unsuspected and well-hidden clown and he had just uttered the *most* amusing jest. But 'twas no jest! *This* was indeed Hever Castle, the manor over which I, Elizabeth Howard, the Duke of Norfolk's adored only daughter, was to preside as mistress, ruling the servants like a queen in miniature.

It was hardly worthy of the name *Castle!* Small as manors go, it was a horrid boxy thing of sandy-colored stone with a drawbridge, moat, and battlements. It had been built in the thirteenth century, my husband informed me, to which I replied with biting arrogance, "I am not blind—I can see that!"

"The crenellations and other improvements were made in 1384," Thomas continued, to which I thought it best to merely nod and force a smile rather than inquire as to what other *improvements* he referred. My eyesight must after all be failing, for they completely eluded me.

I could tell that the shopkeeper's grandson, proud of his little so-called *castle,* sensed my disapproval, so I decided to throw the dog a bone and pronounced it "rather picturesque and quaint."

"I am sure the gardens are lovely come spring," I offered with a conciliatory smile. After all, I did have to live here and sleep with him whenever he was here, which I hoped would not be too often.

Thomas beamed and said, "Aye," especially the rose and knot gardens he had had made in the latest fashion, and rode on across the drawbridge with a satisfied smile.

In the cobbled courtyard, I met my mother-in-law for the first time, the formidable Lady Margaret Butler, who was to share our abode and watch me with a hawk's eye. Standing stoop-backed in the doorway, she was weighed down with gold and jeweled necklaces; ropes of beads and pearls; talismans; protective and good luck charms, some of them rather rough-hewed and crude, tied to leather or frayed woven cords; gem-studded brooches; heavy bracelets; and rings on every finger. She wore a gown of deep green velvet over a kirtle and under-sleeves of the most brazenly bright and god-awful gaudy purple damask I had ever seen in my life, and in the waning winter light, her gray hair, rather haphazardly pinned and sans a proper headdress of any kind, appeared distinctly *blue.* To my great astonishment the crookbacked old beldam was smoking a *pipe.*

My jaw dropped. In my cosseted and sheltered existence, I had never seen a woman smoke before.

"Coltsfoot," she said in a nigh incomprehensible Irish brogue. "To ease me asthma," she added, blowing a puff of foul smoke right in my face.

A poultice reeking of lavender and weeping down her wrinkled cheeks into the dingy, sagging folds of her neck was tied over her brow, "for the misery in me head," she explained. In her other hand, the one not encumbered with a clay pipe, she clutched a large golden goblet of crab-apple wine, which a doctor whose name I didn't catch had recommended for some indistinguishably uttered ailment the old blue-haired witch was afflicted with, which hopefully, for my sake, would carry her off to sleep perpetually in her tomb very soon.

As she ushered me inside, she took from her overskirt a pretty little enameled box with a design of pink and white water lilies and offered me a pinch of lily root snuff. "There's naught better for clearing the head," she said and then frowned when I declined and said with the most frigid, stiff-backed politeness I could muster that my head was *quite clear* and that I *never* partook of snuff, ending with a sniff that I hoped indicated that I did not think much of those who did.

I felt a tugging at my skirt and heard a fiendish gibbering and leapt back as a hairy little goblin climbed Lady Margaret's skirt and began dancing on her shoulders and gleefully pulling the pins from her hair and flinging them every which way. A monkey! I pressed a hand to my pounding heart and sighed with relief. I had thought it was the old witch's familiar! But, no, it was her beloved pet. "Prince Piddle Pants, like another son he is to me," the crazy old crone introduced him to me, beaming with pride, though the creature in question wore no pants, probably because he soiled every pair that was put on him, hence the name. She acted as though she were presenting me to royalty and, when I failed to respond in the expected manner, glared daggers at me and barked loudly like a mongrel cur that God, or perhaps the Devil, had gifted with speech. "*Curtsy!* Where's your manners, girl? Do you not know to curtsy when you're presented to a prince?"

I spun around and stared at my husband. Surely he did not expect me, the Duke of Norfolk's daughter, to curtsy to a *monkey?* When I was at court, in the daily presence of the royal family, even they did not expect us to bow and curtsy to their pets, yet this Irish heiress, the Earl of Ormonde's daughter, who, by her look and manners I surmised had been stolen at birth by gypsies before being restored to the bosom of her noble family just in time to marry Thomas's father, expected me to curtsy to a monkey, a most undignified creature who had just proven I was right about how he had acquired his name by unleashing a thick yellow stream of urine over his mistress's velvet-clad shoulder and her clanking, tangled cascade of necklaces.

Thomas leaned near and whispered into my ear, "My lady-mother is getting on in years, and we must humor her little whims and caprices if we want a peaceful house, Elizabeth." With those words, he put a hand upon my shoulder and, with a subtle downward jerk of his chin, pressed down hard, compelling me to do my duty and dip my knees. So I forced a frigid smile and curtsied to that god-awful creature and her pet.

I nearly vomited on the threshold, so overwhelmed was I by the commingled odors of monkey urine, lavender, coltsfoot, crab apple, aged and unwashed flesh, a hint of dying rose perfume, and dirty hair. I teetered and reeled for a moment, vainly trying to steady myself as the undaunted Lady Margaret cackled, "Perhaps your wife is breedin' already, Thomas?" and slapped me on the back to propel me over the threshold. I felt even sicker at the thought, though I knew this was what was expected of me. When the golden wedding ring was slipped onto my finger, I became an expensive broodmare; it was the role every wife assumed, and I must accept and endure it as best I could, as every woman must.

To my surprise, the interior of Hever *Castle* was far superior to the exterior; it permeated an air of comfortable luxury, warm instead of chilly as one would expect in a larger, statelier abode like the ones I was accustomed to. Everywhere polished woods gleamed; there were diamond-paned windows and even some stained glass, fine tapestries Thomas boasted that he had brought back from diplomatic missions to Brussels and the Low Countries, and a quantity of good gold and silver plate displayed on gleaming tabletops and inside elegant, carved wooden cabinets and cupboards. Not a speck of dust did my discerning eye spy. The candles were of beeswax instead of rank tallow, and strewing herbs gave the air a pleasant scent as did the applewood logs glowing and emanating a toasty warmth from the large, elaborately carven fireplace. Well-trained servants in clean and impeccably tailored liveries hovered at the ready to take my cloak and gloves and offer me a cup of mulled wine and sugar wafers. At least I would not be *entirely* deprived of comforts. I sighed gratefully and let the cloak fall from my shoulders onto the floor.

Weary from the road, we retired early. But Thomas did not spare me. Even if I might already be breeding, he was taking no chances in leaving my womb to languish empty. So the bull was in again. *Bull-In.* He rode me relentlessly, without passion or fervor—

it was a business transaction for both of us, and he was very eager to ensure the succession of his line; he wanted to do all that was possible to ensure I was pregnant before he rode back to court.

The next morning I found I could not rise. A dark depression had fallen over me and lay heavy as a stone upon my breast.

I was trapped. I was Thomas Bullen's wife, his broodmare, and nothing but death could set me free. Through this marriage, which had brought my husband esteem and glory, I had fallen far from the star I was meant to be. I was a diamond lost, buried in bucolic mud.

Here I was stuck in rustic Kent, queen of my husband's larder and laundry, empress of the stillroom, storerooms, and stables, instead of shining bright in London, dancing, splendidly appareled, satin-shod and diamond-bright, at masques and balls, drawing every eye. I would even have been content in god-forsaken Wales amidst ice, naked trees, and bleak marshes—after all, it would not be forever. London would soon enough beckon, and then I would be attending Princess—someday Queen—Catherine, winning her friendship and favor, bathing her fingers in rosewater and brushing her long golden hair out at night, sitting above the salt at the royal table, and being courted and admired.

I refused my breakfast tray. When Matilda insisted that I *must* eat something, I threw it across the room. I lay there contemplating the dark wooden pillars of my marriage bed, carved to depict the Seven Deadly Sins, grotesque, leering, and ugly, until I could no longer bear the sight of them and ordered the sniveling, anxiously hovering Matilda to draw the sapphire and silver damask bedcurtains shut tight around me, to block out the morning light streaming through the diamond-paned windows, and envelop me in darkness as black as my own hopeless soul. I had no desire to get up and play my unwanted role of lady of the manor, so I simply refused to do it and went back to sleep.

My husband came in around noon and found me sleeping. He grasped my dark hair, wound it around his fist, and jerked me awake. My knees banged hard against the floor, bleeding through my shift, and the pain in my scalp brought tears to my eyes.

Tightening his grip upon my hair, Thomas yanked me to my feet and drew my face close to his, staring hard into my eyes.

"You *will* get up and order my house, mistress!" he said, thrusting me toward my maid as he barked an order at her to get me dressed.

"A lady leads by example," he said, "and you will *not* lead my servants into laxity and sloth!"

His fists found my ears and his palms stung my cheeks, and I could not hear his retreating words, so loud was the ringing that filled my head, nor whatever rubbish that sniveling fool Matilda was spouting as she nervously hovered and fidgeted, darting a hand out to wipe the blood away with her apron as though she were afraid to touch me.

As she was lacing me into my buff velvet gown, the same one I had worn the day I found out I was betrothed to Thomas *Bull-In,* Lady Margaret staggered in with a knowing cackle and Prince Piddle Pants capering on her shoulder and shoved a poultice made from the exquisite shy little white flowers of Solomon's seal onto my swollen ear, making me wince and cry out at the sudden throbbing pain that nearly made me faint.

"It takes but a day or two to cure any bruise, black or blue, gotten by falls or woman's willful carelessness in stumbling upon her husband's fists," she trilled, and even had the audacity to wink before she shuffled out in what were clearly a man's old well-worn cracked leather slippers several sizes too large for her dirty feet.

❧ 3 ❧

And so my life began. I swallowed my pride and let my inner fire be doused. I stopped fighting. I smiled and traipsed gracefully through my days, always beautifully dressed, kind and stern by turns with the servants as the moment warranted, and smiling and gracious to our guests, ensuring their every comfort and need was met. I ordered my husband's house and took my ease, reading, embroidering, or playing my lute in the gardens when spring and summer came, walking aimlessly through the fall of autumn leaves in a billowing cloak until the nip of winter drove me back indoors again to brave the loathsome company of my mother-in-law and Prince Piddle Pants.

Yet long before the seasons changed, I, that slim and beautiful, beguiling sylph of a girl, had become a matronly mother-to-be and efficient and proper housewife.

After ensuring that I knew my place and would behave myself accordingly, my husband rode away to London again to rejoin the court. With a glad heart I waved him off. Happy beyond words to be rid of him, I privately toasted his departure by drinking alone in my chamber the better half of a bottle of cherry wine pilfered from my mother-in-law's secret store she kept hidden beneath her bed just so I could hear her running about shrieking that the fairies had taken it and we must purify the house with salt and have the priest in to bless it.

Four months later, word reached me that Prince Arthur was dead. Princess Catherine was a widow of uncertain future and means. There was quite a bit of ungentlemanly haggling about the unpaid portions of her dowry between her father, King Ferdinand of Spain, and her father-in-law, King Henry of England. But absent from the court, it all meant little to me. I felt so remote from it all, it might all have been happening in Turkey.

By then, I was well into my first pregnancy and didn't really care about the world and the fact that there were other people in it besides my fat and swollen miserable self.

"You're not the first woman to be pregnant." Lady Margaret found cause to waggle a finger and scold me nigh every day with Prince Piddle Pants perched on her shoulder and aping her antics. But I went on acting as though I was, making extravagant, unreasonable, and irrational demands that kept the household in a frantic uproar as they rushed about to fulfill my every fancy for the sake of their master's unborn heir. Lady Margaret had swung her sewing needle dangling from a length of thread over my stomach and was certain that I was carrying a boy. "And I," she stoutly declared, "am *never* mistaken!"

I had great fun thinking of ridiculous things to have an unbearable craving for, like roast duckling candied in marzipan, pickles rolled so thickly in cinnamon and sugar I could not catch even a glimpse of the green beneath, sugar-glazed piglet stuffed to bursting with candied figs, capon stuffed nigh to bursting with strawberries and cream, rare and bloody roast beef crowned and glazed with quinces, and sugar sculptures of myself in the guise of water nymphs and classical goddesses that I promptly shattered and burst into tears whenever I spied even the slightest imperfection. One day before the sun rose, I crept out and gathered all the eggs I could find and dyed them blue with woad and red with madder before I replaced them safely in the nests beneath the hens. What a fit Lady Margaret had crossing herself and running about screeching that the fairies had been at work during the night. And another day while my mother-in-law was napping, I gave Prince Piddle Pants a henna bath so that she awakened to find what she thought was a little red devil capering at the foot of her bed and pissed herself in terror even as she crossed herself and reached for her rosary. Then, just as suddenly, I grew bored with it all, ceased all my pranks and capricious cravings, and settled down to calmly await the birth of my baby.

Nearly bursting at the seams with his increasing importance, and the growing reliance and trust that the Crown, and the Tudor men who wore or would one day wear it, bestowed upon him, Thomas came home long enough to have our portrait painted. When he was abroad representing English interests at the court of the Archduchess Margaret of Austria, he had admired a portrait of a wealthy Bruges merchant and his green-gowned, swollen-stomached wife with her devoted little dog at her feet standing amidst the opulent trappings of luxury and status. With the rapidity of lightning, he decided that we should be painted in like manner.

In somber-hued velvets and sable, Thomas stood rigidly at my side, stiff-backed with his own self-importance. I wore the same sapphire velvet gown banded in black with gold lovers' knots and black velvet hood I had worn the day I witnessed Princess Catherine's triumphant progress through London; it was still nearly new after all, and though the bodice fit a trifle too snugly, the skirt flowed smoothly as a placid blue waterfall over the round ball of my belly.

Before we assumed our pose for the portrait painter, Thomas, like a man putting the collar on his newly acquired pedigreed bitch, fastened round my throat the heavy, wide golden collar with the Bullens' ornate, raging ruby-eyed bull. I *hated* its constricting weight and the way it bit into my flesh, but the gracious, docile smile upon my face gave nothing away.

As the artist posed me, with one hand clasping the flowing folds of my skirt demurely over the small round mound of my stomach, to show the petticoat of pomegranate satin I wore beneath, which was richly embroidered with roses of gold and silver, I caught a glimpse of myself in my silver mirror—a highborn sixteen-year-old bride, an emblem of success, a trophy of sorts my husband preened and prided himself over winning, a bitch wearing her master's collar replete with his golden insignia, her belly and breasts swelling with certain proof of her fertility, the first of many pups he planned she would whelp, so that his name would be sure to endure another generation.

Behind us, my sapphire and silver bed shimmered and the grotesquely carven figures of the Seven Deadly Sins grimaced and leered over my shoulder, and light poured in through the diamond-latticed panes of the window to illuminate a pair of gleaming golden bowls piled high with oranges, rising like pyramids, studded with cloves, snowy blossoms, and glossy green leaves.

My husband *adored* oranges as a symbol of wealth and opulence. He liked people to know he could afford them and to share his bounty with those he deemed important enough to deserve a seat at his well-appointed table. Never mind that eating them made his chest ache with a deplorable burn that kept him awake all night guzzling tonics his old witch-bitch lunatic of a mother brewed in a cauldron, incomprehensible gobbledygook spewing from her mouth like some foul incantation as she threw in handfuls of pulverized elm bark, licorice, chamomile, dandelions, peppermint, rosemary, juniper, whole cups of red wine and honey, and a baby lizard for good measure, while Prince Piddle Pants gibbered and danced on her shoulder like one of Satan's imps. But to Thomas Bullen—or *Boleyn* as he was by then styling himself—image was *everything;* discomfort be damned.

Ferdinand, a handsome and most sensual gardener with bronze skin, sleek black hair, a devilish mustache, and dark dagger of a beard, was specially imported from Seville to do nothing but nurture my husband's precious oranges in a specially built hothouse. Each tree was planted in its own silver tub emblazoned with the fierce Bullen—I mean *Boleyn!*—bull crest, cooed over, and pampered like a royal infant, even serenaded with Spanish love songs and lullabies. The precious fruit they bore was kept in locked boxes in the larder to which only I, as lady of the house, had the key lest the servants pilfer themselves a rare and costly treat.

Thomas delighted in displaying the fruit elegantly arranged in gilt bowls, piled in pyramids punctuated with black cloves and orange blossoms, and serving our guests orange slices and orange water to wash their fingers or cleanse their palates between courses. Our cook was famous for preparing a bitter orange sauce for our meat, fowl, and fish. Marmalade made from the best bitter oranges of Seville always graced our table, and curls of orange peel crowned our otherwise bland custards, imbuing them with a lively touch of color and a hint of zesty citrus flavor, which our guests always pronounced "a heavenly delight!" Whenever he hosted hunting parties, Thomas would order our cook to fry orange slices to garnish the fresh kill or spear them raw and juicy to the roasting meat as it spun on a spit.

Every year the two of us, clad in orange from head to toe with accents of black and gold and embroidered or silken petaled snowy orange blossoms, presided over a ball to celebrate the precious yield from my husband's orange trees and dazzled our guests with a menu of sumptuous dishes sauced, spiced, garnished, or flavored with oranges, with a massive orange cake rising out of the midst of it all, decked with candy orange blossoms and candied orange slices.

Around our feet as we posed, a fluffy little white dog, with a tail like a jaunty plume curling over the brim of a gentleman's round velvet cap, yapped and pranced. It was all I could do not to kick it across the room and scream for the servants to take it away. Thomas had brought it home from Austria as a gift for me, not out of any genuine husbandly affection, mind you, but for outward show, to impress those who beheld me with my new pet, the breed being then quite uncommon to our English shores. It yapped and broke wind constantly, and whenever Thomas was about I could not wait for him to depart so I could banish that yapping, stinking snowball to the kennels.

Thomas tarried only long enough to approve the artist's sketches, then left me to pose alone and rode back to London as the King had need of him. But I didn't care; I was glad to see him go, and even gladder to know that the artist had a penchant for pregnant women, and we were of one mind about that beastly little dog. He dallied at Hever with me as long as he dared, creeping down the corridor to warm my bed at night and enlivening dull afternoons when I grew weary of posing and he of mixing his pigments and wielding his brushes. But he had other commissions awaiting him in London, and, all too soon, he had to go, and I was left alone with my mother-in-law and the servants again, screaming inside and sitting on my hands to keep from tearing the hair out of my scalp when Lady Margaret taught Prince Piddle Pants to ride "like a gallant knight" upon the back of that endlessly barking and farting ball of white fluff, and my ears were brutally assaulted for *hours* with the shrill cacophony of the chattering monkey, the yapping dog, and the witchy cackle and gleeful encouragement of my mad mother-in-law.

As the spring flowers bloomed so did the baby inside me, making me miserable with swollen feet and ankles, aching legs marred by sore protruding veins, and ugly blemishes and unsightly blotches upon the porcelain pale perfection of my complexion. My hair lost its luster. And every day I watched and wept as my formerly trim waist grew thick and stout and my formerly flat stomach even more grossly protuberant. I felt so ungainly and ugly; for the first time in my life, I wished I were invisible. How could God do this to me? He had taken my beauty away when it was all I had!

In unlaced stomachers and skirts with extra panels sewn in, I waddled around in a pair of plum velvet house slippers—the only shoes my swollen feet could abide—graceless as a duck. I didn't go a-Maying that year; I was too fat to fit into my green gown, and I couldn't bear to disfigure it by sewing in panels when I could not find fabric to match that exact same shade of green. No, far better that I keep to my chamber; I was too unsightly even for me to look upon, and I could not bear to see the gloating triumph in the other women's eyes. So I stayed at home and watched all the pretty peasant girls traipsing off to the fair, to gather May flowers and dance around the Maypole with amorous gallants with whom they would retreat into the greenwood afterward. How I envied them and wished I could be one of them! What I wouldn't have given for just *one hour* with a lusty gallant clutched tight between my thighs! But then I thought of his eyes looking down upon the disgusting sight of my aching milk-filled breasts, swollen full-moon stomach, and mottled, pimpled thighs and veiny limbs, and I barely reached my chamber pot before I vomited.

* * *

My daughter was born in deep summer's hottest days, in the bed of the Seven Deadly Sins, with their carved faces leering and jeering at me through the hazy waves of pain. I cursed Eve and the child for causing me such agony. Oh what torture! The way it stretched and burned, I was certain my pretty pink cunny would never delight a man again. After this ordeal, I was sore afraid it might not be such a pretty and pleasing sight anymore and I would have to keep it hidden. But when it was all over and I held Mary in my arms for the very first time, I instantly dried my tears and forgave her everything—she was so beautiful! "This must be just like Helen of Troy's mother felt!" I exclaimed with a radiant smile as I admired my perfect little girl.

She was the most beautiful baby I had ever seen and seemed to grow more so every day. Curls like spun gold, soft as silk, covered her scalp; I could not stop twirling them around my fingers, longing for the day when they were long enough to wear silk ribbons. Her mouth was like a tiny perfect pink rosebud, so exquisite, and equally enamored with giving kisses as well as receiving them. I think to kiss was the first thing she ever learned how to do. Her cheeks were plump and rosy, and her eyes a lively amber, as exciting and enticing as jewels, and God had blessed her with the most delightful dimples. When they came, her teeth were exquisite little pearls, and she seemed to always be smiling. I don't believe I ever saw my little girl frown. She hardly ever cried; instead she uttered the most delightful little gurgles and soon learned to laugh. I would put on one of my prettiest dresses now that they fit again and have her brought to me, and would sit with her cradled in my lap and croon over her, caressing her curls and calling her "my sweet cherub" and "my little doll," telling her over and over again how beautiful she was. And I promised my "precious little pearl" that I would not "suffer her to be thrown down before a swine" as I had been; as long as there was breath within my body I would never allow it. God had blessed my daughter with the most important gift He can give a woman—beauty—and I vowed that she would have a husband worthy of her—handsome, lusty, and rich. As I would not have a valuable diamond set in tin, nor would I see my daughter's golden beauty matched with base ugliness and a boorish, boring personality like the man who had sired her.

The following year brought me a handsome son, fey and moody from the cradle. Black-haired and dark-eyed, I called him my "Dark George" for both his coloring and disposition.

Now that I had given him an heir, I fervently hoped my husband's ardor to keep me constantly pregnant would slack and he would allow my body a much-needed rest and me time to enjoy myself. I hoped he would relent and bring me to live with him at court. I didn't like being pregnant; it was such a brutal assault upon my vanity. It made my body an ugly stranger to me, and each time took a toll upon my beauty, stretching and diluting it until I feared one day I would look in my mirror and there would be nothing left, and I would be old and ugly before my time, worn out from breeding children I never even wanted.

But Thomas wanted a large family—at least a dozen children, and it was his desires that counted in this unfortunate, hateful marriage. He informed me that he expected me to give him a child every year until I reached the age when women's wombs no longer quickened.

I was scarcely recovered from George's birth before I found myself vomiting not just in the mornings but throughout the entire day and insatiably craving figs in red wine syrup, thick and sugary, and red as blood, so that I dubbed them "my bloody figs," even though I knew I would only sick them right back up again. I would vomit them up, then with my next breath scream for more. I was *ravenous* for them in a way I had never been for anything before; I wanted "my bloody figs," morning, noon, and night, and at all hours in between. I would wake in the night to use the chamber pot and not be able to fall back asleep until a servant had fetched me "my bloody figs." I wondered if this was God's vengeance for all the strange cravings I had feigned during my first pregnancy.

My daughter Anne's birth was violent and bloody; she tore through me like a lightning bolt as a storm raged outside, rattling and pelting the diamond-paned windows and lighting up the midnight sky nigh bright as day. She came into this world screaming, her face scrunched, red, and furious. I never heard a child scream so. I feared her incessant crying would drive me mad; the first year of her life she never seemed to stop.

I lost so much blood I very nearly died. The midwife had to stitch my torn flesh and poultice my cunny with cobwebs to staunch the bleeding and put me on a strict diet of rare meat, beef broth, and compotes and juices of red berries, to help restore my blood and vigor. Mercifully, she forbade my husband the intimate use of my body for six months if he ever hoped to get more babes from me. For that, at least, I was grateful.

Anne was the *ugliest* baby I had ever seen in my life. Shuddering, I thrust her from me in revulsion, slapping at the hideous wailing thing and the hands that tried to foist her onto me. *"Take that hideous thing away!"* I screamed. She was as ugly as my mother-in-law's monkey! I would not hold her; the thought of cradling her against my breast made me want to vomit. If I were the superstitious sort like Lady Margaret, I would think a troll had somehow snuck in and stolen my beautiful baby, a dark-haired daughter God had created in my likeness, and left an ugly changeling in her stead.

Instead of golden, fluffy, silky soft curls, her scalp was thickly covered with coarse black hair, her limbs were long, scrawny, and thin as sticks that—God forgive me—could so easily snap, I thought. She had none of the plump pink and white prettiness of her sister. Her neck reminded me of a goose's and, heaven help me, I wished to wring it for the trouble and pain she had caused me. And for what? Another daughter, and such an ugly and useless one too! Yet it was so much worse than mere ugliness; she was disfigured, deformed—a nascent nub of a sixth finger protruded from the littlest finger of her left hand and a growth like an ugly brown strawberry erupted from the base of her throat, right in front where her hair or a headdress with lappets or a veil could not hide it.

"This one, if she lives to grow up, shall be a bride of Christ," I remarked to my husband on one of his mercifully brief visits while I was still in bed, sitting up against a mound of silken pillows in a magnificent midnight blue silk bed gown with sapphires flashing against the alabaster of my throat, drawing an ivory comb through my ebony hair, taunting him with how beautiful I was, yet he could not have me lest he do further damage to my womb and thus imperil the future of his line—the Bullen—I mean *Boleyn!*—dynasty. "We must resign ourselves, Thomas; there's no help for it. Look at her! *He's* the only husband who would ever have her, unless you know of a blind and wealthy idiot—the sort of man who chases rainbows with a spade in hand to dig for gold."

"Time enough to worry about that later," Thomas said and let it be known that he expected me to give him another son as soon as I was able. Then he departed, abroad, on yet more business for the Crown, and I would not have to endure his company again for many weeks to come. I was left alone, contentedly if not blissfully, with my beautiful golden girl and my moody dark-haired boy, who was like smiling, happy sunbeams one moment and thunderbolts and torrents the next, and my grotesque black changeling child, who, even after the passage of many months, failed to improve and remained as ugly as a squashed toad.

Once when Anne lay crying in her cradle and I sat beside her, contemplating her ugliness, it occurred to me that it really would be better, for all our sakes, if she were to die, as so many children did, in infancy. I just could not believe that something so ugly could have come out of someone so beautiful. I was embarrassed to have her near me and left her to the nursemaids' care whenever possible, to spare myself the pain of having others see the monstrosity I had given birth to and compare her with my other two beautiful children. I was ashamed to be Anne's mother.

Her crying grated so upon my nerves; I couldn't stand it. Sometimes she cried for *hours,* for no reason anyone could discern. Syrups and sweet words, lullabies and rocking in her cradle failed to soothe her. Yet the doctor and midwife and wise women I consulted said there was nothing wrong with her. Clearly they were all fools!

That dreary, wet afternoon my nerves were raw as freshly slaughtered meat. Anne would not stop crying. I just couldn't bear it another moment. Before I knew what I was doing, I had taken the embroidered cushion from behind my still-aching back and pressed it over her ugly little screeching dark monkey face. But I couldn't do it.

God stayed my hand by sending George to be Anne's champion, a role he would never relinquish unto death. I heard a movement behind me and turned to see his tiny figure standing in the doorway clutching his wooden play sword, staring at me with silent accusation, eyes burning with a scorching reproach that made me, a grown woman, tremble.

I stood rapidly, tossed the cushion aside, and walked out without meeting his eyes, calling for a nurse to attend the children, and went out into the gloomy garden, to walk beneath the gray sky in the gently misting rain.

When I returned, Anne was gone. Though in my heart I was glad, I half hoped the changeling had been spirited away, back where it belonged, but I knew my duty; appearances must be observed, and the servants and I sought frantically for her. They found her in George's room, sleeping peacefully—*silently!*—upon his bed, in a cocoon of crimson velvet he had fashioned from the bedcovers, to make a safe little nest for her, while he stood sentry beside her, wooden sword in hand as though he had taken a solemn oath to protect her and would slay any who dared try to harm her.

"*My* baby!" he protested when the nursemaid tried to take her, rapping her upon the wrist with the edge of his little sword hard enough to raise a bloody little welt.

"*You* don't love her!" He turned accusing eyes upon me, challenging me to disagree as he brandished his little sword at me.

Though he was but a child, I shrank from him, speechless, cringing guiltily beneath that honest, unwavering gaze. His words were true, and I could not deny them. I loved Mary and George in my fickle, capricious way that behaved as though motherhood were a cloak I could doff and don at will, but I did not love Anne. For not one moment since she had been born had I ever felt a smidgen of love for Anne.

In all the years that followed, we never spoke of that day again, but for the rest of all our lives, it would hover, an unspoken, undeniable truth between us—George, Anne, and I—something we all knew, but pretended not to.

That was the beginning of the unshakable, unbreakable bond between them, a devotion that would never slack or waver, only grow stronger with time. From that day forward, Anne and George stood together, even when the whole world seemed to be united against them.

* * *

Thomas came back when the midwife sent word that my body had recovered sufficiently to again receive a husband's intimate attentions. But something was wrong inside. Though I conceived regularly—too regularly to suit me!—and nearly every time my husband visited, I was soon sending a letter after him to convey the "joyous" news that I was again with child, my womb always disgorged its contents, in blood and pain, before life could truly take root and fight for its right to live. The rare occasions when I carried a child to term, it came into this world still and blue or else gasped once, maybe twice, then died. Twelve names—Thomas, Henry, Geoffrey, Margaret, Amata, Alice, John, Edward, James, Eleanor, William, and Catherine, the children who lasted long enough to be born recognizable as human—came to mark the crosses in the churchyard before my womb grew stubborn and refused to accept my husband's seed at all. My womb it seemed had finally followed my heart's lead and locked and bolted its door against Thomas Bullen.

In this manner, the years passed with him growing increasingly frustrated and angry with our futile couplings that failed to bear ripe and beautiful fruit, only bitterness and rot.

Like any good and obedient Christian wife, I silently suffered the vagaries of my womb, the blood and cramps that disgorged an unrecognizable lump of flesh or malformed child, and the fruitless, frustrating pregnancies that endured for a few weeks or months and took such an unwelcome toll on my beautiful body. I fought it all the way, with diets of plain broth, rigorous walks, and binding my breasts to stop the heaviness of the milk that made them sag; I applied lotions and creams to my skin, to keep it soft and fight the blemishes that came hand in hand with breeding, bewailing the telltale lines that remained as an unpleasant reminder of how each child, no matter how long it stayed inside, stretched my belly; and I acquired a deft touch with cosmetics, painting my face so skillfully and discreetly that it often went unremarked.

When I took my daughter, Mary, a-Maying, both of us barefoot and gowned in green like Queen Guinevere in the tales of old, with our unbound hair garlanded with spring flowers, I felt young and gay, as light and airy as dandelion fluff, and amorous male eyes followed every step I took. I sashayed my hips and smiled and let my dark eyes flash, *Come hither!* I left my daughter to watch the puppet shows and morris dancers and admire the rosary of compressed rose petals the village priest had given her because she was such "a pretty and devout little girl," while I skipped and pranced and danced with handsome gallants heedless of their low degree, their rough hands and peasant blood, around the great beribboned phallus of the Maypole. I was surprised and flattered by how many young men were so eager to dance with me. Without a backward glance, I left my daughter, trusting in the kindness of strangers to keep her safe, and let them lead me into the greenwood to kiss me and lift my green skirt as, together, we gave ourselves up to the heady pleasures of wanton, lusty May.

In matching gowns and hair ribbons of cherry red with pink petticoats and fringed pink shawls knitted with a pattern of cherry blossoms, we attended every midsummer cherry fair.

How we delighted in those boisterous, happy affairs, seeing the trees all decorated with ribbons, and, to try to inject a note of piety, pictures of Our Lord Jesus Christ as a child reaching for a bough heavily laden with dangling ruby red cherries, to symbolize temptation, and also, the bloody and violent death to come, and to remind everyone just how brief life is.

"Life is but a cherry fair," was a proverb Mary and I both took to heart and tried to live our lives by.

While I was busy under the cherry trees with my swains, letting them steal kisses or giving them freely—ah, there is *nothing* like tasting that luscious red fruit upon a lover's lips!—my golden girl would buy one of these pictures with her pocket money to hang in her bedchamber as a souvenir of those happy cherry fair days, to remind her in winter's gloom of the joys and sweet fruits to look forward to.

One cold and boring winter I even stitched those words—*Life is but a cherry fair*—in elegant, deep, red silken script encircled by a border of embroidered cherries and delicate pink cherry blossoms. I kept it on my dressing table, beside the pincushion doll Remi Jouet had given me, as a constant reminder, lest I ever for even one moment forget just how brief life is. I would sit and hug the pincushion Eve to my breast and contemplate those embroidered words and dream of kissing Remi Jouet beneath the fall of cherry blossoms and sinking as one to the ground to make love amidst the fragrant, fallen flowers and of tasting the luscious red fruit upon his sweet lips.

I seized greedily at every chance to enjoy myself, never depending on tomorrow to come and bring me fresh pleasures. People said I was selfish, self-centered, and greedy. Some said I was hot and wanton, whilst others deemed me cold and heartless. But I didn't care and never stopped to consider how much was genuine truth or words just spoken in the heat of anger or spite by a spurned lover or jealous rival. I was still young, in my early twenties, and I wanted to live and love lustily while I had the chance, before my own body, and its age and infirmities, became my enemies.

In those years I reigned as the Queen of Hever Castle. I watched my children grow up and suffered my meddlesome mother-in-law and her increasingly addled wits and eccentric ways as best I could. Our wills clashed many times over the children. 'Tis a marvel she did not kill them with her curatives! Every time they squirmed, she wanted to dose them for worms; any upset of any kind she saw as a "sure and certain sign" of a distressed liver and had a vile tasting potion at the ready to pour down their throats. She chased them down with the dreaded enema syringe and purged their insides until they were squeaky clean. She peered into their chamber pots and scrutinized their urine and stool like a fortune-teller who could see their fates written there, tucked them into bed with their little ears clogged with cloves of garlic to keep the ear pains from visiting them during the night, hung charms around their necks, and dosed them daily with St. John's Wort to keep evil spirits and demon lovers away. She gave my poor George so many spoonfuls of rose honey trying to chase away his melancholy that he grew to hate the taste of it, and she had to chase him down every day with the spoon. It was quite a sight to see them—my black-haired boy sprinting across the gardens with his grandmother lumbering and tottering after him, blue hair flying, waving a spoon as though it were the King's banner.

When I could stand no more of it, I threw up my hands and

walked away from it all. I took refuge in my red rose bower. There latticed wooden trellises thickly covered with climbing red roses shielded my private garden and a small reflecting pool where silver and gold fish swam and a statue of Cupid stood on a sunken pedestal amidst pink and white water lilies. Whenever I was within, I let it be known that *no one* was allowed to disturb me, that this was my private time for contemplation and prayer.

It was here that I discreetly received my lovers on afternoons when the weather was fair. It doesn't matter who they were, and in truth, I don't remember most of their names, and Time has blurred their faces. When I wanted a lover I took one; it was as simple as that. Sometimes I chose them with care, like a lady leisurely scrutinizing the jeweler's wares, intent on making the perfect selection, but most of the time I didn't care and took whatever was within ready reach. They were meaningless diversions designed to relieve my boredom, the frustration and tedium of being Thomas Bullen's wife, forced to endure a bucolic exile from the lively life at court. They were just handsome men who knew how to be discreet. Fine, fun fellows who passed through my life briefly as butterflies— traveling tinkers, strolling players and minstrels, journeyman laborers, peddlers and artisans, swift couriers and liveried envoys, and the occasional gentleman. The only thing they had in common was that they all lingered long enough to catch my eye and fulfill a need before they took their leave.

None of them made a dent upon my heart. After the pleasure was past, they were fast forgotten. And if they remembered me, well . . . that was their mind, not mine. The few who came my way again whom I deigned to favor, I welcomed as though we were strangers meeting for the first time and forgot them when they took to the road again.

I didn't want to remember, or to be remembered; I wanted to be admired, pleasured, and then for them to forget me the same way I forgot them. It wasn't about making memories to cherish; it was about relieving boredom and cuckolding Thomas, giving his precious pedigreed pearl to rough swines with coarse, work-roughened hands and dirt-caked nails, men lower than himself, with whom this pearl rolled in the mud and rutted like pigs, nothing more.

During those years I thought often of the doll maker, Remi

Jouet, dreaming of his shy, sweet, round baby face, the fall of dark hair over his brow, his dark eyes, and deliciously voluptuous form. Every time I sat down at my dressing table, the pincushion doll, the miniature enchantress Eve, he had given me that long-ago day, was always there to remind me.

So many times I wondered, *Was his shop still there in London?* Was that delicious dumpling of a man still there, plying his trade, creating and selling his beautiful dolls? Had he ever made the doll I had so imperiously requested? And if so, what had become of it? Did it languish still upon a shelf cocooned in velvet to protect it from the dust? Or had he long since sold it to delight some little girl, a courtier's or an ambassador's daughter perhaps?

Yet I never bothered to find out. I was afraid of what I might discover—a cookshop in its place perhaps, or a round-bodied buxom blond wife behind the counter. Though it was both ridiculous and naive of me to want to deny him a wife and children of his own when I was myself married and a mother, and, even if I were free, could never, as a duke's daughter, stoop so low as to become a tradesman's wife. Yet I never made inquiries. I preferred to keep the dream alive and avoid the disappointment of watching it die in the face of reality and the cold, hard truths I expected it to deliver like a slap in the face.

Sometimes I would sit and hug that exquisite pincushion doll to my breast and dream of what might have been. His body soft as dough but as warm as fresh baked bread, that heady combination of softness and heat as passion enveloped and overwhelmed us. I would close my eyes and let delightfully erotic fantasies play out in the private chamber of my mind, doing all the things I wished we'd done. In my dreams I didn't waste time. I was sixteen and back inside his shop again, but this time when he kissed me I never let go. Instead I dragged him into the back room where he slept, pushed him down onto the bed, fell on top of him, and covered his mouth with mine. It's what I should have done, and mayhap would have done, if that blubbering idiot Matilda hadn't come barging in. If she ever dared come upon me when I was in such a reverie, woe to Matilda, for I was sure to slap her face.

My own little girls were fascinated by the small, temptation-eyed, pincushion Eve, a miniature study in seductiveness, with her extended apple and sly, embracing serpent of green glass and gold beads twined around her like a clinging vine.

The only time I ever raised my hand or voice to Mary was to slap her hands away and sternly forbid her to touch it, promising the most dire punishment if she dared disobey me. No matter how much she wept and pleaded to hold it, just once, promising how careful she would be, I never gave in. It was mine, and I forbade her, or anyone else, to touch it, even my maid when she was dusting and tidying my dressing table. This was something that was mine alone that I would never share with anyone else.

Anne was also fascinated by that dainty doll. But she never tried or begged to touch it, nor ever gave even a roundabout hint that she would like to. Not once did I ever have to reprimand or threaten her with punishment the way I did Mary. She would stand and stare at it like one entranced, hands clasped tightly behind her back, keeping her thoughts, whatever they were, all to herself. She had already learned the value of keeping her own counsel and to not invite mockery and laughter. And in those days, any childish dream she might have dared confess I would most assuredly have greeted with scorn and laughter, and Anne knew it; she had already learned that lesson.

"Daughter," I would have said bluntly, sage and haughty, as I sat preening at my dressing table, "dreams never come true for one such as you. It would be best to resign yourself to that now, rather than court disappointment later."

But, though this is said in hindsight, I have a feeling that if such a conversation had ever happened betwixt us, Anne's dark eyes would have flashed a challenge, a wager, daring to prove me wrong.

❧ 4 ❧

The old King died, coughing up his lungs in bloody bits in a drafty room that, ever the miser, his penny-pinching ways prevented from being kept properly heated. He would rather have the money in his treasury than spend it on firewood for his own comfort. To him, my husband said, that was the same as burning money, and there was no greater sin in Henry VII's eyes. The man kept his rooms so cold, a popular jest went, the kitchen staff used them for cold storage for things like butter and milk, secreting these out of sight behind the faded old moth-eaten tapestries.

The King was dead! It was out with the old and in with the new! Few mourned the old King's passing and rushed to fawn upon his successor, the boy everyone thought destined for the church until his elder brother, Prince Arthur, died. This Henry was *nothing* like his dull, stodgy, old, penny-pinching father, but young, vital, virile, merry, and eager to dance and have a good time and let coins drip through his fingers like water. No musty, dusty old velvet or ratty old fur for him—only the newest and finest! What good was money when you were in your grave and could not enjoy it? Better to spend and enjoy it while you were young and still had the chance! Aye, I thought, here is a king, a man, after my own heart!

On St. George's day in the year of Our Lord 1509, Prince

Henry, "a youngling who cares for naught but hunting and girls," as my husband somewhat contemptuously described that robust red gold stripling to me behind our bedcurtains one night, became King Henry VIII of England at the age of only seventeen.

Since I was obviously no further use as a broodmare, Thomas decided it was time for me to take my place beside him at court. After all, there was no sense in wasting a wellborn and attractive wife, he reasoned, and there were still ways in which I could be useful to him.

"There will be a new queen soon, and she will want ladies about her, and it will serve me well to have a pair of eyes and ears in her bedchamber," as he so succinctly put it. "Someone I can trust, whose best interests are the same as my own. I always *knew* you would be a credit to me, Elizabeth; you are the best investment I ever made."

But I didn't give a damn about being useful to Thomas. In truth, if the choice were left entirely to me, I would not throw him a rope if he were drowning. But I would do what I had to do because it was best for me, so I smiled and said, "I will need at least a dozen new dresses, and jewels. . . ."

At that moment I was so happy to be going to court I didn't even care what price I would have to pay for it, that I would have to give the Devil his due. I was nearly *four* years past twenty—how fast my youth was flying past!—and seized the chance to *finally,* at long last, lead the life I had always dreamed of, the one that had been so cruelly denied me when I became Thomas Bullen's broodmare bride. Soon I would be where I belonged, in a coveted position close to the Queen, to be admired, worshiped, and adored, desired by all the men and envied by all the women. My vanity preened like a peacock as Thomas rambled on, and I nodded and smiled as best becomes a good and obedient Christian wife while brilliant banners of satin and silk and cloth-of-gold and silver unfurled inside my mind alongside the dazzle of diamonds and pearls, sapphires, emeralds, and rubies. I didn't hear a word he was saying; I was too busy planning my new wardrobe.

So I ordered my trunks packed with all haste, kissed my children good-bye, and pretended not to see Mary's and George's tears as I told them to be good and mind their nurses and, to a certain extent, their grandmother, and gaily waved back to Lady Margaret as she ran after my coach shaking her fist and shouting, "A cat's a better mother than you are!" I ignored that mad, old blue-haired witch and sank back contentedly against the velvet cushions of my coach, luxuriating like a beloved and pampered pet cat on its favorite pillow, and trained my sights firmly upon the future.

As soon as my coach rolled into London, I called the coachman to halt, leaned past my maid, Matilda, opened the door, and shoved her out into the muck and mud. I tossed a penny after her and slammed the door and told the coachman, "Drive on!" ignoring her as she wept and ran after me, beseeching me to stop and take her back.

But I didn't want or need her. Thomas had already found the *perfect* lady's maid for me. A smart English girl named Mary, though she preferred to be called Marie, who had accompanied a diplomat's wife abroad and lived in Paris for a good many years. Her mistress had lately died, and she was in need of a new position when Thomas engaged her to serve me. It was as though yet another of my prayers had been answered. If I was to be a star in the glittering firmament of the royal court, I would certainly need a proper lady's maid, not that sniveling fool Matilda; from the start, she had been woefully inadequate, and I was glad, at long last, to *finally* bid good riddance to her.

True to his word, Thomas took me to live at court, had me gowned and jeweled as splendid as a peacock, and *all* my dreams came true. I was appointed a lady-in-waiting to the new Queen before the toe of my satin slipper had even touched the marble floor of Greenwich Palace.

My father was there waiting to welcome me with a necklace of jeweled honeybees. Though he had frequently sent me gifts, since my marriage I had been icily cordial toward him, but now . . . now that I was where I belonged, I found it so much easier to forgive.

My heart thawed, and I went instantly into his arms. After all, the only mistake he had ever made was in casting his most precious pearl down before that swine Thomas Bullen, and my brother, that dreadful scheming rat Thomas, had probably persuaded him to do that since the Bullen shopkeeper's spawn was his best friend.

Everyone makes mistakes, and if the Lord Jesus Christ could forgive those who crucified him, surely I, Elizabeth Howard, could forgive my father for marrying me to Thomas Bullen. So I embraced and kissed my father and happily let him hang jewels around my neck. And when he told me he had a cloak of silver foxes he had been planning to give to my stepmother, but seeing me again, after all this time, and being reminded of how beautiful I was, he saw that against my alabaster skin and ebony hair, it would suit me far better than it ever would my plump and pallid blond stepmother, I kissed him again and told him how glad, how *happy*, I was to "at long last feel the coldness between us thawing and melting in the warm sunshine of forgiveness."

"Elizabeth," my father said, "you have made me the happiest of men!"

I was also reunited with my old lover—my first lover—the poet laureate of England, John Skelton. But it was not a happy reunion. He was old and ugly now, more cadaverous than ever, with a vinegary old-flesh stench about him, and his touch repelled me. I shrank from his embraces the way I would if a skeleton had walked out of a charnel house and tried to climb into bed with me. I wanted nothing to do with him and soon stuck up my nose, turned my proud Howard back on him, and bestowed my favors on other men more worthy of me. My beauty was too precious a gift to squander lightly.

But I should have known better than to cross a poet, and he soon showed himself a spiteful creature. Writers can, and often do, wield their pens as weapons and are not afraid to use them against those who have spited, slighted, or scorned them. Words of love and passion can all too quickly turn to words of bitter hate and mockery.

To welcome me back to court, he reworked an old poem, written in the first flush of his love for me, and branded me the false Cressida. Everyone knew the story of the beautiful Trojan woman who had vowed everlasting love to one man, then spurned him and embraced another. Her name was a byword for feminine inconstancy. To compare a woman to Cressida was to call her cunning, wanton, and deceitful, the sort of woman who would not hesitate to change lovers at a moment's whim and fancy or betray the connubial couch and crown her husband with a cuckold's horns.

"To My Lady Elizabeth Howard." He stood up boldly before the court at a banquet one night to recite words supposedly written in my honor, in remembrance of the occasion when I, as a maiden of fourteen, had crowned him poet laureate, but that were in truth like a dagger hidden in a bouquet of flowers.

> *"To be your remembrancer, Madame, I am bound:*
> *Like unto Irene maidenly of porte,*
> *Of virtue and cunning the well and perfect ground,*
> *Whom Dame Nature, as well I may report,*
> *Hath freshly enbeautied with many a goodly sort*
> *Of womanly features: whose flourishing tender age*
> *Is lusty to look on, pleasant, demure, and sage.*
>
> *Goodly Cressida, fairer than Polyxena,*
> *For to envy Pandarus' appetite:*
> *Troilus, I vow, if that he had you seen,*
> *In you he would have set his whole delight:*
> *Of all your beauty I suffice not to write,*
> *But, as I said, your flourishing tender age*
> *Is lusty to look on, pleasant, demure, and sage."*

While some might say having a poem written about her makes a woman immortal—I myself used to think that—now I know it isn't always so. This—as false Cressida—was certainly not the way I would have wanted to be remembered; now I say I would rather be forgotten!

After the court had finished applauding Master Skelton's clever verses, I stood up, knowing full well what a beautiful picture I presented in a new gown of glowing sapphire velvet with silver-embroidered silk kirtle and sleeves the pale blue of a perfect sky, and a new necklace of the most exquisite little sapphire birds circling my throat that my father had lately given me, and a diamond crescent moon atop the sleek black coil of my hair.

After most graciously thanking Master Skelton in honeyed

tones, and smiling and nodding to the court, framing my words as a jest, I quoted a line from Chaucer's own poem about Cressida.

"Alas," I dolefully sighed, eyes downcast onto my plate of mutton, "of me until the world's end shall be wrote no good song!"

Led most enthusiastically by the new King, the court laughed and applauded my witty rejoinder, and I smiled and sat down triumphant as my husband nodded his approval. I am proud to say that I resisted the fervent impulse to turn and stick my tongue out at John Skelton. But that would not have been ladylike or becoming of a good Christian woman and wife, and now that I was at court, appearances were more important than ever before.

Smitten with his brother's widow, despite the seven years between their ages, our ruddy-haired young monarch swiftly made Spanish Catherine his bride.

And I, in a swirling pearl-embroidered confection of a cream and gold brocade gown, with ropes of lustrous pearls and chains of diamonds and gold about my neck, and yet more pearls and diamonds braided into the coils of my sleek black hair, and the horrendous broad and heavy golden Bullen bull collar clasped stiflingly tight about my throat, fastened there by my husband's own hands as though he were putting a collar on his prize bitch, was amongst those pleased and honored to walk behind her on her wedding day.

Indeed, I had the supreme honor of lacing her into her boiled leather stays before we lifted the gown of shimmering white sarcenet over her head. And I was also the privileged one who held out the velvet cushion from which her proud Spanish duenna, Dona Elvira, lifted the crown of gilded rosemary and placed it on the abundant cascading waves of her golden hair.

How my shopkeeper's spawn of a spouse smiled when I passed him, following in the wake of Catherine's gold brocade and ermine train. I thought the strain of such a wide smile would surely tear the corners of his lying, hypocritical, yet oh so flattering, self-interested mercenary mouth.

And he was smiling again the day I walked, through a cheering populace, and showers of blessings and flowers, to Westminster Abbey in ermine-bordered crimson velvet behind Queen Catherine on her coronation day.

I was close enough to hear the gold-clad, diamond-flashing King, when he turned astride his gold-caparisoned white steed and called back to the radiant little woman riding in a golden litter drawn by four white Spanish mules, gowned all in gold with her hair unbound beneath a coronet of gold and jeweled pomegranates, "Everyone loves my golden Queen, but none more so than I!"

Thomas smiled. And I smiled too. I had never been so happy. Oftentimes my husband was so busy with his business about the court, currying favor with the new King and court worthies, or gone on missions abroad, deploying his superb French in the service of King Henry, that many nights we didn't share a bed.

What *bliss* it was to lie alone in the marital bed without Thomas Bullen beside me delivering a curtain lecture! And other nights, whilst he slept alone, I was chosen to sleep on a pallet at the foot of Queen Catherine's bed in case she needed something during the night. Thomas deemed this a *very* great honor, and I was grateful to our gracious Queen, for I would much rather sleep on her floor than in the most comfortable and luxurious bed in the world if I must share it with Thomas Bullen—I mean *Boleyn!*

One evening I found myself unexpectedly alone with Queen Catherine in her bedchamber.

She stood in her gold-embroidered amber velvet dressing gown with her luxuriant golden hair rippling down past her waist and an awed expression upon her face. Her white fingers toyed absently with the gold filigree cross at her throat, dripping with pearls and studded with rich amber-gold topazes, as she examined the bountiful array of new gowns, petticoats, cloaks, robes, bed gowns, stays, stockings, blackwork-embroidered shifts of the sheerest white lawn, jewel-bordered headdresses, embroidered and fringed gloves, and the overflowing jewel caskets that covered the huge purple velvet expanse of her immense bed with its tassels and fringe of Venice gold, and every table, stool, bench, and the backs and seats of every chair in the room, and even draped the fireside settle. Dozens of pairs of satin and velvet slippers littered the floor, their toes encrusted with gems and embroidered and beaded embellishments, and riding boots of Spanish leather adorned with gold or silver buckles, embroidery, or fringe.

Everywhere I looked there was the glimmer of gold and the shimmer of silver flashing in the fire and candlelight. I don't think I ever saw so much gilt embroidery in one room in my life.

With a timid smile, she shyly confided in me, "After my husband, Prince Arthur, died, while my father, King Ferdinand, and the late King Henry, my father-in-law, argued over my dowry and what was to become of me, whether I should return to Spain or remain in England and marry Prince Henry when he came of age, my gowns grew shabby and frayed, as did those of my Spanish ladies.

"What a raggedy, threadbare lot we were, all of us ashamed to be seen! I cannot tell you how awful and ashamed I felt! I was responsible for the ladies who served me. It was my duty to provide them with food, shelter, clothes, and dowries so that they might make good marriages amongst the English nobility. That was why most of them had come with me; they were willing to brave a new and possibly hostile land to try to make a better life for themselves. And, to my great shame, I found that I could give them *nothing*.

"I was a princess and yet a pauper; I could not even properly clothe myself. I was a virgin widow who did not know if she would ever be a wife again. In those sad, bewildering days we lived on day-old fish and stale bread bought at a reduced price in the marketplace. My proud duenna, Dona Elvira, went out and haggled for these provisions herself. Oh"—Catherine shuddered—"I shall *never* forget that bread! We wore our arms out sawing through it, and it made our jaws ache to chew it; we all feared we would wear our teeth down to the roots."

She paused by the fireside settle and held up against herself a gown of plum-hued Florentine velvet, a beguiling deep purple infused with crimson, elaborately embroidered with a raised design of pomegranates in rich threads of silver and gold embellished with pearls and rich purple amethyst and wine-dark garnet brilliants. She looked like an angel with her golden hair flowing down around her fair, round face, smiling gently, with a faraway look in her gray eyes, as she caressed the fine fabric and recalled the grim, uncertain, and shabby days that were now thankfully behind her.

"I implored our ambassador to intercede for me, as my servants and I were ready to go out and beg alms in the streets for the love of God, but both my father and King Henry maintained that I was the other's responsibility until such time as I remarried, then my husband would see to my needs. I spent my days writing begging letters, and trying to patch my gowns and undergarments, and darning my stockings. There were holes in the soles of my shoes; I patched them as best I could with folded parchment and scraps of leather when I could find them. I could not afford to buy even a length of linen to fashion new shifts, so that beneath my gowns I was often naked. Those I had brought from Spain as part of my trousseau were worn thin enough to read through; there was nothing left of them to mend, and the blackwork embroidery stitched on their hems had unraveled and frayed so that instead of beautiful flowers I now had a frayed mess of unsightly weeds.

"I lived on the edge of the court. No one was ever quite sure how to treat me; with respect always, yes, but they kept their distance just the same, as my position was so uncertain. They did not dare offend me lest I one day marry Prince Henry"—she took up and caressed his miniature framed in diamonds and suspended from a golden chain, and gazed upon his face with eyes filled with the purest love—"and thus become their queen one day. But as this was yet in much doubt, it would not do to fawn and pay *too much* attention to a person of little importance either. My position was so tenuous no one dared offer me friendship and aid I might never be able to repay. I kept my faith in God, but I confess often I did despair and weep and wonder, *What will become of me?*

"Yet through it all, like a golden beacon of hope, there was Henry. I watched him grow from boy to man. When I came to England he had to look up at me, but now I was looking up at him. He *towered* above me, tall, lean, muscular, and fine, a pillar of strength, mighty as Samson, handsome beyond the poets' words or the painters' pigments and brushstrokes; no artist could ever do justice to his life and vivacity, his zest for living life to its fullest. How I *adored* him!" She clasped his miniature to her breast. "I loved him as I never dreamed I could love anyone! My heart was like a cup overflowing, running over with love, ever replenishing, never exhausted! I prayed every night I would one day be his wife. I never wanted anything more.

"There were stolen moments over the years that I regarded as precious treasures, storing them safe inside my heart, where I could take them out and relive them again and again and remember all those times when he had doled out kind words and given little gifts to me that made me feel special and wanted, like I was important to someone, and helped give me the strength to go on. A little book of devotions, verse, or scriptures; the words of wise holy men and women to give me quiet comfort; a poem or a song he had written; a crystal vial of scent; a pomander ball smelling of cloves and oranges that reminded me of Spain and the trees in the gardens of my parents' palaces; a pair of pomegranate velvet gloves fringed and embroidered in gold with my initials and pomegranates, the fruit of fertility, because I had chosen it as my own personal emblem; a pink coral rosary, and another day one of turquoise beads; a nugget of amber with an exquisite little flower trapped, preserved for all eternity, inside; a necklace of little golden loaves and dangling silver fish to remind me that the bad fare would be much better one day; a bouquet of May flowers tied with green and white ribbons—the Tudor colors, you of course know; a single white rose, its petals still wet with the morning dew, that he climbed softly through my window to lay upon my pillow as I slept; an orange that filled my palm perfectly; a bunch of black grapes; his hat filled with cherries he had himself picked or a damson tart fresh baked from the palace kitchens; once even a dainty red rosebud exquisitely wrought from marzipan he had asked the pastry cook to make specially for me. I have many of them still, those I could keep." She turned and pointed to a beautifully carved chest peeping out from the folds of the velvet, satin, damask, and silk gowns draped over it, smilingly calling it her "treasure chest, filled with those worldly things I hold most dear."

"Each time he brought me a gift," she continued, hugging a pearl-embellished, golden wheat–embroidered gown of harvest gold velvet to her breast, "he would lean in close, so close I shivered and almost swooned at the warmth of his breath and the touch of his lips, and whisper in my ear, 'When I am King, you will want for *nothing,* and no one will ever be unkind to you again or make you cry; I will forbid it. It will be like a law of the land that all must praise and adore and do aught that they can to ensure the happiness of good Queen Catherine.'

"One day when he caught me weeping over the shabbiness of

my best gown, a deep brown velvet, its square neckline edged with tiny gold scallop shells and now badly tarnished and frayed beyond repair golden braid, he took my hand and swore, 'When I am King, you shall have a new dress every day, each one finer than the last, and all of them trimmed with gold and gems. I will give you a whole rainbow of jewels, my Catherine! A color does not exist that will not be found in your wardrobe or jewel coffer!' "

As she quoted her beloved consort, she spun giddy as a young girl and flung out her arms to take in the expanse of splendid jewel-bedecked and gem-hued finery, enough to wear for many months to come without ever donning the same one twice.

"He came to me in his gilded armor one day, ruddy-faced and sweat-streaked, fresh from a turn in the tiltyard, and raised his golden helm and brandished his lance high and cried: 'Someday I will slay *all* your dragons, Catherine!'

"He was my knight in shining armor, as powerful and compassionate as Saint Michael!" She clasped her hands to her breast and smiled fondly at the memory. "He was *determined* to rescue me, to save me from penury, humiliation, and distress. Whenever he could, he slipped coins into my hand. He would pause to kiss and bow over my hand and press a coin discreetly into my palm, and no one ever knew, even when we were in the midst of a crowded room; it was just between us two. He was my earthly savior, my champion, my knight, and I was the threadbare princess he would one day rescue and clothe in gold bright as the sun!

" 'You are my golden princess,' he used to say to me, boldly daring to reach out and caress my hair, to pluck the pins or net from it so he could twine the golden strands around his fingers. 'You should shine and smile to rival the sun, my Catherine. My most heartfelt wish is that you will never be sad again. When you are mine, I shall see that you never weep or frown again, by my life and kingdom, this I swear!' "

"Madame," I smiled and curtsied low, "clearly he has fulfilled his promise. You are radiant, and love shines from your very soul; it lights you up and fills every part of you; even these gowns of silver and gold and all the jewels he has given you seem dim in comparison. None can rival the splendor of your love and happiness!"

"Oh, yes, he has, Elizabeth! He has!" She smiled and reached out to clasp my hand before she spun away to enfold herself in a cloak of tawny brocade and red fox.

"Even if I live a century, I shall never forget the day he came to me, straight from his father's deathbed, and flung a cloak of cloth-of-gold and ermine about my shoulders, plucked the pins from my hair, for I was indeed a virgin about to become a bride again, and set a coronet of diamonds on what he called my 'golden waves,' and announced, 'Your days of want and penury are past, my Queen!' as all the courtiers about us knelt solemnly at my feet, pledging their eternal loyalty and devotion. It was like the happy ending of a fairy story, and I had risen from the ashes, like a servant girl who suddenly discovers that she is a princess. And now"—with a tender smile she reached down and cradled the little round belly that was only just beginning to show and could still be mistaken for her natural plumpness—"now . . . my cup runneth over with happiness, and I am well and truly blessed!"

"Yes, indeed." I smiled back at her. "It is the dream of love come true that every duty-bound little girl secretly keeps locked inside her heart, hoping the man her parents pick for her will indeed be a prince of passion and not a cold fish, a cruel brute, or a toothless old dotard. Madame, your love is an inspiration to us all!"

Flattering words, yes, they rolled off my tongue with the most fluid ease. I was well trained in courtly speech, tact, diplomacy, and the ways of the world. I could hold my own with the suavest of diplomats, and lie without a flicker of an eye to betray me. But this time I meant every word.

❧ 5 ❧

In those early days, the marriage of Henry and Catherine seemed a golden and happy union—a true love match. I could not count the times I saw them look at each other with fond and loving glances or sit with their fingers entwined in a true lovers' knot of flesh and blood, or the many mornings when I attended my discreetly smiling mistress after a night of love and saw proofs of the King's passion upon her fair body and the bed they had shared.

They were a beautiful couple. King Henry, strong, powerful, and ruddy gold, fun-loving and vivacious, yet a man born to command, one who knew how to inspire loyalty, and to hold and capture love in the palm of his hand. And Queen Catherine, tiny and plump and golden-haired, a serenely smiling little round Madonna, a motherly partridge with as yet no chicks of her own, radiating love and kindness, with a beautiful nimbus of tranquility and quiet strength about her that won her an assured place in the hearts of the English people.

Many years later, when I looked back and recalled that moment of privileged intimacy with the now sad and gray Queen Catherine in the presence of my cynical black swan daughter, Anne would lift one finely arched black brow, shrug her slim shoulders, and coolly pronounce over the rim of her wine cup, "The sun *always* sets, Mother."

But in those happy golden days there was only one blot, one blemish, upon their perfect happiness—every babe Queen Catherine bore died either in her womb or soon after birthing.

I was there each time to dry her tears and discreetly carry out the bloody linens, to tell her, "Let go, you cannot stop or save it," when she clutched her thighs tight together against the blood that seeped out like red tears her womb was weeping and gritted her teeth as though through sheer force of will she could prevent the precious life within from leaving her before its time. I sat by her side, held her hand, and whispered encouraging words, urging her to take heart, reminding her that she was still young and there was still time, telling her of the many miscarriages I had suffered, and yet God had, in His *own time,* blessed me with three healthy children. Faithfully, I nursed her until she was well enough for her golden King to come back and fill her womb again even though the ending was always the same.

And I was there when she *almost* succeeded, through every stage of the pregnancy that seemed destined to go the natural, happiest course and end in joy and fulfillment for all. Per English custom, Queen Catherine, her female servants, and the noble ladies who attended her, of which I was an honored and privileged one, withdrew from the eyes of the court a month before her child was due to make his—we all hoped and prayed for a prince—debut.

In the soft, quiet, solitude of the lying-in chamber, where her musicians softly played the comforting, dear, and familiar Spanish songs of her youth, Queen Catherine lay resting, hands lovingly cradling her immense, swollen belly as she whispered loving words to the child within, ensconced in a splendid, immense, gold-pillared bed, covered, curtained, and canopied in sumptuous bloodred velvet embroidered with golden crowns above the entwined initials of *H & C*—Henry and Catherine. Sometimes, I remember, sitting bored over my embroidery, I would pass the time by trying to count that vast multitude of golden crowns. I got as high as eight hundred and eight before I wearied of that tedious little game and turned my mind to something completely different.

Dutifully, yet from my heart as well, I knelt daily with the Queen's other ladies and, led by the Queen's confessor, prayed that God would see fit to send Queen Catherine "a good hour," as labor was then commonly called, though *every* woman knows this is a very cruel jest, most likely thought of by men, as we all know a birthing can go on for a great many agonizing hours and be akin to Hell on earth.

The Queen's son, Prince Henry, was born in triumph after many hours of red, ripping pain. The whole time, she grasped the silver crucifix her mother had given her before she left Spain, in which was set, in a little bubble of glass, a precious sliver of wood from the true cross upon which our savior Jesus Christ had suffered and died; she held it so tight that it left a deep red impression in the palm of her hand. Before the doors were thrown wide to welcome the King and court in to greet their newborn prince, we bathed our weary but smiling, triumphant mistress with rosewater, combed the tangles from her golden hair, and I was the one privileged to drape a mantle of ermine-edged crimson velvet over her shoulders to modestly cover the near nakedness of her fine linen birthing shift.

All London celebrated. The church bells seemed to never stop ringing or the wine to stop flowing. How many pairs of shoes did we all wear out dancing? Bonfires were lit and fireworks exploded in a myriad of jewel-colored sparks in the nighttime sky above the Thames. There were tournaments, balls, masques, pageants, and banquets galore, and though she remained abed, Queen Catherine basked in her triumph, glowing with pride; she had finally done it—she had given her husband, and England, an heir.

On New Year's Day, King Henry ordered the palace gates thrown wide to let the common people in so that they too might dance and rejoice in the birth of England's newborn prince.

I was one of many who danced in an elaborate masque, arrayed in a fantastical shimmering tinsel gown of the Tudor colors, green and white; towering jewel and silk flower festooned headdress; and mask, ablaze with ruby red and diamond white paste-gem-petaled roses. Our costumes were sewn all over with large silver and gold *H*s and *C*s stitched but loosely and bulging with little gilded trinkets and toys, whistles and pendants shaped like birds and gilt little boys with proud phalluses, Tudor roses with red and white enameled petals, or medallion portraits of the King and Queen and such, so that we might toss these dainty baubles to the crowd, to give them a special remembrance to take home with them.

Amidst us stood King Henry himself, towering, larger than life, above us all, dressed like the other dancers, his whole great, handsome, robust, and virile body covered with gilt initials bulging with tiny trinkets.

The common people became overexcited at finding themselves so near, within touching distance, of their robust young King. They stretched out their loving fingers to be warmed by his majestic presence as though he were the sun. They stripped the favors from his form, taking the gilt letters and the trinkets they harbored home in remembrance of this glorious day when they had been close enough to touch their King.

Henry threw back his head and laughed, planted his feet wide, and flung out his arms, welcoming them all, trusting himself to his people's goodwill. But there were not enough gilt letters and favors upon the King's person to satisfy the crowd, though we dancers were well stuffed with them; the people wanted something from the King, not us. When his person had been entirely stripped of these, their eager hands didn't stop; they tore his costume to bits, seizing greedily on every scrap and ribbon, until he fled laughing with his hands cupped modestly over where his codpiece had been as the guards moved in to—"Gently!" as the laughing King insisted—herd the people from the palace.

As he passed me, King Henry paused, pulled me into his arms, and grasped me tight. I was startled when he kissed me as he spun me around, using my full shimmering skirts to shield his nakedness, maneuvering me backward until he could reach up and snatch down a gold-fringed banner. He wrapped it around his loins, flopped back against the purple velvet cushions of his throne—the picture of a man at home and completely relaxed in his favorite fireside chair—and called for wine. I laughed and curtsied low, flattered to have been embraced and kissed by a king, then I let myself be swallowed up by the merry crowd, whirled and spun about, and pawed by many manly hands, and thought no more about it. It was merely the joyful madness of the moment, I supposed. When the wine came, King Henry raised his cup high and toasted his "good and loving people" and thanked them all most heartily for their prayers and good wishes on the behalf of himself, his beloved Queen, and the baby boy who would, God willing, be their next King—Henry IX!

With my mask tilted awry, blocking one eye, I was halfheartedly fending off a randy straggler, a great, big, strapping red-haired fellow, who had just ripped a golden *H* from my breast, spilling party favors all over the floor to be crushed or snatched up by the retreating crowd. He wanted to go further, to let his avid, roving fingers explore and find the flesh within, and I was willing, but it was then that word came from the nursery, throwing a black pall over the celebrations. All ended instantly, like a sudden downpour on a picnic, and all dispersed, all the guests going home or to churches to light candles and pray.

Prince Henry was in peril. A fever had come on very suddenly. Already the little prince baked in his gilded cradle, as hot as a piglet turning on a spit above a roaring fire. His breath came in rattling gasps, and the way his chest struggled to rise it was clear that he was fighting for each breath. Doctors, apothecaries, and wise women all came and went, and in the end, so did the prince, and the land was again without an heir.

Inconsolable, Queen Catherine closeted herself in her private chapel, kneeling amidst a hundred glowing candles; she prayed fervently to the Holy Virgin with all her heart. King Henry tried to drown his sorrows with wine, women, and song. But a day finally came when, all his grief spent, he strode boldly into the quiet, candlelit chapel. Queen Catherine peered up at him through her black mourning veils. Gently, he raised her, lifted her veil, put his hands upon her frail black-clad shoulders, and stared deep into her tired, sad, tear-swollen gray eyes.

"We are still young and life must go on," he said. "The time to mourn has passed, and we must try again." And with those words he led her to her bed to do just that.

She was smiling the next morning when I brought her her breakfast tray, and when the time came to dress her, she chose a gown of glowing silk the color of the sunrise instead of black.

* * *

Two months later, she felt certain that a seed had again been planted, but the coming of her monthly courses soon dispelled that hope. Wilting beneath this fresh disappointment, she returned to her chapel to pray all the harder, leaving the King to find other, more cheerfully disposed, ladies to dance with. "Look more to your husband, and less to your womb," I wanted to tell her, but I dared not, and a queen's primary function is to provide heirs, not weep and castigate her husband over his infidelities.

It would be Her Majesty's wily and ruthless father, King Ferdinand, who would proffer the best distraction for this bereft young couple. He urged King Henry to join him in a campaign against England and Spain's shared enemy—France.

Like every young man eager to go to war and blood his sword, King Henry zealously embraced his father-in-law's scheme, spending long hours poring over his maps and being fitted for new armor, while Queen Catherine, aided by her ladies, supervised the sewing of banners and badges of silk, and the business of the realm was left to the man they called "the King's right hand," the Lord Chancellor, Cardinal Wolsey, a man whose star was always rising higher, to the extreme dismay of the old nobility, especially my father and brother, and newer men like my husband who resented anyone getting above them.

Wolsey was an ambitious fellow, rather like my husband, the son of an Ipswich butcher who, lacking any true vocation, and having a mistress and two sons on the side, had used the Church as a path to worldly power. But he was a useful fellow who got the tedious business of the realm done, leaving King Henry free to play and make merry. The King relied on him implicitly and would not hear a word spoken against him, and, at that time, Queen Catherine still held pride of place in his trust, so all seemed well in our world. Her compassion tempered wisdom—neither all heart nor all head—was much respected, and the King was always pleased to have her beside him and often asked her opinion before he rendered a final decision. Whenever anyone had a petition, especially one pertaining to mercy, to lay before the King, they always tried first to reach the ear of Queen Catherine.

When King Henry came to show Queen Catherine his new armor, smiling and preening beneath the oohs and ahhs of us adoring ladies, he caught her close against his steel-clad chest, letting her feel the metal codpiece poking through her full skirts, and asked her to be his warrior queen and safeguard the realm against the Scots while he was away making war upon the French. They would most assuredly take advantage of his absence to make mischief, he said, for such had always been their way.

"Sire, I am my mother's daughter," Queen Catherine declared, standing stiff-backed as a soldier herself in her gown of pewter satin with a bodice of silver that reminded us all at that moment of a gleaming breastplate, and the stirring and inspiring tales of how her mother, Queen Isabella, had donned armor and ridden out to defeat the Moors. "Never fear, if the Scots dare cross England's borders they will find me waiting for them."

We watched delightedly over our sewing as Queen Catherine, more playful than we had in such a long time seen her, consented to play his squire and unbuckled and unstrapped his armor and giggled delightedly when he scooped her up in his strong arms and carried her to bed, calling back over his shoulder that we ladies were dismissed and might go and enjoy some pleasurable disport with our own husbands if we so pleased before they were called off to war.

When King Henry set sail for France, we were all confident that Queen Catherine once again carried his child.

I stood beside her as she waved farewell. When the royal flagship was no longer even a tiny speck upon the horizon, she lowered her hand and laid it to rest protectively over her belly. Now she had not only England but its future sovereign to safeguard, and she was determined to fail neither.

When I gently touched her arm and cautiously suggested she might like to lie down and rest, she laughed.

"Do not cluck over me so, Elizabeth. I have God to watch over me, and the blood of Queen Isabella in my veins. Like my mother, I am as strong as Castilian steel, as the Scots will soon discover if they dare try me!"

* * *

The very next day she went as a barefoot pilgrim to the shrine of Our Lady of Walsingham, the popular patroness of mothers and babies, as many barren and bereft women did, to pray that they be made fruitful and their wombs be filled and blessed, as well as those whose prayers had been answered, to rejoice and give thanks after they had been safely delivered. Many also came to pray for sick children or absent loved ones.

Queen Catherine knelt before the beautiful blue and white statue of Our Lady and the infant Jesus and prayed most fervently for the child she carried and for the safe return of her husband. The nuns there even let her hold the vial containing milk from the Holy Virgin's breasts and joined her in her prayers as did the other women, who were pleased and proud to see their Queen come barefoot and plainly clad as though she were one of them. All were impressed by her honest and humble piety. Though she was Queen of England, she never put herself above the other women who came to Walsingham. When they tried to move away, to give her the place of honor before the statue, she shook her head and moved to the very back. "I come to serve, not to be served. Whosoever will be first amongst you must be last, and the servant of all," she said as she carefully knelt upon the hard floor, disdaining the pillow I offered for her knees. It was no wonder they all adored her.

With the King away at war, striding bravely into the face of danger, and no living heir, no son, or even as yet a living daughter, at home, the dangers were doubly great. She fasted and spent many hours in prayer before the statue of Our Lady, surrounded by dozens of softly glowing candles. Despite our urgings, she often denied herself sleep in order to spend even more hours at prayer.

As I knelt with the other ladies a few feet behind her, my knees aching against the stone floor, so cold I feared the onset of rheumatism, my weary eyes dazzled by the dancing yellow-orange flames, fighting sleep, which nodded my head and threatened to carry me off as a beautiful hostage to the Land of Morpheus, I heard her implore, "*Please,* God, let me bear a son this time, a son who will *live. Please,* do not let me fail!"

True to tradition, the Scots soon seized upon King Henry's absence. Their own King, James IV, husband to King Henry's own sister, Margaret Tudor, marshaled his troops and began marching toward the border even as our army prepared to march out to meet them.

Before they went, Queen Catherine wanted to do something special to inspire our troops. Knowing that some of them were fated to die upon the field of battle and never return to their homeland, it was important to her that they know that their sacrifice would not be in vain; it would be for the greater glory of God and England.

"I will ride out and speak to them," she declared.

"Are you sure you should ride?" her most favored and devoted Spanish lady, Maria de Salinas, asked as we reluctantly helped her prepare. I agreed, reminding her that it was considered *most* unwise for a breeding woman to ride, especially so early on; it could be fatally injurious to the child within.

"Have you forgotten I am my mother's daughter?" Queen Catherine gently chided us. "On the night I was born, my mother had spent all day in the saddle. The next morning at dawn's first light, she rose from her bed as if it were any other morning and she had not just passed the night in childbed, fastened a towel betwixt her legs to staunch the blood, dressed and donned her armor, and rode out at the head of her army to face the enemy. If my mother could do that, then I can surely ride out to address our men." Seeing the concern that filled our eyes, she reached out and took each of us by the hand and gave our fingers a reassuring squeeze. "I promise I shall go gently. Because of His Majesty's absence, this child is doubly precious to me, and I must, and will, take all the care that I can. Smile now; God is with us. And He will watch over me as He has always done."

When we brought forth her brown velvet riding habit, Queen Catherine pushed it away and called instead for a plain white linen gown, and over that, she bade us fasten a silver breastplate such as her mother had worn.

Without her layered petticoats and full velvet skirts, her little round belly showed prominent and proud, bulging gently with the promise of a prince for England. Some might have thought her immodest to show herself so, but I understood; she wanted the men to see, to give them yet one reason more that was worth fighting, and dying, for—the future.

Disdaining her favored headdress, the gable hood, with its boxy, face-embracing frame, she shook out her long golden hair, letting it hang down her back free as a virgin's, and asked me to brush it for her until it shone like the sun. Then she asked Maria de Salinas to fetch a long mantle of Our Lady's blue silk. This she draped over her head so that it flowed down over her body like a gently rippling pure blue river.

Her ankles were badly swollen because of the child, and we found, try as we might, her boots just would not lace. "Take them off," she said, "and my stockings too." And, in a show of humble piety, she went barefoot just as she always did when she went to pray at the shrine of Our Lady of Walsingham.

My father, looking splendid and silver-haired in his gleaming new, polished silver breastplate, gasped at the sight of her, blinking aghast at the sight of her little naked feet. But by the time he knelt to cup his hands and boost her into the saddle of her white steed, he had quite recovered himself. When he rose, he saluted her and gave a nod of approval. "God be with Your Majesty." He understood what she meant to do.

"Your mistress is a brave woman and a very great lady," he said as he helped me, in my silver-braided sapphire velvet habit and feathered hat, into the saddle of my nervously prancing black mare.

"The Lord smiles on those who stand in defense of their own." Queen Catherine raised her voice, clear and steady, as, from the saddle, she addressed our brave troops, gazing out into a sea of many thousand faces, refusing to raise a hand to shield her eyes even though the sun bouncing off their armor was blinding and we would all complain of headaches and scorched eyes later. Yet she, our proud warrior queen, betrayed no womanly weakness at all.

"Remember that English courage surpasses that of all other nations!" she cried.

How they cheered! Those nearest pressed forward to reverently kiss the hem of her blue mantle and white gown; some even dared kneel and press their lips to her naked feet, cupping them tenderly as doves in their big, rough, manly hands in a way that made me shiver and long to feel the touch of those hands against my own naked skin. If an opportune moment presented itself, I vowed, I would find a fine soldier and whisper an invitation in his ear.

When we returned to the garrison, Queen Catherine gasped and bent double as she dismounted, crying out that she had just felt a stabbing pain between her legs, like a knife being thrust up and twisted inside her. But she refused to let the men see her weakness, not after she had just shown herself a great warrior queen like her mother. Pushing free of our hands, she steeled herself against the pain and forced herself to stand erect and walk calmly back inside and up the stairs to her chamber. By then the blood was dripping, like fat droplets of red rain, staining her white gown and leaving a telltale trail behind her on the floor.

We summoned doctors and midwives, but it was too late. The child was dead before it ever had a chance to draw breath.

From her bed, propped up against a mound of gold damask pillows with a lap desk balanced upon her knees, Queen Catherine wrote to King Henry of our resounding victory. Ten thousand Scots lay dead upon Flodden Field, amongst them King James himself, and the greatest of his noblemen and soldiers, the finest flowers of Scottish manhood all cut down. King James left a babe in the cradle as his heir, so England would be spared the menace of Scottish invasions for many years to come. Queen Catherine sent the Scottish king's bloodstained coat as a tribute to her husband across the Channel in France.

At the same time, we received word that King Henry had scored a triumph of his own—the Battle of the Spurs they called it because the French took one look at the superior English forces and drove their spurs into their horses' flanks and galloped fast away. God had indeed been good to us, but we all shared Queen Catherine's sorrow; once again, she had failed to give her husband and adopted nation an heir.

I was quick to remind her that she was still young—they both were—and His Majesty was, I took the liberty of saying, a robust young bull who never left her womb empty for long. There was still time, plenty of time. But now, as my own midwife had advised me after the violent agony of Anne's birth, she must rest and let her body heal. "Enjoy this respite while it lasts," I counseled. But she ignored me and rose from her bed, to fast and pray. As soon as she was able, she donned a rough, white linen gown and walked barefoot to pray before the shrine of Our Lady of Walsingham again. She kept in her private rooms a painting of the Holy Virgin appearing before the devout, but childless, Saxon noblewoman, Lady Richeldis de Faverches, and blessing her womb upon the spot where that grateful and fruitful woman would later build the shrine with a beautiful statue of the Holy Virgin holding the infant Jesus inside. When she returned from her latest pilgrimage, she began donning a hair shirt beneath her splendid gowns that would chafe her beautiful porcelain pale skin raw and open ugly oozing red sores. But the suffering would be worth it, she insisted, if she could only give birth to a son who would live.

"When I hold Henry's son at my breast, these red sores will be as precious and dear to me as rubies," she said. "And when my husband returns from France, I will be ready; I will be waiting to welcome him with open arms, to draw him deep inside my body to make our prince."

And that is exactly what happened. When Henry returned in triumph from the battlefields of France, there she was, waiting for him, and she did give him a son, a one-month's babe who clung to life by a tether and soon closed his eyes forever. He turned blue as the Virgin's mantle even as poor Queen Catherine tried to breathe him back pink again with air from her own lungs.

How bitterly she wept and lamented her failure. *"Why?"* she sobbed again and again. "Why can I not give my husband a son, the only thing he wants that he does not already have? The *one* thing all his wealth cannot buy. I am a woman and meant to bear children, so why have I failed at my purpose in life? Why does God take each of these precious little souls up to heaven to Him and away from my loving arms? *Why?"*

I watched her weep in sorrow-filled silence for I had no answer to give her.

One night soon after her last loss, the Queen asked me to accompany her when she left the Great Hall rather abruptly, claiming a sudden, all-encompassing weariness she could not shake off. We left while King Henry still frolicked and danced. I did not think we would be missed, and when I asked if I should send a messenger to tell His Majesty that she had retired for the night, Queen Catherine said nay, she did not wish to spoil his pleasure.

She sent all her ladies but me away and went to stand before her silver mirror. I stood behind her and lifted the pearl-edged gable hood from her head. In the candlelight, as I plucked out the pins, I noticed what I never had before—strands of silver swimming like eels through the golden sea of her tresses. Our eyes met in the mirror.

"Mirrors do not lie, Elizabeth," she said, appraising the lines the years and sorrow had wrought upon her brow and around her eyes, nose, and mouth. "The feet of Father Time march on." She sighed and stepped back to scrutinize her figure. Even though I had laced her tight into the boiled leather stays beneath her silver and pomegranate velvet gown, I could still see that her waist had thickened with every child she had carried yet lost. Queen Catherine saw it too. "I have become old, fat, and faded! He is still a young man, but I . . . I have become an old woman. How great a difference suddenly seem the seven years that lie between us! What was once a stream has become an ocean!"

She was eight and twenty, the same age as myself. Only *I* was still beautiful . . . for now.

I heard the door open behind us, and in the mirror I saw King Henry, clad in cloth-of-gold and deep red velvet, blazing with rubies and diamonds. I curtsied and stepped quickly aside as he came bounding into the room, a broad smile lighting up his handsome face. He went to stand behind his Queen and brushed the thick curtain of silver-veined golden hair aside, over her shoulder, and bent to press his lips against the nape of her neck as he reached around to cup her breasts. Reflected in the mirror, I saw the fear in Queen Catherine's eyes. I could tell she was wondering if he noticed the change in them, how they sagged a little more after each disappointment she endured.

I felt a sudden sadness as I stood back in the shadows and contemplated the couple before me. Queen Catherine was right—mirrors do not lie. When they had married the difference in their ages seemed paltry and insignificant. Four years ago, they had both been young and golden, but, suddenly, seemingly overnight, only one of them was young and golden. King Henry was still in his lusty, golden prime, while my beloved Queen Catherine had become an old woman with silver strands amongst the gold and deep lines upon her face I doubted any cream, lotion, or elixir could erase.

Old gold is still gold, I tried to tell myself. Beneath the tarnish, silver is still silver. But no, I could not make myself believe. Mirrors do not lie. And I had seen with my own eyes the ravishes time and childbearing had wrought upon my person. I was a woman too; I *knew*.

I shivered with foreboding. I knew in my heart that they were doomed. They had grown apart in other ways too. It was folly to pretend otherwise, to try to play hide-and-seek with the truth, when the mirror's reflection was staring me in the face.

The passion that had once burned so brightly between Henry and Catherine had dimmed to a mere flicker through time and familiarity; duty had long ago eclipsed desire. The desperate need for a son had surpassed their desire for each other. And Queen Catherine had spent so much time sitting out dances when she was with child that, between pregnancies when her womb was empty and she was able, she had forgotten—and in her sorrow lost all desire—to dance again. So she let other women—willing, amorous, and ambitious women younger and prettier than the golden Queen, who had now lost her youth and luster—partner her husband instead. A grave mistake, I thought, but I said nothing.

Then King Ferdinand undid all the good he had done them. He chose to abandon the French campaign and leave Henry in the lurch. When Henry found out, he blasted Queen Catherine with his anger, like a dragon belching fire, while we ladies quailed back, fearing his wrath would burn and blind her. But she stood straight and stoically endured her terrible shame, taking the blame because she was there and her father wasn't.

"Henceforth, I alone shall rule England with Wolsey to help me!" he bellowed. "I want no more advice from you, or your damnable, duplicitous, interfering father, madame! England shall be all for England, not a vassal of Spain as your duplicitous father would have it! I am master here, and the King of England bows to no master save God! And you may tell your father that, madame!"

The damage was irreparable. She had lost all his confidence. The trust was broken. He would no longer discuss statecraft and strategy with her as had always been his custom. Now Wolsey would take her place, shaping the destiny of England, while she was set aside as just another royal ornament, a decoration, sitting on her pretty gilded throne, to smile and nod and dispense kind words and welcome visitors and ambassadors to the court, bestow smiles and charity on the English people, and give alms and gifts of shirts and shifts to the poor that she, alongside us, her devoted ladies, had labored long in sewing. All her *real* power and influence were gone forever, and everyone knew it.

❧ 6 ❧

Although I truly sympathized with all Queen Catherine's sorrows, by then I had my *own* happiness to think of, and I refused, as selfish as it may sound, to let the Queen's sorrows dampen or taint it.

I was what I had always wanted to be—admired and adored. Many men wanted to be my lover, and some I deigned to discreetly favor. But there was one I set above all others, one whose embraces and the rare, sweet times we spent together I truly savored. For me, it was *much* more than my usual, casual carnal diversion; those were all mere indulgences of the flesh to while away the boredom and fill the tedious hours of one who had so easily grown jaded.

The doll maker, Remi Jouet, was now my lover, the one I favored and desired above all men. I called him "my *jou-jou*," "my plaything," speaking those words in the sweetest, most affectionate sense.

His warm as new baked bread, doughy soft, pink and white body was the *most* delightful toy to while away the languid afternoons with. I *loved* exploring it, watching the way shyness warred with boldness inside him. I *adored* every ample inch of him, and the sweet, tender soul inside. He made my pulses race as no one else ever did. I reveled in his pillowy soft embrace and the way he filled and fulfilled me in a way that no one else, neither highborn nor low, ever did. To me, he was truly, uniquely, in a class all his own. I loved to playfully nip the sweet fleshy lobes of his ears, half-hidden beneath the waves of his rich brown hair, so dark that in some lights it might have been mistaken for black, and to tease him about the talisman of red coral, carved into the shape of a tiny horn—"or perhaps a red pepper; which is it, my dear?"—that he wore on a leather cord about his neck alongside a little silver cross. I asked him which he trusted in more—"Luck or God?" and smiled when he explained that he wore the coral in fond remembrance of his grandmother, a very superstitious Frenchwoman, yet marvelous and magical, and so very kind, who had fastened the bit of coral about his throat to protect him from all harm and evil before the midwife even had a chance to wash the birthing blood off him and lay him in his mother's loving arms.

And yes, oh yes, honesty behooves me to confess, I *gloried* in cuckolding my parvenu spouse, that shopkeeper's grandson, so eager to shed his mercantile origins, with an actual shopkeeper, an artisan whose large, powerful hands were work-roughened and coarse from making play pretties for little children, yet capable of the most infinite tenderness when they caressed me—unless I was in a mood for roughness, to be bruised by his kisses and the grasp of those powerful hands around my slender wrists, or on my limbs as he raised them to his shoulders just before plunging into me, doubling me up, until I didn't know if it was breathlessness or pleasure that made me feel so gloriously giddy and faint, as though my head might fall off the edge of the bed and roll away like a child's toy ball. What fun we had! It was the best bed sport ever (and I have had experience enough to make that claim with some authority).

Our affair began shortly after I took up residence at court, when, while spending an idle afternoon shopping in London, I suddenly turned onto the street where his shop had been. It was still there! How my heart raced. But was *he* still there? Shops are bought and sold, or inherited, and change hands all the time. There was only *one* way to find out.

Boldly, I squared my shoulders, thrust my chin haughty high, and barged brazenly through the door. And there he was! All dressed in rusty, rumpled black, just as I remembered him, leaning on the counter, brow puckered in concentration beneath a wing of dark hair, intent on some bit of carving, a face taking shape beneath the blade of his knife. Was it possible? He seemed not to have changed at all! Time is so much kinder to men! I silently pouted, cursing the marks childbearing had left upon my beautiful body. He was just as I remembered him. *Exactly* like the picture I had carried in my heart all these years.

I walked right up to him, my head held high and proud, confident as a queen, my blue velvet skirts swishing over the rough wooden floor.

"Whatever became of the doll you promised me?" I demanded as though mere weeks instead of several years had passed since I had last been inside his shop. "Do you always take this many years to fulfill your commissions? If so, it is a wonder that you are still in business, Master Jouet!"

"A moment, my lady," he said softly with a shy smile and bowed and withdrew into the back room.

He emerged cradling a bundle of celestial blue silk that he sat carefully upon the counter. Slowly, he unwrapped it, revealing the most elegant and exquisite doll I had ever seen—it was me! It was an *exact* likeness of myself at sixteen, with a face of patrician perfection and beautiful hands of carved and painted alabaster, a weighty cascade of night-black hair crowned with a chaplet of sapphire blue glass beads, gold lovers' knots, and white pearls, and a gown of sumptuous sapphire blue velvet bordered with black velvet upon which rows of gold braid lovers' knots were stitched. The full skirt fell gracefully over layered silk petticoats, and this miniature me was daintily shod in black velvet slippers with gold braid lovers' knots on the toes and deep blue stockings with a gold lovers' knot embroidered over each ankle. She even wore a strand of pearls with a sapphire shaped like a vivid blue tear dangling in the hollow between her alabaster breasts and a gold lovers' knot brooch set with pearls.

He would have placed her in my arms, like a midwife proudly presenting a newborn to her mother, but I moved faster. I grasped the soft, well-worn collar of his black doublet and kissed him with a furious hunger as I pulled him after me into the back room and we toppled together onto the disarrayed motley-colored quilt that covered his humble bed. We shed our clothes, I with wild abandon, and he shyly and maddeningly slowly at first until I threatened to rip the buttons and ties and tear the cloth that kept his flesh from me away with my teeth if he didn't strip himself bare for me and quickly. I was *ravenous* for him! I pushed him onto his back, ignoring and kissing away the self-deprecating jest he made about his soft, fish-belly white body looking like a beached whale.

"You look *delicious!*" I said. "Your body is as warm, soft, and comforting as fresh baked bread." I straddled him like a wishbone, my thighs straining, feeling poised to snap but *gloriously* glad of it, because my wish was already coming true. He loved me hard and fast, rough and then exquisitely, achingly tender, and when he paused uncertainly and asked me if he should withdraw without spending his seed, I grabbed his hair in two hard handfuls and yanked him back down to me and held him tight until he cried out my name—*Elizabeth!*—in a passion-choked whisper.

Afterward, we lay together and slept, our lust spent. The stars were poised to come out when at last I stood, letting him lace me back into my corset and gown. I was never less eager to say the word *farewell* or to return to the court I had spent years yearning to be at, when he kissed me tenderly and stepped out of his shop to hail a coach to take me back to my husband and my life as a lady-in-waiting to the Queen. That day brought new meaning to those three words—lady-in-waiting—for this lady would be most impatiently awaiting the next time we could be together, I told him, squeezing his hand as he helped me into the carriage.

One day shortly after that first delicious afternoon, I took my children to visit his shop during one of their rare and infrequent visits to London. I hadn't planned to; it was one of those sudden impulses I was prey to. "The only thing certain about Elizabeth Boleyn is uncertain," those who knew me often said.

Mary was then about seven, if I remember rightly—dates and figures have never been my strong point—and George and Anne were six and five.

My golden girl, with her pink cheeks, rosebud mouth, amber eyes, and vibrant, bouncy, spun gold curls, was so beautiful in her new gown of rose brocade that the moment the nurse brought her prancing in to me, skipping and spinning to show off her new array, with green-gowned Anne and dark, moody George following hand in hand sullenly in her wake, I knew I wanted to ask Remi to make a doll of my sunshine girl, so that even when she was an old woman, crookbacked and haggard, with her gold all turned to silver, her pearly teeth lost or turned to ugly, blackened stumps, cruel lines marring the face that had formerly been porcelain smooth, and her breasts and belly sagging from a life spent in childbearing, her beauty would never be entirely lost; she could look at that doll, cherish it, hold it in her arms, and remember just how beautiful she had been in her glorious youth. I wanted to give her that gift just as Remi had given it to me. I wanted her beauty to become something she could, in this unique way, keep forever and pass on to her children.

As my little brood flitted about his shop, eyes wide with wonder, forgetting their good manners as all children in the presence of toys are wont to do, Remi's hand moved, swift and sure, sketching them from various angles. He gave equal attention to all three. To my surprise, he didn't seem as enamored with my golden girl as I had expected him to be. I was so accustomed to people gushing and making a fuss over her beauty, I was astonished that my lover, a true artist with an eye for beauty, didn't put her on a pedestal and sing her praises.

"Your children are beautiful," he said softly.

"Well, *two* of them." I shrugged and sighed, shaking my head yet again over my ugly dark duckling Anne.

"*Three,*" Remi corrected me firmly. "Give her time; she will surprise you. A moment will come when you expect the ugly duckling and will see instead a beautiful, graceful swan, but not just any swan—a *black* swan!" I blinked and stepped back, incredulous at his enthusiasm. "Beauty is not always at first apparent," he continued, "and, when it blossoms too early so too it often withers; it rarely lasts a lifetime, but elegance and grace, such as yours, Elizabeth, endure forever."

It always amazed me that Remi could see such promise in Anne when no one else did; it was as though everyone else was blind or none of us were looking at the same little girl.

"I will believe it when I see it," I said and went on to tell him that I suspected my youngest daughter was destined for the nunnery, to be a bride of Christ since no other man, certainly not one of wealth, breeding, and discerning taste, was likely to want her.

At these words, Remi laughed and said he would wager his shop that the bleak future I predicted for Anne would never come to pass.

"Just you wait"—he nodded knowingly—"she will astonish you all! That ebony hair will *never* be shorn beneath a wimple; I would stake my shop upon it!"

"If so, 'twill be a *very great* surprise indeed. I'm far more inclined to suspect you need spectacles, my love." I snorted my disbelief, leaning against the counter and watching Anne cradle a doll that was everything she wasn't—blond and beautiful with a complexion like pink roses and cream—while George cantered about on a black velvet hobby horse with a mane and tail of flowing gilt tinsel, and Mary marveled, her mouth a perfect pink *O* framing the dainty pearls of her teeth, at the exquisite, tiny dolls that decorated sewing boxes, needle cases, trinket boxes, and pincushions, like the one on my dressing table that I cherished and had so many times slapped her hands away from.

Soon I grew weary of watching the children play. After allowing them each to choose something for themselves, I sent them away with their nurse and spent the rest of that sweet afternoon with Remi in the back room of his shop. Such were the delicious delights of an afternoon in London!

And so the years passed for me, condoling with the Queen, flirting and dancing with the King and his courtiers, provoking the jealousy and envy of the ladies, being the beautiful, gracious ornament my husband expected me to be, and loving Remi in secret.

Then a moment came when it all seemed poised to change—for better or worse, I could not then of a surety say.

On May Day, King Henry, accompanied by the gentlemen of his bedchamber and a troupe of musicians, all of them masked, crowned with sprightly feathered hats, and dressed from head to toe in Lincoln green, as Robin Hood and his Merry Men, came dancing into Queen Catherine's chamber.

In the center of the room, with his musicians and Merry Men behind him, King Henry stopped and sang.

> *Pastime with good company*
> *I love and shall until I die.*
> *Grudge who likes, but none deny,*
> *So God be pleased, thus live will I.*
> *For my pastance:*
> *Hunt, sing, and dance.*
> *My heart is set!*
> *All goodly sport*
> *For my comfort.*
> *Who shall me let?*
>
> *Youth must have some dalliance,*
> *Of good or ill some pastance*
> *Company methinks then best,*
> *All thoughts and fantasies to digest.*
> *For idleness,*
> *Is chief mistress*
> *Of vices all.*
> *Then who can say,*
> *But mirth and play*
> *Is best of all?*
>
> *Company with honesty*
> *Is virtue, vices to flee.*
> *Company is good and ill,*
> *But every man has his free will.*
> *The best ensue.*
> *The worst eschew.*
> *My mind shall be,*
> *Virtue to use,*
> *Vice to refuse.*
> *Thus shall I use me!*

When he was done, we all applauded. What a talented man our sovereign was, we all most flatteringly marveled; not only could he sing, but he wrote lyrics and set them to music as well. He was, we averred, the finest singer and writer of songs at court, mayhap in all of England. "And France," my husband, ever the favor-currying diplomat, added, knowing full well how much this compliment would please His Majesty.

"Oh, sire!" one lady cooed as she sank into a curtsy before him, bending forward as much as she dared to display as much as she could of her milky bosom. "I daresay if you had not been born to the blood royal you could have made your fortune as a singer!" And we were all quick to raise our voices in agreement, lauding him with praise, feeding the monster of his vanity until its glutted belly threatened to burst.

Queen Catherine was then great with child and her dancing days were already long behind her; she had given it up, fearing that even the gentle exertion of treading even the slowest measures might bring on a miscarriage or premature birth. She smiled like a tolerant mother at her husband's boyish exuberance, but shook her head and gently put him from her when he embraced her and tried to coax her to her feet.

"Rise and dance with me, my Queen!" he cried. "Robin Hood must have his Marian!"

But she would not, laying a hand upon her belly and chiding gently, "Now is not the time for me to dance, my lord."

So he sought a more willing partner amongst her ladies instead.

"Someone must want to dance with me!" he cried, puckering his little mouth into a petulant red rosebud pout.

It was then that his eyes lighted upon me.

As it was May Day, I was gowned in spring green satin embroidered from bodice to hem with white flowers, and on my head I wore a matching green gable hood bordered with pearl flowers with long lappets hanging down in front, past my shoulders, embroidered with yet more May flowers. It was the perfect gown for May Day, but I hadn't reckoned on a royal flirtation. On the contrary, I was hoping an opportunity to steal away to be with Remi would present itself as the day progressed.

I demurred, modestly hanging my head, but Queen Catherine urged me to dance in her stead, insisting that my gracefulness always gave her so much pleasure. So, most reluctantly, I gave in and let him take my hand.

The musicians struck up a merry measure, and King Henry led me out into the center of the room as the ladies and gentlemen moved back to clear a space for us. As the music grew faster, and our audience began to clap their hands in time and call out their encouragement, we lost ourselves in the dance and competed shamelessly over spins, leaps, and kicks, trying to best each other with complex jigs, during which I shamelessly hoisted my skirts to show off my fast-moving feet, my limbs encased in green stockings and emerald-beaded slippers of white velvet. By the end of the dance, I was flushed and breathless, my stays pinching my sides, and my hair, modestly braided and coiled at the nape of my neck beneath my hood, had been shaken down from its pins.

King Henry laughed and reached out to capture my long black braid, "like a rope of black silk," he said, coiling it around his strong fist, to draw me to him for an affectionate embrace and only a chaste kiss since Queen Catherine was watching. As he held me, he declared that I was the best Maid Marian he had ever had.

By the way he spoke these words, and the way his blue eyes bored into mine, I knew he meant to have me for far more than just a dancing partner.

"Only after Her Majesty." With a low curtsy, I demurred. "*She* is your *perfect* partner, sire."

I quickly returned to my seat beside Queen Catherine, while the King's gentlemen gallantly gathered up my fallen and scattered hairpins so I could make my hair right again.

I tried so hard to laugh it off, to dismiss it as nothing, a mere May Day flirtation, court gallantry, the sort of meaningless and idle flirtatious banter we all indulged in to pass the time, nothing more, yet I *knew* I was lying to myself. I knew he wanted me. It was unmistakable. When King Henry looked at me, it was as though his eyes burned my clothes away, leaving me bare and scorched pink by a fire that burned from outside as well as from within. Yet it froze me too. I feared his ardor even as it excited me. A part of me wanted to run to him, to lie down at his feet and lift my skirts, to invite, entice, and excite him, and use every erotic talent I had to hold him for as long as I could; my vanity wanted to wield the heady power of royal mistress, to rule as the uncrowned queen of the court. Yet another, and, surprisingly, I think a larger, part of me wanted to run away in icy dread and hide from his powerful lust, as well as the throbbing sizzle pulsing through my blood, knowing nothing good could ever come of this.

What did I want? I searched my mind for the answer, yet found it finally in the serene gray eyes of Queen Catherine—a woman who understood the flaws and foibles of humanity yet still sought to see the good in everyone. I would not let vanity and hot-blooded lust, for passion or power, be the weapon to wound her. I would not be the one to wield that sword as some of her ladies had already done and others would doubtlessly go on to do. Even though my husband would urge me to grasp that sword, as though it were the fabled Excalibur, I would not betray and injure that gracious lady who had been nothing but kind to me. Not even for a king's ransom in jewels or the deeds to a dozen manors would I do it.

Yea, he was a powerful, passionate man, and I cannot deny that he stirred me. So vibrant and virile a man was Henry Tudor he could have roused a woman from her deathbed with a caress. I remembered that long-ago day, when I stood amidst the crowd, as a girl of sixteen with her head full of dreams, watching him riding by as a boy of ten, smiling and waving to the crowd. I had dreamed then of having him for my lover someday, of kneeling before him and playing the repentant Magdalene to his Jesus Christ. But the boy had not become a churchman, but a king—a king who had married a saintly and devout woman who, in her goodness and loving kindness, reminded everyone of the Holy Virgin. And when such an opportunity was in my grasp I found—to my surprise—I did not want it. Every time I imagined us naked in bed, with the whole muscular-hard and virile length of him stretched atop me, I saw, looking over his shoulder, the pained and wounded face of Queen Catherine, gowned in white, draped in a flowing mantle of Our Lady's blue, tears rolling down her sad face as she clasped a pearl rosary over her broken heart.

I had seen her try to hide the hurt, to turn a dignified blind eye to the little dalliances her husband indulged in when she was with child, or recovering from the loss of one, and must of necessity bar him from her bed. No, I would not be numbered amongst his amours. I would not sacrifice the Queen's friendship. Nor would I give up Remi for a royal lover who would demand my complete fidelity though he might stray as often as he pleased until he grew bored with and discarded me, as was bound to happen sooner or later; few royal mistresses held a king's affection and amorous attention for a lifetime.

But my motives were not entirely altruistic; I am too honest to let those who read this turn the page with that impression. I am no angel of goodness, but I am no she-devil either. Hatred and spite shared the stage alongside love and good intentions. I knew how happy it would make Thomas if I let the King have me. How he would preen and strut like a proud little rooster, king of the barnyard, crowing at the triumph, tallying up all the riches and glory this liaison would bring, praising me to the skies as the best bargain the Bullen shopkeepers had ever made.

In the end, it wasn't such a difficult decision after all to shove vanity aside and ice my lustily simmering blood. I hated Thomas, and I loved Queen Catherine and Remi. I didn't need a lusty king to fulfill me; I already had everything I wanted. I was a reigning beauty of the court, greatly admired, sought after, and ardently wooed by many gentlemen as well as visiting foreigners. And, best of all, I had Remi, soft and sweet like a great, big, sugared dough-baby, far more comforting and pleasing to me than the King's hard muscularity and the disturbing coldness lurking inside his beady blue eyes ever could be. In the end, it was a much easier decision to make than it at first seemed. I found I didn't need, or even want, King Henry, and the triumph over thwarting Thomas Bullen's greed and avid, salivating desire to climb the social ladder ever higher would be *so much* sweeter than a tumble in the royal bed ever could be. Now I didn't want to change my life; I wanted it to go on *exactly* as it was. I was happy. I was content. I had made the best of it.

But though I had made my decision, I still had the King's lust to contend with, and that was no easy matter.

One afternoon, shortly after our May Day dance, when I was about the palace on some errand for Queen Catherine, he caught me around the waist and pulled me into an alcove, stopping my protests with rough, hot kisses. Before things could go further, or I could ice my hot blood and regain wits enough to express my resolve, we heard voices and footsteps approaching. He put a finger to his smiling lips, winked, and swiftly ducked out of the alcove, leaving me alone trembling behind the heavy red velvet curtain.

I waited, heart pounding, until the voices and footsteps had passed, then, swiftly, before he could come back, emerged, pretending that I had sought a discreet shelter to tighten a slipping garter in case anyone saw me, and went on about my business. But the encounter left me very shaken. I knew if I didn't find a way to stop them they would continue until he obtained from me the ultimate favor.

There would be other times when he connived and maneuvered to waylay me. There would be other kisses, cupped breasts and buttocks, playful pinches, and bold caresses; our bodies pressed tight together, and a strong hand forcing my own down to cradle his mammoth bulging codpiece. Yet I always found a way to escape or divert him before things went *too* far. I became adept at evading him; it was rather like a game, at times exhilarating, at times wearying, and I tried, whenever I could, to go about the palace in the company of another lady-in-waiting, or better yet a group of them, and, failing that, to have my maid, the wonderfully efficient and worldly wise Marie, accompany me.

One night, as I sat at my dressing table brushing my hair, Thomas leaned over my shoulder, his fingers digging deep, nails biting hard through the blackwork embroidery edging the fine linen of my shift, and hissed in my ear, "*Give in!* If you do, our fortune will be made!"

But I said nothing and kept on drawing the bristles of the heavy gold-backed brush through the abundant blackness of my hair, my eyes fixed on Remi's pincushion Eve all the while, imagining that tiny temptress was I, and Thomas was that slick, ingratiating serpent, coiling around my limbs, hissing temptation into my ear. But I would be stronger; I would resist. I wouldn't bite. I didn't want the apple he was offering me. There was nothing but bitterness and ugly rot beneath the shining red.

* * *

Then came a night when King Henry's ardor reached the point where there was no dodging or naysaying him. He was alert and watchful, and so was I, but a moment finally came when I had to leave the Great Hall, to attend to a pressing matter of nature. I had tried to wait, to choose a time when he was distracted, so he would not see me go, but I could delay it no longer and discreetly left the banquet table.

He came after me and pulled me roughly into an alcove. He kissed me hard, yanked down my black velvet bodice to bare my breasts, and thrust his mighty, meaty hands beneath my skirts before I could tell him my monthly courses were heavy upon me. The need to change the linen that staunched this copious flow was the urgent reason that had compelled me to quit the table.

I saw his hand emerge, the grimace of distaste as he regarded my blood, glistening ruby dark by candlelight, staining his fingertips.

"Madame, I will trouble you no more," he said in cold, contemptuous, clipped words, his voice and eyes blue marble hard. It was a tone meant to wither me, but I stood my ground, uttering not a word as he reached out and gathered a handful of my skirts to wipe his fingers on. And then, a grimace of distaste still marring his dark tempered face, he was gone.

He never laid hands on me again. I knew from serving in Queen Catherine's chamber that he was rather a fastidious and finicky man when it came to women's matters. He would never partake of pleasure with the Queen when it became evident that she was with child nor after a birthing or miscarriage until she had been fully cleansed and restored; thus it was only natural that he should be repelled by my monthly blood.

Had I not been so content with my life as it was at that time, I confess, I might have been angry that he should abandon me over such a trifling matter. Something that need never have happened at all if he had only given me a chance to discreetly explain before thrusting his hands beneath my petticoats. Ah, the pleasure we might have had! But I chose, I preferred, to be kind to Queen Catherine, and cruel to Thomas, and to preserve my cherished and blissful happiness with Remi.

Whenever such thoughts dared rear their ugly heads, or I found myself wondering, and imagining, what might have been, I dealt my vanity a savage kick and sought respite in the arms of my ravishingly rotund lover. I would sit cross-legged and naked on his bed, suddenly ravenous after our lovemaking, and share his humble repast of oat cakes and stew, roast chicken, or meat- and cheese-filled pasties with a sweet treat after of honeyed buns with raisins or cherry or apple tarts, and only half-tease him about how "ferociously jealous" I was of all the highborn ladies who came to his shop to buy pretty dolls for their daughters until Remi took me in his arms and kissed all my fears away and assured me that he wanted no one but me.

❧ 7 ❧

When May Day next came around, King Henry again staged a Robin Hood masque, with himself, as usual, in the starring role. This time the scene was set outdoors, in the greenwood at Greenwich Palace. A beautiful blond-haired girl, her complexion all roses and cream—she was very young; I would say she was not more than fourteen—played Maid Marian. Her name was Bessie Blount. She was gowned in Lincoln green, and as she partnered the King, he playfully caught hold of her long, heavy, flaxen braids threaded with green ribbon and, tugging gently at them, playfully coiling them around his fists, began leading her away, to the dark and shady privacy of a leafy bower.

I sat in the shade beside Queen Catherine, who was still recovering from her womb's latest loss, and watched in silence as, at a hasty gesture from the departing King, green garbed dancers sprang from the trees and converged in the clearing, leaping and cavorting, hoping to divert, with their vigorous dancing, all eyes and minds from the absence of Robin Hood and his Maid Marian and what naughty things they were doing in the greenwood. But no one was deceived.

Queen Catherine tried to hide the pain in her eyes by covering them with her hand and pleading a sudden headache. And my husband, standing behind my chair, leaned over and gave my arm a cruel, twisting pinch and hissed into my ear, "That could have been you! Our fortune would have been made!"

But I merely smiled and stared straight ahead, pretending I hadn't heard him, and giving my full attention to the dancers' fast and frenzied cavorting and the musicians who played ever louder, hoping to drown out the ecstatic exclamations and guttural grunts of passion issuing from the greenwood behind them. I was so glad it wasn't I. I would not have been in Bessie Blount's green velvet slippers for the whole kingdom; for all the riches it might have brought me, none could surpass the exquisite pleasure of spiting Thomas and denying him all the rewards, the pride and prestige, of seeing his wife become the King's mistress. He wanted it *so much!* Denying him gave me far more pleasure than complying ever could have.

And yet . . . in hindsight a part of me must forever wonder, if I hadn't let that peculiar combination of kindness and spite determine my actions, if I had done what I deemed cruel, wouldn't it in the end have been kinder? If I had become the King's mistress I might have prevented that which would shatter so many lives and end in death and disgrace for two of my own children. But I had no way of knowing that then; even if a gypsy witch had gazed into her crystal ball and told me, I would have laughed in her face—those events would have seemed so impossible, too incredible ever to happen. It was preposterous to think that my ugly duckling daughter Anne could change the world as we all knew it!

Later that afternoon when I threw on my green velvet cloak and went discreetly to Remi's shop, I completely baffled my beloved when I fell into a fit of convulsive laughter upon beholding a pair of beautiful dolls costumed as Robin Hood and Maid Marian. As tears rolled down my cheeks, through gasps and the sputtering remnants of laughter, I cried out that I would not be Maid Marian for a kingdom and flung myself into his arms and found heaven on earth there, held close against his cloud-soft body. Shamelessly, I dragged him to the floor rather than let him take me to his bed as a tonsured, brown-robed Friar Tuck doll clutched his wooden crucifix and frowned down upon us.

* * *

When Queen Catherine, after so many miscarriages and still-births, at last gave birth to a daughter she named Mary in honor of the Holy Virgin, I stood with the other ladies clustered around her bed and smiled, watching as she cradled the infant princess against her milk-leaking breasts and stroked her sparse carroty curls. When the wet nurse reached out to take the child, I saw her shrink back against the pillows with fear in her eyes. I knew she was afraid to let her go, lest her daughter's life slip away like all the other little souls who had come before to so briefly fill her arms. But Queen Catherine knew her duty. Her spine stiffened, and she pressed a kiss onto her daughter's brow and whispered a tender blessing, then relinquished her.

I watched as, with bated breath, Queen Catherine counted the days and prayed as she had never prayed before. Even after a month had passed, still she did not relax her vigilance or let the fear fall from her. Her little lost prince, England's great hope, had lived a month before he left us. But then another month passed, and then another, and another, and slowly, she began to believe that this time, perhaps, her child was here to stay.

Princess Mary became Queen Catherine's greatest treasure, her consolation and chief delight as the gulf between her and King Henry continued to widen. Even the news of her father's death, which we had, at the order of King Henry, kept from her until all the dangers accompanying childbed were well past, could not diminish her joy. She had a living daughter!

Although he was pleased and rejoiced at his daughter's birth, King Henry wasn't able to completely hide his dismay. Everyone could tell when he looked down at his little daughter lying swaddled in fine linen and lace beneath a blanket of ermine in her silver cradle how disappointed he was that she was not a boy.

"A daughter this time, but, by the grace of God, sons will follow. We are both still young enough," he said. As soon as Queen Catherine was able, he came back to her bed, hope renewed by his daughter's survival, and his ardor fueled by the furious determination to get a son.

As before, Queen Catherine's womb soon quickened, then, in the all too familiar pattern—it hadn't been broken after all!— emptied again in blood and pain a few weeks later. Another pregnancy soon followed, but it ended with another girl child, born too soon, who never drew a single breath.

Flaxen-haired, flirty-eyed Bessie Blount seized the opportunity I had spurned. She had a competitive spirit and soon did Queen Catherine one better and gave King Henry the son he hungered for. The boy was christened Henry Fitzroy and given the title Duke of Richmond.

Every time Queen Catherine saw plump, golden-haired Bessie bouncing her baby boy on her hip, her raw, red wound reopened anew and stung as if rubbed hard with coarse, burning salt. Henry had proven himself capable of siring a living, healthy son, thus the finger of fault was pointed straight at Queen Catherine. She alone would bear all the blame.

After her last failed confinement, Queen Catherine began to suffer a most distressing, and embarrassing, feminine ailment; her womb began to leak a stinking white fluid, sometimes tinted pink by a persistent trickle of blood. The King, wrinkling up his nose and grimacing with distaste, dubbed this disgusting discharge "milk of fishes" and declared that he would lie with her no more even though her physicians assured him she was still capable of conception and there was still hope, as Princess Mary continued daily to prove, that Her Majesty could produce healthy, viable children. If they continued to try, the doctors insisted, a prince was certain to follow. But King Henry was adamant. He was done and putting his Spanish broodmare out to pasture. His patience was exhausted, and his desire long dead; he would come no more to her bed.

Queen Catherine was inconsolable. How she wept! Day after day she prayed for a miracle. She was tormented by the knowledge that while she had failed, Bessie Blount, "the King's Whore," had triumphed. And there was some speculation particularly galling to Queen Catherine being bruited about that her son, despite being illegitimate, might someday become King of England. If it came down to a choice between Princess Mary, a girl, and Henry Fitzroy, a male, the cock was certain to prevail.

But Bessie herself didn't last long. Poor dear, she hadn't the strength to hold the reins of such a powerful mount as the man his adoring people called "Bluff King Hal." She was one of those pallid blond women whose time in the sun is brief. Her beauty faded quickly; that beguiling ripe and round, juicy as a peach plumpness settled quickly into matronly lines, and a sad, sagging face peered out of tired green eyes from beneath hair no longer golden but dull, dark, and dingy as dishwater. Darkened tresses were one of the perils fair-haired women faced during pregnancy. How I feared for my golden girl Mary when she married and her own breeding years began! Lemon juice and chamomile can only do so much, and many of the recipes for bleaching hair are ruinous to the scalp and can turn hair to straw so that it grows brittle and prone to break. I have always been very glad that I was not born a blonde; the struggle to retain my beauty would have been so much the greater.

Henry soon married his Bessie off to an obliging country gentleman and sent her to lead a dull and placid existence as lady of a pastoral manor where she could trouble him no more. Her son he took away, to be reared like royalty by tutors and servants, a prince in all but name, so that whenever he saw the woman who had given life to him during her rare visits to London, it was always like meeting a stranger. And soon poor Bessie ceased coming at all and resigned herself to a rustic oblivion.

My husband never let a chance go by to remind me of my failure and how grievously I had disappointed him. Bessie was a naive young girl, with no higher ambition than having plenty of pretty dresses to wear, but I was a wise and seasoned woman, worldly and sophisticated, the daughter of the highest peer of the realm; I would—with my husband to guide me, Thomas insisted—have made the most of such a grand and golden opportunity. I would have looked past the latest fashions to the future. Deeds, sinecures, licenses, lands, manors, and wardships would have taken precedence over frills and furbelows and pretty trinkets. I would have garnered cold, hard coins instead of cloth-of-gold.

I let my husband talk; I nodded and smiled and said, "Yes, Thomas," while I pretended to listen and agree with everything he said like every good and obedient Christian wife should. But in those days my mind was on other matters. My children were growing up and soon would leave me, though in truth it was I who had been largely absent from *their* lives for years.

Whilst on a mission abroad, Thomas had arranged what he called "a golden opportunity" for our daughters, to serve as *filles d'honneur* at the court of Margaret of Austria in Brussels, to give a continental polish to their education, an elegant veneer to their manners, and perfect their French. I feared they were too young. Mary was but twelve, and Anne, though nearing ten, still only nine. But Thomas scoffed and said they were exactly the right age.

"You've never played the mother hen, Elizabeth," he said, fixing me with a stern, unyielding gaze. "So, *please,* for *all* our sakes, spare us the embarrassment and don't start now. The role ill becomes you, and you'll *never* do it justice. If you know you can't succeed, why bother to even try? Never invite failure into your life if you can possibly help it," my sage husband counseled. And I knew, as much as I loathed to admit it, that he was right.

As for George, he continued, after first favoring me with an approving nod after I smilingly agreed to defer to his superior wisdom, my only surviving son was to come to court, to serve as a page boy in the King's household and proudly wear the Tudor livery of green and white with badges of red and white roses on his chest and sleeves. At least one of my children would be left to me, where I might see and embrace him from time to time whenever a sudden maternal mood struck me.

The truth was—and we all knew it, so it was silly to pretend otherwise—I was apt to neglect the children and forget them in pursuit of my own pleasure, until, like a lightning bolt coming out of nowhere from a clear blue sky to strike and split a tree in twain, I would remember them and send for them to come to London posthaste, and try to atone with gifts and sudden spurts of intense affection, but all too soon I would put them aside again, like toys I had grown bored with, and they would be packed into the coach with their nurses and on the way back to Hever again. I was just not a very good mother; I suffered a want of maternal feeling except when it came upon me like a short, sudden, swiftly passing fever.

In my heart, I knew it was for the best; this was one of those chances it would be the zenith of idiocy to refuse. Thomas was right; our daughters deserved this splendid opportunity, and it would be good for George to enjoy the company of other highborn boys, to begin in callow youth to cement alliances that would prove useful and influential allies when he grew to manhood. It might indeed prove the perfect cure for his sullen, sulky dark moods. He had always been so melancholy, seemingly without good reason. He was the only person, Lady Margaret said, who failed to benefit from regular dosing with her rose honey that no fit of depression had ever before been able to withstand. With work to do—Thomas was aiming to see him appointed the King's cupbearer in a few months' time—he would have even less time for brooding and scribbling those strange little verses of his that my mind never could quite fathom; there always seemed to be an elusive, secret meaning hiding inside the words that, try as I might, I could never ferret out.

I remembered how I had felt like a prisoner condemned to rusticate at Hever, and though my daughters had known no other life, I wanted to spare them the same fate. I wanted greater and grander things for my girls; even if Anne must go to a nunnery, I didn't want Mary to squander her beautiful youth as a bucolic broodmare while her husband was away in London, caught up in the merry whirl of court with his mistresses, or, even worse, see my daughter married to a ambitious, mercenary, favor-currying zealot like Thomas Bullen—I mean *Boleyn!* They had gone as far as they could with their governess, and though Mary, never a one for books, seemed not to mind it, Anne was stagnating. I sensed, and sympathized, with her impatience; she wanted to go further and learn more. And their mad old witch of a grandmother filled their heads with all manner of nonsense—Irish folktales, fairy lore, and stories of goblins, ghosts, mermaids, and monsters. Though these had no apparent ill effects upon George and Anne—on the contrary, both seemed to relish such tales and delight in composing their own little dramas, stories, and songs based on them, which always delighted Lady Margaret—they had poor Mary afraid to go to bed, wetting it with fright and calling out every few hours imploring her nurse to bring a candle and look under the bed or in the clothes press to see what evil was hiding there. Lady Margaret insisted on dosing her thrice daily with a syrup of Saint John's Wort to keep evil spirits and demon lovers away from her; Mary being such a great beauty, she explained, she was in even greater danger than most of being visited at night by such creatures. No wonder my poor daughter was afraid to lay down her head and close her eyes at night!

I knew it would be good for them to get away; after all, it had been for me. I was no longer there, and even when I had been, I was at best an indifferent mother who always put herself, her own capricious whims and carnal pleasures, first and foremost. How many days had I passed in my private pleasure garden, my red rose bower, where wooden trellises densely covered with roses red as blood concealed my naughty deeds, never knowing where my children were or what they were doing, blindly trusting the servants and their grandmother to keep them occupied and safe and out of my way until I had time for them again? I was far too selfish to ever make a good mother. Now was the time for me to make a sacrifice and do something for their greater good.

In the end, it was easy, not much of a sacrifice I must say, nothing worthy of the Bible, drama, or epic poetry; all I had to do was smile and agree with my husband that yes, this was indeed "a golden opportunity" for our daughters, not cut out my very own heart or shed even one drop of blood—only a tear or two perhaps. But they were soon dried, and I had Remi to console me. I wept in his arms and then, overcome by the fervor of our kisses, forgot what I was crying about.

My daughters had been gone only a few months when an even more splendid opportunity came their way, engineered, of course, by their ambitious, avaricious father.

The King's beautiful sister, Mary, the one everyone called "the Tudor Rose" for her white rose complexion and red gold hair, was betrothed to a loathsome old man probably suffering from the pox—His Majesty King Louis XII of France.

I remember standing beside my husband in the Great Hall of Greenwich Palace, watching the peculiar ceremony in which the ravishing red-haired Tudor princess was wed with the French ambassador, the debonair, silver-haired Duc de Longueville standing proxy for the poxy bridegroom, when Thomas leaned in and whispered in my ear that our daughters would soon be joining her household in France.

"An appointment at the court of France trumps *anything* Brussels and Margaret of Austria can offer," he said.

"But surely they are far too young for such a lascivious court!" I protested, watching, wide-eyed, as a mammoth gilt-posted bed covered in quilted purple satin edged with fringe and great tassels of Venetian gold was wheeled in.

Princess Mary and the Frenchman, wearing matching robes of checkered gold and purple, knelt before the crimson-clad Cardinal Wolsey and solemnly exchanged marital vows, replete with rings and kisses, then walked to stand on opposite sides of the bed. Aided by an attendant, each stepped out of their velvet slippers and doffed their robes, revealing their white lawn bed gowns beneath. They lay down side by side atop the quilted purple coverlet and joined hands. The Duc de Longueville reached out a bare leg and let it rest, for just a moment, against the princess's bare ankle. Then it was all over. The marriage was declared consummated, and thus legally binding, and each rose from the bed, bowed to each other across its great width, and donned their robes and slippers again, and went to change into more festive finery for the feasting and dancing that was to follow.

"Nonsense!" Thomas scoffed. "This will be the start of a *glorious* career of court service for *both* of them. We may have to re-think sending Anne to the nunnery, but time enough for that later. The Mother of the Maids has vast experience in these matters and will look after them; I've already spoken to her. Your fears are groundless, Elizabeth. It is settled, and I will hear no more about it." With those words he left me and went to offer his heartiest congratulations to King Henry for arranging such a dynastically advantageous marriage, one that would ensure peace and prosperity for both England and France, and prevent them from ever again making war with one another.

My husband's ambition-driven assurances failed to completely quiet my fears. Everyone knew that there was no court more wanton, lascivious, and immoral than that of France. Rarely did any maid who served there leave it with her virtue intact. The heir to the throne, the Dauphin Francois, was a notorious sybarite, a sensualist nonpareil, an insatiable satyr, who lived for lust and pleasure; they said he could not go an hour without a woman and sampled everything from barmaids to duchesses. And virgins newly come to the court were a particular favorite of his, like a box of candy he must dip his greedy fingers into and take a bite out of each to test its flavor. And, being young, dark-haired, diabolically handsome, and endowed with a powerful and charming virility, these innocent young girls, especially those from foreign courts, found it impossible to say no to him and readily succumbed, willingly, in one wild moment discarding the teachings of their little lifetimes to guard their virtue as the most precious gift they would bring to their husbands.

But I was powerless to save my daughters, and I knew all too well that I had set a poor example when it came to feminine virtues like chastity and fidelity. If they ever made good and obedient Christian wives, it would not be because of me or anything I had taught them.

$\approx 8 \approx$

The years danced by, and the cherry fair that is life went on. I danced and flirted and was an ornament to the court and a credit to my husband, despite my single, unforgettable, unforgivable failure in his ruthless, mercenary eyes, the one he continued to rub my face in every chance he got. I enjoyed Queen Catherine's confidence and friendship. And, best of all, I had Remi. On the whole, it was a happy life. I grew accustomed to my daughters' absence and learned not to spend too much time brooding about it or to let my fears for their virtue and well-being get the better of me. *What will be, will be,* I sighed and went on with my life.

I had miniatures of my three children painted and set in a gilt frame with pretty enameled forget-me-nots encircling some words of scripture-based wisdom I had stitched in purple silk inside a border of seed pearls and my exquisitely embroidered violets and forget-me-nots, words that I found most comforting whenever my fears resurfaced or idle gossip disturbed the hard-won peace of my mind.

> *Do not worry about tomorrow,*
> *Leave tomorrow to worry about itself,*
> *For today's troubles are enough.*

> *And who of you by worrying*
> *Can add a single moment to your years?*

And aye, I knew all too well that worry ages like nothing else! I tried not to, but I could not help worrying about the lines I saw forming around my eyes and mouth. Time, and worry too, I knew would only make them deeper. Whenever I saw a strand of silver standing out stark against the ebony of my hair, I would cry out in horror and pluck it out. Later I resorted to rinsing my hair in walnut juice to keep it dark. I wasn't ready to be old and gray. I was still young inside, so why should I not do everything in my power to appear youthful on the outside as well as within? Besides, I owed it to my daughters to remain beautiful for as long as I could. Any prospective bridegrooms would be sure to look hard at me, to get an inkling of how my daughters' looks would fare as they aged.

Vanity, I sighed, as I sat before my mirror, leaning my elbows on my dressing table. *All is vanity!*

When my daughters came back to me, they were no longer the little girls I remembered but grown women of eighteen and sixteen. Anne was the same age I had been when I was forced to swallow my pride and become the Bullen shopkeeper's grandson's broodmare bride. Already my husband was eyeing the gentlemen at court to prune out the perfect bridegrooms for them. There was no longer any talk of the nunnery for Anne.

But my worst fears had come true, and Mary, my golden girl, came back to me with her reputation badly tarnished; tattered like a beggar's ugly, dirty rags. She had been initiated into the arts of love by none other than the Dauphin Francois himself, who had succeeded to the crown when old King Louis died, leaving Mary Tudor a widow merry and free to do as she pleased. The French had dubbed my sweet and beautiful daughter "the English Hackney" or the King's "English Mare," and she had gained a reputation for being an "easy ride," natural and unrestrained when it came to the carnal act, one who freely bestowed her favors on any handsome gallant who caught her fancy or asked nicely. All it took, they said, was a pretty compliment to get Mary Boleyn into bed.

Like mother, like daughter, I sighed and left it to Thomas to chastise her, for I hadn't it in my heart to play the hypocrite and scold her for sins I had committed myself. He blamed me, of course; I was her mother, and it was my duty to teach her proper feminine behavior and mold and shape her into a good and obedient Christian wife, and I had obviously failed. The fact that I had objected to my daughters going to live at the French court, beyond the sphere of my, or any other, restraining influence, was conveniently overlooked.

"Your golden girl has proven base and brass," Thomas said to me, "not *true* gold after all. You used to sit her in the sun with chamomile and the juice of lemons on her hair to keep it golden; it was your way, you said, of helping Mother Nature along. But a little gilding, madame, does *not* make tin a precious metal worthy to stand side by side with solid gold!"

Yet the tarnish did not show upon her face and figure; she didn't look like a soiled dove at all. To the naked eye, this was no rampant, ready whore. When I first saw her standing before me, round as a dumpling in butter yellow satin, with her hair piled up in rich gleaming mounds of golden curls dotted with yellow silk and gilt buttercups, diamond brilliants, and ropes of creamy pearls, she took my breath away. It seemed impossible that such divine beauty could truly be of this flawed and all too human world; my voluptuous golden girl was earthy yet ethereal. The rich fare of France, all the cakes and creamy sauces, had rounded her figure, upholstering her with soft, womanly curves, including a bodice-bursting bosom and bountiful hips that promised any prospective husband that she would be a good breeder as well as afford him countless hours of carnal pleasure, all of which only served to enhance her alluring doll-like beauty even more. She presented the most beguiling combination of innocence and sensuality, like a little girl trapped inside a woman's body. The men found this simply irresistible. I think the problem was her sweet nature. Mary was too amiable and obliging, a naturally nice girl who in the end was just *too nice* for her own good; she lacked that strong, hard inner core of steel, and it left her too soft, too pliant, vulnerable, and easy to bend, especially by a man bent on satisfying his own base pleasure.

But it was Anne who presented the greatest surprise. Remi was right—she *did* astonish us all! My ugly brunette duckling had be-

come a graceful and elegant black swan. I could not believe my
eyes when I saw her standing there, clad in a dramatic gown of
black velvet and dark wine satin embroidered with a flamboyant
array of black-hearted heart's ease pansies, with a choker of black
velvet and pearls about her neck, and a great golden *B* with three
milky teardrop pearls hanging below it resting in the hollow of her
throat, hiding the unsightly brown strawberry she had been born
with. Long ropes of silvery black pearls flashing rainbows of pink,
purple, and blue hung about her long, gracefully slender swanlike
neck—my, how she had grown into it; she no longer looked like a
gangly-necked goose! And she had adopted the most cunning
sleeves, fitting tight to the elbow, then belling out gracefully over
her full under-sleeves and hands to hide that hideous nubby defor-
mity on her littlest left finger. Her black hair hung glossy and free,
thick as a cloak of inky satin, all the way down to her knees, and she
had eschewed the boxy gable hood for a charming crescent of
pearl-bordered wine satin called a French hood to crown her
dome.

She was not beautiful, and never would be in the classical sense,
or even by English standards that celebrated partridge plump
blondes as the epitome of feminine beauty, with those with ruddy-
hued tresses running a close second. But by the time the critical eye
realized that, it was already too late; the trap had been sprung. Her
eyes—large, lustrous, and dark, flashing like black lightning—cast
a powerful spell only a few seemed immune to in those days.

I could not believe it, but I was *jealous,* actually *jealous* of my
own daughter! The one I had thought so irredeemably ugly and
destined for the nunnery! How it stung me to realize that I was actually *jealous of Anne!* No longer would she live and languish in my
or Mary's shadow; she had surpassed us both, and I couldn't quite
figure out how. She wasn't beautiful, yet she had something more,
something inexplicable and indefinable that was uniquely hers.

The Anne who returned to England exuded an exotic charm.
Those years spent in France had left her more French than English
and blessed her with the most enchanting accent, lilting and musi-
cal, yet all too capable of a sword-sharp cynicism. An aura of the
most supreme confidence, such as one would equate with an empress, enfolded her, and she didn't just walk, she *glided,* gracefully,

serenely through life. Every step she took, every gesture she made, was like a dance, carefully and perfectly choreographed yet at the same time, most maddeningly, vexingly, contradictorily, au naturel. And how she dressed! Rather than follow the flock, Anne wasn't afraid to take chances and rise above the ordinary. She made every woman, even elegant and graceful me, seem overdressed, fussily or even dowdily overdecorated in comparison. What a sense of color she had—black cherry, damson plum, dusky rose, spicy orange, regal amethyst, various shades of green running the gamut from spring to seaweed, and of course vibrant emerald, tawny, midnight blue, deep heart's blood crimson, and amber filled her wardrobe, sharing space with burnished and brilliant gold, copper, bronze, silver, pewter, bold scarlet, and shimmering satiny or velvety black. And those oh so cunning sleeves! Soon not a woman at court would dare be seen without them, and everyone was calling them Boleyn sleeves. They even imitated the chokers fashioned from broad ribbons, pearls, or beads she wore about her throat to hide that unsightly strawberry even though their own milky throats were blessedly unmarred. Because of Anne, gable hoods were disappearing too; every day it seemed I saw fewer of them and more French hoods about the palace. And her pearls! Rarely was my daughter ever seen without her pearls, her favorite gem, great, long, creamy, lustrous ropes of them, often wearing a silver or gold initial pendant, *AB* or just *B,* from which a teardrop pearl or two or three usually dangled. Pearls had been popular for years, even in my mother's and grandmother's times, yet Anne made them seem all of a sudden new again. There was just something about her!

"Who wants to appear as everyone else?" she would laugh whenever anyone questioned the choices she made, arching an elegant, plucked black brow. "I please myself; if others are pleased as well"—she shrugged—"so be it."

Many thought her a heartless creature who cared for nothing and no one but herself. But that was not true; there was one she loved more than any—her brother George. From the moment she returned, he was at her side and rarely left it. I don't know how they did it, but they could say more to each other with a look than most people could in whole reams of words. It was uncanny the way they could read each other's minds and finish each other's sentences. They joked that they were twins, only Anne had arrived fashionably late, a year after George, who had gone ahead to prepare the way for her; words that would come back to haunt me at the end of their lives when they took on an even more poignant meaning when George would again go first.

Together, they gathered around them a close set of friends, a clever little band of wits and poets, all happy-go-lucky and devil-may-care. Closest of all were the flamboyant red-haired Sir Francis Weston; tall, dark, and handsome Sir William Brereton, who at first sight seemed awfully staid and serious, the calm voice of reason until you got to know him better; and baby-faced blond Sir Henry Norris, a man many thought too gentle and endowed with too much heart to ever succeed at court, yet was amongst King Henry's most intimate and highly favored body servants.

In no time at all, the finest poet of the court, Sir Thomas Wyatt, was infatuated with Anne and composing sonnets by the score in tribute to her beauty, wit, and grace, declaring his love for her in every word just as John Skelton had done for me. But Anne only laughed, clicked her goblet against George's, and declared, "It is good to be alive!"

As for my golden girl, Mary would redeem herself in her father's eyes when King Henry, always a one for a buxom and obliging blonde, took her into his bed after seeing her in a gown of silver that made her golden hair shine all the brighter. Thomas embraced her and called her "my darling" and magnanimously assured her "all is forgiven," and paid for several beautiful silk and lace bed gowns and crystal vials of costly perfume to entice and excite King Henry. "An investment," he said to me as he nodded approvingly over Mary's selections.

But Mary was too sweet-natured to ever make her fortune as a courtesan. Indeed, I think she would have failed as a ha'penny whore if she had been turned out to walk the streets of London. She asked for nothing and got it, declaring that she loved the King and lay with him as an expression of the great love she bore him. Even when her exasperated father threw up his hands and insisted, "Love is ephemeral. Assets are tangible," Mary refused to use her position to barter for favors or fill the family's money boxes.

"Enjoy your time in the sun, daughter; it will be brief," I told her in words cold and clipped and followed my husband out of her luxuriously appointed palace apartment with a secret passage discreetly connecting it to the King's bedchamber so he need never be seen creeping down the corridor to visit her. I was glad of that paltry attempt at discretion. How it grieved me that my own daughter should be the one to cause Queen Catherine pain by embracing wholeheartedly what I had spurned out of loyalty, love, and marital spite.

When they danced together, their desire for each other blatantly apparent, Queen Catherine, despite her pain, sought to comfort me. She took my hand and, gazing kindly into my eyes, said, "Do not blame yourself; I know it is not your fault, Elizabeth. You have always been a good and faithful friend to me. Your daughter is a sweet girl caught fast in the grip of love; she means me no harm. She will be the one who is hurt in the end, and for that, I am sorry. I pray for her each day."

In the end, Mary's own tranquil, domestically inclined nature would be her undoing. She did not understand that the kings, and other great men, she bedded were not interested in *her,* that they came to her for sensual delights, not the bland and cozy domesticity of hearth and home. They wanted naughtiness, unabashed nakedness, pumice stone–smoothed bare limbs, not woolen stockings; a woman comfortable in her own skin who knew how to cast modesty aside as though she were a naked Eve for whom clothes didn't exist and who wasn't inclined to try on fig leaves; a mistress endowed with an adventurous, spicy sensuality and a zealous, zesty passion that wasn't afraid to take chances, to experiment and play, to revel in hot sweaty lust, whisper dirty words, and perform daring deeds upon the satin sheets; a playful kitten who might at any moment unsheathe her claws; not a placid, proper lady sitting by the fire embroidering and inquiring, "How was your day, dear?" with amusing little anecdotes to tell about children and servants and tidbits of palace gossip. They wanted a tigress in a diamond collar, not a fireside tabby. But Mary's mind never could grasp that. I broke it down for her in a simple equation that even the most mathematically inept should have been able to comprehend: *Time + Familiarity = Boredom,* but still understanding eluded poor Mary.

*   *   *

When she became pregnant, King Henry lost all interest. I knew he would. He always did. If it would not have appeared in such bad taste—I was after all the mother of the mistress of the moment—I would even have cast a wager upon it along with the other court gamblers staking their coins on how long it would be before the King tired of Mary and changed partners again.

It was just like when Bessie Blount conceived and the numerous times when Queen Catherine's womb quickened. Henry simply was not attracted to breeding women. As much as he wanted children, to ensure his line lived on and provide Tudor heirs for England's throne, his fastidious nature was repelled by the changes pregnancy wrought upon a woman's body. And in truth, woman though I am, with all my vanity and pride, I could not blame him; I *hated* the gross transformation pregnancy wrought upon my beautiful body and the sagging and lined mementos it left behind. To my mind, it always seemed too great a price to pay for the miracle of creation.

When the end came, it was swift. A little clinging, pleading, and tears, then it was done, and Mary meekly accepted her lot.

She lacked the force of will to persuade the King to acknowledge her child as his own and amiably allowed herself to be married off to one of his courtiers, the kindly Sir William Carey, an Esquire of the Body, who would gladly give his name to the royal bastard growing in the warm nest of her belly. Luckily, he and Mary were well matched. A pair of golden heads and golden hearts, they were both too nice for the sphere they had been born to inhabit; you have to be ruthless and driven, shameless and willing to do anything, to smile and flatter those you hate or trample and disparage those you like or even love, if you want to succeed at court. You have to be callous and hard, and embrace or discard people heedless of personal feelings as the moment dictates, and not everyone can do that. For some of us it comes all too easy, but there are others who have a conscience that will not allow them to sleep at night if they do not heed its urgent and insistent pangs and the whispered warnings of the little voice inside.

*   *   *

In pale pink and buttercup yellow watered silk, all embroidered with gold, with a wreath of gilded rosemary, marigolds, spicy pinks, and bright yellow gillyflowers crowning her wealth of golden ringlets, my daughter, the most beautiful bride of all, was married in the royal chapel at Greenwich Palace.

As I watched, I wept and wished the King had seen fit to provide her with a worthier and wealthier husband. Though a sweet, kind man who clearly adored Mary, Will Carey could never give my golden girl the life I had envisioned for her.

She smiled coyly as she became Sir William's wife and dipped a little bunch of marigolds tied with pink and yellow ribbons into a gilt goblet filled with rosewater and nibbled at it daintily, then dipped and held it out for him to do the same. Marigolds dipped in rosewater were a popular aphrodisiac in those days, common and harmless unlike some of the more outlandish remedies made with rare and costly or deadly poisonous ingredients one must handle with the utmost care, and it had become fashionable to provide the bridal couple with posies of these quaint orange-gold flowers and cups of rosewater at all the best weddings.

King Henry stood by, resplendent in purple velvet and cloth-of-gold, pearls and diamonds to represent majesty and wealth, not sorrow and tears, spangling his person. Throughout the ceremony he stood there pursing his lips and looking mildly annoyed; if my mother-in-law had been there doubtlessly she would have diagnosed a distress of the liver and been avid to dose him with some noxious brew containing basil and bat entrails. He was, I could tell, at war with himself—loath to relinquish a favorite mistress, though it was his own finicky fastidiousness that prevented him from keeping and enjoying her further.

Mary had run straight to me, poor girl, expecting some comfort from her mother, bursting into my bedchamber in a flurry of weeping, rumpled blond curls, and gold satin, and blurted it all out between wracking sobs and showers of tears. Henry had just told her that they must, because of her condition, part. She confided that though she was well schooled in France in methods to safeguard against conception and had always used them successfully, something had gone wrong this time. The tea of tansy and white poplar had, for the first time, failed, and, for this, King Henry blamed her.

"You should have been more careful," he said. "I thought you sufficiently experienced in such matters and would know well how to avoid this."

My tenderhearted daughter, recalling how delighted King Henry had been when Bessie Blount gave him the son he longed for, had wept all the harder, unable to understand why this fruit of their love was so unwelcome. Why were she, and her baby, not as good as Bessie Blount and her boy? Why indeed? That was an answer that also eluded me.

Poor Mary, she wept and wallowed and buried her face in my lap, leaving behind a smeared imprint of her features painted on my nightgown, before she slunk away, hurt and bewildered, wondering why her mother had failed to give her the comfort she had expected and so desperately needed.

"There are other teas, daughter!" I called after her. "Some pennyroyal, perhaps mixed with . . ."

Mary turned on my threshold, regarding me with wild-eyed horror, shaking her head uncomprehendingly, as though she could not believe those words had passed my lips. I wondered for a moment if she thought me ignorant of such methods. But no, it was horror, true, unadulterated horror I saw in Mary's eyes.

She stopped her ears, pressing the palms of her hands hard and tight over them, and fled from the same woman she had come running to hoping for some comfort and kindness.

And what did I do? Did I run after her? Did I cringe beneath the incredulous amber eyes that regarded me as though I were some kind of monster? Did I try to counsel her or change her mind? Did I comfort, love, hold, and kiss her, and assure her that I, her mother, would love her no matter what? No. I did none of those things. I changed into a fresh nightgown, massaged a little rose-scented cream into my face to keep my skin supple and soft, blew out the candle, went to bed, and slept soundly.

Once again, I had failed and disappointed a child I had brought into this world. I might say in my defense that I was preoccupied with my own grief, mourning my father. He had in failing health retired from the court, passing all his titles and posts on to his namesake and heir, my brother, Thomas Howard, and spent the last year of his life in the country, at Framlingham Castle in Surrey, jesting that he would spend the rest of his days tending his beehives and sending jars of his fine honey to all his acquaintances. He was in his eighty-second year when he perished. I was chief mourner at his funeral, one of the most expensive and extravagant England had ever seen, and walked, gowned in black velvet and long, trailing veils of diaphanous black, at the head of a procession of four hundred black-robed and hooded men bearing torches to see my father splendidly entombed beneath a white marble effigy in Thetford Priory. I *could* claim that grief left me ill-equipped to be a comfort to my daughter, but we all know I would be lying. Even if there had been naught a drop of sorrow in my soul, the scene would have been played out exactly the same.

As I stood in the royal chapel, so gracious and elegant in my gold-edged amber velvet, gold chains, and ropes of pearls, the perfect portrait of an elegant and poised wife, Thomas Bullen's prized and pedigreed trophy, beside my dour, dark-clad husband, who, like His Majesty, placed all the blame and burden on Mary's shoulders, I looked at my eldest daughter and thought, *There but for the Grace of God go I,* and thanked Our Heavenly Father with all my heart for giving me the strength and stubbornness to resist King Henry's advances.

Yes, I also condemned Mary. I had dreamed of a golden future for my golden girl; she was *so beautiful* I wanted her to have the best of everything, a life worthy of her; one doesn't after all take the finest diamond and set it in brass or tin. I blamed her for failing to make the dreams that I had dreamed for her come true.

Mary's glittering career was finished. She was Will Carey's responsibility now, Thomas said, not ours, and we, her family, I am ashamed to say, all washed our hands of her. I would never be there for Mary as a mother should, when her daughter is hurt, heartsore, and has need of her, even if it is only for the comforting balm of an embrace or a few kind and tender words, all the things she had expected from me when she ran to me that fateful night. In this way, I failed her grievously and always would. I should have stood up for her, spoken out on her behalf, and always, always stood by her, but I did not.

Later, I would plead a headache and leave the wedding banquet, and go velvet-cloaked upon soft soles to Remi and in his arms rejoice all the more that I had not gone the way of my daughter. Even though I, being made of sterner stuff, would have succeeded where she had failed, I would not have been in her shoes for a kingdom.

"I'm so glad that wasn't me!" I cried as I lay sweaty and spent in my beloved's arms.

But I didn't want to talk about it. When he started to speak, I silenced him by pressing my mouth hard over his for more insistent and ardent kisses to divert his mind from the matter. I knew Remi would see things differently and say things I knew but did not then want to hear. All I wanted at that moment was to be held; I wanted to be loved, hard and fast, then so gently it made me cry, not debate the ways of the world we lived in and whether I was right or wrong, and if Mary had been condemned unjustly. Only now, in hindsight, when it is too late, can I give voice and due consideration to those things and admit that I was indeed wrong. I failed my daughter. I failed all my children in the worst way a mother can. I was never there, even when I was physically present. When they needed me, I always let them down.

By this time George was also married, but not all the marigolds and rosewater in the world could save that unhappy union. It was a sinking ship from the start—the marital equivalent of a songbird sharing its gilded cage with a serpent. Lady Jane Parker, the spoiled only daughter and sole heiress of Lord Morley, was the proverbial snake in the grass, and I curse the day my son, most unwillingly, married her. Despite her rich dowry, Jane would bring nothing but pain, sorrow, and suffering to all of us.

Indeed, as they stood together at the altar, I thought I could see shackles, heavy iron balls and chains binding them together like a pair of condemned prisoners sentenced to share a cell for the rest of their lives.

Though to look at her one would think her a harmless, plain, mousy, little thing, with no sense of style or what was flattering to her figure, such as it was, Jane was in truth a villainous rat, sharp-toothed and plague-carrying. She was such a spiteful, jealous creature that there was neither a hope nor a prayer that they could ever find a way to live amicably together. George could not love her, and this knowledge sent Jane flying into the most violent, terrifying rages, in which she behaved like a madwoman, and cursed and blamed each and every person George ever liked or favored, even servants he smiled at and spoke a kind word to in passing; Jane would carry on until they quit or were dismissed or send them packing herself, without a reference, if it was in her power to do so. She accused everyone George showed even the smallest sign of liking of stealing away the affection that should have been hers. Jane wanted the whole of George's heart, and he gave her none of it. She didn't want him to smile at anyone else but her.

Most of all she hated Anne. Anne became the particular target of her wrath. Sometimes she spoke wildly, accusing brother and sister of being sin-drenched partners in an unnatural love affair that went against all the laws of God and Man. But George just laughed at her, right in her face. He flung up his hands and declared, "The woman is mad—stark, raving mad!" and went on his merry way, most often with Anne, which only added more fuel to the blazing bonfire of Jane's hate.

Instead of confronting her, trying to play the diplomat and seek a peaceful compromise, George ran from her and took his pleasures elsewhere. Though my husband often reminded him that, as his only living son, it was George's duty to sire heirs to perpetuate the Boleyn line, George merely looked at himself in the nearest mirror, raised his wine cup high in a mocking toast, and said, "Here's to the last Bullen boy!" and continued to shun Jane's bed as though she were a leper and her touch would make his prick fall off. "Living with Jane," he often said, was "pure, unadulterated Hell," and he would not wish his wife on his worst enemy. "I don't hate anyone *that* much!" he quipped, though in truth it was no jest.

He drank, gambled, and took lovers, *many* lovers, both male and female. At first, I was saddened and appalled to discover that my sole surviving son dallied in the sin of Sodom, but he was my son, and I loved him, so I had to accept him as he was. And when I sat and thought about it, I found it didn't really matter all that much. When he drank, and George often sought solace and escape in wine cups, he came to me, instead of Anne, in a mood to confide the "deepest, darkest secrets of my damned soul." He would chuckle as he said it, but I wasn't entirely sure he really meant it to be a jest.

I asked him once when he was deep in his cups why he bedded men.

"They don't bore or disappoint me the way the women do," he slurred over the gilt rim of his goblet, "because they aren't Anne or anything like her. And when I'm done with them, being men, most of them are too proud to cry and cling and try to hold on to me; they let me go even if they hate me for it ever afterward. I make enemies out of my lovers; that's why I never sleep with my friends." He ended with a wry little laugh, though by the look on his face he seemed close to tears.

I sat in awkward silence and patted his black head as he watered his wine with his tears and said nothing. What could I say? What sage words of maternal or worldly wisdom could I offer my son? I only wanted to pretend that I hadn't heard, that I didn't know the secret torment that afflicted my son's sad, dark soul and that he was destined to spend his life searching for something that could not be found. People often say things they don't mean when they're drunk, I told myself, vainly seeking comfort in lies; the wine makes them maudlin and out of sorts. I never broached the subject with him when he was sober, and I think, if he even remembered his confession afterward, George was grateful to me for letting him pretend it never happened. That was the *one* thing my children could always count on me to do, to ignore anything I deemed too difficult or unpleasant. I excelled at overlooking what I didn't wish to see; I was remarkably nearsighted, or farsighted, or even stone blind, depending on the circumstances.

Anne alone of all our children remained unwed, but not unwanted. Soon King Henry's ardent eye would light upon her too. Indeed, he would later tell her, "When I saw your eyes flash like black diamonds on your sister's wedding day, that was the moment I first fell in love with you."

As she stood, serene in shimmering blue black satin dripping with pearls, watching her sister's nuptials, I saw, more than once, the King's beady blue eyes rove up and down her slender figure. If Anne noticed, she gave no indication, though I daresay she would not have wanted to give him the satisfaction. Anne was *not* her sister; they were as different as the color of their hair. Anne was all glittering, hard obsidian darkness, and Mary all rosy softness and golden light. Anne would not give, or sell, her favors to anyone, not even a king. She could not be bought. She made it known that she prized her honor and virtue above all else; her virginity was a gift she would give only to her lawfully wedded husband and no one else. "All ardent wooers and seducers be warned," she quipped, "it is a fruitless waste of time to trifle with Anne Boleyn."

King Henry soon made his interest known by riding in a tournament with his chest emblazoned with the motto "Declare, I Dare Not," and giving many pointed and pining glances at Anne, sitting beside George in the stands. But she ignored him, yawning and treating him like a boring boy in whom she had not the slightest interest. When the King unhorsed his opponent and scored a resounding victory, Anne didn't even notice; she was busy primping the wide rose brocade cuff of her sleeve.

Soon afterward an elaborate masque was staged for the entertainment of a visiting ambassador. It was yet another attempt to marry off Princess Mary that would come to naught. But any excuse would do to show off the richness and grandeur of the court.

Anne was chosen to portray one of eight white-gowned maidens known collectively as the Virtues in a specially constructed green and white plaster castle called Chateau Vert who were being besieged by the black clad Vices, a tribe of fiendish flying-haired devil women who danced like savages in their bare feet.

By hurling down dates, candied fruit, and nuts, the Virtues tried vainly to defend themselves against the onslaught. Then, just when the battle seemed about to be lost, King Henry appeared, leading a group of gentlemen, all of them dressed as knights, in feathered helms, clutching shields emblazoned with flaming hearts, to rescue the fair maidens.

It was all rather charming and quaint. But, frankly, it made me yawn. It was entirely predictable. Everyone would dance and sing, and it would all end happily, as is always the way with such things.

As Lady Perseverance, Anne stood upon a parapet, gazing down as the knights fought a duel of dance with the Vices and whipped and subdued them into meek defeat, and they slunk away, heads bowed in shame and submission. Then the King, with Sir Ardent Desire embroidered on a gold and scarlet banner draped across his broad chest, bounded over to the Chateau Vert and boldly, recklessly, scaled the castle walls, while all below, seated around the banquet table, caught their breaths and prayed the plaster walls would not give way beneath his weight lest he fall down onto the hard marbled floor and do himself a great or even mortal injury.

As he neared the top, King Henry's hand shot out and snatched the white silk net from Anne's hair. Pearl- and diamond-tipped pins rained down about his face as her long braid unfurled like a rope of ink black silk. He caught and twisted it around his fist and pulled her head down to his.

I gasped and sat forward, oblivious to the fact that I had just spilt my wine all over my new moss green velvet gown. In that instant, my mind catapulted back to the days of the Robin Hood masques when King Henry had first captured my braid then, the next year, Bessie Blount's. Now he held my daughter's hair wrapped tight around his mighty, meaty pink fist. He gave it a sudden sharp tug, to pull her head farther down. He would have kissed her lips, but there was something in Anne's dark eyes that froze him.

Abruptly, he released her hair, and Anne stood erect, turned her straight and rigid virginal white–clad back on him, and, without a backward glance, descended from her lofty perch and smilingly gave her hand to her brother, "Sir Loyal Heart," and let him lead Lady Perseverance out to lead the other dancers in the finale, leaving the King behind to find himself another dancing partner.

The other ladies were already taken so it was his misfortune to have to settle for my daughter-in-law, Jane, who was so intent in staring daggers at Anne's back that she tripped and fumbled her way through the dance until she fell, catching her foot in her hem, and badly tearing her gown.

I came upon Anne and George in the corridor as I was on my

way to change my wine-stained gown, laughing in each other's arms.

"Well done, Lady Perseverance!" George exclaimed.

"I hope so, Sir Loyal Heart!" Anne answered.

"The look upon his face!" George laughed, playfully recreating the scene and wrapping Anne's free swinging braid around his own fist, but much more gently than the King had done. "When he caught your hair and drew you down to him . . . I shall never forget it! For a moment I thought you were going to spit in his face!"

"If he had not let go, I would have taken the dagger from his waist and cut the rope, and my vanity with it. I shall *not* go the way of my sister!" Anne said fiercely as George released her braid. "Let him find someone else to play with; it shall not be me."

And, laughing, they danced on down the corridor to find their friends and an all-night card game.

Hearing Anne's words, the stab of dread I had felt earlier left my heart like a dagger being pulled out amidst a flood of warm blood. My youngest daughter, I felt confident, would, like me, be able to withstand the ardent overtures of England's king. I slumped against the cold stone wall and breathed a great sigh of relief and murmured a prayer of thanks. Now there were no more Boleyn women left, except George's vile Jane, for King Henry to trifle with.

Anne soon let it be known that she favored the Earl of Northumberland's shy and gawky son, "sweet Harry Percy," above all men and wanted no one else. She had given her heart to that great, big, clumsy, stuttering baby in a man's body whom anyone with a heart could not help but love.

Everyone was astonished at her choice, except those worldly, jaded, and cynical enough to claim she clearly coveted his title. They seemed such an odd mismatched pair—the witty style setting sophisticate newly come from the French court and the shy, soft-spoken bumbler. But they were very much in love.

Anne's days as an ugly duckling had taught her to look beyond appearances and fix her sights on what is inside instead—that was the way to find love, *real* love. And I, a slim and still beautiful patrician woman, whose body only sagged in certain places due to years of childbearing, who adored a dear, voluptuous dumpling of a man, could well understand. I am not *entirely* shallow.

"Anne aims high," my husband said approvingly when Percy and Anne sought permission to wed. But the King had other plans for Anne. He ordered his crimson-clad minion, Cardinal Wolsey, who now ruled England like a second king, doing all the *real* work behind the scenes and leaving Henry free to frolic and be the nation's handsome figurehead, to break the match and send Percy home to his father, to marry another girl, that harpy in human form, Mary Talbot, the Earl of Shrewsbury's shrewish daughter. If anyone ever aptly had *shrew* as a part of their name, it was that girl!

Anne was banished to Hever, heatedly swearing eternal vengeance against the Cardinal, whom she mistakenly blamed for breaking her heart, vowing that if ever an opportunity presented itself she would work the Cardinal as much displeasure as he had done her.

"I will have my revenge ere I depart this earth!" she swore, shaking her fist up at Wolsey's window one last time before she slammed the carriage door and yanked down the leather shade, so no one else would see when she fell weeping into George's arms.

All too soon the King came calling, as I knew he would. Thomas could not have been more pleased. Ecstatically, he ordered Hever Castle cleaned from attic to cellar, all the wood and plate polished to a high brilliance, and vases full of fresh flowers everywhere. He was there waiting in the courtyard, in his best brown velvet doublet, with a gilt basin of orange water for the King to bathe his hands in, all ready to play the gracious host. And I was there, dutifully curtsying beside him, a good and obedient Christian wife, resplendent in burnt orange velvet trimmed with gold and black silk braid and a black velvet gable hood trimmed with gold braid, but Henry had ceased to notice me long ago, for which I was most grateful. My moment had passed, as had my eldest daughter's; now it was Anne's turn to bask in the royal sun. God help her! I hoped she would not be burned.

Like the Master of the Revels costuming and choreographing a court masque, Thomas set the scene, gowning Anne in green silk and sending her to await the King's pleasure in the rose garden.

But Anne was the greater artist and wit, and against her, Thomas Bullen—I mean *Boleyn!*—didn't stand a chance. Anne needed no one, least of all her father, a shopkeeper's parvenu grandson, to put words in her mouth; she was fully capable of composing her own speeches. Instead of the obedient and obliging, "Yes, Your Majesty, I live only to please you," Thomas would have had her utter, even as she lifted her petticoats and spread her legs and prepared to sacrifice her virginity to the panting and lusty royal bull, Anne spoke the words that would change the world as we all knew it.

"Your wife I cannot be, as you have a wife already; your mistress I will not be. I will sacrifice my honor for no man, not even a king. My virginity is the precious gift I shall keep to give to my husband upon our wedding night. I shall lay it down on no other occasion. If God does not see fit to vouchsafe me a husband, then I shall die a barren, virgin spinster."

By the way she shrugged and tossed the words off her tongue one would have thought she felt no qualms at all that it might indeed be her misfortune to suffer such a sad and lonely fate.

King Henry was dumbfounded. Blinking and befuddled he could not speak. It was as though Anne were a witch and had cast a spell to strike him dumb. She said, *"NO!"* when any other woman would have flopped on her back and cried, *"YES! YES! YES! Thank you for this honor, sire!"* This was what her own father had ordered her to do, knowing that Anne was more practical than her softhearted sister and would know well how to make the most of the experience while it lasted. But Anne, I had discovered, was a gambler; she and George loved cards and dice with a passion, and most nights at court they could be found with their friends hovering over the green felt–topped gambling tables, heads close together, seemingly mesmerized by the roll of the dice and the fall of the cards, eyes avid and afire as they watched fortunes being won and lost, changing hands, and sometimes lives, in mere moments. But Anne knew when to risk and when to walk away and how not to end up with nothing. She won more often than she lost. There was no one in the Tudor court like my daughter.

Thomas was livid when he found out that she had dared spurn His Majesty, his whole body quaking and his face so red I felt sure he would keel over dead of an apoplexy; he threatened her by turns with the convent and beatings. But as George most approvingly said, doubling over with laughter and slapping his thigh, when he heard about the intended romance in the rose garden their father had staged but his sister had turned into a farce instead, "God broke the mold after He made Anne!"

❧ 9 ❧

I watched, an incredulous and increasingly horrified spectator, alongside everyone else, powerless to change anything or interfere, as the world we knew changed entirely over the course of the next seven years.

I saw my daughter assailed with ardent love letters from the King, which she perused with the most casual glance and refused to reply to. She never acknowledged, much less tendered her thanks for, the costly gifts that accompanied them. He sent her jewels; lengths of costly materials to fashion new gowns; sumptuous soft furs; fine gloves; rare perfumes made of rosewater, musk, and ambergris; fine-tooled leather saddles for her horses with gilt embellishments or silken fringe; and ornate leather bindings for her books replete with her initials worked in gold. Many of these she never even bothered to wear or use, setting them all aside without a second glance. More than once, His Majesty sent her his own likeness painted in miniature and ringed by diamonds set into bracelets, necklaces, lockets, and rings. Yet not once, as far as I know, did these trinkets ever grace my daughter's person.

He sent her an ornate brooch of a little gold gem-encrusted lady with long black enameled hair holding a ruby heart and wearing a golden crown in her hands while Venus and Cupid coyly peeped over her shoulders.

Anne laughed and called in the goldsmith to set this little lady in a storm-tossed boat in a wild whitecapped blue and green enameled sea and sent it back to His Majesty.

"Let him think what he will about that!" she laughed. "I hope he stays awake all night trying to figure out what it means!"

And what did it mean? I asked George, who had acted as Anne's messenger and delivered it to the King, while Anne chose to remain at Hever, tantalizingly elusive, and out of reach, to further taunt His Majesty with her absence. But George merely shrugged his shoulders and laughed. "Not a damn thing! Anne got the idea when we were out walking and saw some men scraping the bottom of their boat."

Anne treated the King's palace like her own private residence from which she might come and go as she pleased, regardless of her duties as one of the Queen's ladies. She would return, stay a day or three weeks, and then depart upon a moment's whim, leaving the King to drop everything and go running after her. Even then there was no guarantee that she would deign to see him. She might play the gracious hostess and welcome him with a smile and a basin of orange water with white blossoms bobbing on top to wash his sweaty fingers in or bar her door and plead a megrim or the sudden onset of a summer fever and leave him to sulk and cool his heels until he gave up and rode back to court again to take his disappointment out on his poor servants and sit petulant and scowling in the Great Hall every night, glaring at every woman, making her squirm and regret that she was not Anne Boleyn.

One could never tell what Anne might do. I think that was part of what made her so exciting. The King, accustomed from birth to being surrounded by those ready and eager to please, to flatter and fawn, and do anything to obtain, or retain, his favor, had never known anyone like Anne before. She just didn't care. She treated him like a lackey, and he was ready to lick her boots and dance to her tune.

Soon it was being said of King Henry that "he sees nothing, and thinks of nothing but Anne Boleyn; he cannot do without her for an hour." And it was true. He was a man caught fast in the mighty, powerful grip of blind and mad obsession. He was even willing to risk his kingdom and own immortal soul to have her.

What did Anne have to say of all this? I heard her remark to her brother one day, "He's so obsessed; he's becoming a bore."

To which George cocked a brow and countered, "Only *just* becoming?"

"*Touché!*" Anne laughed, and they danced along the corridor together, laughing as though they had just shared the most amusing jest.

Sometimes I thought it was all a joke to her. When King Henry bade the royal confectioner construct an ornate sugar and marzipan subtlety of himself in the guise of Saint George slaying the dragon, Anne smiled at him and snapped off his sugar candy lance and sucked on it boldly as His Majesty watched and drooled, no doubt imagining that that candy lance was his own member. Then she sank her sharp little white teeth in and bit it clean in half, smiling as King Henry shuddered and winced as though he were actually in pain. She left the rest of it for George and their friends to feast upon while they danced and gambled the night away in Anne's apartments, disdaining to join the King in the Great Hall, preferring to keep their own merry company instead.

I saw Anne rouse the King's jealousy to the boiling point as she continued her gallant and, unbeknownst to all but her closest friends, entirely innocent, flirtation with the poet Sir Thomas Wyatt. Until, fearing the King's wrath, after the two nigh came to blows on the bowling green when each man gloatingly displayed a trinket he had taken from Anne—each stealing the love token he thought he deserved—Wyatt did what he did best and composed a poem in which he renounced his pursuit of my daughter. But he did more than just pen a popular poem; with his words he also made Anne immortal.

Aided by George and their closest friends, Anne set Wyatt's poem to music and staged a masque for the entertainment of the court.

With her knee-length hair plaited into myriad tiny black braids embellished with beads hewn from precious gems, pearls, and textured gold, and crowned with a rearing regal ruby-eyed golden cobra, Anne dressed herself in pleated cloth-of-gold overlaid with a full-skirted and flowing sleeved diaphanous robe of pleated white gossamer, belted in gold beneath her breasts, with a wide golden collar inlaid with lapis lazuli, turquoise, and carnelian, and bracelets and necklaces and rings of scarabs carved from these same stones, as well as green and white agates and black onyx, and danced the part of Cleopatra.

George's flamboyant friend Francis Weston, who loved playacting more than any man I ever met, and would have surely been a strolling player if he had not been born a nobleman, set a wreath of gilded laurel leaves upon his rambunctious red curls and donned a gilt-bordered toga of white linen and a royal purple robe and stepped into the golden sandals of the mighty conqueror Julius Caesar.

George, Will Brereton, Henry Norris, and a few of their other friends oiled and bared their chests, draped their loins in leopard skins and vibrant silks, and hid their hair beneath striped linen headdresses or jeweled and feathered satin turbans. They layered their wrists with gold bangles, donned gilt sandals or bared their feet and gilded their toenails, lined their painted eyes with black kohl, hung their necks with heavy gold chains or beaded collars, and had a high good time playing the Serpent of the Nile's devoted courtiers, fawning at her feet, kissing her hems, and competing shamelessly for her favors as they showed off their fine sweat-slick physiques in a display of vigorous and athletic dancing.

Wyatt, opting for a simple and much more modest, white tunic and sandals, struck a pose with a golden harp and, to music composed by Anne and George, recited what would become his most famous poem.

> *Who so list to hunt: I know where is a hind.*
> *But as for me, alas, I may no more:*
> *The vain travail hath wearied me so sore,*
> *I am of them that farthest cometh behind.*
> *Yet may I by no means my wearied mind*
> *Draw from the deer, but as she fleeth afore*
> *Fainting I follow. I leave off therefore,*
> *Since in a net I seek to hold the wind.*

Who list to hunt, I put him out of doubt,
As well as I may spend his time in vain,
And graven in diamonds in letters plain
There is written her fair neck round about:
Noli me tangere, for Caesar's I am,
And wild for to hold, though I seem tame.

King Henry applauded wildly. He ripped gold medallions from his purple velvet doublet and flung them at Anne's feet as he cried, "More! More! More! Let us see that dance again!"

Anne stood straight before him, with only the banquet table between them, and, hands on hips, defiantly tossed back her braids, thrust her chin high, and proudly pronounced one emphatic word: *"Beg!"*

Like her most faithful and devoted servant, King Henry obeyed, applauding until his palms were sore and smarting pink, tearing more gold from his coat, and roaring, "More! More! Please, let us see it again!" imploring an encore of that wild, sensual performance.

But Anne gave an insolent toss of her head, sending black braids flying like whips with jeweled and gold barbs at the ends. With a wild and wicked laugh, she caught George and Francis Weston each by the hand. As they, standing on each side of her, bowed, she sank into a deep curtsy; then, giggling like a trio of mischievous children, they fled the Great Hall as Norris, Brereton, and the others quickly followed, sweating from their exertions and wiping the kohl and green, blue, and gold paint from their eyes. Only Wyatt diplomatically lingered to regale the court with another recitation of his poem.

More smitten than ever before, King Henry sent for Anne, begging her to return to the Great Hall, but she refused. From the safe haven of her chamber, where she and her friends laughed over their wine cups and lounged like languid cats upon well-padded velvet couches and cushions strewn about the floor, Anne pled a headache.

Back in the Great Hall, King Henry sulkily resigned himself to the fact that he must wait until morning to see his beloved once more. But before first light, Anne was already gone, having waited until our sovereign lord had retired for the night, then she galloped off in gales of laughter, riding back to Hever with George by moonlight. When King Henry awoke the next morning and, even before he had availed himself of the chamber pot, sent an invitation to Anne, requesting her to breakfast with him in his chamber, and some brave servant informed him that she was gone, he threw a mighty tantrum. He boxed the bearer of bad news's ears, flung his heavily laden tray across the room, scattering food, gilt dishes, and breakfast ale everywhere, then kicked over the table and his chair, and bellowed for his riding clothes and his fastest horse even as Thomas shoved me into the saddle and the two of us raced on ahead—so frantic was he to have all in readiness to receive the King, ignoring me when I tartly, yet truthfully, informed him that His Majesty was so smitten with Anne that he was hardly likely to notice if the servants had been lazy and lax and had neglected to beat the dust from the tapestries or clean the cobwebs from the corners.

"All he will see is Anne," I said, but Thomas was too busy babbling of gilt bowls and oranges to listen to a wife's pearls of wisdom.

When Henry arrived at Hever, sweat sodden and caked with road dust, and went like a supplicant, head bowed, his feathered and pearl weeping cap clutched humbly in his hands, to the rose garden, my crimson-clad daughter cocked a finely arched black eyebrow over the beribboned lute she had been strumming as the King of England knelt at her feet and confided that his marriage was barren and cursed in the sight of God and cited a verse from Leviticus as proof.

"If a man shall take his brother's wife, it is an unclean thing; he hath uncovered his brother's nakedness; they shall be childless."

To Henry, a king in desperate need of a male heir to inherit his throne when he departed the world, having only one living daughter was tantamount to being childless.

While her quick mind countered with a verse from Deuteronomy enjoining a man to marry his dead brother's widow—*"If brethren dwell together, and one of them die, and have no child, the wife of the dead shall not marry without unto a stranger: her husband's brother shall go in unto her, and take her to him to wife, and perform the duty of an husband's brother unto her"*—the gambler in Anne counseled her tongue to keep a golden silence.

It was then that my daughter took the second greatest gamble of her life. She had already dared say no to a king; now she went further. *All or nothing!* In my mind's eye, I could see Anne and George standing, black heads close together over the card table, eyes sparkling, chests heaving, as Anne decided to risk all on the turn of a single card.

Anne calmly plucked a vibrant coral rose, one that exquisitely married orange and pink within its fragrant petals, and, with a steady hand, held it out to King Henry, thus symbolically dangling the proverbial carrot before the royal ass's nose.

"I am young and fertile, and I will give the man who marries me a houseful of strong and lusty sons who will live and thrive to a ripe old age! But *all* offspring born of my body shall be legitimate and lawfully begotten," she added, emphasizing the point in case it had eluded the smitten monarch. "I would rather remain barren than give birth to a *bastard,* even a *royal* one!" she said heatedly, tossing a black wave of hair back over her shoulder.

Henry, of course, driven mad by lust, instantly agreed. He wanted to cement their bargain then and there with a binding of their bodies, but Anne witheringly refused, reminding him that *only* upon her wedding night would she part with the precious gift of her virginity. Though chaste, my daughter knew only too well that "say anything to get her into bed" is the creed most men live by; keen observation and her years in France had served her well, leaving her not only elegant but wise beyond her years.

❧ 10 ❧

I was surprised the earth didn't shift beneath all our feet then and there. *Nothing* would *ever* be the same again. Did Anne know or even suspect that her words would change the world?

Thomas thought she was just being mule stubborn, contrary, frivolous, and flighty, to quote a few of the words he used when railing and raging against Anne for refusing to succumb and become the King's mistress, and to get all she could now rather than end up with nothing in the end like her sister.

But I think it was more than mere stubbornness or mule-headed contrariness. And I think I deserve some share of the blame for what happened. I was not a good mother; I always favored one daughter above the other, banishing Anne to live in Mary's shadow, dreaming great, big wonderful dreams for my golden girl and, on the rare occasions when I even mentioned her future, sighing about the bleak and doleful existence that awaited Anne in the nunnery. I never paid much attention to Anne until she returned from France and suddenly became interesting. But by then it was too late, the damage was done, and she didn't need a mother to give her advice or to confide in—she had George and didn't want, or need, me. The gulf between us was just too great; too much damage had been done, and pain inflicted, for us to ever be a true mother and daughter to each other, much less friends. To me, Anne would always be aloof, cordial yet distant, like a wary cat that would never come close enough for me to pet.

In the days and years to come, when the people cursed and reviled Anne, calling her such names as "the she-devil" and "witch," Remi, who like me, remained loyal in his heart to Queen Catherine, said Anne was more to be pitied than despised.

"I do not see a she-devil when I look at her," he said. "I see instead a sad, frightened, and angry little girl, one who grew up believing that she was ugly, inferior to the so-called golden girls of our world, and is now determined to prove her worth to everyone who ever doubted or discounted her. And how better to do that than by doing what they dare not, by saying no when they would be so quick to say yes, by disdaining what they deem an honor, and snaring the ultimate prize—the Crown—exchanging inferiority for superiority, so that all who have ever been mean to her or made her feel shunned and unworthy must bow to her."

I think in those days of hysteria, bias, hatred, and heated discord, Remi was one of the few who remained calm and saw everything clearly from all sides and angles.

So I lay in my lover's arms and let the world bicker and go mad and fall to pieces all around us. Remi said that politics and religion caused enough discord in the world, and we did not need it to intrude and try to leave its mark upon us and our time together. If I wished to argue, there were people aplenty I could do that with at court, and if he was of such a mind, all he had to do was step out into the street or walk into the nearest tavern. Sometimes all it took to get one's nose bloodied was to mention the name of Anne Boleyn. So we let it all fall away from us with our clothes and just enjoyed each other in every way a man and a woman could.

I saw the court, and people I had known my whole life—family, lovers, acquaintances, and friends—divide into factions, like the biblical separation of the sheep from the goats. They were either for the Boleyns or against them, giving their support either to the daughter I had given bloody birth to or the kind and devout woman I had faithfully served for so many years.

Everyone was taking sides, and everyone assumed because I was a Boleyn by marriage and Anne was my daughter that I was on her side. I was forced to withdraw from Queen Catherine's service. My husband said it was not seemly for me to continue to serve my daughter's rival. Yet I did not transfer my allegiance to my daughter, though Thomas did demand I be on hand whenever she needed me to fill the role of chaperone.

Though I did nothing to outwardly oppose Anne's grand scheme, I could not embrace and support her either. I kept silent and did not embarrass either of us by trying, at this late date, to play "the good mother" and give my daughter the benefit of a worldly mother's advice; Anne would have only laughed if I had tried, just as I had once laughed at her girlish dreams. The truth was, by the time my children grew up and became interesting to me, it was too late for me to play any real role in their lives; my attempts at mothering or befriending them were often awkward at best and disappointing, for all of us, at worst. They had grown accustomed to me not being there for them; they had learned not to need or depend on me, and to live without me, and were not inclined to fling the door wide in welcome now when I had been the one who had kept it closed all during their childhoods.

I lived in a sort of twilight world, of the court, yet not of the court, there, but not there. I sat and ate in the Great Hall and dutifully attended hunting parties, picnics, banquets, balls, and masques, knelt and prayed in the royal chapel, partnered all who asked me to dance, and obediently slept beside my husband at night. As I had always done, I played the role that was required of me to the utmost perfection. When Anne had need of me, I was there to act as chaperone; the rest of the time, as far as my husband and youngest daughter were concerned, I could go hang myself for aught that they cared, as long as I did not create a scandal. I'm not complaining, make no mistake about that—that was *exactly* the way I liked it. And I was used to it—I had never really known any other life; neither the Howards nor the Boleyns, with the exception of Anne and George, were ever a close-knit family. When they had no need of me, my time was my own, and I liked being free to spend it with Remi.

I was, in truth, still reeling at the enormity of what my daughter had done. I was astounded and appalled. I *never* believed she would succeed, that a day would come when my ugly dark duckling daughter turned black swan would be crowned and anointed England's Queen. I was certain it was but a tempest that would soon blow past and all would, in time, return to normal, and Queen Catherine would be on her throne beside her husband again, and he would no doubt continue to dally with any pretty girl who caught his fancy. But that was the way of the world. King Henry was a man with a temper, not renowned for his patience, and he would of a surety soon tire of the way Anne treated him, the veiled or openly barbed insults, sharp retorts, bored indifference alternating with temper tantrums, and her refusal to grant him any intimacy greater than the occasional kiss. The court was filled to the rafters with obliging women, all of them eager to give him anything he pleased. They would readily spread their legs wide or open their lips to that monumental member, and devote themselves wholeheartedly to fulfilling the King's Pleasure. *I live only to please you!* they would scream in the throes of ecstasy.

Anne was a woman of ice, cold and frigid, in comparison. Some who, like me, saw this obvious truth opined that it was only by witchcraft that she could hold a man like King Henry. Mayhap there was some truth in such speculations? Who can say? I am not a superstitious woman, like my mother-in-law, and yet . . . kings did not risk their kingdoms, throw their wife of some twenty years away, or boot the Pope out of England because he refused to grant a divorce, and assume command of the Church like snatching the wheel of a ship from the hands of a drunken, insane, or mutinous captain, all for the sake of a black-haired Boleyn girl. Things like that just didn't happen! In heathenish lands like Turkey perhaps, where sultans kept harems filled with beautiful and conniving women who would not hesitate to resort to poison or murder a rival in order to reign supreme in their sovereign's favor, but *not* in England. We were a staid and proper people, creatures of habit, who cherished our traditions and turned our backs and turned up our noses at change like a leper or a parvenu arriving at our court with trumped-up pretensions to nobility, like when the medieval King Edward II bestowed upon his catamite lover, the Gascon son of a witch boy-whore Piers Gaveston, the royal title of Duke of

Cornwall. The King's passion for Anne was a momentary madness, an obsession that would run its course and, in its own sweet time, pass, it just *had* to; it could be *nothing* else!

What was at first known as "the King's Secret Matter" did not remain a secret for long. When it became common knowledge at court, Anne, accompanied by George and their friends, all clad in fiery shades of red, orange, and yellow, walked brazenly into the Great Hall that night in a black gown embroidered with flames and boldly declared a verse of scripture: "Behold, how great a matter a little fire kindleth!"

Thus it became official—not just speculation and wild rumor— the King meant to put aside Queen Catherine and marry Anne Boleyn.

When that dreaded plague known as "the Sweat" came in the sweltering summer of 1528, many saw it as God's judgment crashing down upon us like a great fist.

It was a strange affliction that killed the young and vital but spared the aged and infirm as well as those newly born. It began with a trifling headache, the sort of thing one might shrug off or chew a little willow bark to remedy, then think no more of, then all of a sudden the sweat began, pouring hot and prickly, accompanied by a fast burning fever, shivering fits, and pain in all the limbs. A doctor was useless. As the saying went, "Merry at dinner, dead by supper." Survival was accounted a matter of luck, for there was no certain remedy; all potions and pills were apparently in vain. You lived or you died; it was God's will or the luck of the draw.

When first Anne, followed by George, then my husband and son-in-law, all in short order succumbed to "the Sweat," those still enjoying the bloom of health nodded knowingly and were quick to declare that this affliction was certain proof that God's wrath had descended upon the Boleyns.

Cardinal Wolsey himself went on bended knees like a penitent before the King in the tower where he had secluded himself at Hunsdon House, a dozen miles from London, with his physician and but a single servant, the loyal Henry Norris, surrounded by vinegar-slicked walls and roaring fires in the belief that heat would keep the disease at bay, and begged him to renounce Anne and abandon all thought of divorcing Queen Catherine. That this plague had fallen upon the land and stricken Anne and her kinsmen down, he said, was certain proof of God's displeasure, and he feared the King would be the next to fall.

But Henry rose up from his chair, glared down at the pool of rotund silver-haired redness at his feet, and thundered, "No other than God shall take her from me!" and even dared to kick the Cardinal and order him from his sight. Henry Norris, Henry's most trusted and intimate body servant, and a good friend of Anne and George, was there and saw it with his own eyes.

The King immediately dispatched one of his own physicians, a Dr. William Butts, to Hever Castle, and gave his own favorite great sapphire, nigh big as a man's fist, to be pulverized into an exotic potion to be mixed with humble beer, treacle, various herbs, crushed pearls, and Pills of Rhazis, a popular concoction created by an Arab physician, to dose Anne and her beloved George with, and, of course, his "much esteemed and valued servant, Thomas Boleyn."

While my husband's life and those of two of my children hung in the balance, I sought solace with my beloved in my red rose bower, pillowing my head upon his chest and letting my fingers toy with the coils of black hair that grew there and the little red coral horn and tiny crucifix resting in the hollow of his throat. Sometimes we ate cherries and, wistfully, I reminisced about those happy cherry fair days I had spent with Mary, both of us whirling in red gowns, and the days when, barefoot and green-gowned like Queen Guinevere, we had gone a-Maying and gathered flowers and danced around the beribboned Maypole with handsome gallants. Days that could never come again.

I had resigned myself to the sad and bitter truth that my disgraced eldest daughter and I could never be friends. In those happy, long-ago days of fun and frolic, I realized now, I had used my golden girl as just another pretty ornament, rather like those ladies who carried little dogs with jeweled collars, but now that she was old enough to speak her mind and assert her personality, I saw just how different we really were.

I had persuaded Remi to forsake London in this time of pestilence and come with me to Hever. Thomas was too ill to know he was hosting my lover beneath his roof, and I was always discreet, and the servants, who liked me far better than they did my husband, were well accustomed to such dalliances and knew how to keep their mouths shut. Mayhap it seems callous and shows a want of feeling, my dallying with Remi while the lives of my husband and children hung in the balance. But what else could I do? They had the attention of one of England's best physicians, sent by the King himself, though everyone knew all remedies were useless and only time, luck, and God cured "the Sweat." We could only wait, hope, and pray, which of course I did, albeit with Remi. Though in the secret heart of me I knew what all England said was true—if Anne succumbed, it would make a quick end to this scandalous "Great Matter"—I did not desire my daughter's death. I prayed fervently that she and George would be spared, and, of course, I prayed for my husband and Will Carey. One might say I resigned myself to "what will be, will be," and left it all in God's hands.

Soon Dr. Butts was writing to King Henry that Anne and her kinsmen—with the exception of poor Will Carey, who had sadly perished—were "past all danger" and well on the way to making "a perfect recovery." Soon the jubilant and grateful King was sending gifts galore to the invalids and showering Dr. Butts with accolades and golden coins. He even deeded him a manor, but stipulated most sternly that the doctor was not to stray too far from London as the Crown would ever have need of his skill in any medical crisis.

Will Carey's death left Mary destitute with two young children—a daughter, named Catherine, by the King, and a son, Henry, whose parentage was uncertain.

There had been a night when the royal loins were pulsing with a lust Anne refused to satisfy—on the contrary she had once even gone so far as to "accidentally" spill a flagon of iced water on the royal codpiece, "to cool it off," after the drunken and aroused monarch made so bold as to grab her slender wrist and forced her hand down upon it—and Henry had encountered Mary in a quiet corridor. The torchlight upon her golden curls and gold-flowered silver gown had reminded him of all he had once found so alluring and exciting about her when she was new at court and fresh from France, and, without pausing to think, to ponder that this was the sister of the woman he intended to marry, he drew Mary into the shadows and hoisted her skirts.

Mary docilely endured the encounter without a murmur, then went back to her husband. She said nothing of it to anyone until some months later when she found herself with child and uncertain of its paternity as she had lain many times with the husband she called her "Sweet Will" both before and since that chance encounter in the corridor.

While mourning the husband she had come to love, Mary despaired about what would become of her and her children. When Thomas was well enough to sit up in bed, he refused her even a penny or a roof to cover her head. He was adamant that he wanted her to quit Hever as soon as she was able.

I found her in her old room, her formerly plump, round, rosy-cheeked face gaunt and pale, her eyes deep-sunken and dark-circled from days without sleep, and her gilt hair—darkened to deep burnished gold by her two pregnancies—hanging lank and lifeless, like the black gown that hung loose and limp as a shroud on her, worry having smoothed away her ample, womanly curves. She was standing before the picture of the little Lord Jesus standing on his sandaled tiptoes reaching up his hand for a bough of enticing glossy red cherries, the one she had purchased at one of the happy and carefree cherry fairs of her childhood many years ago.

"This life I see is but a cherry fair," she softly sighed with tears streaming from her tired amber eyes. "Poor Will!"

"Aye, daughter," I agreed and left her to her woes.

A part of me knew I should have gathered her in my arms and uttered some words of comfort. I should have found *something* to say that would have given her heart and the hope to go on. But such a role seemed so foreign to me, and if I tried to play "the Good Mother," I felt certain both of us would see how poorly it suited me. One of the few things Thomas and I agreed upon completely was that when one is apt to fail it really is better to not even try.

To everyone's surprise, it would be Anne who would cajole a yearly pension of one hundred pounds out of the King and, through him, command my husband to give Mary a home at Hever Castle.

After all, Anne reasoned, mayhap while inwardly gloating at this chance to shove the golden girl into the ash heap, I was so often away and Lady Margaret's wits were waning, so Hever was often bereft of a proper lady of the manor; more often than not it was left to the housekeeper to oversee all. If Mary were to take up residence there, she reasoned, their father might save a few of his precious pennies by dismissing the housekeeper and allowing Mary to don the key-hung girdle of the castle's chatelaine.

Confronted with the King's command and Anne's clever plan, my husband could do naught but agree. Thus Mary and her children found a safe haven at Hever, where she could grieve and grow strong again, and endure daily doses of Lady Margaret's rose honey to remedy her depression, while the world as we knew it continued its furious descent into chaos with the combined threat of war, excommunication, and religious revolution hovering over our heads, while my youngest daughter, like a bewitching black-haired, black satin–gowned Circe, stood in the midst of it all, calmly twirling her pearls, like a candle burning steady at the heart of a storm.

Lawyers, churchmen, scholars, and theologians all entered the fray as though it were a wrestling match, using words instead of muscles to strike their blows. Then the Pope's emissary, a gouty old man, Cardinal Campeggio, arrived to try the case, in essence bringing the Pope to London by proxy, hoping to lay "the King's Great Matter" to rest once and for all.

Many thought the whole thing the height of hypocrisy. Henry wanted to divorce Catherine on grounds of affinity, because she had been the wife of his late brother, yet the woman he wanted to marry was the sister of his former mistress. Some, remembering that I had once briefly caught and captivated the King's eye, even dredged up old rumors claiming that I had at one time briefly been his mistress. Some even said that I, a sophisticated older woman, had been the one to educate His Majesty, when he was yet a prince, in the arts of love. The gossipmongers were master embroiderers adept at adding salacious embellishments. Some even went so far as to say that Anne was Henry's own natural daughter. And my old love, John Skelton, chose that moment to drag my name through the mud by putting his poem, comparing me to the false Cressida, back in circulation. This he did from the safety of his sanctuary in Westminster Abbey, where he had gone after running afoul of Cardinal Wolsey, whom he had attacked in a satirical ditty about the Cardinal's palace Hampton Court being finer than any the King himself possessed. It was all nonsense of course, but it shook the King's credibility to its very foundation.

Though it was true that Henry desperately desired a son, an heir to rule England when he was gone, everyone knew what this was *really* about—*lust,* plain and simple *lust* and the aphrodisiacal effect the word *no* has upon some men. If Anne had said yes that day in the rose garden at Hever, smiled, and obligingly lifted her petticoats, none of this would have ever happened. Catherine would have remained England's much beloved and uncontested Queen until God called her home to Him.

Thousands thronged the streets and crammed inside Blackfriars Hall, the Dominican friars' charter house in London, avid to hear every salacious, hypocritical word the King and his counsel would utter before the papal legate Campeggio.

Anne and her court in miniature stayed away, sipping cold wine and lounging like oriental potentates in the garden of the splendid London town house the King had given her, while musicians played and fountains splashed, coins clinked, and the dice rattled and rolled. It was almost as though she did not care about the verdict. Or mayhap she was merely confident of the verdict. Cardinal Wolsey had promised the King he would be a free man anon, free to wed and bed whomever he pleased. And my bullish spouse was certain he would soon be the father-in-law of a king and was bursting with pride at the seams; he was there in the court, lapping it all up like a cat does cream, certain that by the end of the day his youngest daughter would be queen in all but name, and that would come too in but a few days' time.

I had planned to stay away. I did not like to brave the crowds or subject myself to hours of tedious legal and theological debate. I believed Queen Catherine when she said her marriage to the late Prince Arthur had never been consummated. And I believed the desires of the flesh rather than the sometimes contradictory words of the Lord were motivating King Henry. Anne was his Satan-sent temptress; perhaps she was a changeling after all? No ordinary woman could assert such power.

The palace was nigh deserted. Like gluttons for scandal, the entire court had gone rushing off to Blackfriars. Something drew me back to Queen Catherine's apartments, where I used to serve, now so sadly deserted. I found her sitting alone at her dressing table. Her hair now more silver than gold, flowing loosely over the shoulders of her black damask dressing gown, a gold-backed hairbrush lying absently in her lap as she fingered her pearl rosary.

"Madame!" I cried impetuously as I rushed toward her, boldly meeting the sad and weary gray eyes of her reflection in the silvered looking glass. "Why are you still here? You *must* fight for your rights! You'll let your case go by default! Quickly, I implore you; I will help you dress!" And I, the mother of her sworn enemy, for what would be the last time, had the honor of attending England's one true Queen.

I laced her stout waist into her boiled leather stays and helped her don a gown of stark black velvet.

"I wear mourning," she explained, "as testament to my grief, to show the English people how sorely my heart aches and grieves that I have lost my husband's affection."

I hung an elaborate golden crucifix studded with sparkling black spinels and peerless white diamonds about her neck and silently pressed her pearl rosary back into her hand and whispered, "Christ be with you."

"He always is," she assured me with trembling lips and tears shimmering in her gray eyes. "Our Lord Jesus Christ, unlike mortal men, *never* falls by the wayside; He is *always* constant in His affections."

When I draped a gold lace veil over her silvered hair, she laughed. It was such a brittle, bitter, heart-stabbing little laugh. "I first saw Henry through a veil of golden lace, through the swirls and whirls of gilded threads; his was the first open and friendly face I saw in England. I know he did not love me at first—how could he? He was just a little boy—but the love came later. This I know.

And, in his heart, buried so deeply that he has lost all sight of it, it is still there."

There was a faraway look in her eyes as she recalled the first night she had spent on English soil, when old King Henry VII, impatient to see the Spanish princess, to see with his own eyes if she was really as beautiful as the ambassadors claimed, barged into her lodgings, dragging both his sons, her betrothed Prince Arthur and his little brother Prince Henry along behind him. They presented a sorry trio, in rain-soaked riding vestments with wilted, bedraggled feathers on their hats and hair beaten flat and plastered against their cold, pale cheeks.

The old King ordered Catherine's indignant duenna, Dona Elvira, to roust Her Highness out of bed or he would plunge boldly between the bedcurtains and drag her out himself all but naked in her shift if he had to. The horrified governess had hastened to rouse Catherine and, fearing the King's impatience would cause him to kick the door down and come bursting into the room at any moment, she didn't dare take the time to properly clothe her charge, so, thinking quickly, she draped her in a long veil of rich, dense golden lace instead and led her out to face her destiny.

"And now"—Catherine sighed—"again—destiny calls! It is like a battle cry to my ears, and I find myself the warrior queen once more, fighting for what is right and all I hold dear."

At Blackfriars, I stood in the back, crammed against a wall I feared the crush of jostling bodies might cause to collapse, and watched as my queen was summoned to appear like any common litigant in a lawsuit.

She ignored the protocol of the court and went to her husband. She knelt at his feet and spoke to him straight from her heart, entreating most earnestly to know how she had offended him. She insisted that she had done her duty as a wife; she had done it gladly and with *all* her heart. She had given him numerous children, though it had pleased God, for reasons we mere mortals could not know or hope to comprehend, to call them from this earth. She swore again, as she had so many times before, that when she came to him, as a bride on their wedding night, she came innocent of the touch of man, a virgin, even though a once-married and widowed one, she remained *virgo intacta*.

She tried so hard to sway him, to move him; my heart ached for her. It hurt to see such a proud and dignified woman groveling before this ruddy-haired icy-eyed ogre who sat there on his throne like a statue carved out of solid ice or stone. He would not even look at her. It was as if his ears were deaf and his eyes stone blind to her. His heart must have been made out of marble, not flesh and blood. How else could he sit there glowering unmoved in the face of such eloquent and earnest love? But he never spoke or moved, betraying not the faintest flicker of emotion. He sat in silence on his gilded throne and stared straight ahead and right past her.

I saw Remi in the crowd. Our eyes met. Though we were too far apart to even discreetly touch hands, I knew he felt the same. All his good wishes went out to Queen Catherine.

I knew, as Queen Catherine knew, that she could not expect justice in this court peopled by King Henry's foul creatures, men like my husband who would say or do anything to retain royal favor and reap even greater rewards.

Heaving a great, heart-heavy sigh, she rose from where she had prostrated herself at King Henry's feet and went to kneel before the gouty, red-robed Cardinal Campeggio and threw herself on the mercy of Rome.

"To Rome and the Pope I commit my cause!" she cried.

Proudly, she rose, curtsied twice, once to Cardinal Campeggio and then to her husband. With her head held high and her back straight, she turned and walked out. She never looked back. Even though the court crier called after her three times, "Catherine, Queen of England, come into court!" she ignored him.

"God grant my husband a quiet conscience," she said softly as I rejoined her.

Outside the good people of England waited, to warm and embrace their beloved Queen with their words. "God save Catherine, the one true Queen!" they cried. "God grant you victory over your enemies!" and "We'll have none of Nan Bullen!"

Even after so many years, the people's love for her bore not one tiny speck of tarnish. Their love for her was still bright and golden and, in the court of public opinion, she was clearly the winner.

* * *

In the end, it all came to nothing; the court recessed for the summer, as was the custom in Rome, without rendering a verdict and never reconvened.

Pope Clement was still caught and torn between the King of England and Queen Catherine's powerful nephew, Charles, the Holy Roman Emperor, who was likely to declare war rather than stomach seeing his aunt discarded and disgraced.

The Pope wanted to delay making a decision as long as possible; like everyone else, I think he hoped that Henry would soon tire of the whole business and have his fill of Anne Boleyn. But he, like everyone else, discounted the dark enchantment of my daughter. Henry's soul was possessed by the dark demon of lust; it enflamed his loins and burned all reason out of his brain, leaving him determined to move heaven and earth if he must, all for the sake of the dark-eyed girl he was hell-bent on possessing.

❧ 11 ❧

Everyone expected that to be the end of it. They assumed that King Henry would give up. It was just *too* difficult; too much to lose and too little to gain was the common consensus. No one believed my daughter was worth a kingdom and eternal damnation. After all, she was not the only woman in England; there were so many more much prettier and sweet-tempered girls ready to oblige their beloved monarch. But Anne had something up her fashionable, self-styled Boleyn sleeve.

But first . . . first she had to remind the King what he was fighting for and silence all those naysayers and doubting Thomases, including her own father, who, like a weathercock, had suddenly turned and stood, once again, convinced that she could never win.

"Submit now or lose him forever, and end up with nothing like your foolish sister," he insisted, reaching out to grasp Anne's shoulders and give her a hard shake.

But Anne would do things *her* way.

That very night, when King Henry sat down to dine, he found the Great Hall transformed. Great lengths of glimmering tinsel cloth in shades of silver, pearly white, icy and deep greens, and aquatic blues, both pale and dark, were stretched across the immense room, gripped at the edges by concealed attendants who moved them up and down in gentle undulating ripples to simulate waves. The whole scene was lit by lanterns with clear, blue, or green glass globes set upon a spinning wheel to create an eerie, mysterious world one might imagine existing under the sea.

A great silver painted papier-mâché oyster shell was carried in by George, Francis Weston, William Brereton, and Henry Norris, all of them garbed as handsome, bare-chested sapphire- and emerald-tailed mermen with their legs cunningly concealed inside the great pearly white and pale blue seahorses they rode, with wheels cleverly hidden beneath blue waves at the base of each mount. They had rubbed their skin with oil containing gold and silver dust and donned wigs of wild wavy green and blue locks threaded with pearls and crowned with diamond-encrusted starfish and exquisitely jeweled shells, and even put golden rings in their ears and hung thick ropes of creamy pearls and vivid pink, red, and orange coral about their necks.

As the music played, the melody undulating like waves, they slowly opened that great oyster shell. Reclining on a bed of coral satin, Anne slowly sat up, tantalizingly veiled in her long satiny black hair. As she swung her bare feet over its rim, it appeared at first that she was wearing nothing beneath her hair but rope upon rope of lustrous white pearls, some hanging all the way down to her slim, naked ankles. But no, when she took George's hand, and he, shed of his seahorse, with his legs encased in shimmering hose with a pattern of blue and green scales, led her out to dance, we saw that she wore a sheath of sheer white linen sewn all over with thousands of pearls, some draped across her body, others hanging down in loose swaying ropes.

King Henry sat forward, entranced, gripping the edge of the table, unable to take his eyes off her. All she had to do was dance. That's all it took. At the end, when she sank down, gracefully, to her knees, and George set a towering crown of pearls upon her head, we all knew, no matter what it took, even if the very earth must move, she would have her way; and another crown, set upon her head by an archbishop in Westminster Abbey, would come her way very soon.

Only then, after she had danced, to remind the King and rekindle his lust, did Anne lay down her next card.

Anne and George and their circle of friends were fascinated by bold and new ideas, particularly those espousing religious reformation. Martin Luther, a former monk in Germany, and his cry for church reform, blocking the sale of indulgences and allowing the scriptures to be translated into each nation's native tongue so that everyone, common and great, ignorant and educated alike, could understand them, instead of hoarding those sacred words like precious treasures as the priests with their scholarly, elite Latin did, had struck a chord with them.

One afternoon Anne lay on a chaise, boldly perusing one of her forbidden books, a banned volume, William Tyndale's *The Obedience of a Christian Man,* the possession of which Cardinal Wolsey had decreed a criminal offense. Most cunningly, she brought a particular passage to His Majesty's attention wherein it was stated that the king was the highest power in his dominion, and it was treason to acknowledge any other authority as higher than his.

"So . . ." Anne purred, stroking her wide fur cuffs. "Who has more power here in England, I wonder? King Henry, who is actually here, or Pope Clement, who is far away in Rome? Interesting, is it not?"

She tapped her chin like one perplexed by a very great problem, though she wasn't confused at all. Anne knew *exactly* what she was doing—she had just given King Henry the key to make *all* his dreams come true.

Thus she set the wheels of his mind in motion. Soon King Henry was envisioning himself as Supreme Head of the Church of England, with no more tithes and tributes flowing out of England into Rome's already rich and overflowing coffers, and with all the wealth of the monasteries at his disposal.

Anon, she set those wheels turning even faster when she introduced him to a churchman called Cranmer who advised Henry to take a poll amongst the learned doctors in the universities regarding the validity of his marriage to Queen Catherine. And Henry was delighted when—as we all knew it would—the verdict, when it came, was exactly the one he wanted to hear—his marriage to Catherine was, by the world's great universities, deemed invalid. King Henry, the scholars opined, should be free to divorce Queen Catherine and marry whomever he pleased. As a reward, Cranmer would later be appointed Archbishop of Canterbury.

Then it was time to leave on the Summer Progress, where the King would tour the rustic reaches of his realm, visit the country houses of his nobility, and show himself to his adoring people, those poor country folk who never got up to London.

Before, Queen Catherine had always accompanied him. But this time word came she would be going elsewhere—alone, never to return to the King's palace or favor. Anne would be taking her place on the Progress, and her apartments when she returned at summer's end.

King Henry refused to see Catherine before he left, and when she sent a servant scurrying after him to convey her good wishes and undying affection, he thrashed the fellow soundly with his cap while Anne sat, cool and serene, in her gilded saddle, in a riding habit the color of quinces, twining her fingers in the rich rope of grass green emeralds Henry had that morning hung about her neck, smiling beneath the brim of her beguilingly feathered hat.

Defiantly, Queen Catherine stepped out onto the balcony overlooking the courtyard and called down to him.

"Come what may, I shall love you and remain your true wedded wife and queen until my dying day! Even though you have broken the promise you made to me, that no one would ever hurt me, and I would never cry again, once we were married, my love for you endures, unbroken, always, until the day I die!"

Henry made no answer; he merely turned his back and rode away with Anne beside him.

Though my husband and son were quick to join King Henry and Anne on the Summer Progress, I did not accompany them. I pled illness, implying it was of the unpleasant female variety, the sort of ailment men are most unlikely to press for details regarding, and took myself off to Hever with Remi. I did not like what was happening and wanted no part of it. That day I wished I had been brave enough to smother my daughter in her cradle.

The rest of Queen Catherine's life would be spent in crumbling country castles, cold and dank, and deleterious to her health, until her dear heart at last gave out. She went where Henry ordered her, without a murmur of complaint, saying only to the minions who came to enforce the King's orders, "Tell *my husband,* the King, that go where I may, even unto the ends of the earth, until my heart stops beating, I will remain his true and lawful wife and queen of this realm; time and distance cannot change that. Tell him also that I pray daily for his soul and that of his concubine as well."

Henry hoped to break her proud spirit, and if he could not do that, to punish her for refusing to set him free to follow where his lust led. He wanted to show her how hard he could make things for her, to emphasize the contrast between what might have happened had she been more agreeable. He had offered her the title of Dowager Princess of Wales and a life, spent in quiet seclusion away from the court, of course, with all the trappings of luxury befitting her rank. But Catherine would not deny her marriage and see her only surviving child, Princess Mary, declared a bastard. She would hold firm until the very end, even when they refused to let her see her sick daughter and took her jewels away, and her clothes grew raggedy, and moths devoured her furs. And even when a nasty cough racked and rattled her chest and she burned with fever, Catherine would persist in declaring herself Henry's wife and Queen of England until her dying day.

That Christmas Anne presided over the court as though she were indeed Queen. She sat resplendent in holly berry red satin, sipping hot spiced wine and idly nibbling upon sugar wafers and mincemeat tarts, surrounded by George and their friends, all of them clothed in evergreen velvet and silken hose of the same hue, and listened as King Henry sang a song he had written in her honor, as testament to his true and everlasting love for the woman he vowed would soon be his wife.

Green groweth the holly, so doth the ivy.
Though winter blasts blow never so high,
Green groweth the holly.

As the holly groweth green
And never changes hue,
So I am, and ever hath been,
Unto my lady true.

As the holly groweth green,
With ivy all alone
When flowers cannot be seen
And greenwood leaves be gone.

Now unto my lady
Promise to her I make:
From all others only
To her I me betake.

Green groweth the holly, so doth the ivy.
Though winter blasts blow never so high,
Green groweth the holly.

When he was done, Anne applauded and, as he had done so many times after her own performances, implored an encore. King Henry obliged, gallantly bowing and declaring, "Anything for my beloved! Eternal and evergreen shall ever be my love for you!" And while he sang, Anne danced in a swirl of brilliant red satin, bright as the finest ruby, surrounded by the men she had just laughingly dubbed her "Evergreen Gallants."

Gazing down upon them from the top of the stairs, seeing my red-gowned daughter, surrounded by these four gentlemen in green, it was like looking at a holly berry cradled in the midst of its evergreen foliage. Again and again, each time King Henry finished, Anne implored him to sing it again, and again, and again, and went on dancing with her brother and their true and constant friends, the ones, time would prove, who were truly eternal and evergreen in their devotion to her.

I stood and watched for a while and then, doubting that I would be missed, I put on my cloak, took the little bundle of mincemeat tarts I had bade my maid pack for me, and went to Remi. As I walked softly through the snow I thought about Queen Catherine and wondered how she was faring alone on this the first Christmas since she had become queen that she had spent without her beloved Henry.

Queen Catherine was the first of Anne's enemies to fall. The next would be the great and powerful Cardinal Wolsey. It had been a few years coming, but she had not forgotten her vow of vengeance.

Wolsey had been confident that he could sway Cardinal Campeggio to deliver the desired verdict when he sat in judgment in the Pope's place at Blackfriars. And he had failed.

Anne had not forgotten. And she had not let Henry forget it either. She found evidence that the crafty Cardinal, who always swore he served the King before all others, was secretly in league with the Pope, that he opposed the divorce, or, if it was granted, he wanted a French Catholic princess for Henry instead of "a nobody like Nan Bullen."

Anne was determined to make him pay. She had him sent from the court, shorn of his greatest titles and possessions, including the Great Seal of England and his sumptuous palaces, Hampton Court and York Place. She twisted the knife in further by sending her old love, Harry Percy, to arrest the tired, broken, old, silver-haired man at the humble country bishopric where he had retreated in his shame and disgrace.

But Wolsey would rather risk his immortal soul than public humiliation on the scaffold. He died en route to London. Some said he secretly took poison; others that he simply willed himself into the grave. His last words were that he should have served God better than he had the King; perhaps then He would not have abandoned him in his gray hairs.

Meanwhile, a new creature, a clever, ruthless lawyer named Cromwell, came to take Wolsey's place, one who would not scruple or suffer even a twinge of conscience at putting the King's will before God's. Cromwell was one of those crafty men who got results and made things happen. Henry had only to snap his fingers and speak his wishes and his will would be done; Cromwell, or "Crum" as he fondly called him, would see to it, never letting little things like a conscience or his immortal soul stand in his way. Something of a ruffian in his youth, this son of a Putney blacksmith had roamed about Italy soaking up the teachings of Machiavelli. He believed feelings like love, loyalty, and lust were liabilities that only stood in a man's way and he was better off without them. He was devoid of fear, pity, or remorse. In the blink of an eye or a snap of the King's fingers, Anne would later find, a friend could become an enemy, to be persecuted relentlessly unto the ultimate destruction.

When the news came of Wolsey's demise, Anne and her friends gleefully celebrated by staging a ghoulish, macabre masque they called "Cardinal Wolsey Goes to Hell." What fun they all had capering as skeletons, leering demons, incubi, succubi, witches, and fallen angels amidst flaming torches and clouds of opium-scented incense and black and red smoke. Francis Weston particularly relished playing the role of Cardinal Wolsey.

Anne and her friends did a lengthy, unabashedly sensual dance as black-winged fallen angels. When Anne and George danced together, floating and gliding sensually through clouds of black and blue incense like a pair of black swans, in their sleek ebony feathers, dark hair, and black satin, I saw George's wife, Jane, sitting beside me, clench her teeth and stab a gilded fork into the palm of her hand until it drew blood.

In truth, I could not blame her. The way they danced together that night, they looked like lovers, passionate, devoted, and made for each other.

After that disturbing interlude, when my daughter and her black-winged adorers had departed to make a quick costume change, the legions of Hell returned for more frenzied cavorting; they even had trained monkeys in to caper and dance with them with black wings and red devil horns strapped to their ugly little furry forms, and black goats with their horns painted red led about on leashes butting and bleating amidst the red and black smoke, and dancers clad as nuns and priests miming copulation with fanged, horned, and forked tailed red-skinned demons. They borrowed fierce jungle cats from the royal menagerie and had them put in cages with servants stationed beside to poke them with sticks to make them emit furious roars throughout the evening, blending with music that was by turns frenetic, chaotic, furious, slow, sensual, caressing, and erotic; it rose and fell, crescendoed and crashed with such suddenness and violence that not a one of us who sat in obedient attendance and watched that grotesque spectacle didn't leave the Great Hall that night without our nerves sorely jangled and linger a little longer over our bedside prayers before we blew the candles out.

But even that—God help us!—was not enough! This night, it seemed, excess was *everything!* They brought in extra dancers to flesh out their numbers as they danced the Seven Deadly Sins, to tempt and taunt and caress the damned Cardinal Wolsey.

Anne—gowned in red satin, and a mantle of wire stiffened orange and yellow flames, with gold paint around her eyes—exquisitely danced the role of Lust, pausing to caress the Cardinal's thigh through his red robes.

The court sat silent and aghast, sickened and appalled, but not a one of us could tear our eyes away. Though Cardinal Wolsey had been much hated, and many gloried in his destruction, *this,* we all agreed, was in terribly bad taste.

I shook my head and wished myself anyplace but here as my daughter, returning to enact the role of Avarice, appeared before us resplendent in a gold and silver tinsel gown sewn with gold and silver coins, and George, Brereton, and Norris, with gilded baskets filled with jingling coins sewn onto their costumes, and Weston as Wolsey in his voluminous red robes, joined her in a vigorous dance as her adoring, worshipping slaves, showered her with gold and hung jewels about her throat and draped ermine around her shoulders.

When it ended, with George as His Satanic Majesty, stabbing Wolsey in the posterior with a ruby-studded red-painted pitchfork and sending him plunging, screaming, into the Pit of Hell, I was never happier to see the conclusion of any performance in my entire life.

I could see by the expression on his face that King Henry—even though he applauded and praised the dancers' talent and the novelty, artistry, and inventiveness of the evening's entertainment, declaring it "wondrously brave," "incredibly bold," and "most ingenious"—also thought it was too much and in exceedingly bad taste. Perhaps, now that he had lost him, he was remembering how much he had once loved Wolsey; my husband, who feared Anne had *finally* gone *too far* with this epic production of grotesque gloating over an enemy's demise, said there had been a time when the man was like a father to him; Henry had entrusted him with the daily governance of the realm and had turned to him whenever he had felt troubled or in need of advice.

Maybe Anne, seeing King Henry's face, thought she had too.

That night she rewarded Henry by giving him "a little taste—a *foretaste*—of heaven." She let him into her bed—a fat white feather bed covered in quilted white satin, hung with white lace curtains, like a tantalizing veil, where she lay, a black-haired angel in alluring, clinging white satin, whilst in each corner, blindfolded, white-winged and gilt-haloed harpists played, and I sat, unsmilingly, doing a mother's duty and acting as my daughter's chaperone, in a straight-backed gilded chair outside her open bedchamber door.

But she did not grant him the *ultimate* favor—*that* she continued to deny him. As a precaution against the King's mad lust propelling him over the edge of sweet and tender lovemaking into rape, beneath her angelic white bed gown, Anne had girded her loins in white satin covered with delicate silver mesh, held in place by an exquisite little heart-shaped silver lock studded with diamonds.

How she laughed at Henry's dismay when he discovered it! When he pressed too far, pleading for the key to "heaven's gate," she pushed him from the slippery white satin sheets and, rocking on her knees, her wild laughter ringing hysterically, clapped her hands to imperiously summon a host of white-gowned, haloed, and angel-winged servants to toss white rose petals over his head and escort him out the door to the ethereal tune of harps, more certain than ever that he would make Anne Boleyn queen, and that she would be the mother of England's next king.

"Anne, you go *too* far," I felt compelled to warn her, frowning down at my daughter as she lay, convulsed with laughter, wallowing in her white satin and long black hair.

But Anne just smiled, stretched like a cat against her satin sheets, and laughed at me.

"Nay, Mother, he shall move heaven and earth, if need be, to turn my *no* into a *yes*. He only needed a little reminding. 'Tis only a matter of time now, you shall see. . . ."

☙ 12 ☙

One cold mid-January morning, my husband, the newly created Earl of Wiltshire, shook his countess sharply awake and ordered me to dress in great haste. It was still dark outside. The fire had gone out, and he would not even let me summon my maid to light it. Such was the need for secrecy and haste that he fumblingly laced me into my stays and gown himself.

"This is not a royal banquet or a ball, Elizabeth," he said as he struggled with the manifold complexities of feminine garb with all their layers and lacings. "All that matters is that you be decently covered in such a way that does not attract undue attention, not that many are abroad to see you at this ungodly hour."

He refused me sufficient time to arrange my hair. "Just put a hood over it!" he barked. Seething with impatience, itching to be off, he hurriedly, sloppily, coiled up my long, sleep-fuzzy braid, shoved a few pins in to hold it, then crammed the jewel-bordered gable hood I had worn the night before onto my head. Then he flung a fur cloak over my shoulders, grabbed my hand, and dragged me out the door even as I wailed that he must wait; I had forgotten my slippers, and the stone floors would surely turn my feet to ice. But Thomas refused to tarry—"Hang your feet; they will not show!"—and dragged me determinedly down the quiet, dark-shadowed corridor, the torches casting our shadows, larger than life, onto the cold gray stone walls.

We followed the steep, torchlit twists and turns of a stone staircase leading up into a dusty, cobweb-festooned attic turret in York Place where disused palace furnishings, rolled tapestries, trunks of outmoded finery, and unwanted portraits were stored.

There we found Anne, standing before one of the diamond-paned windows, calmly watching the last stars fade from the sky, in pearl-encrusted black velvet. Only her fingers, toying with the great golden *B* dangling from the rope of pearls about her throat, betrayed her nervousness. The three large teardrop pearls dangling from it clacked between her anxious fingers.

George, clad like her male twin in black and white, festooned with pearls and exquisite blackwork embroidery, stood behind her, his hands, calm and steadying, resting on her shoulders, as his bearded chin lightly grazed the row of pearls that edged her black velvet French hood.

King Henry, magnificently arrayed in evergreen velvet and gold brocade dripping with diamonds, emeralds, and pearls, stood nearby, having some hushed and hurried words with his chaplain.

And Henry Norris, Francis Weston, and William Brereton, yawning and sleepy-eyed, hair tousled, in rumpled garments clearly hurriedly donned after being tossed carelessly on the floor the night before, sat huddled in a corner over a game of dice.

"To keep us awake, my lady," Weston volunteered, bleary-eyed with a weary smile as he rattled the dice when my curious gaze lighted upon them.

I stood beside my husband and bore silent witness as my daughter married King Henry while he was still officially the exiled Queen Catherine's husband. A mere technicality soon to be dissolved, my husband assured me, as Francis Weston sneezed behind us, red and watery-eyed amongst the cobwebs.

After that swift, surreptitious ceremony, the King pressed a hasty kiss onto Anne's lips, and then departed with his weary gentlemen, my husband amongst them, and the befuddled chaplain, to begin the business of the day, as though this were any other.

I was left alone in strained and awkward silence with my daughter, who had just become the secret, uncrowned queen of England.

We returned to her chamber and had one of our rare private conversations over an early breakfast where Anne, still nervous and fidgety, pushed her plate away and turned her back on me as I ate.

I admit I often stood in awe of my youngest daughter, the one I had been so disappointed in and expected so little of, thus I knew her the least of all my living children. Anne kept her cards close to her chest and rarely confided in anyone except George. No real closeness ever developed between us, only a cool and formal cordiality, and to the end Anne Boleyn remained an enigma even to me, the one who had given bloody birth to her.

I asked her why she had been married in such secrecy and haste, in this hole-in-a-corner affair. I had always imagined if Anne achieved her aim there would be a royal wedding such as England had never seen before.

Standing at the window, with her back to me, silhouetted against a yellow and gray sky, Anne turned, showing me herself in profile, and drew her full skirts back, holding them taut against her stomach.

"Does it show much?" she asked.

Astonished, blinking and unable for a moment to believe what my eyes were seeing, I let my knife fall with a clatter and stared openmouthed at the soft, gentle swell of her burgeoning belly.

"No!" I gasped. I could not believe it! She had surrendered? Laid down her virginity, sacrificing it to the King's lust without a golden band on her hand first! Risking all, boldly throwing all her cards down onto the table, knowing all too well that after he was sated, Henry might easily find some way to weasel out of his promise and dance away to find another partner, a newer and easier lady, one who did not aspire to become Queen of England.

"When?" I gasped.

"Calais." Anne shrugged, releasing her black skirts to bell full and gracefully around her, and once again conceal her infant secret.

My mind hurtled back to a recent visit my daughter and King Henry had made across the Channel to connive with King Francois, to garner his support for their marriage. Nothing really had seemed to come of it. And, though George and my husband had gone, I had stayed away, feigning illness again, so I could retreat to the sweet haven of Hever for a much-needed respite with Remi.

The disgraced Mary had taken my place and accompanied Anne as a nominal chaperone her sister for the most part disdained. The weather had been bone-bitingly cold; so cold it burned, those who had been of the royal traveling party claimed, with wild winds that had churned the Channel like a witch wildly stirring her brew and delayed their return to England. This—Anne's unexpected pregnancy—was obviously the result. Which Anne, with her words, now confirmed.

"The weather was bad, and we were bored and cold, and it seemed as good a time as any, an apt diversion to pass the time, and it kept us warm." She shrugged it off as though her surrender—this thing which she had for so long denied King Henry—was nothing at all.

I clapped a hand over my eyes and shook my head. I had been a blind fool! There had been rumors of course—there were *always* rumors—which I had ignored. There were so many outlandish tales about my daughter that I no longer believed anything about Anne unless I saw it with my own eyes, heard it with my own ears, or she, or George, confirmed it with their own lips.

It had been bandied about the court that Anne had an insatiable, ravenous, craving for apples, which she had never especially liked, but now she simply could not get her fill of them. But I thought it merely a rumor. *How could I have been so blind?*

I recalled the laughter in Anne's eyes, the sly, mischievous smile that had graced her lips, when, shortly after her return from Calais, she had donned a flesh-hued gown, overlaid with lace sewn with pearls and diamond brilliants, that made me sit up and gasp as I instantly realized that she had brought my pincushion Eve to life. With Francis Weston slithering about the floor in an emerald-scaled costume and green hose as the wily serpent, and George costumed in the same fleshy satin and sparkling lace as Anne's gown, with a large, splendid green satin fig leaf fastened prominently over his codpiece when that shameful need for modesty arose, she danced in a masque telling the story of the temptation of Eve.

There had been such a mirthful, knowing look in Anne's black diamond eyes when she sank her teeth into that ruby-fleshed apple. And George! The way his expression mirrored hers, especially when she cajoled him to share, to take a bite of that forbidden fruit with her; it was as though they shared a secret and were laughing at the rest of the world, because they were the only ones who knew it, and the rest of us were consigned to dark, blind, and deaf ignorance.

Of course he knew her secret! *He* was her confidante; she would have told George before she even told the King. Though the others might suspect and speculate, guess and surmise, and Anne herself might even drop hints, no one *really* knew, and wouldn't until Anne decided to bestow the gift of knowledge and enlighten us. As Anne often said when confronted with criticism and complaints, "That's the way it is, and ever will be; grumble if you like, it will change nothing."

I sat there, staring stunned into my breakfast ale, my mind whirling, remembering the way George had taken a cloak of green velvet fig leaves cleverly stitched together and draped it around Anne's shoulders, embracing her, the two of them swaying together, sharing a secret, mischievous glance, laughing at the world together.

They were such beautiful, graceful dancers, the best I had ever seen, like a pair of black swans mated in perfect harmony.

Then George saucily clapped a cap of black velvet upon his head, as Anne donned a broad-brimmed black hat, each crowned with a single jaunty, curling white ostrich plume, and, arm-in-arm, they had sauntered out of Eden, with the superb serpent Weston slithering, belly flat upon the floor, following them like a pet, causing the court to rock in their seats with laughter.

All except George's wife. Jane dug a fork into the palm of her hand beside me and stifled a silent scream until the applause was finished. Then she rose and, blood dripping from her hand, heatedly denounced such eroticism in an enactment of a biblical subject.

"It should edify souls and educate, *not* titillate! It is no laughing matter!" she howled, as tears raced down her face, before she fled the Great Hall, leaving nods and knowing whispers behind, some cruel, some kind.

Though we deplored her lack of self-restraint, this public venting of private emotions, not a one of us, I suspect, did not feel some sympathy, or even pity, for that plain, pathetic creature, so much in love with George she hated everyone he gave his attention or affection to. Everyone knew it was green-eyed jealousy, not piety that had roused Jane's ire.

On the rare occasions when George and Jane danced together, out of duty, as husband and wife should, the performance was leaden and lackluster, and always ended with Jane fleeing in tears because there was no magic; that only happened when George danced with Anne.

On Easter Sunday, I was one of the favored women who followed in new, pastel-hued gowns behind Anne, dazzling in shimmering white tinsel cloth and diamonds, carrying the flowing hem of her surcoat of bloodred velvet and ermine as she walked majestically into the royal chapel and made her first public appearance as Queen of England.

No one in the chapel uttered a word. They just sat in silence—some glum, some stupefied—and stared. All over England, when the people were enjoined to pray for Queen Anne, they walked out on the Easter service rather than pray for any queen other than Catherine. "We'll have none of Nan Bullen!" they muttered darkly, reviling the woman they called "The Concubine." Though I was never the superstitious sort, I thought it an ill omen.

"Where will it all end, I wonder?" I sighed later when I lay draped languidly across Remi's bed, dreading the hour, coming all too soon, when I must rise and return to court. I wished I could stay there forever, my body wrapped in his humble, faded, and well-worn quilt as though it were the finest, softest ermine or a divine coat of many colors, reveling in its feel against my naked skin, how years of use had worn it soft, loving it just because it was his and covered him, and touched him, every night as I never could.

"Only time will tell," he softly answered, running a gentle hand down the length of my spine. "As for myself, I pray for both of them, and I have so all along; I did not wait to be ordered or asked. There is no one on this earth, I think, whether the highest or the lowest born, who does not need, or deserve, our prayers."

"You really are *too* good." I smiled and drew him down to me, glorying in the warm weight of his body upon mine and wishing I could banish all the clocks from the world.

❧ 13 ❧

By the time my daughter was crowned, storm clouds were already gathering over the supposedly happily married couple's heads.

That humid May day I rode in a gilded coach through streets lined with silent, sour, and surly people who refused to take off their caps, bow their heads, or bend a knee to Queen Anne as she was carried past, resplendent in her golden litter, her six months' belly round as the golden orb that would soon be placed in her hand at Westminster Abbey. I sat crushed and sweating in ermine-bordered scarlet velvet between my daughter Mary and my daughter-in-law Jane, listening worriedly as the first with sweet-natured sisterly concern and the other with relish and mean-spirited glee discussed the signs and scenes of matrimonial discord they had seen themselves or heard tale of.

Only Anne's pregnancy—the precious son she and King Henry believed she carried within her belly—kept a fragile peace between them . . . but only just barely.

True to form, as pregnancy transfigured my daughter's sleek and slender body, and raised her already hot temper, King Henry turned away from her in disgust. I knew he would. *Everyone* knew, except my bold and confident daughter; Anne thought she could succeed where all other women had failed and hold him even when the changes Mother Nature wrought dampened his desire. For once, she overestimated her powers. But she could not concede defeat gracefully and just sit and wait and hope for the best once she regained her figure.

Anne was not one to feign ignorance and turn a blind eye. She would not suffer in dignified silence as Queen Catherine had done. She would not pretend and make excuses. She confronted him boldly, flinging his infidelities right in his face. When King Henry told her to shut her eyes and endure as her betters had done before her, and reminded her that it was within his power to lower her as much as he had raised her, Anne flew at him, claws bared, and only fear that she would harm the child inside her kept his rage from boiling over into violence. Rather than strike her down, King Henry subdued his wrath and tried to smother it under sweet and soothing words that rang false to both their ears. *"Liar!"* Anne spat and stalked away from him.

The love affair was over. It had survived seven years of wooing but hadn't even withstood a single year of wedlock.

Henry expected my mercurial and fascinating black swan daughter to transform as soon as the ring was on her finger, to cease her frank and outspoken ways, to curb her brashness, bridle her tongue, doff her bold, brazen acts, and put them away like a wedding gown tucked in a chest with lavender sachets, and become instead a meek, mild, little hen with no spice or pepper, no pluck or verve.

"Well, more fool, Henry!" Anne declared. "I am not about to sit at his feet like a dog; *his little pet!*" She sneered and tossed her head contemptuously, though she knew better than any that she had already fallen from the pedestal upon which the King had placed her. She didn't need her father to tell her, as he was ever wont to do, "It is easier to fall than to rise." She already knew.

In truth, such words didn't matter. They were only rubbing salt into wounds; this marriage was already doomed, and I think it had been from the start. It was a colossal mistake born of ambition and thwarted lust, and once both were sated, they found there was nothing else to hold them together, except for the child, the expected prince, in Anne's womb.

Henry wanted a submissive, demure, docile, and sweet-tempered little wife who never contradicted or challenged him. Suddenly, he had had enough of spice and wanted blandness.

But the kind of woman he now wanted simply was not who Anne Boleyn was. She didn't have it within her to douse her fiery spirit and become that humble creature or even make the attempt. There was no pretense or artifice about her; she was simply, from the cradle to the grave, Anne Boleyn and no other. The only roles she ever played were in masques, and even these, she infused with her own unique and indomitable personality. "I cannot be other than myself," she always said when others counseled her to tread a safer path. Her spirit was too proud to be broken or bow beneath the yoke or the angry lash of the whip.

Why, I could never understand, did Henry suddenly expect her to become someone else? After all, it was that special, mercurial, and fascinating self that he had fallen in love with. Yet, perhaps, it was as simple as this—what men want in a mistress, they despise in a wife.

Anne wasn't like me; she couldn't go through life pretending. She could never be that exaggeratedly docile paragon of wifely virtue and perfection that men encouraged their sisters, daughters, and wives to mold themselves after, the eternally amiable, smiling, subservient Patient Griselda, always agreeing, always obedient, ready to live or lay down her life if her husband's will decreed it, whether he decided to slay her children one day or turn her out of his kingdom naked but for her shift the next. No, that was not Anne; it never could be. Anne argued with, challenged, contradicted, denied, and defied him as her mood and convictions dictated, never thinking that it might place her very life in peril. She simply was not the "nod and smile," good and obedient Christian wife like I had been reared up to be by governesses and etiquette books.

I rarely talked to my husband. I didn't want to. Nothing he had to say was of the slightest interest to me; court gossip I could get from my maid. As for arguing with him, it really wasn't worth it; I could live the life I wanted without resorting to open defiance. All I had to do was be discreet. But then *I* was not the Queen of England like my daughter. I wasn't fighting to prove myself, or to hold on, to keep my grip from slipping from a scepter or a man's cock. I

had already established myself. I was secure. I, the proud pedigreed bride, was the best bargain the Bullen merchants ever made,
and Thomas knew it. So why dither about the details? The garment
looked good on the outside—every eye that beheld it admired and
praised it—so what mattered if inside the seams and stitches were
flawed and imperfect? None but a privileged few, who knew how
to be discreet, would ever see the inner truth.

On the seventh morning of September 1533, I was shaken from
a sound sleep by my anxious husband, shoved hastily into my
clothes as I had been on that hole-in-a-corner wedding morn, and
sent to Anne's lying-in chamber, where she gave birth, after a long
and grueling labor, to a little red-headed girl who came bawling,
with fists balled, into the world.

How heavily the silence hung after the midwife had announced
the child's sex. Anne knew better than any that she had failed. She
had promised Henry a son, the first of *many* sons to ensure the
continuation of the Tudor dynasty, and with this daughter, she was
off to a sorry start. He was certain to be angry and disappointed
and moved to question everything he had ever done for Anne Boleyn. Henry had had enough of failure. He hadn't gone to hell and
back, and changed the world, to wed and bed Anne Boleyn for a
girl-child to be the result. Henry wanted, and needed, a son. And
with that fluid and susceptible conscience of his that seemed to
change the way the wind blows, he just might see this as God's
judgment being visited upon him; a neat and tidy excuse to set
Anne aside, just as his conscience had decreed that he discard
Queen Catherine. The time was ripe for another brave woman, if
she dared, to enter the field.

Anne tried to brazen it out. She dried her tears and bade the
maids change the linens and hangings on the bed to the most regal
ones of royal purple velvet, fringed and tasseled with Venice gold
and embroidered with golden crowns above the lovers' knot entwined initials *H & A.* Her ladies obediently combed the sweaty
tangles from her hair, crowned it with a circlet of gleaming bright
gold and ruby-set roses, perfumed her person with her favorite
musky rose scent, clothed her in a clean, fresh white linen shift
edged with blackwork embroidery, and hung her pearls with her

favorite golden *B* pendant weeping a trio of teardrop pearls about her throat. Only then, reclining regally against a mound of plump pillows, with the newborn princess swathed in purple velvet and ermine in her arms, did she allow them to open the doors and let her royal husband enter, followed by a throng of curious courtiers, avid to see if Anne could overcome her disgrace.

Imperious as ever, Anne did not even defer to him in the matter of the child's name, but boldly announced that she had borne him a daughter and named her Elizabeth, to honor his mother as well as her own—luckily we both had the same name—and that she would give her little girl a brother, hopefully as loyal and loving as her own—she smiled up at George hovering protectively at her bedside—the next year.

She didn't let a crack show in her confidence, and not a drop of vulnerability or fear seeped out. Rather than wait for the royal bull to attack her, she plunged ahead boldly and grasped him by the horns. I thought the scene very well played, and even Thomas, glowering and frowning beside me, had to concede that Anne deserved some minor congratulations on how she had so neatly averted a potentially ugly situation.

"Mayhap motherhood will be good for her," Thomas pronounced dourly, "and subdue her inner harpy."

I nodded and smiled, but inwardly I doubted it. Anne might be a good mother, but I doubted anything would ever change her. And, at times, I rather liked and admired and even envied that "inner harpy," as my husband dubbed our daughter's tempestuous and rebellious nature.

King Henry glowered but chose to restrain his temper and not make a scene that would be reported, with great relish, by the gloating naysayers, to the foreign ambassadors. How the whole world would laugh! All this supposedly for a son and now . . . what was left? Dead lust and another useless daughter! Henry knew it was in his best interests to plaster a smile upon his face and brazen it out just like Anne was doing. Still in his hunting clothes and reeking of sweat, he bent and planted a chaste kiss, a grudgingly given peck, upon Anne's cheek, then took his leave, calling for roast meat, wine, a warm bath, and a change of clothes.

All the celebrations planned in honor of the expected prince

were canceled. For the newborn Princess Elizabeth there would be
no bonfires or tournaments, grand balls, banquets, free-flowing
wine in the city conduits, or dancing in the street for the common
people. An extra *s* was hastily appended, by secretaries supervised
by my husband, to the birth announcements that had been written
in advance, announcing the joyous news that a prince had been
born to the King and Queen of England. And while Anne and her
baby slept, her royal husband sat glum and moody over his wine in
the Great Hall that night and not even the court beauties parading
before him with beckoning eyes and enticing smiles could arouse
him. He was too worried about the future.

After my daughter and newborn granddaughter were asleep,
cocooned, however uneasily, in regal splendor, I threw a dark
hooded cloak over me and went to Remi.

He had rubbed a chicken with garlic and herbs and roasted it,
and we shared it with red wine, a small round of cheese, and a loaf
of fresh bread by candlelight in the little kitchen at the back of his
shop.

How out of place my court finery—my gold and silver vine- and
flower-embroidered pomegranate Flemish velvet; silver-threaded
blue-gray damask; deep, wide, silver fox-fur cuffs; gold and silver
chains; brooches, rings, and ropes of pearls; and jeweled gable
hood—always seemed there, at least on a grown woman, not a doll
fashioned to fit a child's arms, and yet . . . I felt right at home there,
more than I had ever felt in any manor or palace. I was a diamond
who had forsaken her precious setting and mayhap, I sometimes
thought, in doing so I had found something better.

But could I have made that change permanently, given up being
a noblewoman for love? I very much doubt it. As much as I loved
Remi, I doubt it. The love of the finer things, the feelings of superiority and entitlement, and pride in my pedigree, were too deeply
ingrained in me. I could never forsake velvet for homespun.

We sat and talked long into the night, pondering Anne's, and
her little princess's, fates, and Remi, with a piece of charcoal and
light scrap of wood, drew the newborn Elizabeth as I described
her. "Ah, here is the proud grandmother, after all!" He smiled as a
hint of pride crept into my voice. Though I knew it was only the

fortunate coincidence of names that had led Anne to name her daughter as she did, I was nonetheless proud to be the grand-mother of a princess and have her named after me.

Later, from that sketch, he would make a little red-haired doll of her that would ever remind me of a fierce little lion cub, gowned in gold-braided spice orange velvet and tawny damask with pearls and beads the color of honey golden topazes. It never failed to amaze me how perfectly he captured her zesty little spirit and fine features, even the hue of her hair, without ever having laid eyes upon her.

And then we went to bed, and it was love, love, love until dawn's first light.

I hardly ever slept when I was with him in London. That was the one sad note that crept into our beautiful love song; I could rarely curl up and enjoy the sweet pleasure of slumbering in my beloved's embrace, feeling the warmth of his breath upon my bare skin, and his soft and ample flesh warming, cushioning, and comforting mine all night long.

When I knew I must return to court, that my husband, and oth-ers, would be expecting me, I didn't dare sleep lest I—lulled into such sweet contentment by the feel of Remi's arms holding me and his sleeping body pressed close against mine—overslept and re-turned late to court to face suspicious and inquiring glances and outright questions about my whereabouts and what had happened to delay me.

With the morning light, feeling that same accustomed sadness, the tiredness mingling with the regret that I must soon depart, I wrapped his threadbare white linen sheet about my nakedness—he was too proud to accept a set of fine silk from me—and sat and watched the first trickle of sunlight trace over his plump bearded cheeks and thick-lashed, dark-browed eyes beneath which his warm brown eyes, veiled by delicately veined lids, danced in a dream.

He looked so young lying there, a chubby dark-haired cherub, angelic and smiling in his sleep, curled upon his side, facing the window so he might feel the sun upon his face gently coaxing him awake, hugging tight against his chest the old, faded quilt of many colors, of fabrics flowered, striped, spotted, and solid, that his grandmother and mother had made together when his mother was first learning to sew, the coils of dark hair that lightly covered his breast and one rosy-haloed nipple just peeking out over the quilt as he embraced it. I had to clasp my hands tight, to keep from reaching out and caressing him, as the frail buttery rays did. I wanted to kiss him, to lean over and playfully nip that pink nipple, but I didn't want to wake him. A part of me wanted to let my hand delve mischievously beneath the faded quilt and find his manhood, slumbering pink in a nest of short black hair beneath the soft, doughy shelter of his stomach, to rouse him again for more play, but I was too tired, and my accursed vanity was always afraid to let him see me looking anything but my best even when my weariness came from a wonderful night of love. With all the others, I never cared what they thought, or if each tryst would be our last, but with Remi I *did* care; I didn't want it to end. I wanted him to stay with me forever.

Soon he too must also rise, to open his shop, and begin the business of the day. There were dolls to make and dolls to sell.

What jealousy, and, I admit, fear, what blind, fluttery-belly dread, that kind of unshakable panic that wants to take flight but can't, I felt whenever I thought of the noble ladies who would come into his shop, to browse idly and buy trinkets and trifles for their little girls and boys. Did they flirt with him? I was certain they did. Were some bold enough to dare as I did and drag him to the floor or take him to his bed? Did they arrange for Remi to deliver certain goods to their boudoirs at appointed hours? He was so sweet, so polite, so shy, yet bold sometimes, in his own special way, it was hard to believe he could resist such temptations.

I saw men at court succumb every day to the wiles of bored and jaded, capricious and amorous ladies whose eyes lighted interestedly and admiringly upon them. From kitchen spit boys, grooms, liveried servants, and stable boys, to handsome minstrels and tradesmen visiting the palace to display or deliver their wares, I saw them one and all lie down and surrender when a pair of tempting eyes flashed and beckoned, *Come hither!* Hadn't I, after all, deployed such charms often enough myself? And still did whenever the mood struck me and a handsome prospect stood before me. I knew how the game was played.

Remi assured me that these things never happened, that men as ample as himself seldom held much attraction for ladies. Time and again, he told me that there was no one like me, and no one else in his life, never calling me out as a hypocrite and flinging in my face my own varied and many fleeting amours. Sometimes I worried that I was standing in his way. What right did I have to keep him from marrying and having a family when I had these things and could not give them to him myself? But when I tried to talk to him about it, to fully comprehend the situation, to discover what kind of ground I stood upon, Remi would only smile and, in his soft, quiet way, assure me that "all is well" or "fine." It was maddening as well as sweet because I never *truly* knew what he thought and felt. I would always wonder if he was just being kind and polite. Maybe he truly was content, and I, in my selfish way, really did fill a need? Even after all these years, I still do not know. I wanted to believe him, that everything was fine, and sometimes I think I did, and yet . . . I could never entirely banish the fears; they were relentless pursuers I could never shake off but for an occasional pleasant hour or two.

It is one of life's truths that a vain woman accustomed to adoration, especially an aging beauty, is often, in her heart of hearts, an insecure one; some just hide it better than others. Some are better at slamming the door shut upon their fears and keeping them from peeping through the keyhole or the shutters and intruding upon, and spoiling, their pleasure. Alas, that was an art I never fully perfected. The perfect, pedigreed wife with all her beauty and elegant, refined airs wasn't perfect at everything, especially the things that *really* mattered, the things that weren't all show and grandiose pretension.

With a reluctant sigh, I left the bed and gathered my rumpled clothes from where they lay upon the floor and went to stand before the mirror hanging over my lover's humble washstand. This looking glass was the one luxury I had insisted upon providing—I must be able to put my hair and garments right lest I return to court looking like a milkmaid who had just been tumbled by her swain in a haystack.

The morning light is not as kind as the gentle golden glow of candles. My eyes, the ones men often described as black and bewitching, looked like they were resting in beds of crinkled gray silk, like sheets a pair of passionate lovers had kicked to the floor and left for the night.

I tried to tell myself that it was only fatigue, and when I was well rested . . . but I knew better. I was then eight years past forty, and Father Time is seldom kind to vain coquettes like me. Ethereal beauty, the beatific kind that suffering and sorrow only enhances, is a rare and precious gift given only by God to a certain privileged few such as saints. It is a gift that money cannot buy, nor a pretense of piety either. I could walk barefoot to the shrine of Our Lady at Walsingham until my feet were raw, and it would not turn back time and restore the youthful smoothness and pearly luster of my face.

I bent closer to the mirror and scrutinized the lines upon my brow and around my eyes, nose, and mouth. My rouge and red lip paint had been worn away by the passion of Remi's kisses the night before. I was glad my lover was still asleep and could not see me without my paint. I never appeared in public without it; I deemed my cosmetics as vital as air to me.

I bared my teeth to the mirror's unyieldingly honest gaze and flinched back as though I had been slapped. They were the color of old, yellowed ivory. Vainly, I had endeavored to whiten them with vigorous daily scrubbings with a concoction of white wine, vinegar, and honey. I had even resorted to my mad mother-in-law's so-called "sovereign cure to turn ugly, yellowing teeth snow white," and brushed them with a paste made of grated pumice stone, stag horn, and cuttlebone, the acidic aqua fortis, burned iris root, and the urine of a white mare, but all to no avail. I had nearly died retching over the evil taste it left in my mouth and spent nigh two days afterward rinsing my mouth and gargling with lavender, terrified whenever anyone came near me that they would recoil at the stench emanating from my mouth.

Another aging beauty of the court swore by the urine of a Portuguese man liberally mixed with the juice of ripe lemons—full yellow without a spot of green on them—chased by a gargle of warmed white wine and honey.

In desperation, I donned a cloak and found myself a swarthy Portuguese sailor and went with him to a dockside inn. Though he laughed at me when I insisted on "hard pissing" before the carnal act—I was obviously past my childbearing years so there was no need to attempt contraception with what many considered a tried and true method—but he indulged me just the same.

After he left me, I carefully poured the contents of the chamber pot he had used into a bottle and took it with me back to court, so I could send my maid to procure the other ingredients and attempt the restorative in the more comfortable confines of my bedchamber. But it was all to no avail.

After I lost a tooth last year, one that just barely showed an empty space when I flashed my brightest smile, I had begun practicing before my mirror until I had perfected a closed-lipped smile. And none too soon; I was terribly concerned about a wobbly incisor. Every time I bit down hard or felt it sway in its socket, I feared its loss was imminent.

I had seen a quack in London about it, and he had attempted to steady it with a metal binding. But it cut my tongue so badly when I talked, and, to my great embarrassment and dismay, one of my lovers when his tongue delved inside my mouth, so I had to return to that mountebank and have it carefully cut out. The whole time that charlatan's hands were at work within my mouth, I was terrified that my tooth would come away with the metal that had failed to anchor it firm.

Thomas was *furious* that the man would not return his money and even dared demand payment for undoing his shoddy, incompetent work, but I left it to my husband to sort the matter out; I was far more concerned with my tooth.

Nor had I fared any better when another medical man, claiming worms had been fast at work boring holes into my teeth, had attempted to fill the aching cavities with a mixture of pulverized ox bone and white clay. His handiwork had me adding poppy juice to my wine more often than I cared to and drinking cup after cup of sage tea to try and soothe my sore and bleeding gums.

I suppose there's really nothing one can do about teeth! I lamented and, with a sigh, resolved to keep practicing my tight-lipped smile.

But my face . . .

Perhaps mad old Lady Margaret was right and a lotion made of minced horseradishes and milk slathered upon the face followed by the cleansing lather of soapwort was the best remedy for restoring its youth and vitality, closing up pores, and curing all manner of blemishes. And that cream of cowslips she always swore by, citing it as a sovereign remedy for taking off spots, wrinkles, and other vices of the skin, might indeed be the very thing to iron these wrinkles out. And that vexing unevenness of tone! Though I was always careful of my complexion in the sun, I had lately noticed that there were spots and patches upon my face where my skin appeared a trifle darker; it was hardly noticeable in dim, flattering light, but in stark sunlight . . . that was a different story. Perhaps I really should try the infusion of elderflower she recommended after all.

Maybe there was some magic in Lady Margaret's strange remedies? Thomas had listened to his mother when he noticed a bare round spot atop his pate, rather like a monk's tonsure in the making, and upon her advice had begun nightly applying an ointment of goose droppings she had made, slathering the reeking greenish black paste on thickly with a butter knife while I tried hard not to laugh. So far, though the bald spot had not diminished, it had not grown wider either.

If her witchery failed me, there was always a mask of white fucus that I might try. This was a popular recipe for whitening flesh I had heard other women at court, desperate to restore or prolong their beauty, often resorted to in which the burned jawbone of a hog was ground and sieved, then mixed with the oil of white poppies, the milk of an ass, alum, egg whites, powdered eggshells, vinegar, the milk of green figs, birch tree sap, and just a hint of sublimate of mercury, then layered upon the face and left to sit for a time.

With a sigh, I let the sheet fall. I had already appraised my face, so I might as well see the rest. It wasn't *really* as bad as I feared, well . . . not quite. Except for a lined and sagging belly and breasts—the result of all those years of playing the Bullen broodmare—the swags of pure white flesh sagging from my upper arms, and a mottled curdling effect upon my thighs, I was well enough for a woman fast approaching fifty. My buttocks were still plump and round, and the men who saw them always said the dimples upon them were delightful.

I shook my head and heaved a doleful sigh, then straightened and quickly yanked my embroidered shift over my head. It was then that I noticed a few skeins of silver snaking treacherously through my ebony tresses. *Had Remi seen them?*

In a panic, I glanced at the sun, now streaming bolder through the window, and, without waking Remi to help me, hurried into the rest of my clothes as best I could, cursing under my breath, and devil damning the manifold complexities of hooks and laces a lady was required to endure in order to present a pleasing figure.

If I hurried, there would be time for my maid to prepare a walnut juice rinse to hide the silver in my hair before I must face the world again. I had tried other concoctions, washes of crushed poppy petals, betony, sage, and ivy berries to cover the gray, and even a handful of crushed calendula petals from time to time to lend my tresses a beguiling reddish sheen when I was in the mood for something different; but walnut juice, I found, always worked the best for me. Afterward, I always used a lavender rinse, as it was my favorite scent, and so that whenever I walked past anyone his or her nose would receive a welcome whiff of sweetness. I also gargled with a mouthwash made of lavender after scrubbing my teeth to sweeten my breath. I also found a good, brisk rubbing with the oil beneficial when I noticed a slight, aching inflammation in my knees and hands.

While I soaked in a warm bath perfumed with lavender petals, I could rest with a poultice of rosewater over my eyes to relieve the puffiness, rub some lavender oil on my temples to soothe my nerves and the headache I felt tentatively hammering on the inside of my skull, and send Marie to inquire in the palace gardens and kitchens, to see if she could find the horseradish and cowslips and the other ingredients Lady Margaret deemed vital to a lady's regimen of lifelong beauty.

I had been most remiss in not trying sooner; I rebuked myself sternly as I threw on my cloak and hurried out, so consumed with my vain and self-centered worries that I forgot to kiss my beloved adieu. What did it really matter if the old woman was mad? About this, she might be right, and, if there was even an almond-slim sliver of a chance it might reverse the damage, and restore and re-vitalize my complexion, it was well worth trying. And what risk could there possibly be in horseradishes and cowslips? To my mind it seemed much safer than sublimate of mercury!

❧ 14 ❧

Anne tried again as soon as she was able. What else could she do? Although she doted upon her red-haired daughter, spending hours fashioning exquisite little gowns for her, and wept when the King refused to let her nurse Elizabeth from her own breast— she had to give him a son or else . . . the consequences were too horrendous to contemplate. Scandal, another divorce, or exile and confinement behind the bleak gray stone walls of a strict convent? Oh no, such was not the way for Anne! She would never agree, much less swallow her pride and submit humbly. That proud and haughty spirit would *never* pick herself up from a fall and go quietly into oblivion.

But failure, I fear, was the new and frightening pattern my daring daughter had fallen into and didn't know how to recover from. Luck had turned against her and, for the first time in her life, she didn't know how to turn it back. A successful pregnancy, ending with the birth of a healthy son who would grow and thrive to lusty manhood, was the *only* thing that could save her.

Now her womanly wiles counted for nothing except to lure King Henry back to her bed so that she might conceive, and also safeguard her daughter's rights by persuading Henry to create a new law, the Act of Succession, making it an act of treason, punishable by death, for any man to deny any children born of their union as England's rightful heirs.

At the same time, Henry decreed the same fatal penalty for any who refused to acknowledge him as the Supreme Head of the Church of England. Many grappled with their consciences, and a great many died, amongst them Sir Thomas More, the devout, gentle scholar, who had formerly served the King as chancellor. King Henry later lamented his death and blamed Anne for it because she had been so adamant that he enforce these laws. The people hated her even as they feared her; the great and powerful Queen Anne, they said, had witchcraft in her black soul; she made heads fall, and thunder roll.

But Anne was only thinking of Elizabeth, and the brothers and sisters she believed would soon join her little daughter in the royal nursery. She was fighting like a lioness to protect her red-haired cub, and, for that, no one should blame her; she was only doing what a mother—a *good* mother—is supposed to do.

As though to rub salt in Anne's wounds, though I know in truth that was not what she intended, Mary appeared at court, round-faced and smiling and swollen great with child beneath the faded sage green damask of a gown that had seen better days. As she fidgeted with the pearl-tipped pins that held her dark gold curls matronly trapped beneath her hood, she casually announced that she had married, for "love, sweet love," a soldier named William Stafford, who was a good ten years or so younger than herself. Some of the court gossips and men who had known him when he served at the garrison in Calais insisted the difference was greater, and more like twelve or thirteen years, not that it really mattered; the deed was done, and there was no undoing it.

Time had not been kind to my golden girl. Living at Hever, serving as housekeeper, except when Anne summoned her to court, she had found consolation in food, as she had when the rich fare of Brussels and France had been laid before her as a young girl, and her curves were even more seam-bursting and bountiful than ever before. Her hair had darkened to a deep burnished gold; long gone were the lazy, languid days of sitting idly, as a lady of leisure and pampered royal mistress, in the sun with her hair soaked in lemon juice and chamomile spread out over the wide brim of an open-crowned straw hat. The busyness of life had long ago taken precedence over my daughter's vanity.

Anne was *livid*. We all were. How could she do this? Marry for love! A common, lowborn soldier! A man with no money to speak of! Now that Anne was Queen, Mary, as her sister, might have at last made the kind of marriage she should have in the first place with a man of wealth and station who would appreciate a curvaceous blond bride with a pleasant disposition, the talents of a courtesan, and who was still of childbearing age and had twice demonstrated her fertility. But no, she had gone and let "love overcome reason" and married a ne'er-do-well soldier of fortune.

Anne flew into a wild, weeping rage. The sight of Mary's bulging to bursting belly seemed to taunt her, and she banished her from court, shouting, "You *disgust* me! I never want to see you again!"

The pension Anne had procured for Mary when she was widowed was instantly withdrawn; she had a husband to support her now and thus no longer had need, or was worthy of, the King's charity. And this time there was no one to stop Thomas from turning her out of Hever. Anne was now her enemy. And I, her own mother, could not comfort or condole with her when I felt like shaking her and battering her head against the wall for ruining yet *another* chance with such gross stupidity. How could she go and do such a fool thing?

Hypocritical and cruel though it may seem given my affair with Remi and the many casual and meaningless dalliances I had indulged in throughout the years with other men—lowbred and sometimes years younger than myself, especially as I aged and men of my own years or older grew even less attractive to my jaded eyes than they had been in my wide-eyed, wanton youth when I craved the worldliness and sophistication of older males—I *deplored* Mary's foolish choices. I could never abide a fool, and it was clear to me then as the finest Venetian glass that this was what Mary was—a stupid and irredeemable fool!

As I saw it then, Mary had been given opportunities aplenty. From birth she had been the golden girl, and yet, she had failed each and every time; she had turned her back on every golden chance, even when they came as easily as reaching up and plucking them like golden pears right off the trees, and let each and every one of them pass her by. Not once, but *twice,* she had been the mistress of one of the greatest kings in Christendom; she had shared the beds of first the King of France and then the King of England. Yet what did she have to show for it? Not a blasted thing! Had she ever ruled the court as an uncrowned queen? Had she been powerful, influential, her patronage and favor eagerly sought, had people come clamoring to her door with petitions they hoped she would lay before His Majesty? No! Mary hadn't even had the influence to set fashions as her younger sister, a veritable nobody newly returned from France, did. And the bastard daughter, and mayhap son, she had borne King Henry went unacknowledged, cheerfully claimed by the loving and doting Will Carey. Where were the sinecures, the titles, the deeds, the manors, the lucrative wardships, money boxes overflowing with coins of gold and silver, and the jewels and furs and splendid gowns every mistress worth her salt garners? They were not even gone, blown away on the wind, or squandered through carelessness; she never had them at all!

Mary was a fool; no one could deny it, and we were happy when she finally slunk away, like a whipped dog with its tail tucked between its legs, an outcast set adrift and banished from the bosom of her own family, weeping on her young husband's strong and sturdy shoulder, to lead a quiet life in the country in a thatch-roofed cottage with tansy, marigolds, and daisies blooming in the little garden outside. That was the only type of life Mr. Stafford could afford to give the new Mrs. Stafford and their unborn child, and it was a far cry from the glittering and sophisticated world of the court or the rustic semi-splendor of Hever Castle. The new Mrs. Stafford didn't even have a washerwoman or a maid to help her! When her baby came, it would not even have a wet nurse or a nursemaid!

Mary's other children remained at court as Anne's wards to be reared up properly lest they too disgrace us. And of Mary herself, we would hear, or see, no more. I don't even know if the child she gave birth to was a boy or a girl, or if it lived or died. True to her word, Anne never saw her sister again. And I didn't either. I want to, but it's too late now, I fear, to make amends. As much as I want forgiveness, I cannot bear to risk the rebuff, even though I know in my heart that I deserve it.

Twice after Elizabeth's birth, Anne thought herself pregnant, only to suddenly discover herself, weeks after announcing the joyous news, sitting in blood.

Were these mistakes, merely the onset of her courses, their natural, habitual rhythms disturbed, delayed, or altered by her one successful pregnancy, or were they indeed truly miscarriages? Had her womb been damaged by the birth of Elizabeth as mine had been when I brought Anne herself into the world?

Two years in a row this happened, during which time the King grew increasingly querulous and disenchanted. They quarreled more than ever. Discord now far surpassed desire. What little passion remained in their marriage was spent in arguing. Bedding Anne had become a loathsome duty Henry submitted to only out of necessity. He now *hated* the one he had once loved and worshiped so madly. He blamed Anne for making a fool of him.

There were murmurs about the court that King Henry believed he had been bewitched, and not in the sense a man usually means when he is wildly infatuated with a woman. No, Henry sensed Satan had been lurking behind Anne all along, waiting to put out a cloven hoof and trip and snare him. How absurdly ironic that my daughter, who read the scriptures so fervently, and wholeheartedly embraced the idea of English translations so that all might understand them and grow closer to the Lord, should now be suspected, by her own husband, of signing her name in the Devil's black book and of selling her own immortal soul for a crown and a throne.

My daughter was doomed, and more than ever I was afraid of what would become of her. As the scriptures say, "Pride goeth before destruction, and an haughty spirit before a fall." A lifetime in the thrall and governance of powerful men had taught me it is far easier to fall than to rise; indeed my own husband frequently parroted that phrase. It was a truth I had seemingly known from birth and lived by all my life. And I did not doubt it then or now. Anne was already falling.

Dreams began to torment my sleep in which I saw Anne plummeting from a great height, black skirts and hair flapping like wings on the wind, before the bone-shattering crash followed by blood and stillness, black eyes blank, wide, and staring, the last vestiges of horror fading from them with life itself, and that long, graceful swan's neck bent at an awkward, impossible angle. I would start awake, consumed by guilt, remembering the day I had been tempted to take my daughter's life, a life I now feared for as I never had before.

I just *knew* something terrible, something horrible, was going to happen to Anne, and I was powerless to prevent it. I could not save the life I had once contemplated taking. I could only be, like in the dreams that plagued me, a helpless and horrified bystander. I could watch my daughter fall, but I could not catch her, stop her falling, or in any way cushion that fatal fall. I was helpless. We both were.

Henry had a new love now. A fair and fragile lady who was everything my daughter wasn't and never would be—soothing, still waters, a placid blue gazing pool, instead of turbulent, cascading, rapid waters, crashing waves, and strong currents; clear blue skies instead of darkness, thunder, torrential, cascading rain, and flashes of diamond-bright lightning. She was like a plain little oatcake served on white porcelain set down next to Anne's luscious and tangy, cream-dolloped, black cherry tart enthroned in sumptuous gourmet splendor atop a gilded plate.

Jane Seymour was demure, sweet, and pure, without a dash of cinnamon to enliven her bland custard nature. She was quiet as a church mouse, soft-spoken, and shy, one of those women born to always nod and agree, to go through life, from her cradle to her grave, without muddying the waters with even a hint of discord or contrariness, content to play the role of good and obedient Christian daughter, sister, and, later, wife and mother as ordained and written for her. She was wholly in the mold and of the mold; she didn't have it in her to break it as Anne had done.

Some women go through life never knowing who they truly are; they only know who and what their fathers, brothers, husbands, and sons want and expect them to be. Such was Jane Seymour. When she replaced Anne in the King's affections, some people tried to imbue her soulless blank blandness with an air of mystery, depicting her as some sort of living feminine cipher too deep to fathom, when the truth was, rather sadly, that not even Jane Seymour herself truly knew who Jane Seymour was; she had never dared delve that deep and probe for her own opinions, thoughts, and feelings. I would say she was like a puppet, for in truth that was what she was, the puppet of ambitious men—her father; conniving, clever brothers; and, of course, the King. Only the puppets with their carved and painted faces that Remi made had more personality than that prim and proper miss ever possessed. She was merely a vessel others emptied and filled. And yet, King Henry saw everything he wanted in her.

Vainly, I tried to reassure Anne. Rather ineptly assuming a maternal mantle, I sat beside my daughter on her bed, trying to play the role of consoling and condoling mother, and awkwardly rubbed her shoulders as she wept while, over her tear-shuddering back, I batted flirtatious eyes at the lute player sitting in the corner on a velvet-padded stool strumming his instrument, and silently mouthed the hour for us to meet to share some secret pleasure.

A great talent and handsome in a rather fey, ethereal sort of way, young Master Smeaton, or Mark, with his pale heart-shaped face, curly chestnut locks falling like kisses over his brow, great, luminous blue eyes, and elegant, oh so talented hands, adept at provoking the most exquisite sensations out of the human body as well as notes from his lute, was yet another of George's meaningless dalliances; one whom, anxious to be rid of, for reasons I would soon all too well understand, he had been eager to pass on to me.

Poor Smeaton, he was very much in love with Anne. He wrote songs and music for her that he was too afraid to dedicate and openly declare were inspired by her, songs which Anne applauded as she would any good composition performed by a talented musician, which was all Mark Smeaton ever was to her. She never thought of him as anything but a musician, albeit a favored one whom she often chose to play for her when her head was aching or her nerves disquieted and she wanted some soothing music in her chamber.

Knowing he could never hope to possess her, except in his dreams, Smeaton let himself be seduced first by her brother, and then by her mother, as a way of bringing himself a little closer to the one he loved best. Then he wept all the harder when we each in turn rejected him and refused to provide further fodder for his fantasies.

Mayhap that was why he tried so hard to hold on to me, because in the shadows, I was *almost* like her. At one rendezvous, a hurried tryst in a quiet, dark-shadowed corner, I laughed in his face when he so far forgot himself as to call, *"Anne!"* I left him standing, weeping, with his prick wilting, as I smoothed down my skirts and went back to the bright lights and merriment in the Great Hall. I hurt him, but he *always* came back for more. Sometimes I gave it to him, and sometimes I didn't. He never knew which tryst would truly be our last.

"This *will* pass, Anne," I said with a confidence that fooled neither of us. "Have patience," I counseled, "and you will see. She will go the way of all the other lights of love he has dallied with. His love lights upon these women like a hungry honeybee does upon a flower, and once he's sated and has supped his fill, off he goes, flitting off to the next flower, and then the next. . . . You will see, this drab country wallflower will not hold his interest for long. She's *boring!* One might as well try talking to a sheep!"

But Anne was too desperate and afraid to believe me. Rounding on me impatiently, she cried, "Even dull, dirty ditch water can, under the right circumstances, cool and refresh a parched and thirsty throat or hot, flushed face!"

And, as time would soon reveal, I was wrong. But I had my own problems to preoccupy me at that moment, namely ridding myself of the worrisome Master Smeaton, who had become too cloying and clinging for words. I simply could not *abide* to have him touch me or anywhere near me! He demanded too much attention. The poor lad thought that because of what we had done together we were now a loving and devoted couple. I let my son know I did not thank him for passing this nuisance, this *pest,* on to me. I had been a fool to dally with him and regretted the momentary lapse that had led me to betray Remi, but fortunately he knew nothing about it, and I hoped he never would. I have always been very discreet.

Desperate to conceive a son and keep her fragile hold upon her husband and crown, Anne knew she had to lure him back to her bed. But how could she do that when the King had turned against her and now favored a woman who was everything she was not? Indeed, that difference was Jane Seymour's trump card and sole attraction. When an antidote is offered to one in the grip of an agonizing death from the poison they have just ingested, they care very little whether an ugly hag or a fair and beautiful princess holds the lifesaving vial in her hand.

In the end, Anne did what she always did, resorting in her weary desperation to the tried and true. When she wanted to entice King Henry and remind him of her allure, she set herself like a rare and precious gem in the center of a spectacular masque and danced as though her life depended on it. This time it really did.

When she sat with her circle of friends, all of them offering up ideas calculated to rekindle the fickle sovereign's lust, George said, "Why not remind him that women like Jane Seymour can be had by the dozen, like buns for a penny in a London bakeshop, whilst you, my darling Anne, are unique and one of a kind?"

She took his advice. While Henry sat and supped with Mistress Seymour, and Queen Anne pled a headache and kept to her chamber, he suddenly found himself confronted by a dozen dowdy, whey-faced, beak-nosed celestial blue silk–clad Jane Seymours, all dancing dully, bobbing and swaying, in a row before him, meek and pure, with partlets of blue-embroidered white lawn filling in the square necklines of their gowns and their pallid blond heads boxed in by old-fashioned gable hoods.

Anne had paid an artist to surreptitiously render a perfect likeness of Mistress Seymour's face and had then had masks made for the dancers, so they in truth appeared like those penny a dozen buns George had mentioned. They executed the steps adequately enough, rather like a children's dancing class, but without verve or especial skill to music as dull and unimaginative as the dance steps themselves. As the music met its meek conclusion, the row of dancing Janes clustered together, curtsying in a close-packed group, perhaps aiming for the illusion of a bunch of country daisies, gathered together in a bouquet as a gift to give His Majesty.

Then a trumpet blared a sudden, jolting, discordant note that made us all sit up and blink as Anne barged her way through, with shoulders and elbows, sending the simulated Seymours scattering like pins on a bowling green.

She was splendid as a peacock gowned in shimmering green and blue satin and black lace overlaid with those fascinating eyed plumes, sparkling with what must have been thousands of jet, sapphire, peridot, honey golden topaz, emerald, and diamond beads. A mask of jet-beaded black lace tantalizingly veiled her black diamond eyes, and a fan of peacock plumes swayed atop her head as her hair swung free like a cloak of black silk all the way down to her knees.

I had never seen her like this before. So energetic and vital, performing bold moves, feline leaps, sudden spins, and high kicks, swirling her skirts and shaking her feathers to lure her mate. One moment she was like a black panther, a lithe and lethal dangerous black beauty, and a graceful, gliding black swan the next, slowly swirling, gracefully swaying, like an exotic blue and green flower floating on a reflecting pool. But the black lace couldn't hide the desperation in her eyes. I saw the terror underneath every move she made, the fear of what might happen if she failed to woo the King back to her bed and conceive a son.

George and their friends, the ever loyal Weston, Brereton, and Norris, danced around her, masked in shimmering black lace, in brilliant and befeathered costumes of peacock-hued satin, fluttering great fans of peacock plumes. But this time was different—the men danced only as a group, to showcase Anne, like a jewel; none of them came forward to partner her. Every move they, and she, made was calculated to draw the King's eye to Anne, to rouse and kindle his lust into a blazing carnal bonfire that would lead him straight back to her bed long enough to plant his seed within her.

It worked. At least it seemed to. King Henry rose from the table, moving like a man under a spell, pushed his way past the fluttering fans of peacock plumes, seized Anne, and crushed her hard against his chest. He kissed her with a bruising intensity, then swept her up into his powerful arms and carried her out.

We remained in awkward silence at the table staring after them, then a babble of voices began, talking all at once.

Jane Seymour sat next to the King's now empty chair and looked blankly around, not sure what to make of it.

Francis Weston leaned cattily over the back of her chair and hissed, "Take that, you whey-faced bitch, the King obviously prefers a more peppery wench!" then blew a cloud of black pepper into her face, stinging her pale blue eyes and making her sneeze several times.

Only a little time had passed before my husband nudged me and whispered, "Go to her; Anne may have need of you."

Though I could not think why, if things were going as Anne planned, I obeyed and went softly into the anteroom outside her bedchamber.

I was never a one like George's wife to press an avid ear to a door or an eager eye to a keyhole. But this time there was no need for either. I heard voices raised, ripping cloth, and flesh striking flesh. These were fast followed by the unmistakable sounds of passion punctuated by slaps, shouts of "Whore!" and "Bitch!" followed by a woman's sobs and words too muffled by tears to be heard clearly through the thick oaken door.

"YOU CAST A SPELL ON ME!" Henry's outraged bellow came loud and clear through the door, making it seem flimsy and sheer as gossamer, before it crashed open, kicked by the King's broad and mighty foot encased in a gem-encrusted white duckbill velvet slipper.

Panting hard, his face livid pink and sweaty, King Henry stopped and stared hard at me, as though all this were my fault for bringing Anne into the world, yet said nothing, then continued on his stormy way.

Beyond the broken door, I saw Anne crouched, crying on the floor, her face, half-veiled by a curtain of black hair, hidden in her hands, her peacock finery hanging in tatters, trailing from her bare shoulders, on which livid red scratches stood out, puffed and raw, like clumsy red stitches on alabaster satin, her skirt in luxurious shimmery beaded shreds that gave tantalizing glimpses of white limbs marred by bruises and the same ugly, angry red scratches.

Before I could reach her, George was there, moving swiftly past me, to take her in his arms.

Unnoticed, his wife trailed slowly after him, like an annoying younger sibling whose presence is undesirable, and came to stand beside me.

Together, we watched as Anne clung to George, whimpering and trembling, and soaked his shoulder with her tears. They spoke in voices too soft for us to hear. After a few moments, he bent and, putting a hand beneath her knees, gathered her up, tenderly, into his arms. He came toward us. For a moment I thought he was bringing her to us, for us, fellow females, to tend. But when I saw the look in his eyes, I knew he did not even see us. Much quieter than the King had been, he gently shut the door. And we saw no more of them. I would later learn that he laid Anne upon her bed and stayed all night with her, lying across the foot of her bed, leaving only with the dawn. This would later be viewed through the red veil of adultery, a sin that would be used against them in a court of law.

Beside me, Jane quaked, her face red, beaded with sweat, hands clenched tight at her sides, balled into fists that dripped blood from where her nails had bitten through the skin of her palms.

"I HATE YOU, I HATE YOU!" she seethed in a deadly quiet whisper that was somehow more frightening than a bloodcurdling scream as her hands clawed at the sides of her head, tearing at her hair, as though she might somehow manage to dig through her skull and claw out the worm of jealousy burrowing deep into her brain, driving her mad, and causing her such terrible pain.

With a sudden shriek, she wrenched her hands away, taking with them two great hanks of mousy hair, and ran from the room in tears. I would later learn that she ran straight into the arms of Cromwell, to deluge his eager ears with delusional tales borne of jealousy, hate, and a lust for vengeance, to punish one for giving a love, and the other for receiving a love, that could never be hers.

But no matter what vile tales that venomous little snake told that loathsome toad Cromwell, Anne was safe for the time being. King Henry's ardor, though expressed in hateful, hurtful words and violent fury, had left her with child.

I could hardly believe that any good could come of that violent, ugly encounter. But my daughter's womb was filled, and, for now, she was safe and none of her enemies or rivals could touch her.

Once again Anne reigned supreme over the court, the Queen

triumphant. Her enemies must wait and see what fruit her womb bore before they could try to tear her down again.

When word reached us that the woman now known against her will as the Dowager Princess of Wales, but always, in my heart, as the saintly and beloved Queen Catherine, had died, summoning the last vestiges of her strength to put pen to paper and declare that her eyes desired Henry above all else, and sign herself, one last time, "Catherine, Queen of England," I smiled, bittersweet, at her audacity, and in the secret chamber of my heart, where none could venture unless I let them in, I wept and greatly mourned her passing. I would always regret that it had been my own daughter, flesh of my flesh, who had been the instrument of her destruction and caused her so much suffering. Queen Catherine was a good woman, and she deserved so much better than she received at the hands of King Henry, the husband who promised she would never cry again or ever be unhappy after they were married.

Instead of mourning, the court celebrated. A decree went out that all should deck themselves from head to toe in jolly yellow and gather in the Great Hall for dancing and feasting. Even the little Princess Elizabeth was dressed in sunny yellow and brought in to join her jubilant parents. When he saw her, King Henry laughed and swooped her up onto his massive shoulder and carried her around for all his courtiers to admire, drawing all eyes to her vivid Tudor red hair and proudly proclaiming her "the living spit o' me!"

Anne, her belly round as the sun, was at his side, radiant as I had never seen her before when she was breeding. During her last two pregnancies—if they were indeed pregnancies—she had been so gaunt, sickly, rail thin, pale, and frail. But this time was different; she was glowing, and her face and figure were healthy and round.

They seemed the very picture of a perfect happy family. Holbein should have been on hand to paint them. The three of them standing there, smiling, until their teeth and faces must have ached, arrayed in sunny yellow.

Anne's hand, I noticed, rarely strayed from where it rested protectively upon her belly, as though she were patting the son she was sure rested within, secretly urging him to take all her strength he needed to see him through to his triumphal entry into the world where he would someday reign as England's King, speaking softly so that only he could hear, telling him that a golden destiny was waiting for him; all he had to do was *live*.

And Henry beside her, a bloated golden sun of a man, robust and pompous, with a feathered cap encrusted with pearls and golden beads that he kept on to hide his balding pate, thus making it fashionable for men to keep their splendid hats on indoors, and his yellow doublet and surcoat tricked out with a blinding dazzle of gold braid, beads, golden topazes, yellow diamonds, and pearls creamy and gold, and artful puffings and slashings of cloth-of-gold designed to distract the beholder's eye from his ever-expanding girth, only slightly restrained by the boiled leather stays he now wore beneath his gaudy garb, which poor Henry Norris had the unenviable task of lacing him into each morning. Even his mammoth codpiece was jeweled and studded with honey topazes and pearls.

Elizabeth sat, perched regally upon his broad shoulder as though she were Queen of the World and this was her throne, wearing the jolly yellow gown Anne had herself lovingly embroidered with a flight of golden butterflies.

Laughing, Henry tore off her little cap and tossed it high into the air, and called for everyone to look at his daughter's fiery Tudor red hair.

But it wasn't destined to last. A moment came when the King discreetly disappeared. Around the same time, it was noticed that Mistress Seymour was also absent.

When Anne went in search of her husband, she found him with Jane Seymour's skirts spread like the petals of an upside-down buttercup over his lap, giggling as he jiggled her up and down—"Riding the Maypole," as he called it—while he twirled the yellow ribbons on her bodice around his fingers and tugged them gently to reveal her milk pale breasts. "Even her nipples are colorless!" Anne would later declare most scornfully.

Never one to hold back, Anne strode forward and grabbed hold of the golden chain around Mistress Seymour's neck and snatched "that hussy" from Henry's lap, sending her sprawling flat on the floor with her skirts flying up over her shame-flushed face, leaving her floundering on the floor with her thighs splayed wide and her most intimate parts on display.

When Anne looked down at the broken chain she was holding, she saw her husband's fat and florid face dangling from it, ringed in diamonds.

"Well, well, Mistress Seymour, I see your virtue is not beyond price, after all," she said tartly, parroting the Seymour slut's false modesty as she twirled the pendant around, swinging it in swift circles on its broken chain. "Apparently you two have agreed upon a price—bad art and little diamonds."

Henry tried to make excuses, to keep Anne calm and the child within her safe, but Anne would have none of it. She cursed the King as she never had before and lashed him with his own likeness, so that he had to guard his face against being cut by the paltry diamonds he had given his mousy little whore.

Suddenly she rounded on the whimpering girl again. Jane Seymour was then trying to crawl quietly away. With one swift move, Anne kicked her and sent her sprawling flat on her face, "banging her big beaky Seymour nose on the floor," she later boasted.

When Henry tried again to pacify her, deftly snatching the dangling pendant from her hand in a moment of distraction, then reaching out his arms, to embrace her, calling her sweetheart, swearing that Mistress Seymour meant *nothing* to him, blaming it all on a jousting accident he had suffered recently, in which he had lain stunned for some two hours and had been taken briefly for dead. The whole experience, he averred, had left him shaken and eager to grasp at life, to live and love, and since Anne's condition precluded them from engaging in any amorous consort, he had gathered up the first willing rose that presented herself.

Anne snorted her disbelief, rolled her eyes, and spun on her heel, pausing only long enough on her way out to deal Jane Seymour's lemon yellow–clad backside another swift kick.

The next morning Anne found in her sewing basket a crudely bound booklet, of the sort that are sold on the streets of London, no doubt put there by Mistress Seymour or one of her friends. It was a so-called "Book of Prophecy."

Curious, she perused its pages until she came to an image of King Henry, standing in his favorite and familiar pose, hands on hips, with his feet planted wide apart, glowering out at the world as if he were its master and none but a fool would dare cross him. Beside him stood a woman dressed in elegant black. She was headless. She wore a rope of pearls with a *B* suspended from it. It was Anne's favorite necklace; George had given her that pendant, and she was seldom seen without it. Even as she sat there, eyes wide with horror, staring at that crude and vulgar drawing, her fingers reached up to fiddle nervously with the big golden *B* resting in the hollow of her throat, the three large creamy teardrop pearls dangling from it clacking against her fingernails. A head that was clearly Anne's lay in a pool of blood at the King's feet, her long black hair sopping up the blood.

Abruptly, Anne stood up. Nervously, she began to pace restlessly about the room, back and forth, trying to laugh it off.

"Oh, Mother, it is all nonsense! The fools are only trying to frighten me! And with this!" She snorted and flung the book down, laughing when I quickly snatched it up and threw it into the fire. But her laughter rang false. Then all of a sudden she gave an anguished cry and bent double, hugging her stomach tight, just before she fell at my feet in a dead faint, blood soaking through her plum satin skirt to stain the floor.

She lost the son who would have saved her. The same January morning as Catherine of Aragon was laid beneath marble for her eternal slumber, a little blue boy gushed out from between Anne's legs on a wave of crimson blood. He would never draw a single breath. The cord was wrapped tightly around his little neck like a hangman's noose. That was the end of it. There would be no more chances for Anne. She was finished.

After we had put her in a fresh shift and braided her hair into neat, smooth ebony plaits that hung down upon either side of her pale, tear-stained face, Henry barged in, ignoring Dr. Butts and the midwife, who both counseled gentleness and quiet. Anne wept and promised him a son next time. She had come *so* close only to fail at the very last!

King Henry went straight to the bed and grasped one of those long black braids and twisted it savagely around his fist to pull Anne's head up even as he bent down to her, his icy blue eyes boring hard as nails into her dark ones.

"There will not be a next time," he informed her, giving her braid another cruel twist. "You will get no more boys by me!" Then, abruptly, contemptuously, he released her hair and straightened. "I will speak to you when you are up," he said, then turned his back on her and slammed out, leaving Anne weeping inconsolably amongst the fat, feather-stuffed pillows until she fell back into the black bliss of oblivion and slept, letting it swallow her, until she was strong enough to get up and face the world again.

As he stormed past me, standing huddled with Anne's other attendants, I heard the King declare that if he had it all to do over again, by heaven, he too would have "none of Nan Bullen!"

"I should have listened to my people; no monarch should ever stop his ears to the voice of his people!" he fumed. "See what I have come to by ignoring them? In this case, the subjects had more sense than their sovereign!"

Anne kept to her chamber for several weeks. George would come to her; he would sit on her bed for hours, and she would lay her head on his lap and let him hold her as the tears seeped from her eyes to soak his silk hose. There was no need for words between them. They sat in silence while George stroked her thin, sob-shaking shoulders and her hair, which he sometimes combed the tangles from and braided. When he came, he always brought Mark Smeaton with him. The smitten lute player would sit upon a padded stool in the corner or cross-legged on a plump plum velvet cushion on the floor at the foot of Anne's bed, gazing with love-struck eyes at the grieving woman in George's arms, and endeavor with his music to calm the fear that raged like a caged tigress inside her.

❧ 15 ❧

It had been a slow rise, but a swift fall. After it was all over, when I would sit and weep and ponder and tally it all up, I would discover that Anne's reign as England's queen had lasted for only one thousand days.

The court began to distance itself from Anne. She now knew just how few friends she really had and how many enemies. The latter far outnumbered the former. So many flocked to surround Mistress Seymour, to be on the all-important winning side, to fawn over and flatter her, and that little hen soon became queen of the barnyard with a big, brawny, Tudor red rooster strutting along proudly beside her, unable to take his eyes, or keep his hands, off her.

A day came when my husband discreetly drew me aside and "suggested" that I follow Mistress Seymour's example instead of Anne's when it came to matters of dressing, that I forsake the French styles my daughter favored, the bold or subdued jewel-hued shades, and opt for the more modest and respectable English fashions and drab and muted shades her rival clearly preferred, replete with yokes of plain white or delicately embroidered lawn to fill in what he now regarded as my immodestly low bodices. In those days you could tell where a lady's loyalties lay by her head-dress—the crescent shaped French hood Anne favored or the old-fashioned, cumbersome, and boxy gable hood that Queen Catherine had always preferred and Jane Seymour had never forsaken.

Thomas also made a point of waylaying George on his way into Anne's chamber and sternly advising him to distance himself from his sister and to do so at once, *"instantly and openly,"* insisting that this was the only way George could hope to save himself from certain disgrace.

George laughed in his face and advised him "with all due respect," words spoken in a withering tone that implied his father was due no respect at all, that he would have better luck trying to persuade the sun to forsake the sky. "I'm not like you," he added. "I know how to be true; winning isn't *always* everything."

"Remember, I warned you," Thomas called after him and made a motion suggesting he washed his hands of him.

When Anne at last emerged from her chamber, she put on a brave face and tried to pretend she didn't care.

"It's not my heart that hurts," she declared, "only my damnable pride!"

But it was not easy for her to see herself supplanted by a boring little nobody, "that swooning, calf-eyed Seymour slut!" who had by some astounding miracle enchanted the royal bull.

She spent extravagantly, ordering numerous beautiful and bewitching gowns, all calculated to kindle a man's lust; exotic, heady perfumes; rare and costly gems; and won and lost fortunes at the gambling tables, recklessly risking all on the turn of a single card or the black-spotted ivory dice. She laughed more and louder than ever before, and danced, and drank, and flirted with a new abandon. It was as though she thought that if she could only convince everyone else that she didn't care, it would become the truth. Every night she threw the doors of her chambers open wide to welcome in any who wished to come in and make merry, until, exhausted, she fell into bed with the dawn and slept through mass, leaving her place vacant, for Mistress Seymour to fill, beside Henry in the royal chapel.

These wild nights of dancing and gambling, known about the court as "pastime in the Queen's chamber," soon became notorious. The respectable stayed away in droves. And each night the number of those who dared show their faces in Queen Anne's apartments dwindled until a night came when there was only Anne, George, Henry Norris, Francis Weston, William Brereton, Thomas Wyatt, his sister Meg, and a friend of his, Sir Richard Page, a kinswoman of ours, Madge Shelton, George's vile viper Jane, and me, with musicians, including Mark Smeaton, to play for us, and a couple of servants to pour the wine. Unbeknownst to Anne, or indeed to any of us, that night one of this downhearted and shrunken-numbered company would betray her.

Anne was all in white, a gown so thickly encrusted with pearls it seemed to be made of them, woven together thickly with shimmering silver threads, with thick white fur cuffs belling gracefully over her hands.

Seeing her, a bittersweet smile tugged at my lips. I remembered her as a little girl, the ugly duckling standing back, hands clasped behind her, to hide the deformed finger she was so ashamed of, morosely watching as her beautiful golden girl sister sat at my dressing table and reddened her cheeks and lips with my rouge pot and drew out long ropes of pearls from my jewel coffer and wrapped them around her neck, waist, and wrists. Finally Anne spoke up, boasting that when she was a grown woman she would have a gown made entirely of pearls.

Of course, we all laughed at her—Mary; the nursemaids; witchy old Lady Margaret; Matilda, my incompetent fool of a maid; and, of course, me, her own mother—all except George.

"But, Anne, you're going to be a nun," Mary said with a quizzical frown as she thrust jeweled combs into her hair and daubed messy streaks of gold paint onto her eyelids. "What need would a nun have for pearls? Besides, I don't think things like pearls are allowed in convents. Are they, Mother?" She turned to me with a questioning glance.

Anne stamped her foot and tossed her black head, slinging her long hair like a whip, while she tried vainly to hold back the furious tears that seeped from her eyes.

"Just you wait!" she cried, and in a flurry of spring green-and-white-flowered damask skirts, fled from our mocking laughter.

"A gown made of pearls!" Lady Margaret cackled. "Who ever

heard of such a thing? Someone has been filling this child's pate full of nonsense!"

I boggled at that pronouncement and bit my tongue to keep myself from blurting out, "If anyone has, it's you, you old witch!"

She was the one who was always wanting to torture the children with her bizarre curatives, like dosing them for worms when they squirmed in the pews at church when the sermons droned on overlong, and telling them tales of goblins, banshees, and ghosts, water sprites, fairies, giants, ogres, mermaids, demons, hellhounds, phantom coaches, screaming skulls, and pacts with the Devil.

"Don't you *dare* laugh!" George roared, stamping his foot down so hard his nurse would later report he bruised it and would limp a little for a few days afterward. "If Anne says she'll have a gown made of pearls, she'll have it! I *know* she will!" Then he ran after her.

It seemed, at long last, Anne had attained her wish.

I marveled at the weight of that magnificent dress. Always slender, Anne had lost much flesh since her last pregnancy, and I wondered that she could bear the weight of that sumptuous gown; it was like no other I had ever seen at court, but it was too late to have any effect upon King Henry. He was beyond being lured by dresses and dances and intoxicating perfumes and incense now.

Ropes of pearls coiled around her neck, and her favorite golden *B* pendant rested in the hollow of her throat, and her hair hung down, virgin free as always beneath her pearl-encrusted French hood, flouting the convention that decreed a married woman should put up her hair and save that sight for her husband in the privacy of their bedchamber.

She was very melancholy. Her nerves clearly frayed and her eyes dark-circled and full of fear. She looked as though she hadn't slept at all in many a night. Over our wine cups, she related how she had been walking in the garden with Elizabeth that afternoon, chasing butterflies and gathering flowers, teaching her beloved little girl snippets of French, when she had spied the King looking from a window above.

"Glowering down on us like a thundercloud." She shivered and frowned. She had tried to make him smile by lifting Elizabeth up to wave at him and call, *"Bonjour, Papa!"*

"But he slammed the window shut, so hard a pane of glass cracked, and turned his back on us."

As she spoke those words she began to shiver. "I felt as though someone had just walked over my grave."

She shuddered uncontrollably and hugged herself as though she were suddenly icy cold, rubbing her arms through the pearls as though she were trying desperately to warm herself. I don't think I ever saw so much fear on a human face before. Her lips trembled, and she looked close to tears. Like someone standing on the edge of a cliff, pondering whether to take that fatal leap, trying to decide if things are *really* as bleak and hopeless as they seem, wondering if they can hold on, survive one more dark night, and if the dawn will bring fresh hope along with the new light.

I trembled too. I could see Anne so clearly in my mind's eye, standing, looking down, poised on the brink. I was half afraid to look at her. I was so afraid to see her fall in truth, as she seemed to do nightly in my dreams.

Anne leaned her head wearily against the wall, her usually diamond-bright eyes glazed by tears and looking so very tired.

"My soul is overwhelmed with sorrow to the point of death." She sighed.

George, his eyes dark-circled, as though sleep had been eluding him also, set aside his wine cup and stood up.

Despite his obvious fatigue, I smiled, with a mother's, and a vain woman's, pride at how handsome he looked in his black velvet doublet, so elegantly cut, with blackwork embroidery standing out starkly elegant against the snowy white lawn of his shirt collar and cuffs, and his long legs sheathed in black silk and shod in black velvet.

Gently, he took the cup from Anne's hand and, without bothering to look, trusting that it would be taken, passed it into the nearest hand.

"Come," he said, "dance with me."

Mutely, Anne nodded. She took his hand, stood, and let him lead her out, slowly, to the patch of floor that had been cleared for dancing, with the floor-length windows behind them thrown open wide to welcome in the light of the full moon and any hint of an evening breeze.

Together, brother and sister stood alone, leaning within the circle of each other's arms, their faces showing a shared sorrow so deep I feared they would sink and drown in it.

There were no other dancers. So few were our numbers now, and so heavy our spirits, no one felt like dancing. The musicians played idly in the background, without spirit, only to fill the silence that threatened to become oppressive and to have something to do with their hands. Tonight, the instruments they held were like toys they had lost all interest in.

"Play our song," George said, snapping his fingers sharply as though he were giving a command to a dog, without even bothering to look at Smeaton. If he had, he would have seen the mixture of longing and resentment that filled the eyes of his discarded plaything. But George only had eyes for Anne.

And then it began, a melody that was like *nothing* I had ever heard before. They must have written it over the course of all those sleepless nights. It gripped the heart with fear yet gave it an encouraging pat all at the same time. It was haunting, bleak, moody, melancholy, yet so, so sublime. It was *magnificent!* A *true* masterpiece! If any of the songs Anne and George wrote together survive down through the centuries, this should be the one. It captured so perfectly their shared spirit of proud defiance in the face of looming disaster. This was a song that thumbed its nose at desperation, and sneered and shook its fist in the face of fear. It was made for them to dance to...while they still had the chance. Boldly, they faced that uncanny music and danced as they never had before. It was as though they both knew that this was the last time they would ever dance together.

Slowly, arms gracefully undulating, thrust to the side, first to the left and then to the right, Anne's heavy pearl-encrusted, fur-cuffed sleeves hanging gracefully from her thin arms, they swayed, face-to-face, moving as one. Slowly, they spun, circling one another, her little diamond-buckled silver slippers flashing as they parted, then turned and faced one another again and repeated that entranced, mesmerizing sway that reminded me of a snake in the power of its charmer I had once seen at a cherry fair, many years ago, in my wanton youth.

I sat and watched, entranced by the sinuous, willowy sway of their two bodies in motion, matching step for perfect step while across the room Mark Smeaton devoured them both with his eyes as he strummed his lute over those elegant yet eerily melancholy strains, as though he were unable to decide which of them he desired most—Anne or George, the one he dreamed of having and the one he had already had and been spurned and discarded by.

Beside me, George's horrid wife trembled and blazed with the fierce green fire of jealous hate, sick with a fever that would burn what little was left of her reason right out of her brain. No sane person could ever have done what she was about to do. She had always been unstable, but tonight she too was teetering on the brink, standing on the edge of a precipice from which there was no turning back.

Holding hands at arm's length, Anne and George slowly circled the floor. He would draw her close, clutching her hands against his chest, and, just for a moment, their brows would touch, and they stood close enough to share breath, and then she would pull away, her hands still in his, as they continued circling the floor. Each movement was so fluid and graceful, so perfectly matched, it was hard to believe they had not practiced this, like a routine for a masque, dozens of times, striving for perfection. Yet this was the first time they had ever danced to that haunting melody. It would also be the last. There would be no time to perfect what was already perfect. And I know now, in their hearts, they knew it. Everything was about to end.

They moved apart. Side by side, they glided, dipped, and swayed across the floor. Arms about each other's waists, they circled the floor, executing a flawless series of little leaps and steps as the music swelled, nimble feet crossing in the air, then landing deftly and moving seamlessly into the next series of steps. Faster and faster they went, moving together in a graceful blur. I worried that Anne's heavy, hanging sleeves would catch George in the face; they were weighty enough to deliver a powerful, stunning slap that would leave him staggering and seeing stars, but that was one fear of mine at least that was never realized. And indeed I should have known better; George had enough practice dancing with Anne to know how to expertly avoid those famous sleeves whether they were diaphanous, airy and light, or weighed down with a fortune in precious pearls and white fur.

The men sitting around me sat up straight, as though in an abrupt awakening. They forgot their wine cups and began to clap their hands in time to the music as though they too had fallen under its spell.

Anne and George swayed together, side by side, thrusting out their hands, as though to block or ward off a blow or push an invisible foe away—death, I now know. With this dance they were acting out their struggle against fate, a tug of war between hope and despair, alternately denying and accepting that they had no choice in the end, that this was the way it had to be; whether they fought tooth and nail or submitted gracefully, it wouldn't change how the story would end—their destiny was preordained and about to play out its final act on the stage of life for all the world to see.

Again and again, they came together, then separated, spinning away from each other and then returning, unable to bear to let go, until a moment came, as the music swelled and grew even faster, more frantic, and desperate, when Anne stayed in George's arms, and they circled together, round and round, faster and faster, spinning in a blurring swirl of sleeves and pearls, midnight black, lustrous white, and shimmering silver. Faster and faster, in perfect step, they swirled and spun, leapt, swayed, and dipped, in each other's arms, side by side, or standing face-to-face. Until, as the music reached its defiant crescendo—one that spoke of hope in the face of hopelessness, defiance in defeat, of thumbing one's nose at fate—they held each other close and made the greatest leap of all, like one of faith, a leap that, although magnificent, chilled my heart, for it was as though each was saying to the other, "If you are going to jump off this cliff, I am going with you." I shivered, and instinctively I crossed myself and whispered a silent prayer. I felt as though I had just watched my two children leap to their deaths.

As one, clasped tight in each other's arms, they spun out onto the moon-silvered white marble terrace, Anne's pearl-heavy skirts wrapping around George's long, slender black silk–clad legs. There they stopped, frozen forever in my memory, though in truth it only lasted a moment, facing one another, lips parted, breasts heaving, catching their breath, as Anne's sleeves and skirts settled and stilled, and George took a kerchief from his doublet and wiped the sweat from his brow.

Deaf to the applause and the praise and compliments called out by their friends, George slipped his arm tenderly around Anne's waist and she laid her head gratefully upon his shoulder and put her arm around him, and they walked out into the garden, where the fountains plashed and white roses glowed like ghosts gently billowing in the silvery moonlight.

Abruptly, spilling red wine, like blood, all over her hands and pale blue gown, George's wife leapt up.

"I have to go!" she cried and departed quickly before anyone could cock an inquiring brow or question her. The little Judas, I now know, was scurrying off, straight to Cromwell, to collect her thirty pieces of silver.

Yawning, Tom Wyatt, his sister Meg, Richard Page, and Madge Shelton, as well as the musicians and servants, said their good nights and went to their beds. But Weston, Norris, and Brereton lingered. They tossed their velvet cloaks over their shoulders and gathered up the wine bottles and their gilded cups and followed Anne and George out into the garden and arranged themselves in a circle upon the grass. Smeaton lagged behind, cradling his lute and staring longingly after Anne and George, but when he started to follow the others out into the garden, I stopped him with the curt and cold pronouncement, *"You may go, Master Smeaton!"* and he had no choice but to obey, as I was the Queen's mother and a noblewoman high above him.

Before the cock crowed he would be in the custody of Cromwell, singing the desperate song that only caged birds do, hoping to save his life. The poor fool!

I had been troubled lately by a persistent cough that sometimes brought up a trickle of blood or two. I should have stayed inside. Yet I too went out into the garden, to sit upon a bench on the terrace with my shawl draped, but loosely, over my shoulders so that it did little to defend me against the night's dampness and chill.

The circle of friends sat and drank until, yawning and heavy-eyed, they wrapped themselves in their cloaks and lay down amongst the flowers.

"The spirit is willing, but the flesh is weak," Francis Weston said, his words, punctuated by a yawn, only half a jest, amongst agreeing murmurs, before they fell asleep.

Anne and George remained awake. Standing amongst dew-dampened white flowers, they watched the sun rise, leaning in each other's arms, with Anne's head pillowed on George's shoulder, and his resting against hers, their black hair mingling, weaving together in such a way that anyone looking at them would be unable to tell where one ended and the other began.

When the sun was fully in the sky and the palace behind them bustling with life, servants coming in with inquiries about breakfast and whether Anne would like a bath, which I took the liberty of shielding her from and shooing them out, Anne and George turned and faced one another. They stood and stared for a long time into each other's eyes. He cupped her face in his hands and bent and gently kissed her lips.

Jane was back, having come in with the servants; she stood behind me, looking over my shoulder. She saw them kiss. But I, the mother who gave birth to them, can swear, in spite of what that lying little snake would tell Cromwell, there was *nothing* carnal in that kiss. They did not touch and mingle tongues as would be claimed in a court of law where they soon would both be fighting for their lives and to clear their vilely slandered names.

As Jane smoldered behind me, a quaking volcano of rage so soon to erupt, seething, hissing through tightly clenched teeth, "You'll be sorry; soon you'll *all* be sorry!" Anne flung her arms around George's neck, and for a long time they clung together, desperate and shaking, as though neither could bear to let the other go.

At last, they stepped apart. With tears streaming down her face and lips trembling, Anne caught his hand, desperately, clutching it between both of hers, against her heart, as though she could not bear to let him go. Gently, George took one of her hands in his and drew her arm straight out.

"To life's last faint ember," he said as he bowed gallantly over her trembling hand and pressed his lips reverently against its flesh as though there were nothing in this world more precious to him.

Anne nodded. Seemingly too overcome to speak. She shut her eyes and swallowed hard.

"Good-bye—*no!*" She hastily amended as a frown creased George's brow. "We would *never* say good-bye! Adieu, Sir Loyal Heart."

"Adieu, Lady Perseverance." George smiled through his own tears. "Adieu," he whispered and swiftly kissed her hand again before he tore himself from her side.

Halfway to the terrace, he turned, pausing where their friends still slept, snoring, cocooned in their velvet cloaks, amidst a litter of golden goblets and wine bottles cradled by the dew-damp grass and May flowers. He plucked a white flower and, with a cocky smile, stuck it in his black hair, behind his ear, and picked up a wine bottle that was still half full and drank from it. How typical of George, to try to introduce a note of levity into the saddest song.

"I am with you always. . . ." he called back to Anne.

She nodded, smiling through her tears, and finished with him, "until the end of time."

After George had gone, Anne rushed past me, in a blur of clacking white pearls, shimmering silver threads, and white fur, with her black hair flying out behind her like the tail of a comet, and ran into her room and slammed the door.

I never saw either of my children again.

I went to my room. I was of a sudden very hot and wanted to bathe my face with cooling water and strip off my velvet gown and lie down in my shift for a little while. My head ached abominably and felt heavy as stone, though I had not drunk much wine at all. I felt my face and found it afire with fever. My throat also burned; every swallow pained me, and I wanted to ask Marie to make me a tonic of lemon juice and honey to ease it, but I lacked the strength even to pull the tasseled silk rope beside my bed to summon her.

I will lie down, just for an hour or so, mayhap two, I said to myself. *Then I will rise and go to Anne and give her what comfort I can.*

But it was not to be.

❧ 16 ❧

When I next opened my eyes I was in my own bed at Hever, stripped down to a sweat-sodden shift that I had worn for many days with my hair an oily, sweaty, matted mess rats might have nested in and showing more gray than ever before.

"My lady, you mustn't!" Marie pleaded as she tried to hold me back as I struggled to sit up and floundered amidst the tangle of bedsheets.

Slapping my maid's hands away, I bolted from my bed. Without sparing a care for dignity or modesty, I ran in my bare feet and dirty, stinking shift with my ratty-nest hair down the corridor to my husband's chamber.

I found him standing before his silver mirror, attended by his valet and tailor, as he tried on a new bloodred velvet robe edged in ermine.

"Elizabeth!" he rebuked me sharply. "You should be in bed. Andrew!" he barked at his valet. "Fetch a robe to cover my lady-wife. She forgets herself; the fever has clearly addled her senses."

I ignored the rat gray—what a fitting color given who it belonged to and the circumstances!—velvet dressing gown Andrew draped over my shoulders and approached my husband. I put out a trembling hand to touch his red robe.

"What are you doing, Thomas?" I asked. "What occasion is this for?"

"The trial," he answered crisply. "I am to sit upon the jury."

He went on to explain that Anne and George, along with several of their friends—Henry Norris, William Brereton, Francis Weston, Thomas Wyatt, and Richard Page—were being held as prisoners in the Tower of London. Also imprisoned with them, albeit in worse quarters on account of his common birth, was the lute player, Mark Smeaton, who, though he had given evidence against the others, was himself accused alongside them of having carnally known Queen Anne. The charges were high treason, adultery, and incest. All these men were accused of having carnally known Anne, and the paternity of her children, Princess Elizabeth as well as the babes who had died, was now suspect and under legal scrutiny.

"And you, my husband, you would do this for the King?" I asked even though I already knew the answer. That he was being fitted for new robes made it rather obvious. I sincerely doubted that Thomas, even if he viewed this as a loathsome and unwelcome responsibility he would rather avoid, had the courage to feign illness at the last instant.

"Yes," he answered without hesitation, with an expression in his eyes that conveyed to me that he thought this the most ridiculous of questions, "of course I would."

He did not even have the grace to pretend it would be a sacrifice that cost him dear, that the lives of Anne and George mattered to him at all.

I stood there reeling. It was as though I was seeing Thomas Boleyn, the *real* Thomas Bullen, for the very first time. "Use and then lose" sums up nicely his philosophy regarding people, including his own children. His affection for them lasted only as long as their usefulness, and the profits and glory they could bring him or help him, through their influence, to acquire. Now Anne and George were finished; they could be of no further use to him, and nothing could be gained by speaking out in their defense and declaring their innocence. They were already as good as dead in their father's eyes, and he clearly had no qualms about being the one to bang the last nail into their coffin.

I remember nothing more. It was then that the floor seemed to come up and strike a mighty felling blow to my face. But it didn't matter. No stone floor could ever, I discovered, be as hard as my husband's heart.

When I next regained consciousness, my children were already dead, unbeknownst to me, lying headless in the Tower's crypt, condemned by their own father, as a jury man in robes the color of blood, as "this vile, incestuous pair," who deserved death for the crimes they had committed against the King's person and majesty.

My husband was at Hampton Court preparing for a wedding. He had given it out that I was "diseased with a bloody cough, which grieves her sore," to explain my absence, lamenting on my behalf to Mistress Seymour that it grieved me just as sorely as my mortal illness did that I could not be there to walk behind her on her wedding day. But Thomas knew that if I had been there, walking behind her in a festive new gown—not mourning!—I most assuredly would have kicked her. So it was far better for everyone that I keep to my sickbed and spare my husband any embarrassment and the next Queen of England a sore rump.

And vile Jane—that poisonous viper, the daughter-in-law I now disowned, who had accused Anne of luring George to her bed with her tongue in his mouth, causing George to cry out, "Upon the word of this one woman you are prepared to believe this great evil of me!"—had taken pride of place amongst the soon-to-be Queen Jane's ladies of the bedchamber. It would be she, instead of I, who would don a new gown and smilingly carry Mistress Seymour's ermine-trimmed train upon her wedding day.

But her prize did not come without a price. There is some justice in this world after all. A widow clad in full woebegone black, a hypocrite mourning the death she caused, Jane was destined to lead a friendless existence. There would be no wooer to relieve her widowhood; George's blood was on her hands, and no one would ever forget it. She might as well have been wearing red gloves; that was what everyone saw when they looked at her—a woman with bloodstained hands that could never be washed clean. Given the wild distortions and outright lies she had uttered against George and Anne, all the other ladies who likewise served the new queen shied away from her, fearing a day might come when thoughtlessly spoken words or careless actions might be embroidered upon and used against them for some evil, or even fatal, purpose. Whenever she would approach a gossipy gaggle they would instantly fall silent and break apart, making it clear that she was persona non grata.

They died bravely. Everyone—our chaplain; my physician; the apothecary; the neighbors who came to call bearing gifts, condolences, and remedies for my cough; the servants; Lady Margaret; and even that Judas Jane, who had braved the crowds and borne witness to all the executions, relishing in particular each one of Anne's last moments—said that as though they expected it to bring me comfort. They died bravely. But they died. They *died!* George, Weston, Brereton, Norris, and Smeaton on May 17, 1536, and Anne two days later, on the nineteenth. While my prideful streak applauded them for their bold, gracious, and elegant exits, dignified to the very end, my mother's heart wept tears of blood and stinging salt. That they had died bravely was really no consolation at all. Whether cowardly or courageous upon the scaffold, it was bound to end the same way—they died.

This flood of maternal grief was so great it took me completely by surprise. I had lost so many children before; I didn't expect to feel so much. Yet Anne and George, and Mary too, were different; these three had lived long enough to grow up and become people, individuals I could know and see as *real* human beings, unique in all their foibles and flaws, virtues and vices, passionate in their desires, needs, and convictions, their joys and sorrows, not dead little blue babies I never knew. I knew them all well enough to like, admire, or at least understand, and even love them, and, most assuredly, grieve their loss like no other lives that had ever touched my own. I brought them into the world; I should not have had to watch them leave it. I was old with rotting lungs; they were young, vital and vibrant—I should have been the one to go first.

Anne accepted death with a goodly grace. Who taught my daughter how to do that? Who taught her how to die, and how to live, so bravely, so differently and defiantly? To dance to her own music instead of the same old staid rhythm everyone else did. Certainly not I. What did I, her own mother, ever teach her except to spend her life in proud defiance trying to prove to the world that she was indeed worthy of love, admiration, and respect, that there is more to beauty than golden hair, a porcelain and roses complexion, and buxom, voluptuous curves. The things that I taught her were not very good lessons for a mother to teach her daughter.

I marvel now that I did not destroy Anne in a completely different way. What might her life have been if she had not been somehow imbued with such a proud, fighting spirit? What if she had wilted instead of growing strong and defiant in the face of our disdain? What if she had returned from France quiet and dowdy and never learned to make the most of what she had and let her inner beauty shine in a way that blinded all to her flaws? Would she still be alive today? She would never have danced with kings, set fashions, driven a monarch nigh mad with lust, become Queen of England, and given birth to Elizabeth; the world I had known when Catherine was queen would still be the same, but Anne would, God willing, still be alive. But—I have to ask—would the life that she would have as that meek, ugly, and drab creature, perhaps confined to rot behind convent walls, a life akin to being buried alive, even be worth living? Was the life she had actually lived worth the sacrifice, worth dying for when it all fell apart?

When the verdict condemning Anne "to be burned or beheaded at the King's Pleasure," was read out in court by her own uncle, with her father sitting there straight-faced, she accepted it like a queen, gracious and elegant, never letting her composure slip or crack.

"Gentlemen"—she turned to address the jury, looking each and every man, including her own relatives, boldly in the eye—"I think you know well the reason why you have condemned me is something other than the evidence presented here today. But you must follow not your own conscience, but the King's. My only sin against His Majesty has been my jealousy and lack of humility toward him, which his goodness to me merited. I confess I have had jealous fancies and suspicions of him, which I had neither wisdom nor discretion enough to conceal. But God knows, and is my witness, that I have not sinned against him in any other way. Think not that I say this in the hope to save my life. God hath taught me how to die, and He will give me strength. As for my brother, and the other men unjustly condemned, I would willingly die many deaths to save them, but, since it is the King's Pleasure, I shall accompany them into death, with this assurance, that I shall lead an endless life of peace with them at the foot of the throne of Our Lord."

I laughed through my tears when I heard that Anne had left the Lieutenant of the Tower with a message for the King that he was too timid and terrified to deliver.

"Master Kingston," she had said graciously and fearlessly, raising her voice so it would be sure to carry and reach the ears of the crowd standing clustered avidly around the scaffold she was even then in the act of mounting, "please commend me to His Majesty, and tell him that he has ever been constant in advancing me; from a private gentlewoman he made me a queen, and now that he has no greater honor to bestow upon me, he gives my innocent head the crown of a martyr."

Poor Master Kingston! I could well imagine him quaking in his boots at those words he had been entrusted with. Sorry to break a solemn promise to a dying woman, yet too afraid for his own head to dare deliver the message. The King was certain not to receive it graciously. Yet I, if I had been there, if she had trusted this final message to the mother who had so many times failed and disappointed and even scorned her, I would have taken it to him. When you've already lost everything that matters, sometimes you lose your fears too; I was no longer afraid of the King. And what was left of his favor I would, unlike my desperately clinging husband, gladly lose.

I could see her standing there, midway up the thirteen steps, posed to show herself to best advantage, before she strode boldly up the last few steps, onto the stage of the scaffold itself for the final act of her life. She wore a cloak of regal ermine, which she let fall with a contemptuous, disdainful shrug onto the straw that would soon be soaked through with her blood, as though she was happy to be rid of this royal regalia. As she deftly delivered her innocuously worded but slyly sardonic speech, every eye drank in the sight of her elegant black velvet gown and underskirt of bloodred damask.

As she spoke both her full skirt and hanging sleeves moved with a graceful, bell-like sway and her fingers toyed nervously with her pearls and the golden *B* pendant George had given her so long ago when she was a frightened little girl about to set sail for Brussels, afraid that she was doomed to always be an ugly duckling, to dwell forever in the shadow of her golden-haired sister's radiant beauty, and mayhap even end by spending all the rest of her days cloistered in a convent as a nun, black-robed and bald-pated beneath her stark white wimple. It was her talisman and her way of keeping George with her always, even when they were physically apart. I could imagine her nervously fingering that golden *B* and thinking of him; I could even hear the three white teardrop pearls that hung beneath clacking against her fingernails. I remembered then the very last words they had spoken to each other in the garden at Greenwich Palace—*I am with you always, until the end of time.* And time for Anne was about to end.

Upon her head, she wore a jaunty black velvet cap sporting a rakish spray of black and white feathers held in place by a diamond horseshoe—of all things, of all the talismans Anne might have chosen to don on the day of her death, she chose this, making certain the *U* was upturned to hold her luck and keep it from spilling out. Beneath the soft round brim of her chic little hat, her abundant black hair was tightly braided and pinned so as not to impede "the Sword of Calais," as the headsman was called. Some joked that this was the last Valentine King Henry would ever give my daughter; in remembrance of the great love he had once borne her, he had summoned a swordsman from France to take her head, instead of subjecting her delicate swanlike neck to the sturdy but sometimes blunt and brutal ax of a British executioner. The sword was swift and surer, while the ax sometimes required repeated blows to get through all the bones and gristle. Unless the ax was sharp and the executioner skilled, it was not a pleasant way to die.

"Good Christian people," she said, "I am come hither to die according to the Law, and therefore I will speak nothing against it and accuse no man. I pray God to save the King and send him long to reign over you, for a kinder or more merciful prince there was never, and he was ever a good and gentle sovereign lord to me. . . ."

It was Anne's way of striking one last blow at Henry. Even though she left a defenseless daughter behind whom she had every cause to fear for, Anne unbridled her tongue and lashed the King with it one last time, letting his subjects see just what sort of a man Henry Tudor truly was. He was so kind and merciful, gentle and good, that he was sending his wife to the scaffold to make way for another.

Regardless of how the people felt about her displacing their "good Queen Catherine, the one true queen," they all agreed the travails and tragic outcomes of childbirth are not just grounds for taking a woman's life. But divorce is messier than death, and the King wanted a change; he wanted Jane Seymour—that was what it was all about. King Henry wasn't fooling anyone. And by saying that she accused no man, Anne was hinting, quite brazenly, that there *was* a man lurking in the background who might be accused of her murder and with just grounds.

King Henry had taken full and most cruel advantage of the verdict delivered against Anne and her accused paramours "to be burned or beheaded at the King's Pleasure," and hinted that he was leaning toward the stake; *however*, Anne *might* change his mind and spare herself and the friends and brother she held so dear this hellish and gruesome fate by signing a document attesting to the fact that their marriage was a sham, invalidated by reasons of affinity, because her own sister had warmed his bed first, thus placing his eventual "marriage" to Anne in the forbidden degree.

Fearing the fire, Anne signed, but not without noting that "without marriage there can be no adultery, therefore, if these sentences are carried out they shall be naught but *murder*." She was absolutely right, and as she stood upon the scaffold, preparing to die, everyone knew they were about to witness not an execution but the murder of an innocent woman, just as they had already witnessed the murders of five innocent men. Though I was glad that Smeaton, though innocent of any actual carnal knowledge of Anne, despite his dreams and fantasies, had died for his lies and treachery. Some would counsel me to be kinder and gentler, and remind me that his confession was obtained under torture, that this poor, low-born musician had no high birth and noble title to protect him from all the hellish implements of torture as it had the other men, the men that he himself had named, echoing Jane, as Anne's lovers, but I don't care about that; even if they racked him and broke every bone in his body, I *cannot* forgive him.

Anne wasn't even dead before an army of stonemasons, seamstresses, glaziers, and carpenters descended upon the royal palaces to eradicate her initials and replace them with Jane Seymour's. Anne's white falcon emblem was shot down and Mistress Seymour's phoenix rose in its place.

When I learned that George might have saved himself I wept all the more. The other men had already been condemned, found guilty of treasonable adultery with Queen Anne, and it was a foregone conclusion that the same verdict would be brought against her. For how could they be guilty and she not? It takes at least two to commit adultery.

My own brother, Thomas Howard, who had succeeded my father as Duke of Norfolk, presided over that farcical fraud of a trial as Lord High Steward in his own set of bloodred robes. Besides keeping the King's favor and proving he loved the sovereign more than his own flesh and blood, he had even more to gain by Anne's death—his own daughter, Mary Howard, was married to the King's illegitimate get by Bessie Blount; thus if King Henry died without giving England a legitimately born prince, and Henry Fitzroy, the Duke of Richmond, became king, my brother's daughter would be queen. Truly, it was something to think about, a possibility well worth considering and even laying a discreet foundation for; I could almost hear the wheels of his mind turning even in the quiet country seclusion of my husband's castle in Kent.

Thinking to spare His Majesty undue embarrassment, my unusually considerate brother had written a particularly intimate question touching upon the royal member's potency and vigor upon a piece of paper and given it to George to read *silently* and then consign to the flame of a conveniently provided candle a blank-faced page boy held upon a tray. George was instructed to answer merely with a simple "yea" or "nay" and say *nothing* more.

"Do you understand?" His uncle's hard eyes bored into him.

"Yes, Uncle," George smiled and obediently answered, as

though he were a young lad back in the schoolroom, then bent his head to read the paper that had just been placed in his hand.

I could see that devilish smile lighting up his handsome face, as, over the paper's edge, his eyes found Anne's.

My brother might just as well have handed him a weapon. Words, the poet and wit in George knew, could be as mighty as the sword; they could slay a reputation just as surely as a sharp thrust or slash of steel could end a human life.

George raised his voice so that it would carry to the back of the hall and up to the rafters, so that each and every one of the two thousand people packed inside would be sure to hear it and send it spreading out the door to travel throughout London and eventually across the Channel. He read the question aloud and then said "nay" and went on to add that his sister had never confided anything pertaining to either the limpness or liveliness of His Majesty's private member. And, in any case, he really would rather not give an answer that might in any way cast doubt upon the legitimacy of any offspring resulting from the King's *next* marriage.

Thus, he yanked the veil off Jane Seymour's face and let all London know *exactly* what this farce of a trial was all about. Anne, for all her faults, was no adulteress; she had never cuckolded the King. Henry was merely of a mind to change queens again, and the *one* thing his divorce from stubborn and proud Catherine of Aragon had taught him was that when ridding oneself of a wife the ax is always quicker than the law of either church or state, and, in spite of the blood spilled, an execution really is less messy in the end.

I rocked and laughed and cried until my sides ached and I was breathless.

"My brave George!" I gasped as the tears poured down my face.

I could see him standing there, tall and handsome, all garbed in black relieved only by the whiteness of his shirt, gazing at Anne over that scrap of paper right before he read it, locking eyes with her, the Gemini, together once more, alone against Satan and all his legions, determined not to fall without a spectacular fight—he the one who had arrived early, and she the other twin soul who had been fashionably late coming into this world, the two of them knowing *exactly* what was about to happen, and that, if it must end like this, falsely accused and condemned on the lies of a tortured, spurned, and lovelorn lute player and an insanely jealous wife's lust for vengeance, with both their lives bleeding out upon a straw-strewn scaffold, they wouldn't have it any other way. They would orchestrate their own dramatic exits as though this were just another masque they had devised and were dancing the lead roles in. Even as Anne's eyes must have pleaded with him not to do it, to save himself if he could, she knew that if their roles were reversed and if she were standing there in his stead, no power on this earth could still her tongue from reading the damning words written there aloud for every ear in London to hear so that their voices would carry the truth to the far-flung reaches of England.

For George and the loyal friends who had died with them—Henry Norris, Francis Weston, and William Brereton—I recited a verse from the Book of John that came at that moment like a white dove fluttering through the open window of my sorrow-filled mind. "Greater love hath no man than this, that a man lay down his life for his friends."

They didn't have to do that. They didn't have to die. They could have saved themselves. They could have turned on Anne, the way the King entreated them to do; he gave the accused noblemen, with the exception of George, every chance to save themselves and swim free while Anne sank, even offering them money and lands to betray their friend. He tried particularly hard to persuade his favorite body servant, Henry Norris, to turn on Anne and stay with him, but he was too honorable and noble, too honest a man ever to accuse an innocent person. Henry Norris was a man who valued friendship—real, loyal, and true friendship—more than gold or the worldly goods the King offered him. They were all like that. They could have aped my husband and accepted the King's bribes, chosen him over Anne, stood up in court, and spewed vile lies about attempts at seduction and assignations that had never taken place, portraying my daughter as an insatiable succubus who tried to lure them into her bed with caresses and costly gifts, and as an unnatural creature who lusted after her own brother as he lusted after her. They could have supported Jane in her evil accusations that

Elizabeth was sired by George instead of King Henry, though only a blind fool would have believed that; one had only to look at the child Henry had affectionately dubbed his "red-haired brat" to know that she was a real Tudor rose—a rose with an inner core of steel I believe her father and the world will in time discover. What a pity I will not be there to see it! I would like to have another chance, and to not fail my granddaughter, to be there for her, as I never was for my children in the way that they needed me to be. But sometimes, no matter how much a person desires and longs for a second chance, it is not given.

But they didn't do that. They told the truth. They stood by their friends and, with great courage and verve, refuted and denied each and every foul charge—showing them for the lies they were. They even used their sharp wits like razors to shred through the false and flimsy "evidence" produced against them.

It was all a ragbag of gossip, frayed and rotten fragments of speech and gallant, courtly banter, even snippets of poetry, all taken grossly out of context, wildly misconstrued and misinterpreted. Ludicrous things like dancing with the Queen, or little gifts and trinkets that had been exchanged, were used against them. For one last performance, they made their audience laugh as they deftly punctured each absurd accusation with the clever rapiers of their tongues. They were able to prove that adulteries allegedly committed at certain times and places had never happened at all, and that one or even both of the parties accused of the act were absent from that location or otherwise engaged on that occasion. At the time of one of these alleged adulterous liaisons, Anne was still in bed recovering from childbirth and in no condition to intimately entertain any man, even her own husband.

But it availed them naught. Only the people in the crowd, the dear, vulgar, and savvy Londoners, believed them, not the jury; they were ambitious men bound to serve and obey or forfeit the King's favor, and all they had gained, or hoped to gain, from it. The jury did what they were there to do and delivered up a verdict of "guilty" as a wedding gift to King Henry and set him free to marry Mistress Seymour.

It was hard to believe that they were truly gone, that I would never see their smiling faces or hear their jests and laughter again. They were all such gay and vibrant young men, brilliant, stylish, and creative, the life and soul of every celebration! It was as though the heart of the court had been torn out.

Sir Henry Norris was the gentle, soft-spoken one, but he was not afraid to speak up in the face of injustice, to bravely espouse the truth, nor did his quiet ways mean he was devoid of fun. Ladies liked to run their hands through the silky flaxen waves of his hair, and he liked to let them. He loved gaiety, dancing, music, poetry, and gambling just as much as the rest of them, otherwise he would never have been a part of that staunch circle of friends. After our long-ago wintertime liaison, he married a sweet girl he loved dearly yet lost shortly after she gave birth to his only son. At the time of his death, he had been considering marrying our cousin Madge Shelton. He enjoyed her perky, mischievous charms, but hesitated over the tales of her flightiness and wanton ways. He had a young son to bring up and wanted to provide a proper, and loving, stepmother who would love him like her very own. But Madge showed no sign of settling, of curbing the amorous exuberance she scattered like flower petals most generously over the court, nor had she ever exhibited any fondness for little ones either, much less any of the patience, dedication, and kind and loving wisdom that make a good mother (being a bad mother, negligent and morally lax as a London trollop, has taught me well how to recognize the ingredients that go into making a good one). And the kind of "love" Madge gave to men, both young and old, suggested he would do better to look elsewhere, for both his own and his little boy's sake.

Sir Francis Weston, with his laughing eyes and fire red locks, was known as "Never Say No"; whether it be a loan of coins or a night of coitus he was always game. He was a soft touch for anyone with a tale of woe. With the largesse of a king, as magnificent and magnanimous as an emperor, he went through life spending and giving, racking up debts at an astounding rate. Money flowed through his fingers like water; for him trying to save a penny was like trying to hold back the wind. But he was so likeable no one could stay angry at him for long. To his tailors, goldsmith, and embroiderers he was like a pet peacock, and though he owed them all vast sums of money, they nonetheless adored him and could never say him nay when he came to them, hat in hands, smilingly proclaiming himself "in dire need" of a new doublet or a jeweled chain.

Sir William Brereton, with his blue black hair and sharp, patrician face, was often taken for the serious one at first glance. But I saw him dancing atop a table with a wine cup in his hand and heart's ease pansies in his hair too many times to be deceived. He was the best gambler of the bunch, almost as good as Anne, relying on that serious mien from which he could erase all expression when the dice or cards were in his hands and a gleaming pile of coins was on the table.

Tom Wyatt and Sir Richard Page were, for whatever reason, exonerated. Acquitted of all blame, they never even set foot before the jury. They were held in the Tower until Anne and the others were dead and then released, though neither desired to linger at the court long and opted for diplomatic service instead.

Wyatt, who had watched the executions from his window, would live on to honor his friends with a poem.

> *Who list his wealth and ease retain,*
> *Himself let him unknown contain.*
> *Press not too fast in at that gate*
> *Where the return stands by disdain.*
> *For sure, circa Regna tonat.*
>
> *The high mountains are blasted oft*
> *When the low valley is mild and soft.*
> *Fortune with Health stands at debate.*
> *The fall is grievous from aloft.*
> *And sure, circa Regna tonat.*
>
> *These bloody days have broken my heart.*
> *My lust and youth did then depart,*
> *And blind desire of estate.*
> *Who hastes to climb seeks to revert:*
> *Of truth, circa Regna tonat.*

> *The Bell Tower showed me such a sight*
> *That in my head sticks day and night:*
> *There did I learn out of a grate,*
> *For all favor, glory, or might,*
> *That yet, circa Regna tonat.*
>
> *By proof, I say, there did I learn:*
> *Wit helpeth not defense too yearn,*
> *Of innocence to plead or prate.*
> *Bear low, therefore, give God the stern.*
> *For sure, circa Regna tonat.*

No truer words have ever been written about the perils of seeking royal favor. *Circa Regna tonat*—thunder rolls around the throne! The lightning of royal wrath can strike even the mightiest down within an instant. No one is immune or invulnerable, indispensable, or irreplaceable. It is as dangerous as fondling and kissing serpents to aspire too high and to put one's trust in princes. In the end, vain ambition will avail you naught.

Look at me—I came into this world a vain and haughty beauty striving for admiration and ever greater prestige; marriage to a merchant's grandson hurt my pride. I dyed my hair, painted my face, and resorted to every remedy within reach, no matter how perilous or inane, to retain my youth and beauty, and took lovers, *dozens* of lovers, and even briefly contemplated a dalliance with the King, but I later, through the seed my hated husband sowed inside me, became the mother of a Queen. I watched her impossible rise and sudden fall, and in the end . . . what is left to me? "Pride goeth before destruction, and an haughty spirit before a fall," so says the Lord. And this haughty spirit has fallen so low she will *never* rise again, and doesn't want to.

Like a person born blind who all of a sudden sees, I realize now, in the gloaming of my life, that I wasted it all in vain pursuit of all of the wrong things. All the things—the luxuries and ambitions, the pedigrees and prestige, the admiring eyes, lusty desire, gifts, and flattering words—I thought so very important, and so vital to my happiness and well-being, didn't really matter at all.

Would that I could have back all the years I wasted wanting a "more" that was actually less, and a "better" that was in truth worse. That was the curse I brought down upon myself. God help me.

While my husband danced at Jane Seymour's wedding, Remi came to me at Hever.

He found me sitting amidst the ruins of my red rose bower, the bloodred climbing roses all torn down and uprooted, thorny stems, scattered petals and leaves, fallen everywhere, a great floral massacre, and the latticed wooden trellises hacked to splinters strewn all over the ground, making it a perilous place for anyone to walk in their bare feet.

My strength swollen by the madness of grief, I had shoved the statue of Cupid at the center of my reflecting pool off his pedestal, so that he sank to the bottom and only the tip of his arrow, like an erect phallus, penetrated the still green surface of the pond where the bloated bodies of gold and silver fish now floated blind-eyed and belly-up, baking in the May sun now that there was no longer any rose-covered bower to shade them. The water lilies were gone; I had viciously yanked those graceful pink and white beauties out and flung them onto the ground to wither and die and rot in the summer sun.

I sat on a stone bench carved with hearts and lovers' knots, sweating in my black mourning weeds in the full glare of the sun, my coif and thorn-tattered veil cast aside, caring not a whit for my complexion or how gray my bare head now showed. Disdaining the offering of rose honey my mother-in-law had left for me, in a little glass jar tied with a pretty pink bow, swearing in the note she laboriously wrote that "rose honey can sort out any fit of depression like nothing else," I sat there dreaming, watching the ghosts of my children playing in the garden.

Anne, gowned in green like the spring, and George, smiling, black heads together, their lutes, only momentarily abandoned, lying on a nearby bench, while they instructed the servants' children they had gathered together for the final rehearsal of the play they had written to entertain us in the Great Hall after supper. Beautiful Mary, kneeling like Narcissus beside the lily pond, amber-eyed and rosy-cheeked, her golden ringlets crowned with a circlet of daisies she had woven, wearing about her chubby little neck the necklace of enameled cherries that I had given her to wear at our last cherry fair, lost in admiration of her beautiful reflection mirrored in the placid green water between the pink and white water lilies, shrieking and nearly jumping out of her skin when a little green frog leapt from a lily pad onto her skirt of cherry blossom pink silk.

Why is time always so much kinder to men? the last fleeting vestiges of the vain coquette in me wondered as I watched Remi approaching. He had aged well, removed from the backstabbing intrigue, rivalries, smiling-faced lies, betrayals, and factions of the court, where loyalties shifted as the wind blew. I do not mean to suggest the life of an artisan is easy, but creating dolls to make children smile is a more thankful and enjoyable occupation than navigating the many intricacies of court life and striving always to hold on to what one already has and greedily acquire more, to always be the best dressed and the most admired, and to let no one usurp your place or paramours. It is a constant, complicated struggle that will put gray in your hair and lines on your face faster than anything else I know. I laugh now, albeit bitterly, so bitterly, at the folly of the green girl I used to be who spent her youth dreaming of a life at court and pined for it when she was confined as a broodmare at her husband's rustic castle. If only I had known then what I know now . . . it might all have been a different story.

I smiled through my pain as I watched my lover cross the ugly, ruined, and uprooted garden, carefully navigating his way around holes, matted roots, clumps of grass, shrubs yanked whole out of the earth, and dying flowers languishing in the sun, their roots raised like prayerful hands to heaven, hoping someone would come along and take pity and tuck them back into the nourishing earth to give them another chance at life. He stood and frowned over this devastation, but said nothing, and after a lengthy pause, perhaps to mutter a quiet prayer, moved on.

He was—as he had always been—a quietly handsome, tall and ample man garbed in black, almost as pale-faced as a lady because his work kept him indoors, with nary a speck of gray in his still thick dark hair and the slight beard that bordered his cheeks and chin, and only a few lines around his brown eyes and mouth when he smiled. Even a few years past fifty he still seemed young and boyish, like a great, big, moonfaced, soft, and sweet dough baby that I wanted both to devour and hug, hold tight and never let go of. Mayhap it was that blessedly serene combination of calmness, a quiet, tranquil nature, and a clear conscience that allowed him to sleep easily in his bed every night that worked that magic for him? And having no marital woes or children to worry about losing their heads to a capricious King can do wonders for one's peace of mind and keep worry from carving lines deep in one's visage or weaving skeins of gray through one's tresses. There was nothing brazen, quarrelsome, haughty, or showy about Remi. He led a quiet, contented, simple life and saved all the drama for his magnificent dolls.

I sometimes joked that getting enough words out of Remi to gauge what he thought and felt was somewhat akin to pulling teeth. My lover was such a soft-spoken man of so few words, unlike the chatterboxes at court who could speak volumes, wasting words for the sheer joy of hearing themselves prattle, in love with their own voices, tossing off words to display their cleverness, without ever really saying anything, least of all a single honest or heartfelt word, whereas when Remi spoke it truly meant something.

He was carrying a large, velvet-wrapped bundle cradled in his strong, soft arms.

"Elizabeth," he said as he knelt before me, his brown eyes filled with the most tender compassion. I saw the struggle within him, wanting to say something that would give me some comfort, some measure of peace, but knowing there were no words he could say that would work that particular magic. Grief is one illness that defies all remedies; it must ever run its course.

With a bittersweet smile, I reached down to cup his chin, loving the way his beard gently prickled my palm and the softness of the flesh that cushioned his jaw and chin.

"I've brought you something," he said and set about unwrapping his parcel.

I gasped as the last fold of dark velvet fell away. There, lying at my feet, smiling up at me, were my three children, restored to me in their youth, before the world of foreign courts and the first sown seeds of ambition took them away from me, before they grew into their own unique personalities, adults who had long ago grown accustomed to being ignored and disappointed by their mother and learned to do without her. Back when they were still of an age when I might, if I had only chosen to, have proven to them, and to myself, that I could be a *good* mother, that I could set my own selfish whims aside and truly be there for them whenever they had need of a mother's love, counsel, and comfort.

But here they were again: ringleted, golden, and rosy Mary, a pretty, plump, smiling cherub in gold-worked butter yellow damask with a kirtle and under-sleeves of dark, dusky rose; Anne, a black swan to be, gowned in the green she always loved, and a choker of pearls, endowed with a special and unique beauty that entirely eluded my eyes when she was a child, but Remi showed me now had been there all along; and George, changeable as the weather, smiling one moment, brooding black as a storm cloud the next, here he was garbed in a gold-braided doublet of quince-colored velvet, a cheerful little boy, the way he had been the day he straddled a hobby horse and cantered about Remi's shop.

"Now no one can ever take your children away from you again, Elizabeth," Remi said, the last few words muffled as, with a choking cry, I threw myself into his arms.

He held me tight. His softness and warmth were like heaven to me. And as the painted faces of my doll children smiled up at me, I felt, for the first time since the brutal British ax fell and the gleaming French sword slashed, truly at peace. How could I have ever wanted anything else?

EPILOGUE

March 27, 1538
Hever Castle in Kent

I've been very ill with a cough that gives me no peace. I cannot rest properly; I cannot lie flat lest my lungs flood until they threaten to drown me. The flesh falls from my bones, and I bring up blood. But I'm bored with bed, especially without my lover and something fun to do in it, though in truth I haven't the strength for it. I don't care what my physician and Lady Margaret, or anyone else says; I *need* to get up.

When I came out this morning, the first time I've beheld my snarled and tangled garden of wickedness in weeks, I thought a thick snow had fallen only over this accursed spot. I was *amazed* to find snowdrops, *everywhere* snowdrops, blooming in a thick carpet of voluminous white all over the churchyard, blanketing the graves, and the makeshift monuments to my lost and slain children. Like good triumphing over evil, they had even gained ascendancy over the worst and thickest matted roots and brambles. There was not a patch of ground that they did not cover with their heavenly profusion.

I plucked up one of the dainty bulbous white flowers, like a teardrop pearl hanging gracefully from a shepherd's crook of living green, and sank down upon the nearest bench to contemplate its simple snowy beauty, twirling it betwixt my bony thin, age-coarsened, and lined fingers, my once beautiful nails now grown brittle and yellow in my old age and illness.

I had a strange dream last night, so vivid and intense it almost seemed real. Actually, I've been having it for quite some time. But last night was different.

A coach, clearly not of this world, all spectral and white, glowing in the moonlight, drove up to the front door at Blickling Hall. Gazing from a window above, I could not believe my eyes. The liveried coachman perched atop the box was headless as were the fine white four that drew that elegant equipage.

The door opened, and George stepped down, arrayed all in shining white. He too was headless, but from the crook of his arm, his head smiled up at me and winked. Though now, when I am awake, I have to wonder how I could have seen that at night, even by full moonlight and from such a height. And my eyes are not what they used to be. But strange things happen all the time in dreams.

He reached up a hand, for Anne, and she stepped gracefully down in a radiant, glowing gown of dazzling white, with her head tucked beneath her arm, one fine black brow sardonically cocked, as though she were silently laughing at all the world.

Arm in arm, they turned to face the imposing red brick manor. They glided up the steps and entered the house, passing through the doors without opening them.

I heard their voices, their laughter, but even though I rushed frantically from room to room calling their names, I could never find them; they were always somewhere else. I must have spent hours running back and forth, upstairs and down, in and out of doors, round and round in dizzying circles. Then I heard the crunch of hooves and wheels upon the graveled drive. A cock crowed three times. I ran out, waving my arms, calling after them, shouting at them to stop. But they never did.

Only last night was different—this time they stopped for me.

I climbed into the coach, beside George, and when I looked back I saw the chain-shackled body of my husband, eyes filled with misery, staring up at the dying moon, being dragged behind us, demons in the form of dogs nipping at him, and other fiends, scaly-skinned and fiery-eyed, clawing at him with their long-taloned fingers, and cursing him most foully, leaving his blood behind to stain the gravel until glowing ruby-eyed hellhounds came running to lap it up.

Maybe when justice fails in this world, it atones for it with a vengeance in the next? If that is true, I almost pity Thomas, and my daughter-in-law too.

I've made up my mind; I'm going to Norfolk, to Blickling Hall. I've a sense my fate awaits me there, that this dream was a message from beyond the grave. I must bind the loosened knots and set all in order while I still have time.

I will leave Hever to Thomas—I never liked it anyway—and bid adieu to mad Lady Margaret, who will not suffer her hair to be combed since she believes a bat to be trapped in it yet is too vain to suffer her head to be shaved, which she insists is the only remedy, so has left it to mat and stink these many months while she runs about shrieking, being tormented by a phantom bat biting and clawing and tugging at her scalp. And my poison garden, now garbed in the white flowers sacred to Our Lady, the same ones that adorn lady chapels for the Feast of Purification, when bouquets of them cluster around her statues by candlelight, must fend for itself, evil warring against good, in that eternal, never-ending battle, as it has ever been since God created the earth.

But, before I go, there is something else I want to leave for Thomas....

The *very* last thing before I go, when I am already dressed for travel and the coach is waiting below, I will go into the bedchamber we used to as husband and wife share, bid a final farewell to that hateful bed carved with its grotesque depiction of the Seven Deadly Sins, which I have not shared with Thomas since I became ill. I will leave sitting in the chair beside that horrible bed the doll Remi made for me so long ago, of the young and beautiful sixteen-year-old Elizabeth Howard, the Duke of Norfolk's spoiled only daughter, gowned in velvet the color of the finest sapphires embellished with gold lovers' knots, the dress I was wearing the day I met my husband and the love of my life.

I leave this with Thomas as a reminder, one might even say a trophy, of the beautiful, elegant, refined, gracious, highborn, proud, pedigreed, noble wife he always wanted, the woman I outwardly, always so concerned with appearances, wasted my life trying to be. But one cannot turn back the clock. Now I take my leave. I implore you all to pray for this shallow, vain, and jaded woman who made too many mistakes and realized it only when it was too late.

This memoir I leave behind for Mary, since I cannot find the courage to face her or address her directly in a letter, hoping that, after she has read it, and I am in my grave, she will decide to award me some small measure of forgiveness whether I deserve it or not.

POSTSCRIPT

Elizabeth Boleyn, the Countess of Wiltshire, died on April 3, 1538. She was fifty-three years old. She was found lying unconscious, facedown in her nightgown amidst the gravel on the drive a little distance from the front door of Blickling Hall. There were marks her feet had left behind her in the gravel that suggested that she had been running after something, but no one knew what. Per instructions she had left in a letter, she was taken to London by a gentle barge, to the home of Hugh Faringdon, the Abbot of Reading, beside Baynard's Castle. Despite the efforts of the best physicians, she never regained consciousness.

She left behind a letter, addressed to the Abbot of Reading, in which she refused, most adamantly, to sleep beside her husband for all eternity in the church at Hever Castle, insisting that her soul could never find rest if her final wishes were ignored.

"I was a dutiful wife and slept beside him in life, but my obedience to him ends with death, and I will not spend eternity sleeping beside a man I despise, a father who denounced and condemned his children to an infamous death when he *knew* them to be innocent. False belief I could forgive, but he knew the truth full well. He did what he did solely to retain the favor of the King, and that I *cannot,* and *will not,* forgive."

She chose instead the church of Saint Mary-at-Lambeth, where some of her illustrious Howard ancestors were entombed, as the place for her eternal rest. The site of that church is now the Museum of Garden History.

The night her coffin, draped in black, emblazoned with a large white cross, was ferried by torchlight across the Thames to Lambeth, a single mourner, a rotund, bearded, black-clad figure, sitting bareheaded in a hired barge, followed, quietly weeping.

When the coffin was set down inside the church, he softly approached. He lit a candle and knelt in prayer and stayed there for some time, then pressed his lips to the coffin lid, just where the lips of the woman lying within it would be, and vanished into the dawn. No one ever knew who he was.

As he departed, as silently as he had come, rude jests were uttered amongst the oarsmen and servants who had carried the coffin in. They dredged up all the old gossip about the Lady Elizabeth Boleyn's lax morals and many lovers and said the late Queen Anne must have gotten her wanton ways from her mother, and wondered would the daughter she left behind, the red-haired bastard Elizabeth, go the same way. They marveled that this mystery man who was obviously of humble origins, and being such a corpulent, portly fellow, had ever been the lover of such a beautiful woman. How had he ever coupled with such a slender lady without crushing her bones to powder? Why had a woman reputedly so beautiful in her prime and so vain of her pedigree, with all the gentlemen of the court to choose from, ever have chosen a fat tradesman to warm her bed? But Remi Jouet, even if he had heard them, was not telling. He remained, as he had always been, a man who knew when silence was indeed golden and when to spend a few words; and this occasion, to satisfy the lewd curiosity of some bargemen, was not one of them.

As Elizabeth predicted, Thomas Boleyn immediately dispatched a team of gardeners to restore the churchyard at Hever to a sedate, orderly, and elegant appearance befitting of his station. Hever Castle and a reconstruction of the rose garden where Henry VIII wooed Anne Boleyn remains a popular tourist attraction to this day.

Thomas Boleyn retained his sovereign's favor to the very end. He died March 12, 1539, at the age of sixty-one, a month shy of marrying the King's niece, Lady Margaret Douglas. He was being fitted for his wedding whites when the fatal fever came along and laid him in his coffin. Already in declining health, though he put up a valiant fight, in the end, he could not withstand it.

His steward wrote of his passing, "My good lord and master is dead. He made the end of a good Christian gentleman." King Henry ordered masses said for his good and faithful servant's soul.

He was entombed in the church at Hever beneath the magnificent monumental brass he had commissioned showing himself in his prime clad in the full regalia of a Knight of the Garter.

Lady Margaret Butler lived out her days at Hever, sinking ever deeper into dementia. As her mind returned to her childhood in Ireland, she was given dolls costumed as princesses, fairies, and mermaids, kindly supplied by Remi Jouet, to amuse and divert her. She died at the age of eighty-five and was entombed near her son in the church at Hever.

Mary Boleyn lived happily with her second husband, William Stafford, never wanting for love, though the same could not be said for money. She lost the child she had been carrying when she was banished from Anne's good graces. She and her beloved Will, to their great sorrow, had no more children. They lived for a time abroad as William resumed his military service and later returned to England as part of the retinue of Anne of Cleves when she came to become Henry VIII's fourth wife in 1539.

Mary lived to see both her children make good and—most importantly to her—*happy* marriages in which each found love. She died of consumption in July of 1543, greatly mourned as a beloved wife and mother.

Discounted during most of her lifetime as a fool, even by those who should have known and loved her best, Mary was the Boleyn girl who got it right in the end; she knew how to follow her heart and go after what was *really* important.

Country folk claim that on moon-bright nights Anne and George, clad in spectral white to symbolize their innocence, still ride the country lanes of Norfolk in their elegant, eerily glowing coach and four, reaching Blickling Hall at the stroke of midnight.

George hands Anne down, and they glide, arm in arm, each with their head tucked beneath an arm, into their ancestral home, passing seamlessly through doors and solid walls.

While they visit until dawn, seeing the changes time has wrought, including a completely new house rebuilt from the ground up in the seventeenth century, the legend says, the coach rolls on, dragging the damned soul of their father, Thomas Boleyn, behind. On and on he goes, being dragged through hedges, brambles, and ditches, banging and bouncing over rutted and rocky roads, mud and twigs tangling in his gray hair, fire sometimes shooting from his mouth, scraping and clattering over the twelve bridges that lie between Wroxham and Blickling Hall, as orbs of colored light and fireballs and a horde of screaming demons follow, some in the form of hounds that occasionally pause to lick up his blood, cursing him for betraying his own flesh and blood, damning him to endure this ordeal as penance for five thousand years. They say that anyone witnessing this sight will be instantly dragged down to hell by the same demons that torment Thomas Boleyn.

The coach always returns to collect Anne and George as the dawn is breaking. With a crunch of wheels upon gravel, and the fading neigh of horses and ghostly hoofbeats, the entire equipage vanishes in a burst of white light as the cock crows.

According to a member of the British Folklore Society, writing in the 1940s of the ghostly goings-on at Blickling Hall that had been occurring through the centuries, "the occupants of the house are so accustomed to these appearances that they take no notice of them."

The unquiet spirit of Anne Boleyn has also been seen at Hever Castle and the Tower of London, where, in 1864, a sentry was once almost court-martialed, accused of drunkenness and dereliction of duty, when he fainted after a late-night encounter with the white-gowned ghost of Anne Boleyn, who had walked straight through him and the pointed bayonet he used to challenge her. Luckily, two of his fellow officers had heard his cry of terror and seen what transpired from a window, and he was acquitted.

* * *

Remi Jouet remains, as he was in life, maddeningly elusive, a brilliant artisan, yet one of those ordinary people whose lives are lost in the mists of time unless they happen to rub shoulders with the great. No further details of his life are known. Only a few of his dolls remain in museums and private collections, where they are lovingly preserved as cherished treasures and continue to delight adults and children alike.

THE
BOLEYN BRIDE

Brandy Purdy

ABOUT THIS GUIDE

The suggested questions are included to
enhance your group's reading
of Brandy Purdy's
The Boleyn Bride!

DISCUSSION QUESTIONS

1. Elizabeth Boleyn readily admits that she is a vain woman. What do you think of her vanity and pride and the way they affect her thoughts and actions? Do you agree that she was raised to be this way or do you regard this as an excuse and her attitude as more of a personal failing? Does she remind you of the Tudor era equivalent of the mean, pretty, snobby girls everyone encounters in high school? What do you think of the way she treats people, like her maid Matilda, her husband, children, and the men she has affairs with? Near the end of this novel she describes her husband's attitude toward people as "use and then lose"—he discards them when they are of no further profitable use to him. Though, as far as we know, no one has ever died as a result of Elizabeth's behavior, is this a case of the pot calling the kettle black?

2. Discuss the marriage and relationship between Elizabeth and Thomas Boleyn. Do you believe he deserves the contempt Elizabeth treats him with? She regards herself as superior, sneers when he changes the spelling of his name from *Bullen* to *Boleyn,* and rubs his family's mercantile origins in his face whenever she has the chance. She glories in cheating on him with men of an even lower social status. What do you think of all this? How would you react, if you were in Thomas Bullen's shoes, to a wife like Elizabeth?

3. Elizabeth Boleyn views her life as that of a broodmare, though one of a Tudor era wife's primary responsibilities was to provide her husband with heirs. She endures numerous pregnancies as many women did, many of which end in miscarriages, stillbirths, or the death of the baby soon afterward. In the prologue where she describes her poison garden and later when she advises Mary that "there are other teas," she shows she has knowledge of contraception and abortifacients; do you think, though she never directly tells the reader so, that Elizabeth has resorted to either, or both,

of these measures? She appears to regret the effects pregnancy has upon her body more than she does the loss of these little lives. Do you think, reading between the lines, that she directly caused some of these miscarriages? Discuss Elizabeth's attitude toward pregnancy. In your opinion, is it natural or unnatural? Do you think she is one of those women who is devoid of maternal feeling?

4. Thomas Boleyn tells his wife and children, "If you doubt you can succeed, why even bother to try? Never invite failure into your life if you can possibly help it." This is one of the very few things husband and wife agree upon. Elizabeth believes this is true and good advice. Do you? He also urges them to always be on the winning side, that this is the only side that matters. Do you agree?

5. Discuss Elizabeth's relationship with the doll maker, Remi Jouet. He's the man she claims is the love of her life, yet she continues her casual dalliances with other men, and throughout the story he remains something of an enigma, a soft-spoken man of so few words that Elizabeth and the reader never truly know what he is thinking. What does each of them gain from this relationship? Despite being adulterous, is it a good, healthy relationship or are they merely using each other? Is Elizabeth, as she sometimes worries, holding Remi back from having a normal life with a wife and children? What do you think this man truly wants out of life, and does he get it? The reader never sees his life, except in the moments he shares with Elizabeth; what do you think it is like when she is not there? Do you think Elizabeth has grounds to be jealous and that he has affairs with other women who come to his shop?

6. Since time began women have been on a quest to keep young and beautiful, sometimes going to outlandish and dangerous lengths. Today you can't turn on a TV or open a magazine without seeing an advertisement for the latest and greatest miracle cream. In this novel, Elizabeth Boleyn mentions some of the methods she tries to maintain her com-

plexion, color her hair, and whiten her teeth, even going so far as to brush them with the urine of a Portuguese sailor and trusting her mouth to quacks with none too pleasant results. Discuss the lengths that women, past and present, go to, to preserve or enhance their beauty. Is it worth the fight, and submitting to expensive treatments that are sometimes risky or even fraudulent, or is it better to grow old naturally and gracefully?

7. Elizabeth Boleyn has many affairs with younger men. She says, "I relished the role of instructress. Or perhaps I just liked being the first, the one they would *always* remember no matter how many others came after." What do you think about this? It contradicts what she says about forgetting her casual dalliances and wanting to be forgotten too. Why does Elizabeth have so many affairs with men of all ages from all walks of life? Is it really just to appease boredom and, in the case of those of lower social station, to spite her husband, or is something missing from her life? If so, what do you think that is? And despite these many affairs, she spurns the ultimate paramour, the King. Why do you think she does this? Do you believe the reasons she gives?

8. Discuss Elizabeth's relationships with her three surviving children—Mary, George, and Anne. She admits she has been an emotionally as well as a physically absent and distant mother who always put herself and her own pleasures before her children's well-being. She knows this, even as she is doing it, in the early years when there would have still been time to make a change for the better, yet she never does. Do you think Elizabeth had it in her to ever be a good mother? Discuss how having Elizabeth for a mother affects each of her children. Does her indifference and neglect help or hurt them? Does it make them weaker or stronger? Two of them, George and Mary, grow up to be somewhat promiscuous; do you see Elizabeth's influence in this? Do you see Anne's transformation from ugly duckling to black swan as a result of Elizabeth's treatment of her as a child?

9. Elizabeth is driven, by her disappointment in Anne's appearance as well as her incessant crying, to attempt to murder her daughter in the cradle. If George had not appeared, do you think she would have done it? Do you think Elizabeth Boleyn was suffering from postpartum depression, or were her actions cold-blooded? How would history have been different if Anne Boleyn had died or if, as Elizabeth ponders near the novel's end, she had never transformed herself? How would Anne's life have been different if she had remained an ugly duckling and never captivated a king or had the nerve to refuse him and hold out for marriage and a crown, or if she had gone into a convent? It might have been a longer life, but would it have been a happy, or happier, one? If Elizabeth had loved Anne from the start, the way she did Mary, how do you think this would have affected Anne and the woman she became? Would she have turned out better, worse, or the same?

10. Mary Boleyn is deemed a failure by her whole family. Over the course of the novel, she goes from adored golden girl to pariah. She repeatedly fails to make the most of the opportunities she is given, to reap a profit from the amorous attentions of powerful men, like the kings of England and France. Her own mother thinks she would be a failure even as a halfpenny whore. She incurs only anger and disgrace when she marries a poor man who truly loves her for herself. What do you think of Mary, the choices she made, and the way her family regards and treats her? Is she really the Boleyn girl who got it right in the end?

11. After years of leading the broodmare life, Elizabeth's dream of going to court and serving the Queen finally comes true. Discuss her relationship with Catherine of Aragon. Is it a real friendship or merely a noblewoman proud of her privileged position and of having the confidence of the Queen? When her husband orders her to give up her position as a lady-in-waiting because it does not look right for her to serve Anne's rival, she does so without argument, though she claims to remain loyal to Catherine in her heart. Do you

believe this is true? If so, why? Does Elizabeth Boleyn *really* love anyone but herself? When she says that she would have fought for the lives of George and Anne, do you believe her?

12. Discuss the close bond between Anne and George. Do you believe it is in any way incestuous, as George's wife alleges, or that it is the innocent love of a brother and sister who are best friends as well as siblings? Do you see George's drinking and many affairs, and his dissatisfaction with his lovers, as proof of incestuous longings, as his drunken confession to his mother might suggest, or was he merely talking in his wine cup? Do you think there was any way George could have shaken off his dark moods and led a happy life? Do you believe he suffered from some form of depression?

13. Discuss the role the lute player Mark Smeaton plays in the Boleyn saga as depicted in this novel. Do you believe his affairs with George and Elizabeth Boleyn and their treatment of him in any way motivated his confession? Is Smeaton right to resent the way the Boleyns have treated him or do you think he brought it on himself? Do you believe, as Elizabeth wonders in the prologue, that someone might have seen her in a compromising position with Smeaton and mistaken her for Anne?

14. Near the end of the book, Elizabeth says, "If only I had known then what I know now . . . it might all have been a different story." Do you believe this? What do you think she would have done differently if she were magically given the chance to live her life all over again?

15. With her parting words, Elizabeth leaves her memoir for her daughter Mary. Do you think Mary will forgive her mother after she reads it? If you were in Mary's shoes, would you? Does Elizabeth deserve forgiveness?

Do you love historical fiction?

Want the chance to hear news about your favourite authors (and the chance to win free books)?

Mary Balogh

Charlotte Betts

Jessica Blair

Frances Brody

Gaelen Foley

Elizabeth Hoyt

Eloisa James

Lisa Kleypas

Stephanie Laurens

Claire Lorrimer

Sarah MacLean

Amanda Quick

Julia Quinn

Then visit the Piatkus website and blog

www.piatkus.co.uk | www.piatkusbooks.net

And follow us on Facebook and Twitter

www.facebook.com/piatkusfiction | www.twitter.com/piatkusbooks

piatkus